HIGHEST PRAISE FOR
JOVE HOMESPUN ROMANCES

"In all of the Homespuns I've read and reviewed I've been very taken with the loving renderings of colorful small-town people doing small-town things and bring 5 STAR and GOLD 5 STAR rankings to the readers. This series should be selling off the bookshelves within hours! Never have I given a series an overall review, but I feel this one, thus far, deserves it! Continue the excellent choices in authors and editors! It's working for this reviewer!"
—*Heartland Critiques*

We at Jove Books are thrilled by the enthusiastic critical acclaim that the Homespun Romances are receiving. We would like to thank you, the readers and fans of this wonderful series, for making it the success that it is. It is our pleasure to bring you the highest quality of romance writing in these breathtaking tales of love and family in the heartland of America.

And now, sit back and enjoy this delightful new Homespun Romance . . .

SPRING DREAMS
by Lydia Browne

Praise for other novels by Lydia Browne:

Summer Lightning: "Simply enchanting! This romance is filled with charming characters, a unique twist to an intriguing plot and lots of romance." —*Affaire de Coeur*

Heart Strings: "Witty, charming, and delightfully simple, this story is sure to win your heart." —*Rendezvous*

Titles by Lydia Browne

WEDDING BELLS
HEART STRINGS
PASSING FANCY
SUMMER LIGHTNING
HONEYSUCKLE SONG
SPRING DREAMS

Spring Dreams

Lydia Browne

JOVE BOOKS, NEW YORK

SPRING DREAMS

A Jove Book / published by arrangement with
the author

PRINTING HISTORY
Jove edition / May 1997

The Putnam Berkley World Wide Web site address is
http://www.berkley.com

ISBN: 0-515-12068-5

A JOVE BOOK®
Jove Books are published by The Berkley Publishing Group,
200 Madison Avenue, New York, New York 10016.
JOVE and the "J" design are trademarks
belonging to Jove Publications, Inc.

PRINTED IN THE UNITED STATES OF AMERICA

10 9 8 7 6 5 4 3 2 1

To my sister,
LAURA BAILEY,
with fondest love

Spring Dreams

1

$\mathcal{A}$T THE BOTTOM of the church steps Marshal Faraday put out his hand to stop the doctor from going up. "Trouble," he muttered, casting a watchful glance around.

Instantly the doctor's handsome face froze, his usual expression of confident cheer hardening into something harsh and rigid. "What's up?"

"Looks bad. They're aiming to ambush you after a house call."

"Do they ever give up?"

"Not till they've got you."

The marshal, big and broad, a man who hardly needed the star pinned to his chest to emphasize his authority, nodded to a couple of women hurrying up the stairs. "Afternoon, ladies," he said, brushing the brim of his hat.

The doctor smiled, too, his instinctive charm overcoming his worry. He didn't wear a hat, never having been able to find one to fit comfortably over his thick blond hair. Other than that, he was impeccably dressed in a neat blue suit. He didn't feel that being sloppy would enhance a doctor's reputation, though plenty of his colleagues seemed to believe it. Besides, female patients preferred their physicians to be well turned out, right down to the gold pin in his tie.

"Okay, Jake," he said, turning again to the marshal. "What's the deal this time?"

"Dinner. Lucy George. After you take a look at Mrs. George's sore knee."

Ned Castle, town doctor and, less coincidentally than it seemed, the marshal's brother-in-law, let his broad shoulders slump. "It's a terrible thing to be a hunted man, Jake. I blame the spring. Not a woman in this town gave my unmarried state a second thought all winter long. But as soon as the robin's on the wing, I'm the target of every woman with an unmarried relative or friend. Even my own sister, who should have plenty on her mind, hasn't anything better to do than plot and plan to get me married."

"Marriage isn't so bad," Jake said.

"You won't convince me. I know you're happy . . . and you have only to look at Antonia to know she's happy . . . and the two of you might have been made for each other. But I'm a crotchety bachelor. . . ."

A grin spread over the marshal's face. "You're not seventy, Ned."

"No. But I intend to go on being a crotchety bachelor until I *am* seventy. You would think the women in this town would get it through their heads that I'm not interested in marriage."

"According to Mrs. Cotton, no man ever *wants* to get married. They have to be persuaded."

"Don't talk to me about Mrs. Cotton. She's the ringleader. If it wasn't for her . . . Didn't you tell me she got you married to Antonia almost before you knew it?"

"No, that was the judge's doing. He threw her at me, and I didn't have any choice but to catch her." The bare words would have seemed grumbling were it not for the half-anxious, half-eager looks Jake kept turning in the direction of the church.

Ned knew the marshal's heart walked around outside his body in the person of the former Antonia Castle, now highly pregnant wife to a very nervous husband. Jake Faraday had stood off Indian attacks, Yankee armies, and the assorted desperadoes of the half-civilized Missouri-Kansas border, but the thought of a baby scared him green.

Relenting, Ned said, "Thanks for the warning, Jake. You better go along before Antonia figures out you told me about the Georges. You know what happens to traitors to the cause." Giving a sharp whistle, Ned ran his finger across his neck.

"Oh, Antonia wouldn't kill me. Not till after the baby's born, anyway." Jake hurried away to find his wife.

Alone, the doctor fished a cigar out of his vest pocket and rolled it between his palms luxuriously. The leaf-wrapping crinkled, releasing some of the fragrant tobacco perfume. Two more hours, he thought, and regretfully slid the cigar back into his pocket. He wanted to prove to himself that smoking had no hold over him . . . that he could quit whenever he pleased. So far, he hadn't succeeded in banishing all thought of tobacco from his mind.

Ned considered his other problem. As a man of science, he'd scoffed when he'd learned of the popular misconception about Culverton, Missouri. So what if no schoolmistress had stayed at her post above three months before getting married? What did it matter that he couldn't think of another unmarried, permanent resident male over twenty-three for fifteen miles in any direction, barring old Mr. Scott, who'd buried his third, and Poot Harvey, who hadn't quite all his faculties? And surely he could assign no importance to the fact that men who never considered getting married found themselves happily walking down the aisle within weeks of coming to Culverton?

Let others believe that this town possessed some magical quality. Some spell that enchanted anyone who came near Culverton, making them fall in love and marry their own true mate. He refused to be so gullible.

It wasn't the town. It wasn't the water or the air. And Dr. Castle certainly did not believe in witchcraft. Most of the so-called "love matches" were nothing more or less than the women of the town badgering and tricking a man until his natural resistance wore away. Who wouldn't be glad to say "I do" so only one woman would bother him instead of half a dozen? That the unfortunate man seemed blissfully happy thereafter could be explained as a willful refusal to accept his essential misery.

Besides, even if other people were foolish enough to believe in it and let that belief influence their behavior, Ned Castle knew himself to be the exception. He'd been in town almost eighteen months. Thus far, he'd not met a soul who tempted him to depart from his state of single contentment. He had Mrs. Fleck and her son to cook for him and look after his laundry. He could stay up as late as he pleased, reading his medical journals while his stocking feet dangled over the end of the couch. If he wanted company, there were plenty of transient salesmen also living at the boarding-house. Or his sister and brother-in-law always seemed pleased to see him.

At the boardinghouse no one asked him where he was going or what time he'd be back. No one bothered him with tears or tantrums, outside his professional duties. Though he would have liked to keep a dog to go on his calls with him, he never felt lonely. What did he need or want a wife for? Let the scheming ladies of Culverton answer that one!

"Afternoon, Dr. Castle." The woman who stood before him wore a calico bonnet about fifteen years out of style. But it suited her round face and the laughing wrinkles at the corners of her brown eyes. As charming in her early sixties as she must have been in her girlhood, Mrs. Cotton's whole existence breathed a warmth and kindness that reached out to everyone she met. Even Ned, thinking unpleasant thoughts about her a moment ago, answered her smile with one of his own.

"How are you today?" he asked, mingling the medical attitude with his real desire to know.

"Middlin'." For a moment her brightness seemed to dim. "Just can't seem to get as much done in a day as I'm used to. I get tuckered out over nothing. Why, yesterday I dug the garden, pulled down all that dead creeper from the side of the house, and done the laundry, and I was that close to being too tired to cook supper."

"Well, Mrs. Cotton, we're none of us—"

She shook a playful finger at him. "Now, don't you go tellin' me I'm not gettin' any younger. My momma lived to be eighty-two, and I can't remember her ever sitting down without knitting or mending in her hands. All the folks say I'm just like her, and I aim to live just as long. With you to help me, of course, Neddy."

"I'll do my best." No other human being alive could call him "Neddy" and get away with it. His father and mother called him Edwin, and sometimes, when they were displeased with him, Edwin Dickson Castle! His brother and sister preferred to call him Ned, the name he answered to most readily. To his friends, he'd always been Win. But from Mrs. Cotton, he'd take Neddy and like it.

"May I offer you my arm into the church?" he asked.

"They can say what they like about you, but you do have manners. Oh, my. Oh, yes. But I reckon I'd better wait for the old man."

She turned away and shaded her eyes with her hand against the slanting light of the late afternoon sun. "Where in tarnation . . . ? He was right behind me. Oh." Nodding as though she hadn't expected anything less, Mrs. Cotton said, "Now, ain't that just like him? Comes along late *and* finds a pretty girl."

Ned squinted down the street. He saw the judge all right, a flamboyant figure in his top hat. On his arm he escorted a woman, dressed in black from the dyed straw hat on her head to the high-button boots on her feet. Beneath the squarely set brim, her hair showed as black as her boots. He knew that crow-colored woman, and felt the embers of his anger flare as she approached. She had a way of setting her feet just so, as though she never took a step without thinking it over first.

"Millicent Mayhew?" he asked incredulously.

"Now, Millicent's a pretty girl. You can't deny it. I dare swear she's got the prettiest eyes in these parts."

"She looks like a black cloud. I never see her but I expect it to rain."

Mrs. Cotton chuckled and shook her head in disbelief. "You can't fool me. I've seen the way you look at her."

Keeping his eyes very cool, he glanced at the older woman. "I don't look at her in any special way. Except to wish that she would keep her nicely gloved hands out of my practice."

Despite his dislike, he took pains to be polite when the

others came up to them. "Miss Mayhew. Pleasant to see you again. How are you, Judge?"

Miss Mayhew inclined her head, as regal an acknowledgment of his presence as any duchess could give. Then she turned to Mrs. Cotton and said, "I hear tell you've wrangled some bulbs from Mrs. Stalnaker. You must be a wonderworker."

"She said they were fixin' to take over her garden. Why not ask her for a couple of them big pink lilies? They'd look right pretty over next to your front stoop."

Judge Cotton spoke up, "You gals better get on into church. You got all week to plan your gardens. Come on, Mother."

He all but seized his wife bodily and carried her along. Ned noticed that they'd hardly gone out of earshot before they began whispering to each other. Uneasily aware that the judge's reputation as a matchmaker equaled his wife's, Ned glanced at Miss Mayhew standing beside him. She looked off into the distance, as though forgetting his existence.

"May I escort you inside?" Ned said, still polite.

"I reckon I'll skip church today, Dr. Castle. Thank you kindly just the same."

"Off to pick herbs by the light of the moon?"

She flicked her amber-colored gaze at him then, as though checking the position of something she didn't care to step in. "Not at present," she said levelly. "There isn't going to be a moon tonight."

Ned didn't want her to keep her temper. He wanted her to lash out, to meet his scorn with scorn. Her cheeks were always too pale. Only once had he ever seen her mouth without the tucked-back corners of one who dares not speak her mind for fear of saying too much. She'd been shouting at him, and her cheeks had flown scarlet flags. She hadn't been pretty then; she'd been spectacular.

"Hadn't you better go in, Doctor? I'm sure a prayer meeting will do you a world of good."

That was more like it!

"No doubt," he agreed, reaching into his pocket for his

precious cigar. "But it's going to be a lovely night, moon or no moon. Maybe I'll just stay out here and commune with nature."

"Com . . . commune?" Instantly she covered her confusion with her haughty shrug. "If you prefer the stink of tobacco to the pure Word . . ."

She picked up her heavy skirt in her gloved hands and started toward the church. "Miss Mayhew?" he called, and she turned to wait for him, her face as remote as a queen's.

His long shadow crept up her as he came closer. "Mr. Grapplin's sore hand seems to be cured."

"I'm glad to hear it."

"He tells me that the stuff I gave him for it wasn't any good. But Miss Mayhew gave him some noxious slime in a bottle and it cleared the problem right up." She didn't shrink under the hostility with which he formed the syllables of her name. "Didn't I tell you to stop treating my patients, Miss Mayhew?"

"You did."

"But you're still doing it." Ned told himself that he had every right to be furious. But he feared he sounded petulant, like a small boy pouting after not getting his way. She had that effect on him, and it infuriated him.

She raised her eyes to his for one instant. After a single, searching glance, she looked down again. She had the longest lashes he'd ever seen on a human being. Just because he thought that, he reminded himself, didn't mean he admired her. He could observe her eyelashes, the slenderness of her waist, and the fullness of the rest of her figure in the same way he would observe the physical reality of any patient. The thought of actually being attracted to Millicent Mayhew made his lips twist wryly.

"Well?" he demanded. "Are you going to stop treating people?"

"The last time you ordered me to stop, you said 'my people.'"

"They are my patients. You are meddling with their health with your potions and home remedies. Why can't you get it through your head that it's dangerous?"

"I can't turn anyone in need away. No more than you can, Dr. Castle."

She went on her way, the heavy material of her dress brushing with a soft whisper over the grass. Ned took a step to follow her, but why bother reasoning with a stubborn old maid? Though at times his hands itched to take her by the shoulders and shake sense into her, he knew he couldn't do that. He had a reputation for urbanity to maintain, being the only person in town who'd ever traveled farther than St. Louis. The best thing to do, he decided, was to ignore her. It wouldn't be easy. She could easily be the most aggravating woman on earth, and she happened to live in the same misbegotten town as he did.

Millicent took her place in the pew and opened her hymnal. Though she didn't look up, she knew that Dr. Castle's anger still burned brilliantly, just from the heavy sound of his footsteps as he went by. Amazing how so fair a man could look so dark, just by twitching his brows down. She, though, couldn't be frightened by a mere frown. Other things were far more frightening, most of which she knew by name.

At least Dr. Castle fought fair. Everyone said that he could be a perfect gentleman, and her run-ins with him had proved it. Even when she'd forgotten herself, shouting at him when he'd broken the bottle of cough syrup she'd given Mrs. Ottway, he'd remained calm. It had taken her the better part of a day to brew that syrup and he'd smashed it. A slow stain of red came into Millicent's cheeks when she remembered how fierce she'd become. Of course, if she hadn't been sickening herself . . .

Since then, they'd only met in passing. She'd taken her own remedies for the nasty head cold she'd picked up and hadn't lowered herself to calling the doctor, though she thanked God Mrs. Cotton lived next door. Her hot soup had staved off chest congestion while her laughing conversation kept away the bad dreams.

The congregation stood to sing. Millicent could look down between her neighbors and see the doctor. His thick hair had sprung up in the back, standing up like the hackles on a dog. Deep inside herself, where she kept her secrets and her feelings, Millicent felt a little spark of satisfaction. She'd disturbed the doctor, shaken him up. As long as she could do that, maybe she wouldn't feel so much like a lost and lonely ghost. For that, if nothing else, she thanked Dr. Castle.

After the meeting she could even spare him a pang of compassion. As no one could possibly live in Culverton and not hear at least some of the gossip, Millicent knew as well as anyone else what it meant when Mrs. George went limping up to Dr. Castle to ask him to call at her house.

"This knee!" she said in ringing tones. "Never a moment's peace, Doctor. Just throb, throb, throb, morning, noon, and night."

Millicent saw him nod as he agreed to call on Mrs. George's knee tomorrow. She also saw the smirking smiles and approving whispers of the women as they saw the trap set with bait Dr. Castle couldn't possibly refuse.

"I don't think Lucy George has much hope of landing my brother, do you?" a laughing, husky voice asked. Gentle fingers were laid on Millicent's arm, and she looked down into the slightly swollen but still enchanting face of Antonia Faraday. "Would you mind helping me down the stairs, Miss Mayhew? I'm not as steady on my feet as I once was."

A few inches shorter than Millicent, Antonia looked even shorter because her figure had become so very round. Though Millicent usually felt gawky and awkward, compared to Antonia Faraday she could pass for a willowy, graceful creature of air and fire. "Why do you say Lucy George won't get him?" Millicent asked, telling herself she didn't care but she couldn't get by without making some conversation.

"Because my brother is anti-woman right now, and even if he wasn't, I've never known him to like gigglers."

As though on cue, Lucy George's laughter rippled through the emptying church. A beau had once compared her laugh to silver bells. Millicent thought a lot of the silver had been worn off with too much polishing. Very little of the sound seemed to have any natural shine.

"At least she sounds happy," Millicent said softly.

"But can she make Ned happy?" Antonia shook her head as though that settled the matter. "Men need someone who can stand up to them . . . or you might as well lie down for them to wipe their feet on you."

Millicent had not been in town during the exciting weeks when Antonia Castle had stood up to the man who had since become her husband. Since she'd moved back, however, Millicent found herself constantly refusing invitations from the marshal's wife. Millicent didn't know why Antonia should want to be so friendly; but she could no more discourage Antonia Faraday than she could drive off a puppy, not without the outright cruelty that Millicent shrank from using.

"Lucy George might stand up to your brother. She's said to have a will of her own."

"Not her. She's got doormat written all over her. Now, Mrs. George . . . she's the one with the backbone. This whole idea is her doing. It's a shame she's not thirty years younger."

"And with a sound knee," Millicent murmured.

Antonia laughed out loud, pressing her hand into the small of her back. Though her plain dress had been cut cleverly to conceal the swelling of her pregnancy, very little camouflage could be managed by the eighth month.

"Maybe you should sit down," Millicent said.

"No, no. It feels better to walk . . . or waddle as the case may be. There's Mrs. Cotton. I want to talk to her."

She stood in a little group under the shade trees, talking with Mrs. Wilmot and several other middle-aged ladies. At least two rolled their eyes when Antonia came up, still clinging to Millicent's arm. The marshal's wife panted, trying to catch her breath, and spent a few seconds just smiling around until she could speak.

Mrs. Cotton said, "Mrs. Stalnaker, Millicent here was going to ask you for some of your lily bulbs."

"Well, I don't know," the lady said, running her gaze over Millicent. Mrs. Stalnaker very rarely said anything else.

Feeling Mrs. Cotton's surprisingly sharp elbow hit her

ribs, Millicent stammered, "Th-that's right. If . . . if you don't mind."

Mrs. Cotton said smoothly, "See, our houses being cheek by jowl as you might say, I think it'd be right pretty if Millicent and me both had the same flowers. Now I could give her some of the bulbs you let me have, but they won't look so nice if they're spread out thin."

Antonia, having gotten her breath back, said, "I wish I could grow flowers. Last year even my daisies died."

Mrs. Cotton said, "There's some as can and some as can't. At least you learned how to cook."

A ripple of laughter passed around the circle of women. Millicent blinked, smiling uncertainly, and then glanced at Antonia. Would she be angry that they were all laughing at her? To her surprise, she saw Antonia laughing, too. "I had to, in self-defense," she said. "The only thing Jake knows how to make is stew. And I can't live on stew!"

Mrs. Wilmot, the mayor's wife and Millicent's employer, perhaps emboldened by the laughter and Antonia's response, took it upon herself to say, "Mrs. Faraday, I wonder if I might make a suggestion to you."

"About cooking?"

"No. As you haven't had a child before . . ."

Antonia's hand, where it still rested in the crook of Millicent's elbow, suddenly tightened. Millicent knew she would be black and blue tomorrow. Yet Antonia's voice remained light. "No, I haven't. To tell you the truth, after what I've been through in carrying this child, I may never have another!"

Mrs. Wilmot didn't accept this attempt to change the subject to the fascinating trials of pregnancy. "I thought I'd drop a hint to you, Mrs. Faraday, that most women stay in their homes when they become so . . ." At a loss for a polite term, Mrs. Wilmot simply drew a circle in the air. "I wouldn't mention it, but some of my younger children are asking embarrassing questions."

Millicent felt Antonia's hand relax as the small blonde laughed. Then she said, "I suggest you answer their questions, no matter how embarrassing. I have a pamphlet I can let you have."

"It is customary—"

"My dear Mrs. Wilmot, I'm not about to stay cooped up in my house merely to save you some little embarrassment. Babies don't come out of the cabbage patch, and it's folly to think we can keep children safe by keeping them ignorant."

Mrs. Wilmot drew herself up. "You may think so now, but wait until you have children of your own."

"As you pointed out, I haven't very long to wait, have I?"

Suddenly it seemed as though everyone had a subject to introduce. After a moment Mrs. Wilmot showed her teeth in what might have passed for a smile. Millicent remembered that Antonia Faraday had first come to Culverton to lecture on Sexual Health. Apparently, despite all that had happened to her since, she hadn't entirely given up on her desire to enlighten the world. Millicent had to admire her for it. She didn't have that kind of courage.

Disengaging her arm, she said goodbye in a vague way and drifted out of the circle of women. She paused when Antonia called to her. "I wanted to invite you over for supper tonight. We brought the wagon, 'cause I can't walk so far. Jake'll be happy to run you home afterward."

"Thank you, but I have to trim a hat."

"But you might as well eat with us as eat alone."

"Thank you," she said again. "I really am busy. Besides, it's going to rain."

In a group the women looked up at the endlessly blue sky overhead. Though a breeze rustled the treetops, no clouds threatened. The object of sideways glances, Millicent smiled her soft, retreating smile. "The blackbirds . . ." she explained with a slight shrug.

Millicent slipped away, thinking how nice Antonia could be. But she couldn't trust that niceness to continue. In her experience it made more sense not to trust people at all than to trust them too much.

Ned, of course, had leaped at the chance to eat his sister's cooking. "You've become quite the chef, Tonia," he said, pushing back from the table and sighing in contentment. "Mother would be proud. When I think about the fights you used to have . . ."

"Don't exaggerate. Mother never fights. She just cries until you give in."

Jake, clearing the dishes from the table, said, "You ought to try that sometime, Antonia. Make a change from logical, well-reasoned argument."

"You hate it when I cry. I hate it when I cry. Makes my nose itch."

Her husband winked at her. "But with logical arguments, I never get the fun of kissing away your tears."

Ned coughed stagily. "Don't mind me. Though I must say I can digest better without this sickening display of affection."

"Well, if your stomach's that upset, I guess you can skip dessert."

"I can manage. . . ."

As they sat over their pie, Ned said, "I noticed you'd set another place before. Practicing for when the baby comes?"

"No. I was hoping Millicent Mayhew might come to supper tonight. I don't know why. She never does. I've asked her I don't know how many times."

"Sounds to me like you can stop," Ned said, scraping up the blackberry juice from the plate with the edge of his fork.

"I suppose I should, but . . ."

"Charitable impulses?"

"Don't make it sound so horrible. I *like* her. Or I would if she'd let me."

"Some animals are just natural loners," Jake said. "I think your Miss Mayhew's a loner, too."

Antonia sighed. "Maybe you're right. But something about her . . . maybe it's her eyes. I've seen stray cats who looked that way. Wanting to come inside where it's warm but never quite—"

"Don't waste your time," her brother advised. "She's a frozen old maid and that's all there is to her."

"Just because you don't like her."

"She meddles."

"She helps. You can't deny that!"

"I do deny it. Stewed messes, country remedies! No scientific basis at all, just what someone's grandmother said. Miss Mayhew should limit herself to working at the general store and trimming hats. At least a few wildflowers on the brim of a hat can't poison anyone."

"She's never poisoned anything. Except your disposition."

"Oh, it's not her," he admitted reluctantly. "Or only partly. If the women in this town don't stop their marriage traps, I won't be able to stay on. It's becoming impossible to practice! I've gone out on two calls this week that turned out to be nothing more or less than attempts to flirt with me!"

"Not that you know anything about flirting!"

"Not while I'm on my rounds," Ned said firmly. "If this keeps up, I'm going to have to take a chaperon with me every time I leave the office!"

"Maybe you could offer the job to Miss Mayhew," Jake suggested.

Ned snorted with unwilling laughter. "Even she's not old maid enough to be safe. The tongues in this town would have us married by the end of the first day! Imagine that . . . me and Millicent Mayhew!" His laughter became rich and full.

Jake and Antonia exchanged glances, hers awake with a new idea, his resigned but loving.

2

$\mathcal{M}$ILLICENT CAME HOME with a basket of Mrs. Stalnaker's lily bulbs in her hand. Stepping up onto the porch, she reached out to turn the thin key in the lock. The click as the bolt released seemed to echo. There weren't many people in Culverton who bothered to lock their doors; she never forgot to.

She thought of sunset as the loneliest moment in her empty days. When the western sky still glowed with streaks of yellow and pink, and all around her families went into their houses to eat their evening meal with the sauce of noise and love, she felt her own isolation most keenly.

Silence and coldness breathed out from her narrow house. Millicent took a last glance to the west before going inside and shutting the door firmly. Once again she locked it.

Her footsteps whispered over the bare floors as she headed straight back to the kitchen. Millicent lit a lamp from the banked embers of the black iron stove. The single flame showed a painfully clean room without any frills. The only furniture consisted of a cupboard against the wall and a table with a solitary chair. Everything still and silent, just as it should be. At least, no one else expected her to clean up after them.

Other old maids kept cats. But their fur made her sneeze. Her parakeet had died of old age last year. She didn't want a dog because the rugs in the house weren't hers. They, along with almost everything else, came with the house when she'd rented it from the Cottons. Though she couldn't imagine either of them refusing to allow her to have a dog because it might mess in the house, neither could she imagine herself asking to keep a pet. She had learned long ago that it was wiser to ask no favors of anyone. To be alone, to be independent, a woman could ask nothing more of the world and expect to get it.

With that thought in her mind, she proudly prepared her meager supper—a boiled egg and some winter-stored potatoes. A sparse meal by Culverton standards, just enough to keep body and soul together. Yet every bite of it was the product of her own work and therefore a source of pride.

While washing the dishes, she heard the wind beginning to kick up. It would soon rain.

True to her prediction, by the time she'd finished trimming Mrs. Hertsbrucker's new hat, the splatter of rain could be heard dashing against the windows. The wind had become fierce, banging the shutters across the front of her narrow house. Though her house might lack luxuries, or indeed basic comforts, the roof did not leak and there were no more drafts than might be expected in any house. Millicent could thank heaven for its sturdy shelter. What did she want with embroidered cushions, rose-colored table lamps, or carved woodwork?

After all, she reminded herself, cheerfulness comes from within. You couldn't expect a bright and festive home when the owner was as she was. And even if it were a palace, she'd still live in it alone. Other people made demands, started conversations even when one wished only for silence, and were always dragging up the past.

There had been a time, when she'd first returned to Culverton, when Mrs. Cotton had tried to match her up with a husband. In her room Millicent shook her head as she removed her dress. Washing her face at the spindly-legged washstand, she remembered the older woman's determined attempts.

Dr. Castle thought *he* had trouble with Mrs. Cotton! She treated him with kid gloves compared to the way she'd harried Millicent. For a while there she'd almost been afraid to leave her house, knowing the older woman waited around every corner with some poor bachelor in tow. Millicent had finally sat down with Mrs. Cotton and stated her feelings on marriage without beating around any bushes.

After all, for some women, marriage might as well be another name for slavery. Washing, cooking, cleaning, hoping always to please, and failing more often than not. Backbreaking, heartbreaking labor and nothing to show for it except calluses. Calluses and babies.

Pausing on that thought, Millicent peered at her face. The lamp cast a yellow glow over her skin, deepening the set of her eyes and emphasizing the tiny lines around her mouth. With her hair dragged back to keep it dry, she looked like a witch from a nightmare. Not a cackling hag but a woman whose eyes told of traffic with the devil himself. Not so far wrong, either, Millicent thought. She reached behind her head and searched out the pins that held her twisted hair close to her head.

Brushing her hair vigorously, she tried to think of something else, to block out the pang she felt whenever she remembered how much she'd once wanted children. All her games as a girl . . .

Mrs. Hertsbrucker's hat, Millicent reminded herself, had more value at the moment than a lot of silly dreams. Would that bunch of cherries at the side stress or downplay the fact that Mrs. Hertsbrucker's cheeks were very nearly the same color? Mr. Hertsbrucker liked his wife's high color; Dr. Castle said something fussy about her heart.

As she took off her white petticoats and corset to slip on her nightdress, the corners of Millicent's lips lifted in a tiny smile. Poor Dr. Castle. She could almost pity another poor victim caught in the ladies of Culverton's marriage madness. She knew from experience that sooner or later he would knuckle under. Everyone gave up sooner or later.

There were a half-dozen young ladies who would do for him. Some were pretty, a few even achieving beauty, especially in one of her gayer hats. Others were plainer of face but charming of manner. Actually, except for herself, Millicent couldn't think of a single girl over eighteen in Culverton who wouldn't make a suitable wife for a rising young physician. It would be interesting to see which one of them caught him at last.

Millicent considered telling the doctor the surefire way to get Mrs. Cotton and her friends to stop matchmaking. It would be kind. But no. He had declared again and again that he didn't need her help or want it. Despite her successes with her grandmother's remedies, he turned up his rather beaky nose, sneering at her lack of scientific proof. Everyone else went on and on about his handsome face and winning ways, yet Millicent preferred to think his nose too prominent and his expression far too haughty. The charm all the women chattered about escaped her.

Blowing out the lamp, Millicent swung her feet under the covers of her narrow bed. It had been a long time since she knelt for her prayers. She believed in God, and would pray to him in his house. But in her own home Millicent never prayed. She lay flat on her back in the dark and listened to the rush and worry of the wind.

Sleep beckoned like a night-dark sea. She could feel the drag of the water rushing past her, drawing her in, lifting her off her feet. As always, she delayed sleep, holding off the moment when she would sink beneath the black waves, losing herself. Sometimes she had dreams that took her back to a time when she'd been happy; there were darker waters when she struggled in a nightmare's coils. She never knew what to expect, so she held off the moment until at last her eyelids fell irresistibly over dry and weary eyes.

At first she couldn't be sure what had awakened her. She hadn't been asleep for long—she could tell because she hadn't rolled over yet. She still lay flat, the covers unwrinkled over her body. If the past was any proof of the present, she should have slept on until the sun came in her window, at about six in the morning. Even after a nightmare, she usually lay awake for only a moment before returning to sleep. What then woke her?

It might have been the wind, still driving the rain against windows. Thunder muttered in the sky, hardly more than a vibration, too far off for her to see the accompanying lightning flash. Millicent decided that she'd heard only the echo of an approaching dream and settled down again to sleep.

Then the wind died for a moment, and with it, the rain. Sharp and clear in the pause, she heard a snuffling wail, half-choked, but clear in its note of desperation. Millicent sat up, clutching the bedclothes to her chest. She closed her eyes to listen harder. A cat, she thought, but not the mating scream. A kitten, maybe, caught in the shed, there where some boards had tumbled. Well, it would be safe enough.

Then she heard it again and knew she'd go on hearing it. With a sigh of resignation, she tossed over the covers and sought under the bed with naked feet for her slippers. Worn though they were, they'd keep her shrinking feet from the cold floors. She swung her spring coat over her nightdress—a slovenly habit but excusable under the circumstances. She couldn't go out in a rainstorm in her robe.

Millicent hurried down the steps. Even if she couldn't breathe around cats, she could keep it in the kitchen until morning and then see if any of the neighbors had lost their kitten. But at the foot of the stairs she paused, hearing the cry again. Was the poor thing on the porch?

She opened the door, clutching the coat around her middle as the wind tugged at it. "Here, puss-puss. Here, puss!"

No soaking little figure trotted in over the threshold. "Come on, kitty! Kitty-kitty?" She made *psht-psht* sounds through her lightly clenched teeth—very enticing to small animals.

The rain bounced off the boards of the porch and rebounded into the house, dampening Millicent's feet. Realizing she didn't have any choice but to go out, she sighed and stepped out into the cold and the wet.

"All this," she grumbled, "for some stupid cat! I should go back. . . ." She stubbed her toe, but not on anything hard. On something that crackled and gave. Basketwork, she told herself, well used to the feel and sound of wicker because of her hats. The smell of wet basket came up, mingling with the fragrance of wet earth.

The lightning arrived, a beating glow in the sky behind

the clouds. Millicent saw a basket at her feet, and over the edge a fold of blanket. Even as she wondered who could be giving her a kitten, she heard the cry again.

Dropping to her knees, she drew back the rain-sparkled blanket with fingers that trembled despite herself. Something white moved and thrust out small arms. Then it opened its mouth and let out the funny wail that had awakened Millicent.

"Oh, dear," she said, addressing the person in the basket. "Oh, my dear."

She poked at the fire in the stove, bringing it back to life. Then she wiped her trembling hands on her coat. Slowly she approached the basket sitting on her table.

The baby stopped crying as soon as she brought it into the house. Something about this baby, maybe the pugnacity of the tiny nose or definition of the chin emerging from plump cheeks, told Millicent that a boy lay in the basket. His dark blue eyes stared about him with guileless curiosity. He had no hair, just the lightest softest fuzz imaginable, glinting golden in the lamplight.

With one hand he reached out to her, to make a limp grab at the dark hair that flowed down above him. Millicent smiled. "You like that?" she said softly and laid the strands against his open palm. The impossibly tiny fist closed around, and he gave a surprisingly hard pull.

Millicent laughed, a breaking sound against the silence of her house. Almost without realizing it, she lifted the small, warm bundle out of the basket, her hands under his armpits. He kicked his feet against the folds of his beige woolen dress. Soft sounds came from his lips, along with a few bubbles. He looked at her as if to say, "You understand me, don't you?"

Responding to an ancient instinct, Millicent folded the baby against her heart. He turned his face toward her warmth, nuzzling the folds of her coat. Millicent laughed and then said ruefully, "I haven't any. . . . Let's see what's in your basket."

Using only her free hand, Millicent felt around the faded

pink gingham lining and the still-damp blanket. Paper wrinkled and rattled, but she ignored it. Then her fingers touched cool glass. She lifted out a flat flask bottle, fitted with a rubber nipple, half-full of milk.

The young visitor knew exactly what to do with that. In an instant he began to suck, keeping his eyes closed to better aid concentration.

Sitting down, Millicent looked on in wonder. He was so perfect . . . tiny fingers, long eyelashes, and pink cheeks. Millicent had never been a prey to baby worship, the ritual oohings and aahings over newcomers to the earth. She'd glanced into cots and cribs, made suitable sounds, and departed unmoved.

This time Millicent felt a pang in the area around her chest, and wondered if a corset eye had given way. It felt just like that—the glancing touch of something small snapping under a strain too great for it. Then she recalled. She'd taken her corset off for the night. This must be something else.

One of the side benefits of Culverton's quick and early marriages was that there tended to be a lot of babies around. Sometimes in the store a distracted mother would even hand one to her as she chased after an older child. She'd always thought that taking good care of a baby simply meant exercising a little more common sense than most people possessed.

Therefore, after a moment's thought Millicent knew what to do when the bottle's last drops were drained. She put the baby against her shoulder and patted and rubbed his back—no wider than her hand. After a few moments he gave off a burp that would have done credit to a grown man—if he'd been raised by the roughest of roughneck miners.

Millicent laughed again. "That feels better, doesn't it?"

She became aware that the weight on her shoulder was increasing. Turning her head, she tried to see if the baby had fallen asleep. But his left cheek lay on her shoulder, so she could not see the baby's face.

Walking slowly, trying not to jounce him too much,

Millicent carried the baby out of the kitchen and across the hall to the room she had fitted out as a workshop. Here were baskets with feathers, fruit, or ribbons and a table holding some wig forms.

Turning and bending her knees, Millicent tried to see the baby's face in the mirror. Were his eyes closed or not? She couldn't tell. She thought not.

Millicent began to sing, very softly, her voice rising only to the level of a comforting whisper. "Oh, Heaven's Door, I can't hardly see. Oh, Heaven's Door, won't you ope for me? Too weary are my feet; too dry and drear the way. Lay me down in a bed of ashes; Lord, here ends my day. Oh, Heaven's Door . . ."

As she sang, she realized that as a lullaby, this song would lead to nightmares rather than pleasant dreams. She tried to remember a happy song and couldn't think of any. Frowning at herself, she walked back and forth, her hand lightly pressed against the baby's back.

He grew heavier as though he were leaning harder against her. On the point of getting the lamp so she could see for sure whether he slept, she held still when he began whistling lightly. It couldn't be called a snore; the little gurgle came and went on a note far too soft and high for that. She smiled tenderly as she realized he'd dozed off. After all, it must be all of nine o'clock, far too late for such a little one to be awake.

Stepping just as slowly and softly as she could, Millicent returned to the kitchen. Offhand she couldn't think of a place for him to sleep. If the blanket in his basket felt damp, she could find him another. That yard and a half of dress goods she hadn't made up yet would do for a start.

While feeling his blanket for dryness, she heard the paper crinkle yet again. Millicent pulled it out. Brown, triangular in shape but more as though roughly torn than cut, it didn't look as though it belonged anywhere near a baby. She'd seen paper like that before, only usually it had come in wrapped around a rock.

The carefully formed letters were written in a thick, rusty

black ink with a pen that alternated between scratching and leaving spidery blots.

Missus Cotton he is a good boy Petey he don't have no daddy

Millicent turned the paper over, but the baby's mother didn't write another word. Giving him another light pat on the back, Millicent said with satisfaction, "Petey."

With the baby sleeping on her shoulder and the basket tucked beneath her arm, Millicent went up the dark stairs to her room. She had no blankets soft enough to touch his smooth warm skin, but the brushed cotton flannel in a dusty shade of red would do very well. She'd been planning to make a new wrapper to keep her clothes clean while she worked. It would do just as well as a baby comforter.

She lay the baby down on her bed. He let his arms fall open beside his head, while his fat legs crooked out to either side. Millicent found herself smiling at his little face crunched up with dreams.

Shaking herself, she got out the dress goods. Being careful to conceal every scrap of wickerwork that might scratch him, Millicent made his bed. Then she picked him up and carried him over to it.

The instant she lay him down, his long eyelashes lifted. Out of his tiny red mouth came a sound like the steam whistle on the noon express. Millicent snatched him up again. "What is it? What's wrong?"

In the air he kicked and gurgled. Resting once more against her chest, he quieted. His head dropped to the side.

Millicent squinted down toward her shoulder. He couldn't have fallen asleep that fast! But he had. The tiny lips fell open with a smack, while his fists clutched her nightdress. She let ten minutes go by, while she said the Lord's Prayer five times at the Reverend Budgell's pious pace. She'd noticed often enough in church that it took him two minutes by the clock.

When it seemed that Petey had again become deeply asleep, once more she bent to place him in the basket. Once again, he woke up. "For mercy!" Millicent said.

Putting him on the bed, however, seemed to ensure a restful sleep. Maybe that's what his mother had done.

Millicent sat on the bed and watched the baby sleeping, a surprisingly entertaining pastime. Did all babies have eyelashes that shaded their cheeks? She could see the pulse beating in the hollow above the back of his neck. She found herself doting on it.

For the first time she asked herself why she hadn't instantly awakened the Cottons. As soon as she read the note, she should have been next door, pounding their new brass knocker up and down until one of them came down. When she found the basket, she should have called upon them directly. Strange babies on doorsteps weren't her responsibility; let the judge handle this. That was what the town paid him for.

Really, such tiny fingernails!

After all, Millicent reasoned, the note said "Missus Cotton." Petey's mother had obviously imagined that she left her son on their porch. Everyone for miles and miles around knew Mrs. Cotton had a heart as big as nature. She would have cut off her head with a blunt knife sooner than send a poor orphan away to some soulless orphan asylum.

Especially such an adorable baby.

If she had the mind God gave a goose, Millicent thought, her lips tightening, she would take Petey over to the Cottons' house first thing in the morning, before cockcrow. After all, she wasn't really settled enough to care for a child. Some days it took all she had just to scrape together enough money to buy food for herself. And babies needed lots of things . . . diapercloth, special foods, toys. And they were a lot of work . . . washing things out, changing, playing. Besides, *where* was she supposed to sleep if Petey was going to take over her bed?

She covered him gently with her own blanket. Then taking a pillow, she made herself as comfortable as possible under the circumstances. The dress goods really were very soft, even on the floor.

3

$\mathcal{N}$ED DECLINED TO have Jake drive him home from the Faradays' little house on the edge of the woods. "But it's going to rain," Antonia said. "You'll be soaked through before you ever get to the station."

Ned had a standing arrangement to play checkers with Mr. Grapplin, the stationmaster, every Wednesday night while he waited for the midnight train from St. Joseph. The train only made a water stop, but the stationmaster liked to be there. As everyone in town knew where to find the doctor on Wednesdays, Ned felt an obligation to go, though in every other way he felt like saying the heck with it.

He couldn't remember when he felt so cantankerous. "Rain? Nonsense. The sky's just slightly overcast."

"Millicent said—"

"Oh, the oracle has spoken. Look, it's bad enough I have to put up with her meddling in my practice. She's not going to start meddling with the weather."

"But she said the blackbirds . . . something about the blackbirds."

"Antonia, no one can predict the weather by the actions of dumb animals. That's been proved an absolute rustic fantasy by Professor Jankowicz of Prague."

"Prague's a city, isn't it?"

"Yes."

"Stands to reason animals in a big city wouldn't know how to predict bad weather."

Ned shook his head, wishing he could learn to be as wise

as Jake, who had vanished to care for the livestock at about the time this discussion began. "You used to be so clear-minded," he said. "You even have a degree from a prominent women's college."

"I haven't forgotten."

"Apparently your *mind* has. Of all the circular, inside-out logic!"

"Logic," Antonia said with the air of one who makes an unanswerable argument, "won't do you any good when raindrops are sliding under your collar. At least take an umbrella."

Ned left, grumbling, under a sky that looked more threatening every instant. The skin on his neck prickled with the feeling that lightning charged the air. Maybe that explained why he felt so mean and impatient, as though he'd like to stomp and rage like the weather.

When he considered with what enthusiasm and high hopes he'd first come to Culverton, he didn't know whether to laugh or cry. His cherished little sister lived here, happy with her marshal, and his father, whom he revered but with whom he quarreled whenever they met, lived fifteen hundred miles away in Connecticut, far enough away to let his reverence overcome his impatience.

He couldn't complain about his welcome. The town had refrained from turning out the band only because they didn't have one. However, banners had waved, flowers had been given by a blond little girl, and speeches, pompous and lengthy, had been given by the two rivals for mayor, Mr. Wilmot and Judge Cotton.

On seeing the man he replaced, Ned understood the joy of the town's welcome. Dr. Partridge, a snuff-fingered, grubby old soak, had been a disgrace to his profession. The town had voted him a small pension, to ease the pain of his retirement. He'd been easing the pain steadily at one of the local saloons ever since. Even the small group of prostitutes in Culverton now preferred to take their concerns to Dr. Castle, though a few cowboys still went to Doc Partridge for boil-lancing and ingrown toenails.

As Ned reached the edge of town, the rain began to fall,

a cold, soaking rain. Ned began to grumble. "That blasted woman," he said. Knowing he had not the slightest reason to blame her for the bad weather didn't make him feel any more charitable.

Millicent Mayhew—right again. In another day and time they'd have burned her at the stake, or at least dunked her. Though a man devoted to science, when it came to Miss Mayhew, Ned wondered if his old Puritan ancestors mightn't have had a few good ideas.

He lifted the umbrella Antonia had insisted he take and pushed it open. It gave him a moment's respite from the rain before the wind tugged it inside out. Stopping on the boardwalk, Ned squinted up at the black oilcloth, willing it to return to its proper bell shape. Even when he tried to wrestle with it, it obstinately refused to resume its function.

With a superstitious shudder that he couldn't entirely repress, Ned wondered if his hard thoughts about Millicent had caused it to break. He let go of the handle and it skittered away, rattling over the boardwalk, looking like a black-garbed witch riding a low-flying broom.

"Nonsense!" This wasn't Salem, and he wouldn't be an illiterate religious fanatic for anything in the world. The strengthening wind alone had confounded his umbrella. He'd just congratulated himself on coming to a scientific conclusion when the wind died away entirely. In that moment he heard a baby's cry.

Ned glanced around. Who at this end of town had an infant? There were stores, a few homes, the rebuilt livery stable with the Dakers' new, neat little house beside it. They had a baby, a toddler really, rising all of two years old now.

The cry came again, just when Ned had all but convinced himself he'd imagined it. The wind rose. He brought out his watch from his hip pocket, wiping the rain off the crystal with his thumb. Tilting it to get a good look at the face in the dim light, he said aloud, "Just nine o'clock. Too late to have a baby out in the night air."

Slowly he walked on, listening as he walked. The rain splattering on the walkway and dripping in musical rushes from gutters made a curtain of sound. The lightning pulsed behind the clouds and as the thunder died away, the cry came one more time, more faintly.

What made him look at Millicent's door? Merely that she'd been in his mind? Or a movement glimpsed out of the corner of his eye?

Her white nightgown billowed between the folds of a dark robe. Her long hair mingled with the color of the robe, losing itself. Ned looked at her and thought of a strange, slightly decadent painting he'd seen in Vienna. Medea by night, exalted with love, yet with the tragedy to come somehow foreshadowed in the uplifted wings of her hair.

Millicent bent low and picked up something, a basket, an awkward oval shape that she held in both hands as she looked inside it. He heard her voice, more feminine than he'd ever heard it, saying, "Who are you, little one?"

Then she seemed to disappear into the darkness. He knew, of course, that she had gone into her house, carrying the thing with her, carrying it with the greatest possible care, as though the contents were more precious than a Ming vase or a Cellini saltcellar.

Ned felt curiosity attack him like a sudden burning itch.

Though he'd never been in Millicent Mayhew's house (indeed he could think of no one who had been), he'd spent several laughing evenings at the Cottons' house. Once, he'd heard how both houses were exactly the same, inside and out. Therefore, if the Cottons' kitchen had a window above the sink, there must be one in Miss Mayhew's. Unless he missed his guess, Miss Mayhew would take that basket into the warmest room in the house.

Ned didn't try the gate, guessing that the rain would make it squeal like a trodden cat. He touched one square-topped post lightly as he swung himself over in a lithe leap. Then, after a quick tiptoe through the spring flowers, a few strides carried him through the narrow gap between her house and the blank wall of the house next door, and then around to the back to look for the window.

Miss Mayhew kept no dog. Ned thought fleetingly what a shame to have a snug little house without a dog. But no doubt Miss Mayhew's cold heart had no affection to give to a dumb creature, so it was just as well. That was one drawback to boarding at Mrs. Fleck's. She thought dogs were a nuisance, though there wasn't a carpet in the place that couldn't have been improved by one.

His eyes having adjusted to the night on his long walk, the light that shone out from the back window seemed blindingly bright. Ned squinted as he came closer. He wiped the drops from the glass with the flat of his hand.

Miss Mayhew bent over the fire, poking it up into a livelier blaze. The flame's light seemed to dance among the voluminous folds of her nightgown, making it golden. She'd look good in any color besides the everlasting and eternal black she affected, but gold would best play up the exotic coloring of her skin and hair, while her unusual eyes were already that color.

When she turned from the stove, closing the door, the golden trick of the light faded, leaving her drab again. Ned ducked down as she crossed in front of him. His feet must be crushing some wet plants, for a sweetly aromatic fragrance floated up to caress his face. "Wolfsbane and hemlock, no doubt," he said softly, wrinkling his nose.

When he looked again, a baby nestled in Miss Mayhew's arms.

Ned stared through the window, ignoring the rain that dripped off the ends of his hair, rolling down under his collar. The baby took all of Miss Mayhew's attention. Realizing he could have leaped up and down without attracting her notice, Ned stood fully upright, easing his back.

She never would have allowed him to see her like this. If she'd known he looked in on her, her lips would have pursed, her brows would have twitched together, and her back would have become as straight as a poker. With her guard relaxed, she looked as young as a new bride. He'd seen his share of women with their child in their arms, some worried, some resigned, some exhausted. He couldn't remember one with such an air of bliss. Her face shone as though all Miss Mayhew's dreams had come true. Ned found himself wishing she looked like that all the time, for she had suddenly become as beautiful as his own dreams.

The squeak-slap of a privy door brought home to Ned the dubious nature of his position. He crouched low again. To be caught looking in a lady's window, even her kitchen window, smacked of perversion. Shocking for any man; disastrous for a doctor. Curiosity alone wouldn't be enough of an excuse.

From next door Ned heard Judge Cotton's heavy footsteps crunching the gravel that ran from the privy to the back door. As he went up the back stairs, they creaked under his feet. "Mother?" he called as he opened the back door. "Better break out the lime again. That privy's smellier than a polecat in August."

Ned knew he should go. But he couldn't resist taking one last glance through the window. Millicent could no longer be seen within the picture frame of the window. He hesitated a moment more, hoping she'd come back.

Then the Cottons' back door slammed. Ned snapped his head around to see the judge, his black silk coat pulled on anyhow over his undershirt.

"I see you, you varmit!"

Without a word of warning, the old man threw a squirrel rifle to his shoulder. Ned decided discretion was the better part of valor and quick feet the major factor in any retreat!

He leaped around the far side of the house. His heart pounding like the hooves of a runaway horse, Ned headed for the front yard. With infinite relief he heard the judge exclaim, "Damn blasted powder's wet! But I scared him off, Mother."

Once again Ned jumped over the fence, only to land on one knee. Not waiting to take stock, he sprinted away toward the depot. Though he felt sure the judge didn't see as well as he claimed, Ned still didn't care to be on the wrong end of the gun. The judge might not hit a vital spot, but the odds were just as good that he would. Ned never cared for fifty-fifty propositions. Too many European cardsharps had shown him that a hundred for two doesn't always mean fifty apiece.

Halfway down the street he stopped to take a dozen panting breaths. Recovering, he tugged down his waistcoat and adjusted his trouser legs. Outwardly just as usual, inside him a thousand questions churned in his brain.

As he walked toward the depot, he tried to sort them out. Where had that baby come from? What did Miss Mayhew intend to do with it? He had to find out, not merely to satisfy his curiosity but because he had taken an oath as a doctor, swearing to uphold the public good. A foundling—if that's what the child was—meant somewhere a mother broke her heart over giving up her baby. Plus, she might be in need of his skills.

Though the child had looked to be six or eight weeks of age, Ned had seen the consequences of enough bungled births to wonder what condition the mother might be in. *He* hadn't delivered any babies lately; that meant either Doc Partridge or some woman had attended, possibly experienced in childbirth, or more likely not.

Behind him he heard the slam of a door, the squeal of a gate and running footsteps. "Hey, you there, wait up!"

The judge slowed, lifting the rifle and holding it steadily at Ned's chest. Having never been on the business end of a gun before, Ned marveled at how wonderfully it concentrated his thoughts. He could be proud, however, that his voice didn't shake as he said, "What seems to be the trouble, Judge?"

"What? Is it you, Ned? That's right. It's checker night." He lowered his rifle. "Have you seen a low-down varmint anywhere about?"

"Cat, rat, or dog?"

"Two-legged. Saw some twisty son of a bitch peering through Miss Mayhew's window not two minutes back."

"Outrageous!" Ned exclaimed. He thought it would look better if he glanced around and did so. "Just a few minutes ago? It seems to me I did see someone down the street a few minutes ago. Well, not seen so much as heard."

"Which way?"

Ned gestured loosely in the general direction of the heart

of town. "He was going fast by the sound of his footsteps. I doubt you'll catch him now."

The judge sloped his rifle against his shoulder. "Dang and blast! I would have peppered his backside for him if I had another second to aim. Can't understand fellers who go peeking in windows. Seems there's more comfortable ways to enjoy yerself. Nice set of French postcards, say."

Ned thanked his luck that the dark covered his face, for he could feel an unaccustomed heat in his cheeks. Even when his sister had made a cult of frankness in sexual matters, he still believed in a time and a place for everything. A dark and rainy street was not, for him, the place to discuss . . . French postcards.

"As long as Miss Mayhew is all right . . ." he began.

"I don't want to tell her," Judge Cotton said. "Don't want to scare her. No point in gettin' the ladies all riled up and jittery. I'll drop a word in the marshal's ear though. What're we paying them deputies for if not to keep the backyards free of two-legged peepers?"

"Exactly," Ned said. "Well, I'll be going along. I've already kept Mr. Grapplin waiting."

"Couldn't tear yourself away from Antonia's good cookin'? That gal's improved time out of mind since she come to Culverton. And Jake was just a dried-up old bachelor until they got hitched. You know, there's nothing like marriage for settlin' a man down and makin' him alive to the opportunities . . ."

Ned tried to interrupt. He'd heard this speech before, and it did not improve with the wearing of a soon-to-be-soaking suit. "Judge," he said, "you'll have to—"

The judge did not seem to notice the rain, though his black silk coat must have been getting heavier and heavier by the minute. "Yes, sir, a man who ain't married is only half alive, in my view. Marriage gives a man solid values, something to back him when things get tough, keeps him goin'. Look at me. I never would have risen to the heights of my pro—"

"Old man," Mrs. Cotton said out of the darkness. "You goin' to be jawin' all night, leaving me here with nothing but worry? I been thinkin' for an hour past that you been knifed in an alley or clouted on the head by that sneakin' son of an alley rat."

"Sorry, Mother. Got talkin' to the doctor here."

"Doctor?"

"Good evening, Mrs. Cotton."

The rain had settled into a monotonous drizzle, good for the crops, but very penetrating even to wool. Enough light came from the sky to see Mrs. Cotton, the gay print of her wrapper muted, her gray hair twisted into two tight braids, the curl rags sticking out.

"Well, you may be a doctor, but you'll catch your death standing around out here in the rain listening to this old blowhard. I bet your feet are wet."

"A little, nothing to worry over."

"That's because you haven't seen as many wet feet turn to pneumonia as I have. Vernon, you get along to the depot and tell Mr. Grapplin the doc ain't comin' up tonight. Anybody that comes lookin' for him can come to our house."

"Really, Mrs. Cotton, I'll be all right."

"Do as you're told and come along with me." She seized his hand and began to walk off with him. "Get along, Vernon."

"Ain't I goin' to catch my death?" he asked plaintively.

"You're too tough to kill easy," she said. "'Sides, you got me to keep you warm in the middle of the night. Who's Neddy got?"

Thus, despite his protests, Ned found himself sitting in a scrubbed kitchen, his boots drying by the back door and his pants legs rolled up to his knees. Mrs. Cotton was just lifting a kettle off the stove. Ned flinched and squeezed his eyes tight shut as she poured the steaming water into the big bucket where his bare feet sat defenseless.

"Some for the feet, some for the throat," Mrs. Cotton said, as though repeating a mystic charm. "Drink up that tea, Neddy; it'll stave off the sore throat you're headed for."

"What's in it?" he asked suspiciously.

"Nothing but tea—and a mite of honey. Don't have no lemons yet."

Her merry eyes shot him a teasing glance. Aloud, she mused, "Maybe I ought to wake Millicent. She might have a remedy or two."

"No, don't trouble her." He noticed with what surprise Mrs. Cotton regarded him. Had his tone lacked the heat it usually took on when someone suggested Millicent's "medicine"? Perhaps it had, but he'd been thinking of the look on her face, so tender, so happy. He realized he'd never seen her look happy before, not in all the time since she'd come to town. He didn't realize he wore a smile until Mrs. Cotton said, "There, now. That hot water's startin' to feel right good, ain't it?"

4

IN THE COOL mist of the next morning Millicent crossed the backyard. The Cottons' garden, laid out in neat rows, showed the first sprouts of the coming year. Though she herself had a vegetable garden, she never achieved the yield Mrs. Cotton got.

She grew enough to keep her, though. In summer she ate mostly home-grown vegetables with a piece of butcher's meat two Sundays out of four. But neither turnips nor chunks of cheap pork would do for Petey. Freeing her arm from her black-fringed shawl, Millicent rapped gently at the Cottons' back door.

She saw Mrs. Cotton, her hair still twisted up in curl rags, pull aside the curtains and peep out. Surprise and pleasure mingled in her expression, and her lips, as pink as a young girl's, formed the words, "My lands!"

The doorknob rattled as she turned it. "If it isn't Miss Mayhew! I was just sayin' to myself how I had to stop by later and give you a hand with them bulbs."

As soon as she could, Milllicent rushed into speech. "I'm sorry to trouble you so early—"

"No trouble, honey. Come on in and set yourself!" Mrs. Cotton took Millicent's hand and all but hauled her bodily over the threshold.

Millicent shook free, but gently. "I can't stay. I only wanted to ask if I could borrow some milk."

"Milk? I don't know as I have any."

Glancing uneasily toward her own house, knowing Petey

must be awake by now, Millicent did something she'd never done before. She asked a favor twice. "Do you think you could look?"

She saw surprise brighten Mrs. Cotton's eyes before the older woman's natural courtesy took over. "Sure as you live. I'll go down cellar. Wait just a shake."

Millicent tugged her shawl closer about her shoulders. She'd hustled her old poplin skirt on over her nightdress and had plucked up the shawl instead of taking time to button a blouse. There were no stockings on her feet either, stuffed hastily into her dull black boots. The cool morning air seemed determined to find out all the shortcomings of her clothes.

Mrs. Cotton came back, and to Millicent's infinite relief, she carried a bottle about a third filled with white liquid in her hand. "Here you go," she said, lifting it. "Not much, mebbe a cup or two. Makin' pudding, are you?"

"I—uh—yes, that's right. Bread pudding."

Millicent did not lie well. She blushed, stammered, and tripped over her tongue. But Mrs. Cotton only smiled. "Mr. Cletterbuck will be around later on with his wagon. If'n you like, I can ask him to drop you off a bottle. He's reasonable in his prices, too; lot cheaper'n keeping a cow anyhow."

Mentally counting pennies, Millicent said, "Yes, that will be all right." As an afterthought, remembering belatedly what one said when someone did a favor, she said, "Thank you. Thank you very much."

"My pleasure, child. If'n you have a minute . . ."

Millicent turned back on the bottom step. Though she had a picture in her mind of Petey screaming for breakfast, she couldn't be rude now. "Just that long," she said.

"The judge didn't care to mention it, but I reckon you ought to know. I was sittin' here last night, lookin' at some foolish book Mrs. Little lent me . . . all 'bout dukes and peasant-gels and such . . . and I got up to get a sip of water when I happened to catch sight of somebody in your garden."

"In my garden?"

Mrs. Cotton nodded, the little twists of rag in her braids

bobbing. "Lord, yes. Gave me such a turn! Some sneakin' weasel was a-peeking in your kitchen winder."

Millicent stared blankly at the morning-glory vines sprawling over the back porch. She couldn't seem to take in what Mrs. Cotton was telling her.

"I can't blame you for being took aback," Mrs. Cotton said. "I ain't never heard of such a thing in all my born days, 'cept once and that turned out to be Jess Teckle eloping with Margery Walton. And it wasn't as if her daddy weren't glad to be shut of her, either. She thought it was romantic; that's why they did it 'stead of gettin' hitched Christian in a church."

Soothed by the gentle flow of talk, Millicent could respond more naturally. "What did you do? I mean, about the person in my garden?"

"Oh, you should have seen the judge! Soon as he comes back from the . . . convenience . . . I told him. He snatched up his squirrel shooter and went tearing out there like the devil wanted his shoe leather. Ain't seen him move so slippy-like since the day I waxed the floor with grease by mistake for paraffin."

"Did he . . . shoot?" She hadn't heard anything, but being so busy with Petey . . . Millicent put her free hand to her lips. What if the unknown "peeper" had been Petey's mother, looking to see that her baby had been cared for? "He didn't shoot, did he?"

Mrs. Cotton sighed in resignation. "No. Dern fool let the powder get wet. Was his granddaddy's gun and it's temperamental-like, 'specially in the rain."

"Thank heavens," Millicent whispered.

"Don't blame you for being upset," Mrs. Cotton said kindly. "Bad enough having someone creepin' around without finding his carcass in the collard greens. Why, if it hadn't been for Doc Castle, I would have been scared to stay here alone."

"Dr. Castle? Oh, that's right. Last night was checker night, wasn't it?"

"'At's right. The judge caught him just on his way there, soaked to the bones. I had him here with his feet in a mustard bath soon as I seen him. Just like a doctor not to take care of himself, but I guess the cobbler's young'uns go barefoot."

"Thank you for telling me," Millicent said, still troubled. What if Petey's mother came back? Millicent didn't want to trust to the temperament of the judge's granddaddy's rifle. The next time the night might be fine.

"Like I said, the judge wasn't goin' to say anything to you about it. But I reckon a woman's got a right to know what goes on in her own backyard."

"Yes. I'd rather know. But—"

"Don't you worry, child. The judge and me'll keep an eye on things for you. If'n you get scared in the night, just scoot on over here. No spyin', creepin' hound's gonna tangle with the judge."

"Oh, I don't think he'll come back . . . the 'peeper.' I mean, it's not like he could see anything through my kitchen window. Not like my bedroom . . . not that there's anything to see there, either. I keep my shades drawn, I hope."

Millicent let herself into her house, expecting to hear demanding wails from upstairs. The house, however, remained as silent as an unvisited tomb. Suddenly afraid something tragic had happened to Petey, she darted up the stairs and went straight into her room. The baby lay still and small in the center of her bed.

Each breath a painful blow to her chest, Millicent crept nearer. No sooner had her shadow fallen over him than he awoke. He didn't wake crying, like most babies. The lids over his slate-blue eyes lifted, and he raised his head to look full into Millicent's eyes. She smiled as he yawned and smacked his lips.

"Breakfast coming right up, sir," she said merrily. "But first, we'd better change that diaper."

Her dress goods were sacrificed without a second thought. Peeling away the soiled diaper, Millicent couldn't help making a face but, meeting those innocently staring eyes, forced a smile. "There you go," she said, after cleaning him with water. "That must feel better. Now, just hold still. . . ."

With excellent aim Petey drenched her with a homemade

fountain. Millicent staggered back, swiping at her face. "Ugh! Oh, mercy!" she said, feeling the hot liquid seep through her dress to her shoulder.

She dried off with her towel, then approached the baby again. "Oh, so you think that's funny, do you?" Kneeling down, she blew a raspberry on his round tummy. He kicked his legs and grabbed at her face, babbling little sounds of delight.

Millicent babbled right back. "Oh, yes, that's funny, that is soooo funny."

She blew some more raspberries, inhaling the sweet baby scent. "All right, then, Petey. How 'bout that breakfast?" she offered, when he wore a red cotton diaper and his shirt.

Millicent knew she couldn't keep Petey a secret for very much longer. For one thing, when he cried during the uncomfortable minutes while a burp stuck halfway up, Millicent thought the roof would collapse from the sheer volume of sound. For another, feeding time would come again soon, and she couldn't borrow another drop of milk. Everyone would wonder, as Mrs. Cotton already wondered, why a single lady suddenly needed vast quantities of milk. Yet from moment to moment she put off the inevitable. It was so wonderful to pretend, if only for a few hours, that this baby belonged to her alone.

Then, at about ten-thirty, Millicent noticed that Petey's nose needed wiping. A moment later it needed wiping again.

"It's most likely not serious," she told him. He nodded, not in answer, but as sleep began to creep over him. They'd been playing half the morning; Millicent's back ached with the unaccustomed lifting she'd been doing. Somehow she found it impossible not to hold him.

A little sniffle meant nothing, after all. Children got them all the time, especially when they'd been outside in the rain. It didn't mean a thing, Millicent told herself, pacing slowly back and forth. He'd be over it tomorrow.

She consulted her grandmother's receipts, the grease-spotted pages in the old copybook that had been her only inheritance from that wise old woman. There were many receipts for children's ailments—How to Bring Up the

Spots in Measles, A Sure Cure For Ringworm, To Prevent Biting of the Nails—but not for children's colds. Most of the adult remedies for a head cold called for quantities of alcohol. Millicent didn't know how effective they'd be without the necessary brandy, gin, or cordial to carry the medicine to the bloodstream. Her grandmother hadn't held with giving drink to babies and neither did Millicent.

She hated to admit it, but she was sorely tempted to call in Dr. Castle. She could imagine how he'd sneer and tease, gloating over her. He'd enjoy telling her that obviously she had faith in her receipts only as long as she herself didn't make use of them. As though she hadn't cured burns and breaks without ever asking his advice, and sometimes against his orders.

"He thinks just because he's a man . . ." Millicent muttered.

A man, moreover, who could be said to be good-looking when he didn't have a sneer twisting his firm lips. Millicent could just bring herself to admit that she found Dr. Castle attractive. She sometimes found herself wondering if his hair could really be as thick and soft as it looked. His coloring was so fair, yet yesterday with the sun on his face, she'd seen the glint of golden whiskers on his jaws. Remembering another kiss with the soft scrape of whiskers against her smooth face, Millicent could almost imagine it had been Dr. Castle who had done the kissing.

Millicent forced the pleasant fantasy away. It hadn't been Dr. Castle and it never would be. She couldn't allow herself to daydream. Facts, as hard, knobby, and unromantic as potatoes, were facts. And that kiss had lead to a betrayal. She had thought of it as fraught with meaning; he'd turned his back the very next day.

Petey slept for three hours by the clock. Millicent got some work done, trying to copy hats from the latest catalogs. She couldn't beat the prices of the big companies. The only advantage she could claim was that if a woman liked a hat, she could have it from Millicent in a day or two, depending on alterations. The big catalog places took far longer, and one had to fight a creeping doubt that one would not get exactly what one had paid for.

When Petey woke up, he refused to take any milk. He didn't want to play. He seemed inert, and when Millicent laid the back of her hand across his forehead he didn't try to pull it down to his mouth. Plus, he felt warm to the touch of both her fingertips and her lips.

She did not stop to think now of what Dr. Castle would say. Petey needed more help than she could give him. Millicent changed him again—protecting herself against further christenings—bundled him up in her shawl, and decided to introduce him to the Cottons. Maybe Mrs. Cotton would know what to do. If not, it would be far less embarrassing to meet Dr. Castle in front of people instead of by herself in her own home.

The only difference between knocking on Mrs. Cotton's back door in the afternoon and the morning was that her hair had been brought under control in neat, smoothly waving rows. She even said the same thing as she pulled back the curtain to see who waited on the step. "My lands! Why, Miss Millicent. What's that you've got?"

The judge appeared behind his wife, a large napkin tucked into his shirt collar. "It's a baby, Mother."

"I know it's a baby. I'm not blind or crazy yet."

Millicent said, "I found him, last night. I'm afraid he's sick."

"I wondered why you borrowed the milk!" Mrs. Cotton said in the tone of one solving a bothersome mystery. She stepped back into her kitchen. "Bring him right on in. You found him, you say?"

"Yes, in a basket, at my front door." Millicent held back the fact that Petey had only appeared at her door through a mistake, instead of at their door. She acknowledged that some part of her still hoped against hope to keep him.

Mrs. Cotton laid the back of her hand to Petey's forehead. "Go and get Dr. Castle, Judge. The little sweetie's running a mite of a fever."

Millicent glanced up into the older couple's faces. Mrs. Cotton's looked just the same as always, her eyes a trifle graver than usual but still smiling. The judge, on the other hand, had turned somber. His innocent eyes did not sparkle, and his face had settled into lines of determination. "I'll have to get Jake as well."

"Now, what good do you expect that man to do? He's not even a daddy yet." Mrs. Cotton looked at her husband, her hands on her hips.

"It's a matter for the law," the judge replied. "Abandoning babies is against the law. 'Sides . . ."

"Will you arrest the mother?" Millicent asked. "I didn't see anyone; I can't tell you anything."

"'Course she can't," Mrs. Cotton said stoutly. "Who'd see anything in the kind of weather we had last night? Why, even that feller you was chasin', you lost."

The judge shook his head as he tugged the napkin out from beneath his double chin. "I'm thinking of the mother. She must be awful confused and frightened to abandon this child. The marshal's the man to find her and then this town will help her. Whatever she needs . . . food, care, a husband . . . we'll get it for her. Ain't right, otherwise."

Instinctively Millicent cuddled Petey closer. Mrs. Cotton stood beside them, her birdlike hand resting on Millicent's shoulder. "Talkin' ain't gonna get us anywheres," she said sternly. "You trot 'long and find Jake and Neddy. Send 'em right over and we'll sort out the whys and the wherefores afterward."

When Ned Castle arrived before the others, Millicent blamed her bad luck. She sat up a little straighter in the hard-backed chair the moment she heard his voice. She felt her face stiffen into hard lines, though she couldn't resist a last smile down at the baby.

Therefore, Ned saw her with a light still in her eyes. Her hair did not look as though it had been ruthlessly dominated; smokelike wisps of it escaped her bun. Remembering how feminine she'd seemed last night when he'd peered through her window, Ned could no longer be fooled by her air of cool conceit.

"Well, now, Miss Mayhew," he said, putting his black

leather bag on the table by her elbow. "Who's this young-ster?"

"He has a cold," Millicent replied. She turned Petey around on her lap to face Ned.

"Just the sniffles," he said, stroking a gentle finger down the baby's soft cheek. The blue eyes stared up at him. "Nice to see you," Ned said. "I can always use another patient."

He held open his hands, and Petey launched himself forward, off Millicent's knee. A gasp exploded from her lips as she grabbed for him. "He'll fall!"

But Ned had already swung him up in his arms. "I've held a baby before, at least once or twice. I won't hurt him." Hefting the baby, Ned said, "Seems like a well-fed young-ster."

"He's too skinny," Millicent said. "Babies should be fat."

"Fat babies make fat adults. Can't do all the running and jumping a child needs to do if he has to waddle."

"Everyone knows babies should be plump so they're strong enough to ward off sickness."

Ned chuckled. "Old-fashioned thinking, Miss Mayhew. The latest facts show that weight has nothing to do with health. This young man . . . he *is* a boy?"

"Yes."

"Looks like it. I can tell he's going to grow up full of sin and impudence. Aren't you, young fellow-my-lad?"

Petey gurgled and stuck out a random fist, right into the jaw so near his own. Ned laughed. "And a right cross, too! That's the way to do it! Hit out!"

"Dr. Castle!" Millicent said, rising to her feet. "About his cold . . ."

"Oh, that. Just a little sniffle. Children get them all the time, especially when they've been outside in the rain. He'll be over it tomorrow, most likely."

Millicent noticed how gently the doctor's hands cupped Petey's little head and how he held the baby close to his chest. Something like laughter rippled in his voice when he spoke to the child, but that meant nothing. Dr. Castle had an unfortunate frivolity of mind that meant he always laughed at unbecoming moments.

She held out her arms to take the baby back, stepping closer to Dr. Castle. He didn't tower over her, yet he didn't seem slight. As he handed Petey over, his hand brushed against her flat waist. Millicent's eyes widened in shock when she felt an answering flutter beneath the black linen.

Heat crept into her cheeks, so she looked down to hide it. She heard voices and footsteps coming up the back steps.

Ned looked in that direction as he said, "As long as he's eating, I wouldn't worry."

"But Petey wouldn't eat lunch. I had milk for him. . . ."

"How do you know his name?" Ned asked, turning to her again. "Was there a note with him?"

Millicent wished again that she'd learned how to lie. All the trouble in her life came from telling the truth without thinking about it. "I . . . um . . ."

Another male voice, deeper than the doctor's, said, "I'd like to know the answer to that, too, Miss Mayhew."

Millicent looked up in surprise. She saw the Cottons and the Faradays, the badge shining on Jake's chest. Protectively, she brought Petey closer to her body. To her, Jake and the judge looked like the law personified, trying to do the right thing perhaps, but more likely to cause havoc with its cold-blooded rules. She'd believed in the law once, trusted it to care for her. It had failed her before; she couldn't let it fail Petey.

The trapped feeling lasted exactly as long as it took Antonia Faraday to push past her large husband. Her blue eyes took in the scene, and she rushed over, as quickly as her pregnant state would allow. "What an adorable baby! May I . . . may I hold him, Miss Mayhew? I'll be so careful. . . ."

Millicent couldn't help hesitating, yet she couldn't quite bring herself to refuse. Antonia Faraday had always struck her as a flighty thing, scandalously in love with her husband. On the other hand, she did have principles that Millicent could respect.

Watching Antonia cuddle Petey above the evidence of her own impending motherhood, Millicent felt a pang of jealousy so intense that she turned away. But Dr. Castle broke into her reflection, as irritating and hard to escape as a mosquito!

"About his name, Miss Mayhew . . ."

"Yes!" she said more sharply that she'd intended. "Yes, there was a note. I'll get it."

She fled, knowing they were watching, believing that they pointed disparaging fingers at her. What would they say when they learned the baby hadn't come to her at all but had been misdirected? It had been wrong to keep Petey, even overnight. They were bound to take him away, regardless, but she couldn't stand the thought of being the focus of malicious gossip again.

Back in the house Mrs. Cotton gave Ned a sharp nudge in the back. "Go after her," she whispered. "The gel shouldn't be alone."

"She won't want me. . . ."

"Git! It's your duty as a doctor." Her voice rose. Rather than argue with Mrs. Cotton, for he knew his chances of winning any argument with her were nil, Ned followed Millicent.

5

$\mathcal{N}$ED HESITATED ON the threshold of Millicent Mayhew's house. The size and shape of the kitchen echoed the Cottons' home, exactly. And yet . . .

No comfortable cushions. No mementos clustered on every available surface. No feeling of warmth or life, despite the stove. An abandoned house with the reputation of being haunted would have a more homey feeling. Ned had seen more welcoming residences in the back slums of London, more cheerful kitchens in miners' camps. He couldn't imagine coming home to this place after a long day on one's feet, selling hats.

The pity that rose up in his heart for Millicent equaled his curiosity over why anyone, let alone a woman, would choose to live like this. When he'd first met her, long months ago, he'd been intrigued by the beauty she kept so ruthlessly under control. Then she'd irritated him by her persistent, wrong-headed meddling in his cases until he'd been certain he no longer cared *what* other facets she might have. Last night he'd been eaten alive with a curiosity that had not yet been satisfied.

He heard a thump from overhead and realized she must be upstairs. Uninvited yet compelled, he followed the sound.

As he went up the uncarpeted stairs, he heard a steady muttering that became words when he came closer. ". . . just a fool and I've no patience with you! Why couldn't you have lied and said it was just a name you made up? Blast Ned Castle anyway! Why'd he have to notice I said the name?"

Her door stood open a crack, not enough for Ned to see in. He gave it a slight push with his hand. The scolding voice stopped the instant the hinges creaked.

Ned walked in, shooting a glance around. He half-expected to see a man; he didn't know why. But Millicent Mayhew stood alone in the center of the room beside the bed. She flicked her gaze over him. "I didn't hear you come in. Can I help you with something, Dr. Castle?"

Her voice held no trace of the bitter anger that had marked it before. "You talk to yourself, Miss Mayhew?"

"Certainly not!"

He smiled at her, trying to beguile her into a confidence. "But I heard someone talking."

"*I'm* not to blame for whatever you think you hear." She folded a cloth in half with a smart snap and thrust it into the basket on the bed. "There," she said. "That's all he came with. It's little enough."

"You know, *I* talk to myself, too."

"I shouldn't go braggin' about it, if I was you."

"Sometimes there aren't any other human voices around."

"Maybe if you didn't live like a hermit . . ."

"Isn't that what you do?" Answering a sudden compulsion, he caught her arm as she strode past him. She tensed and tried to pull free. Ned felt the muscles in her forearm flex beneath the smooth black fabric.

"I'm very lonely sometimes, too, Miss Mayhew."

"Too bad for you."

He said in a low voice, "You're lonely, aren't you? That's why you want that baby."

"I don't want him. . . ."

"You don't want him now because you think we won't let you have him."

"You know so much!" Her lashes shaded her eyes as she strained away from him. Suddenly Ned wanted them to lift so he could look down into her smoky topaz eyes. Even with the rigid lines of jaw and cheek, she had an exotic beauty that seemed so out of place in this small town. He could imagine her in Sicily or Spain; not the Midwest.

She yanked her arm, trying to free it. When that didn't work, she dropped the basket to land a slap on his gripping fingers. "Let me go; what do you think you're doing?"

"Nothing." He opened his hand and she half-stumbled, half-stepped away. When she looked at him, her eyes were magnificent in their anger.

"Are you crazy?" she demanded. "You shouldn't even be up here. I've got to think about my reputation."

"I'm a doctor," Ned said, straightening his coat. "I spend a certain amount of time in ladies' bedrooms."

"So I've heard."

Ned chuckled and had his reward, another flash of her angry eyes. "Gossip always exaggerates."

"Not much. You better watch out for Widow Nichols. She nearly got your brother-in-law once, and I hear tell she's looking to marry into his family."

"She's too old for me."

"You like 'em young? Then Lucy George oughta be just your slice of heaven. What's she? Seventeen?"

"Nineteen."

"An old maid."

"What about you?" he asked flippantly.

"Me?" Her fleeting glance this time held not only shock but a sudden hurt. Ned thrust out a hand, as though to heal the wounds with his touch. But Millicent didn't see. She had turned aside with a flip of her skirts. "I'm too old for you, too."

"You're twenty-four," he said, though he knew differently.

"I'm twenty-eight. An old maid for certain and glad of it."

"Glad of it? You don't want a husband?"

"I want a husband 'bout as much as you do a wife. Funny we both wound up here in Culverton. If you're single and sensible, you get away from this place as soon as you can."

"But you came back. I've heard you lived . . . where? Colorado, wasn't it?"

"That's right," she said shortly. "I want to go now, Dr. Castle. *If* you don't mind?"

Ned reached the door first and pushed it closed. Standing with his back to it, he saw what amounted to a storm of emotions crossing Miss Mayhew's normally impassive features. Anger at his effrontery, anxiety to return to Petey, even a gleam of humor tightened her lips and set her cheeks flaming. His earliest suspicions were correct. Under the right circumstances, Miss Mayhew could stun male beholders into unconsciousness with a kind of wild beauty he couldn't recall ever seeing before.

Yet underneath all that ran a vein of bitterness that might very well have its source in sorrow. Was that the meaning of her black clothes? Whom did she mourn for? Herself, or someone else?

"Why are you an old maid?" he asked, and wondered at his own drive to know more. Usually he knew exactly when to drop a subject. A doctor needed tact almost as much as he needed knowledge.

She just glared at him and demanded, "Have you been drinking? At this hour of the morning?"

"There's no point in antagonizing me. Don't you realize that I can help you?"

"What makes you think I need your help? I don't need anybody's help."

"You want to keep that baby? Don't you think someone's going to ask me if I think you're qualified to care for him?"

"That's . . . what do you call it?"

Ned nearly smiled, only controlling his face at the last instant. He wouldn't put it past her to slap a smile away. "Some people might call it blackmail."

"Blackmail! That's it! Well, Dr. Castle, you can just take your help and stick it . . ."

Now he could laugh. He saw her hand fly up and back. Then the open hand clenched into a fist, and she slowly, slowly brought it down under her control. Somehow the fact that she didn't slap his face disappointed Ned. It would have at least been a contact she had initiated.

She walked back to the bed and sat down. Her shoulders

drooped but her snapping eyes defied her fatigue. They told him she'd fight him every inch. "I've had a right busy morning. What do you want?"

"Answer my question."

"What question? I forgot it already."

"Like fun you have," Ned muttered. More clearly he said, "Why are you an old maid?"

A smile unbent her tight lips a moment. "I'm an old maid because I've never gotten married. May I go now?"

"Why do you live like this?" he asked, his gesture taking in the whole of the plain room. "Why do you wear black all the time? Why don't you have friends?"

"That's three more questions," she answered. Looking past him, she said, "I wonder if I forgot anything?"

Ned stepped away from the door, giving her the ability to leave if she liked. "I will find out," he promised.

"Why? Why do you care?" Her eyes held a challenge that forced Ned to be honest.

"I don't know. Only . . . it goes against the grain to see anyone living like this. Such a cold house."

"I don't care for a place to be stuffy."

"You know I don't mean the temperature."

She got up and crossed the room. She bent to pick up the basket at his feet. Her movements held a certain stiff grace, as though she were protecting her body, afraid to let it be free and natural. "I'm sure Mrs. Cotton and your sister-in-law have got to be wondering what's become of me."

"It was Mrs. Cotton who sent me over."

"I would of thought you'd be cleverer than that, Dr. Castle. You know what this town is like. One false move and you'll find yourself hitched up to me. Wouldn't that just fry your bacon?"

"Both parties have to be willing, in a marriage, Miss Mayhew. And you don't intend to be willing, I take it."

"You take it just right. I don't want or need a man in my life. More trouble than they're worth, more often than not."

"But you want that baby."

She hesitated, then nodded. "Yes, I do."

"Why?"

Did she hide her eyes so much because they were so honest? He looked into their depths and realized she didn't have to answer that question in words. Remembering what happiness he'd seen through the window last night, how her every motion gave away her delight in the child, how she had not troubled to hide her feelings behind a stoic mask, Ned knew he'd have to do all he could to help her keep Petey. He suddenly found out that he wanted to see Miss Millicent Mayhew happy, if only to satisfy his curiosity. Would she be as radiant as he suspected?

He asked, "Can you do it by yourself? What about your work?"

As though she'd given this question a great deal of thought, Millicent answered, "I can take him with me. The other women in the shop won't mind. Mrs. Wilmot did it herself when Arthur was born. He spent his first two years behind that counter."

"It may be different, since Petey isn't hers."

"I think it'll be all right. I can ask." After a moment's thought she added, "Besides, I'm the only one in town who can trim a hat right. My hats bring business into the store; Mr. Wilmot wouldn't like it if I set up a store here. He couldn't care for the competition."

"I'm surprised you don't have a store here already. Seems to me that it would pay you to work right here where you live."

Millicent's lips twitched and Ned held his breath. Would she break into a brilliant smile for him? With a sense of disappointment that surprised him by its stabbing keenness, he watched the smile die before it appeared. She said, "You're the one who just told me how drab my house is. Customers wouldn't like it any better than you have. I can't buy no red turkey carpet or fancy candle-stands. 'Sides, I . . . like getting out of here every day."

"That I can understand."

"I bet you can," she said with a wry tone and a twisted smile. "I spent a couple of weeks at Mrs. Fleck's boarding-house when I first came back to Culverton. I got right tired of the smell of cabbage."

"It only smells like that in the fall. In the spring, it's cauliflower; in the winter, beans."

"And in the summer?" she asked.

Ned closed his eyes and shuddered. "Let's not talk about that," he said.

He heard something that sounded like a choked laugh. But when he snapped his eyes open, Miss Mayhew looked as grave as ever. Perhaps a tiny flush of pink had awakened in those olive-toned cheeks. Ned smiled, that slow, knowing grin that had won him quite a few conquests among the ladies of Europe. Miss Mayhew only said, "Let's get going."

As they crossed the grass, Ned took the basket from her hand. He said in a conversational tone, "I will find out about you, Miss Mayhew."

"Don't trouble your head," Millicent said, putting on speed. "I'm just 'zactly what you see."

Watching the sway of her hips and the glossy brown lights of her dark hair, Ned wished that she had no depths beyond what he saw. For her figure, especially from the back, was alluring, even more so to a man who hadn't tasted the delights of the flesh for two years. Miss Mayhew was a bundle of mysteries, not the least of which being how a woman with a figure made for love could reconcile herself to a dim, dull existence like the one she lived.

Petey undeniably brightened when he saw her. He bounced on Mrs. Cotton's knee and opened his arms wide as Millicent came near. "Lands," Mrs. Cotton said. "That child sure has taken a fancy to you, Miss Mayhew. Oh, my. Oh, yes."

"He's just a baby," Millicent said, scooping him up and cuddling him close. She hadn't realized how empty her arms had been until she felt that yielding, squirming baby in them again.

"Babies know things." Mrs. Cotton nodded wisely as she took up a shirt to darn. "They may come into this world without a word to say for themselves, but that don't make 'em stupid."

The older woman looked over at Antonia Faraday, who

sat in a spindle rocking chair, one hand resting on her swollen abdomen. "You'll see soon enough," she said reassuringly.

Antonia looked up with a smile. "It can't be too soon for me. This little rascal's got a kick that would do credit to a Missouri mule."

Mrs. Cotton chuckled. "That's what you get for making babies in this state."

"Next time I'll be more cautious."

"What's this about a next time?" the marshal said, coming in from the hall. He always made a room look smaller, with his broad shoulders and wide chest.

"Oh, just planning a trip out of state," his wife said with a wink. "You might have to get some help to haul me out of this chair, Jake."

"Not a problem. I'll take you and the chair and tuck you under one arm."

Mrs. Cotton said, "You're welcome to it, Marshal."

Jake Faraday thanked her. Then he said with a sobered tone, "Miss Mayhew?"

Millicent braced herself. He and the judge had been in the parlor, where the judge had been used to rendering judgments in the days before the Courthouse had been built. Had they passed judgment on Petey's future?

But Marshal Faraday said nothing other than, "Where's Ned?"

Not allowing herself to sigh in relief that the moment had been put off, she answered, "He was right behind me when I came in. I don't know where he went."

"Out visiting the . . . convenience, mebbe," Mrs. Cotton said.

"He'd better come back soon," Millicent said. "He walked off with the basket Petey came in." She smiled down into the baby's face, her upper body swaying comfortingly.

Marshal Faraday stepped out onto the back porch, holding the door half-open with his booted foot. "What in tarnation is that man doing?"

"What?" Antonia asked. "Who?"

"Your brother. He's in your flower bed, Miss Mayhew."

"He's what?" Millicent asked. Petey let out a yap of protest. Automatically she made soothing noises and began again to sway. In a gentler voice Millicent asked, "What is he doing?"

The marshal came in, shaking his head and letting the door swing to behind him. "Honey," he said, putting his hand on his wife's shoulder. "Honey, I was willing to put up with your daddy's lectures and your mother's trivial conversation, but if your brother's going to start thinking he's a daffodil, I'm going back to Georgia!"

"A daffodil?" all three ladies asking in voices so mingled they might have been a lone woman.

"Well, whatever Miss Mayhew has planted under her kitchen window."

Mrs. Cotton nodded wisely. "Oh, he must be looking at the tracks of that peeper."

"Peeper?" Jake asked. Millicent noticed he had the expression of a hound dog who hears an opossum in the underbrush, wondering if he should take official notice of the trespasser.

She said, "Yes, I had someone in my yard last night, or so Mrs. Cotton says."

Surprising her with his penetration, the marshal said, "Do you think it might have been Petey's mother?"

"Lands," Mrs. Cotton said, alarmed. "I never thought of that. Vernon! Vernon!"

The judge came in at the double. "What, Mother?"

"That person we saw last night. Anything make you think it might of been a woman?"

Judge Cotton considered a moment, then shook his gleaming head. "No, ma'am. Not 'less she was wearin' a pair of pants, beggin' you ladies' pardons."

"Granted," Antonia Faraday said with her fetching giggle sounding through the word.

Millicent looked down at the baby and found him asleep. "Sssh," she admonished the others.

"Come on," Mrs. Cotton said, putting aside her needlework. "I'll show you a spot you can put him down safe as safe."

Antonia struggled up out of the chair. She said, "Jake, you go and get Ned out of the flowers while I put on some water for tea. You don't mind, Mrs. Cotton?"

"Mercy, child. If you don't know to make yourself at home by now . . . !"

At the top of the stairs Mrs. Cotton stopped, still holding on to the railing. She pressed her free hand to her chest and panted for a few breaths. Her color seemed off, too, but that might have been the dimmer light.

"Are you all right?" Millicent asked.

Mrs. Cotton smiled and nodded. Then, still breathless, she said, "I swear those steps are getting higher! Next thing you know there'll be a volcano in the basement, and I'll be walking up the side of a mountain to go to bed."

"Oh, well," Millicent said, not knowing how to play whimsical games like this.

"Never you mind," Mrs. Cotton said. "The only person in these parts who talks more nonsense than me is my husband."

"You've been married a long time?"

"Forty-seven years come July." Her pride showed in the way she tossed her head up as she spoke.

"That's a long time to be with one man," Millicent said.

"It'd be a lot longer with two! I can't regret getting married, but there's something to be said for staying single. Don't have to answer to anyone, for one thing, and for another . . . for more'n forty years I been sleeping with the window open when I like it closed! But one of these here days, he'll get a surprise."

"What's that?"

"I done told him once that he could have the window open for the first fifty years . . . well, that second fifty's a-coming up mighty quick now!"

As Mrs. Cotton cleared out the bottom drawer of her chifforobe, Millicent wondered what it must be like to be married to the same man, day in and day out, for so many years. Wouldn't there come a moment when there'd be nothing left to say, no surprises left in store? Or did human beings go on being complicated and confusing forever?

They tucked the baby in. For a moment Mrs. Cotton stood gazing down at him, her hands folded together on top of her comfortable stomach. "We never had children," she said. Yet her smile held only a gentle wistfulness.

Millicent never knew what to say when people made confidences. So she said nothing.

"Oh, it's an old pain," Mrs. Cotton said. "After a while you don't notice it so much. It was hardest when everyone else was having 'em, but all my friends are past that now, too."

Millicent nodded. "I . . ."

Reaching out her hand, Mrs. Cotton patted Millicent's forearm. "I'm too old to take in a baby that's not kin. And Vernon ain't the type of man who relishes gettin' up in the middle of the night if he don't have to. So don't you worry. I'm not going to make it hard on you. If you want this young'un, you can have him for all of me."

"But . . . the judge and the marshal . . . and Ned Castle . . ."

"Don't worry." Mrs. Cotton smiled again, a shy, very subtle smile that held the secrets of feminine mysteries. "I can still manage the menfolk."

Millicent's education, she realized, had been neglected. A few minutes of watching Mrs. Cotton "manage" the menfolk and Millicent felt as though she'd been to college.

"But does Miss Mayhew know how to take care of a baby?" Dr. Castle asked, looking at Millicent doubtfully.

"Of course she does," Mrs. Cotton answered. "She's a woman, ain't she? It's not like we're givin' him over to a *man*, is it?" Her tone gave him to understand that she couldn't think offhand what anyone needed a man for in this enlightened day and age.

"I don't know, Mother," the judge said. "Maybe a nice family . . ."

"Like who? Mrs. Lansing's already got so many she don't call 'em by name . . . just gives 'em numbers. Mary Lou Budgell's handless; Mrs. Carter's got the scrawniest youngsters in town 'cause she don't feed 'em nothing but skim milk and hoecake. . . ."

"What about Mrs. Wilmot?" the judge suggested, his expression that of a man who trys to stop a runaway train with his bare hands.

"What about her?"

"She's got a few children, but her youngest is almost three. That's a good time to take on a baby."

"If I know Elviry Wilmot, she's got another bun in the oven right now. And I wouldn't give her a baby to take care of in her condition any more than I'd give him to 'Tonia, here."

"I'm grateful," Mrs. Faraday said. She twinkled at her husband. "At least I'm not handless, darling. Ur, what is handless, anyway?"

"'Stead of coming up with other places to send this child," Mrs. Cotton said, sternly bringing the subject back to the matter at hand, "you men ought to get a-movin' on finding out where it done come from. Jake, you got to talk to every man in this town. Find out what they was doing 'bout a year ago and who they were doing it with."

"Mother!"

"And you, Neddy, you check up on who might of come to you."

"I didn't deliver any children in the last two months, except for Mrs. Schaefer and she had twin girls. Neither one of which could possibly be Petey."

Millicent felt too miserable even to glare at Ned. She couldn't even argue on her own behalf, she thought, tired of herself. It had always been that way. Whenever she felt strongly about something, she found herself tongue-tied and frustrated. Far wiser to barricade her heart against strong emotions. She just managed to get along better without them.

"Yes," Antonia said, suddenly coming in strongly on Millicent's side. "You men ought to be able to solve this mystery in no time. Somewhere in this town or environs is a very unhappy young lady. We've got to find her and help her before she does anything rash."

"What could be more rash than leaving your baby on a stranger's doorstep?" her husband wanted to know.

"Jumping in Petawaukee Creek? With all the snow melting in the past couple of weeks, that creek's gotten dangerous."

Marshal Faraday looked thoughtful and then scared as he considered his wife's words. "I better go check that out," he said, rubbing his cheek with his big hand. "Not that I think she did that. . . ."

He started for the door. His brother-in-law stopped him. "Jake, what's your vote?"

"Oh. Her," he said, nodding at Millicent. "I'll be back."

Heartened, Millicent returned Dr. Castle's very steady gaze. She had the satisfaction of seeing his eyes drop first. She knew he didn't much like the thought of her caring for the child alone, and she didn't care for his high-handedness. Yet as they stared defiantly at each other, Millicent couldn't help respecting him, too. He cared for the people of this town, even if they drove him crazy, which meant, she supposed, that he cared about her, too. If only . . .

She cut that thought off. She had no interest in Dr. Castle beyond trying to understand and overcome his opposition to her taking Petey home. She had to either win him over or get the judge to vote for her, so that the doctor would be outnumbered two to one.

Then Ned Castle had the gall to wink at her! Suddenly she didn't know whether or not he could be counted on to support her. And in any case, how dare he be so lighthearted!

6

MILLICENT JUMPED UP from her chair, her face alight with joy. "Really? You're serious?"

"Absolutely," Judge Cotton said. "Until we find the mother, that baby's all yours."

She pressed the baby to her heart and closed her eyes. Ned saw her tremble as though her body resisted the pressure of happiness flowing through her. He literally could not tear his gaze from her face. All the beauty of her great heart revealed itself before his very eyes.

Ned wished he could shield Millicent from the stares of even his dearest friends and relatives. He almost couldn't keep himself from racing forward to throw himself in front of her. He felt hot and angry inside his skin, as though he stood before a shrine only he understood and had to suffer the impiety of other visitors.

He shook off that unsettling feeling, saying, "Remember that when we find the real mother, Millicent, you're going to have to give the baby back."

"Yes, I understand," she said. But her eyes didn't dim. He realized she resisted thinking about the painful future.

Ned stood over her and looked down at the pink and white face of the sleeping boy. "He's a nice-looking baby."

"He's perfect," she said without looking up.

Reaching down, Ned stroked the smooth cheek so close to her bosom. She stiffened, freezing into immobility. "Yes, he's perfect," Ned agreed. "But let's keep an eye on those sniffles. Sometimes having a stuffed-up nose keeps a baby from getting enough milk. . . . Oh, what are you doing about that? I mean, obviously you can't . . ."

"He took cow's milk this morning," Millicent said.

Standing above her, Ned could see the pink come into her cheeks and even onto her neck, there where the nape showed between the heavy coil of her hair and the edge of her high collar. Ned eased the knot in his tie.

He reminded himself that the nape of Millicent's neck could not be considered an arousing sight compared with some things he'd seen. He'd been at dinners where women's bosoms practically adorned their plates, danced with debutantes who would die before showing an elbow but who had no objection to revealing their breasts as far as the nipple, and the restrictions on keeping ankles concealed never applied in the boudoirs of Italy. Therefore he could look at her nape and never feel a desire to drop even one kiss on it.

Miss Mayhew's neck could be thought of as a nice neck, a clean and enticing neck, with the three buttons below it to close up her collar from behind. No doubt her hair smelled of honeysuckle and roses. He could imagine it falling as it had last night, in two heavy streams, while he . . . He closed his eyes tight and counted backward from ten.

Just because he saw some part of her body ordinarily kept hidden didn't mean he had to go crazy, he told himself, forcing a dispassionate view. If a man had any pretensions toward being a confirmed bachelor, he developed early on a certain intuition regarding the approach of infatuated ideas. He then, if wise, embarked upon a course of long, exhausting walks, took cold, healthy baths, or recalled to mind those dear habits which would instantly be done away with by a wife, until the ideas withered and died.

"I . . . uh . . . better get back to my office," Ned said, and backed away. He fumbled up his black bag, aimed a hasty kiss at his sister's cheek, and hurried out of the kitchen.

Mrs. Cotton said, "I'll walk you to the door."

On the way she said in a low voice, "I just hope and pray that girl knows what she's gotten herself into."

"Miss Mayhew seems competent enough," Ned answered.

"Oh, no doubt about it. But taking care of a little one is awful hard . . . awful hard. It sure would be a kindness to her if you'd stop in and see her; kinda keep an eye on things."

"Won't you and the other ladies—"

"Sure as you know. But . . ." Mrs. Cotton shook her head. "Old wives' tales, Neddy. Everyone's got a different idea, seems to me. Now, you can give Miss Mayhew the latest word in taking care of young'uns."

"I'm the last person Miss Mayhew would listen to," Ned said bitterly, all his rancor toward her returning. "She will probably dose that child with 'wool of bat, and tongue of dog.'"

"Well, now, I'm not so sure about that," Mrs. Cotton said, stopping with her hand on the doorknob. "Seems to me folks undergo some change in their thinkin' when the baby's their own. After all, it's a sight easier to say what's to be done with someone else's children than to figure out what your own little ones are needing."

"If Miss Mayhew wants me to call on the baby, I will of course do so." Ned hesitated and decided to speak his thought. In a lowered voice he said, "By the way, I was wondering if you'd give her . . ."

He put his hand into his breast pocket and brought out the five-dollar bill he always kept there for emergencies. "I don't want you to tell her it's from me. She wouldn't take it if she knew, but that baby's going to need things . . . things I don't believe she can afford."

Mrs. Cotton smiled softly and indulgently, a motherly smile. She took the money from his hand and said, "She won't hear it from me. I'll tell her it's my gift." Standing up on tiptoe, she aimed a kiss at the doctor's cheek.

Bashfully Ned ducked his head. Just as he opened the door, the judge said, from behind them, "Gad, leave my wife for one minute and some other feller's kissin' her!"

At the best of times Judge Cotton's voice carried. Today, it carried to the ears of the three women standing on the porch. The leader, Mrs. Wilmot, had her white-gloved fist raised up to knock at the door. The other two held baskets, heavy ones, judging by the way the women leaned to the side.

The awkwardness passed off in laughter, yet Ned went out with his face burning. He realized the truth of the old saying that "the road to hell is paved with good intentions." He had the good intention of secretly giving Miss Mayhew a few dollars. If he'd kept his money in his pocket, he would have avoided an embarrassing moment. Unfairly, and knowing it made little sense, he found himself blaming Miss Mayhew.

"Someone's here to see you, Miss Mayhew," Mrs. Cotton sang out as she came back into the kitchen. Right behind her, hardly giving Millicent enough time to look up, came Mrs. Wilmot, Mrs. Grapplin, and young Mrs. Budgell, respectively the mayor's wife, the stationmaster's wife, and the minister's wife.

Mrs. Wilmot spoke first. "Is that the baby?" She came and stood over Millicent. "Isn't he a little on the small side?"

"He's just beautiful," Mrs. Grapplin said as she put down her heavy basket. Millicent bestowed a grateful glance on the former Maisie Linton, for she hadn't even taken a peep at Petey yet. She came over now, her golden hair gleaming under her simple hat. "Yes," she said. "Perfectly beautiful."

"All babies are beautiful," Mrs. Budgell said sentimentally, but a groove appeared in her youthful brow. Married two years already, on the same day as a matter of fact as Antonia and Jake Faraday, Mary Lou had yet to have a baby.

"Hmph," Mrs. Wilmot said. "When you've had as many as I have, you don't see much in them but hard work and more hard work."

"Oh, I don't know. . . ." Mrs. Grapplin said.

Millicent saw how Mary Lou folded her white-gloved hands and saw her lips move as if in prayer. For the first time in a long time, Millicent felt a spark of anger on another person's behalf. If she were Mrs. Budgell, she'd throw some sharp words at Mrs. Wilmot for her thoughtlessness.

She said, "Would you like to hold him, Mrs. Budgell?"

"He's asleep. . . ."

"Oh, he won't mind."

Millicent stood up and somewhat awkwardly transferred the limp baby to Mary Lou's arms. Instantly the younger woman began to sway in an ancient, soothing rhythm. "So tiny," she sighed.

Mrs. Wilmot sniffed and said abruptly, "Well, Millicent, I was most surprised when I heard about your finding this baby. Naturally, I could hardly believe you meant to keep it."

"So was I," Millicent admitted. "A little."

The mayor's wife glanced at Mrs. Cotton, working by the stove. "I understand the judge and the marshal have no qualms about you keeping him?"

Mrs. Cotton turned, her blue eyes narrowed. "Vernon made the right decision under the circumstances. Or are you sayin' different, Elviry?"

"I wouldn't think to second-guess Judge Cotton. All the same, it's strange they'd pick out a maiden lady 'stead of a married one. Mrs. Budgell for instance."

Mary Lou's face sharpened in surprise. "Oh, I couldn't," she said. Swiftly, but carefully, she returned the baby to Millicent. "I just . . . I mean, you're going to give him back when they find the mother?"

"That's right," Millicent said.

"Oh, I couldn't ever do that! He's so helpless and sweet. I . . . I vow I've lost my heart already. If I kept him for any longer than a minute . . ." Her pretty face had never been meant to look so tragic. The false laugh she gave to convince them that she didn't mean it only made her look aged beyond her time.

Then, taking a shaking breath, she turned and dashed out the back door. They could hear her footsteps splash in the still-soggy flower bed.

"Well!" Mrs. Wilmot said.

"You shouldn't have twitted her about not having any children, Elviry."

"Twitted her? As if I'd do such a thing!"

A knock at the front door, followed by a yoo-hoo, broke into what might have shaped up to be a legendary squabble. Several more women, all bearing gifts, came into the room. Millicent had to wonder at the remarkable efficiency of the town grapevine. It had hardly been half an hour since she'd been told she could keep Petey, and everyone knew of it already.

Mrs. Cotton shook her kettle invitingly. "Anybody care for a little tea?"

Hours later Millicent realized, halfway through supper, that this unsettled feeling that plagued her felt just like anticipation. Considering that once she'd come home, her knocker hadn't been silent a moment all day, she would have thought she'd had enough company. But all her visitors had been women; some brought food, some clothes their own babies had outgrown, some brought useless things like toys too old for Petey. All had come with curiosity. A very few had brought orders for hats.

But all had been women.

Petey slept in a cradle Mrs. Harnottle had lent, complete with bedding. He was a good baby, they'd all declared, chiefly because he hadn't minded being handed around from person to person like a photograph. They'd all gushed over him. He had only cried once, when Mrs. George had him. She'd made a face so alarming in its ugliness that even Millicent had been startled. Apparently, Mrs. George had expected the baby to laugh and had gone away rather huffily when he hadn't.

Now Millicent sat in her front room, binding the crown of a straw hat with ribbon. Sometimes her head nodded over her work, but she always popped upright before pillowing her face on her arm.

She didn't want him to come, she told herself firmly. All the same, there had been times today when she would have been glad to look up and see him there. Ned Castle would have appreciated the humor of two women bringing clothes big enough for a four-year-old, or old Mrs. Crane stopping by to drop off a bottle of her cherry brandy "just in case the little feller can't sleep."

She'd give him half an hour more, more or less.

In all likelihood, Ned wouldn't be bothered. All that big talk about him wanting to know more about her! Just the kind of nonsense bragging men went in for. And hadn't she heard that he had a high opinion of himself? Hadn't she seen it at work?

She had yawned for the fifth time in as many minutes, telling herself that of all the bona fide, gold-plated fools, she took the cake, when she heard a very soft rapping at her front door.

Quickly she ran her hand over her hair to be sure it was neat. Then, taking her time but not dawdling, she went to the front door, candle in her hand. As she reached for the brass knob, she hesitated.

"Who's there?" she called, and leaned forward to listen for the answer.

"It's me. Dr. . . . Ned Castle. May I come in?"

Millicent thought about it. The warm night air wouldn't do Petey any harm; she could leave the front door open. No one would think twice about her having the doctor in the house anyway.

Even through the door she could hear the humor in his tone as he said, "I can send for my references if you like."

Opening the door, Millicent said, "I'm sorry to keep you waitin' out here. I wanted to be sure you weren't the peeper."

"Miss Mayhew, I . . ."

The lamplight showed droplets in his hair, a spangle of flame against the smooth gold of his hair. "Is it comin' on to rain again?" she asked.

"A little mist, nothing to speak of."

"Well, don't stand in the doorway."

The shoulders of his suit were spotted by damp as well. With a gesture as old as womankind, Millicent reached out to feel the sleeve. "You'd better hang that by the stove. It'll never dry in your room. I can make up some tea, too."

"Tea?" Ned asked, pushing the door closed.

"Yes, everyone's been very . . . No, don't close that."

"I assure you, Miss Mayhew . . ."

His eyes would have made his fortune on the stage. They looked so straight, and so sincere. No doubt all he had to do with most girls was gaze into their eyes with those river-blue eyes and they fell down at his feet.

"Leave it open, please. I've heard about you."

"That's the second time you've hinted that I'm not to be trusted," he said, following her into the kitchen. "You have no need to worry; I'm fairly restricted in my tastes."

"*I'm* not worried." She took down a fat-bellied teapot and ran steaming hot water from the stove reservoir into it. Then she took up the teaball she'd used before and dropped it into the pot. Maybe it would be more hospitable to use fresh tea, but she couldn't afford to waste any of her precious stock. Goodness knew when it would be renewed.

She saw him looking around. "What?" she asked sharply.

"The place looks different."

"How different?"

His sideways smile had a spice of the devil in it. "Messier."

Her cheeks heating, Millicent bent to pick up a dishcloth from the floor. "I hadn't got the chance to tidy up. It's been busy. Lots of folks called on me today."

"I've heard. The whole town's talking about you and Petey."

As she poured the tea into her only cup, she said, "They all brought things. That child has enough clothes for an army—and diapers! Doesn't seem possible one child could need so many, but they tell me he will."

"Where's Petey?"

"Asleep. I got a cradle for him now. And Mrs. Wilmot promises to lend me her crib as soon as I need it."

She couldn't help recalling how he'd put his hand on her before, holding her arm. That impulse seemed to have left him. He sat at his ease, sipping from the cup she'd given him. Millicent stood over him, her hands on her hips.

"Do you want to see the baby now?" she asked.

"In a few minutes, perhaps. This is the first chance I've had to be quiet since I left here this morning." He glanced up at her. "Won't you join me, Miss Mayhew?"

"I can't," she said gruffly. "I've only got the one cup and chair." To cover up the awkwardness she felt at admitting that, she said, "Would you care for some of Mrs. Borland's pumpkin cakes? They won't keep."

"Gladly. But you'll join me for those?"

She nodded and bustled around. She hadn't liked the look in his eyes when she'd told him how little she owned. Pity had always been offensive. She'd seen too many people finding it easy to start accepting other folk's pity and too hard to get away from it. She'd be trapped like a fly on flypaper, only in sentiment, instead of arsenic.

While she worked, he stretched out his legs beneath the table and said, "Seems everyone with so much as a sore pinkie-toe called me out today. Of course, most of them just wanted to hear all the latest gossip."

"About me?"

"You're the freshest thing on the menu, Miss Mayhew. I've told the story of last night to about twenty-five people, and goodness knows who they've all told by now. If that young woman's out there, she'll know you have her child and not the Cottons."

"That's good . . . I guess."

"That's not the only good. Mr. Landis was so eager to hear all about Petey that he actually let me examine that lesion on the back of his arm. I think if I operate soon, I'll be able to cut it all away." He coughed as if embarrassed. "I'm sorry, Miss Mayhew. I shouldn't talk about such things."

Millicent shrugged. "I don't mind. I'm not squeamish."

As she came over with the plate, he stood up. She waved him back into his chair. "I'll be comfortable enough. I'm not the one who's been on my feet all day."

"I insist. . . ."

With an exasperated "Oh!" she dropped the plate with a clatter onto the scrubbed tabletop, making his cup and medical bag jump. Marching away, she brought out her old step stool and poked it into place at the doctor's elbow. Sitting down, she said, "There. Now eat."

The pumpkin cakes, like golden saucers, lay arranged around a teetering pot of black currant preserves. The knife had fallen on the table. Ned placed it back on the rim of the plate, steadying the preserves with one finger.

"Do you mind if I have more tea?" he asked, rising.

"I'll get it. . . ."

"Don't trouble." He poured the light amber liquid out and then set the cup down in front of her. "Your turn."

"But I—"

"It may be more blessed to give than to receive, Miss Mayhew, but it's better still to share. Won't you share with me?"

Millicent knew that there must be many women unable to resist the wide-eyed, hurt stare that Ned Castle turned on her. To refuse what he asked would seem not only rude but cruel. Besides, it didn't seem worthwhile to make a fuss over just a cup of tea. It might be different if he were asking for the moon . . . or a kiss.

They shared the cup and the knife. He talked about his cases while she listened. When the last pumpkin cake had become nothing but a memory and some crumbs, she said, "Well, you'll want to see Petey now."

"Yes, of course. Thank you for the refreshments."

As they walked together down the narrow hall, his shoulder bumped hers. He apologized without breaking stride. Millicent said nothing. Strangely, she only just then realized that he stood much taller than she did. For a moment it had been as though she were completely aware of him as a man and herself, a woman.

Going up the stairs in front of him, Millicent found herself wondering if her skirt hung straight. She hoped he couldn't see her ankles, neatly clad in high-button shoes. She didn't know what to do with her hands as he stood looking at the baby, soundly sleeping in his borrowed bed.

"I'll bring by some saline drops if his nose doesn't clear up. You say he took his whole bottle?"

"That's right. Drank it down." She added proudly, "He burped like a cowhand."

Ned laughed, a warm, caressing sound. He glanced at her. "That's an unusual expression for a girl to use."

Millicent felt strange, as though her insides had turned into risen dough. Just from his laugh! Just from the look in his eyes. "I . . . I'm an unusual girl," she muttered.

"I won't need this," Ned said, hefting his bag. He looked down into the cradle for another moment. "At first I wasn't sure about this. But I think Petey is a very fortunate little man to have wound up on your doorstep."

"There are worse places he could have landed." She walked toward the door.

She felt just as odd going down the stairs as she had going up them. It was all she could do to keep from turning to see if he watched her. Of course he didn't, she told herself. Why would he?

At the foot of the stairs, in the hushed breeze that flirted through the open door, he said, "Just a moment, Miss Mayhew."

As she glanced up into his face inquiringly, she saw him draw very near. Without a word, he leaned toward her. She felt the wall at her back. Then he kissed her.

Millicent couldn't breathe or think. His lips were warm, and soft. Then they moved, hardening against her own at the same time his hand tightened on her waist. Millicent felt a little lurch inside herself, though whether of fear or longing, she couldn't begin to guess. Just when she thought she might know, he lifted his head. She had an instant to catch a quick, fluttering breath.

He said in a low, laughing voice, "I'm probably going to regret this, but right now . . . I don't care."

Dropping his bag with a thud, he came back to her mouth, bending to catch her parted lips at an angle. His hand slipped around her waist, bringing her body against his. With his shocking warmth all along her front, Millicent remembered how good a kiss could feel.

She raised her chin, softening her lips, moving them as he moved his. But she kept her arms down at her sides, rigid. Afterward, she found the marks of her nails in her palms. She wanted to reach out, but some remnant of what she called "common sense" held her back.

When he lifted his head again, Millicent turned her face away. Did he know she trembled, the way she could feel him tremble? Would he ask embarrassing questions, feel he had the right now to know everything? How could she make it clear that she had no wish to repeat that kiss, especially as she didn't know that for a fact herself?

"I'll be by tomorrow with those drops," he said. Then he went out into the blue twilight.

Still dazed, she began to close the door when she heard the snap of his fingers. He appeared again on her porch. Without another word, only an apologetic noise, he walked into the hall, took up his bag, and went away.

Millicent stood there, her mind refusing to accept what had just happened. Her loneliness, her damnable spinsterhood, the natural heat of her blood, they'd combined to create a dream for her. She was still asleep, nodding over her worktable. When she woke up, she'd know for certain that it had all been a dream. There'd be no cup, no crumbly plate, no step stool dragged up anyhow to the table. Ned Castle had never come by. That kiss had never happened.

Strange, though, that a dream could be so real. She could still taste him on her lips; how could she know he'd taste of smoky tea and the tartness of black currant? Dreams went by contraries, she'd heard. Did tea and currants have opposites? If she could think of them, then she'd know what this strange dream had meant.

Millicent realized she was cold and shut the door the rest of the way. Then the baby started to cry.

7

$\mathscr{N}$ED LAY ON his thin boardinghouse mattress, the sheet to his waist, and wished to God he could smoke a cigar. He needed the well-known properties of tobacco to help clear his mind. His vow proving not to be discipline enough, Mrs. Fleck fortunately had a strict rule against smoking in bed, though judging by the tiny holes in his coverlet, some previous tenant had ignored the restrictions.

The early sun coming through the windows sketched a delicate tracery on his unattractively papered walls, a moving shadow-picture of the tree standing in the yard. Ned took a moment from his confusion to reflect on the miracle of May. A few weeks ago that tree's branches had flexed as bare as the bleached bones of a medical-school skeleton. Now tiny green leaves made this elegant beauty. And who was there to appreciate it? Only him.

Ned rolled onto his side, away from the shadows, away from thoughts of spring. He must have been out of his cotton-picking mind! What on earth had possessed him? Bad enough his behavior of Wednesday night—he still writhed when he thought how close he'd come to having his hair parted by the judge's grandfather's rifle. Bad enough even to have threatened Miss Mayhew with heaven knew what blackmail when he'd been alone with her yesterday. But to go back and then to . . .

Ned groaned and buried his face in his pillow. He hadn't felt this unwell since the time he'd accidentally inhaled ether. He'd been lucky to have awakened that time; he hoped the daze he experienced now wouldn't last any longer. The headache felt definitely similar.

"Lying in bed won't solve anything," he said a few minutes later.

He sat up, a fold of sheet across his lap. Stretching and flexing his muscles, he tried to force a feeling of well-being into his body and mind. Maybe coffee would help.

After splashing water on his face, shaving, and dressing, he went downstairs, still straightening his tie. Mrs. Fleck's red-haired son, Egbert, greeted him in passing. The seventeen-year-old boy hustled out of the dining room, his skinny arms holding up a tray loaded with dirty dishes. "Morning, Doc! Cut yourself?"

Ned touched two fingers to the scrape on the side of his jaw. "Didn't strop my razor enough," he said briefly. "Any coffee going?"

"Sure as you know! Bring it right out."

"Thanks, Ed."

Ned pushed open the door to the dining room and walked in. One of the men had just started a booming laugh. The cough that came out when he saw Ned shook him so hard that Ned considered offering his professional services. Not the most intuitive person alive, he didn't have to be supernaturally gifted to know that, when a dead silence falls upon one's entrance, people have been bandying the most familiar name in the world.

Ned nodded to Mrs. Fleck, sitting in state at the head of the table, and slipped into his usual place at her right hand. As the town doctor, he had a certain social standing.

Mrs. Fleck nodded her head graciously at him, her smile as stiff as her neck. She modeled her behavior on the great ladies she read about in magazines—Mrs. Cornelius Vanderbilt, Mrs. William Backhouse Astor, and that ilk. The bane of her life had always been that her name did not have some grandly sounding echo like a rumble of distant drums. She could find no music in the plain name of Mrs. John Fleck, widow.

For this reason she'd hung the name of Egbert on her only son. He, without any sense of drama, preferred to be called

Ed. Ned gave him the name he preferred whenever he could, but had learned his lesson about calling him "Ed" in front of Mrs. Fleck. Unchanged sheets, unwashed linen, and unde-livered messages had been the least of it.

The boy came in with the coffeepot. As he poured the hot, fragrantly steaming liquid into the doctor's cup, he winked with the eye that did not face his mother. "Bacon and eggs?" he asked.

"Thanks, er, Egbert."

Down at the far end of the table, Mr. Standish, a whiskey drummer from St. Louis, started a fresh conversation. "Say, it looks like it's definitely gonna be Blaine for the Repub-licans this year."

Ned gratefully did his bit to keep this fairly neutral topic going. "That is news. So you think President Arthur isn't going to have a second chance?"

"Don't look like it. These here big Democrat wins, well, they show the way the tide's a-turning."

"Ah," said another drummer, this time in ladies' goods, "it'll all be decided in Tammany Hall, just like every other jeezeldy 'lection."

A growl of agreement came from the other breakfasters and the conversation became truly general. Ned blinked in surprise when Mrs. Fleck touched him fleetingly on the wrist and under the cover of the chatter said, "I'd be glad of a word with you, Doctor. After breakfast."

"You're feeling all right, Mrs. Fleck?"

"I'm never sick . . . can't afford to be." She never gave any other answer than that. Even last year, when a simple chest cold had to all but turn to pneumonia before she'd take any rest, she'd made the same reply.

Egbert came out with Ned's breakfast, his heels tapping fast on the wooden floors as he carried the crisping hot plate. His bony wrists stuck out from his cuffs the same way his ankles were too long for his pants. "Here you go, Doc. Eggs dry, bacon curly and wet."

"Just the way I like it. You're a good cook, Ed . . . bert."

Mrs. Fleck's lips thinned. Ned hoped he'd get points for a good faith effort.

When Ned came downstairs after breakfast, his medical bag in his hand, Mrs. Fleck stood by the sitting room door, waiting for their conversation. She waved to him, her hand covered with a white cloth, indicating he should join her in the cavelike darkness of her best room.

Without preamble, she said, "I think it's right you ought to know what they're sayin', Dr. Castle."

"Who?"

"The women of this town. You don't mind if I go on with my work?" She flicked her cloth over the multitiered and carved wood of her whatnot shelf. "Dusting don't do itself."

Ned knew nothing short of cosmic calamity would stop Mrs. Fleck from cleaning, unless one meant to try physical restraint. He sat down on the piano stool. "What are the women saying, Mrs. Fleck?"

She clicked her tongue. "Honestly, what's the world coming to when a decent man can't do a decent thing without having bitter tongues laid to him? As you know, I don't get 'long any too well with Mrs. Cotton—she snoops and I like to mind my own business, when I can. But in this case, I gotta agree with her. It's a downright shame!"

"But you haven't said—"

"Just you look outside the door and make sure Egbert isn't listening."

Ned did as she asked. No footsteps fell on the worn red runner in the hall. He heard a distant buzz of voices, but nothing more.

"No one's there." He stepped back in surprise when he found Mrs. Fleck had come within inches of him.

"It's a crying shame and scandal," she whispered hoarsely. "It's just 'cause you're single. If you were a married man, nobody'd be able to say a word against you. Why, even if you was to announce your engagement now, that'd scotch these rumors."

Ned wished he'd left the door to the sitting room open. Mrs. Fleck's blue eyes had a radiant glitter as she whispered, and how had her hand come to be on his sleeve? Casually he dropped his arm and maneuvered so that the low table stood between them.

"I really don't understand. What rumors?"

"'Bout Miss Mayhew. They're saying this baby she is supposed to have found—"

"She did find it!"

"Well, there's nothing stopping a girl from putting her own baby outside her own door and then saying she found it."

"Her own baby? That's preposterous!"

"That's what folks are saying. They're saying it ain't natural for a woman to take on so after some stranger's baby. 'Sides, she was laid up 'bout six, eight weeks ago with what she said was 'influenza.' You didn't happen to pay her a call long about then, did you?"

Mrs. Fleck's company voice, all refined vowels and the kind of careful grammar that reminded Ned of someone talking around a hot potato, had given way to her own natural style. Her airy unconcern with gossip had changed to the kind of avid devourer of unconsidered words that she would have been if her duties allowed her to hang over a back fence.

Ned wondered how he could sound unconcerned with Miss Mayhew's reputation while at the same time protect it. With hardly a pause he said, "I can't recall. I shall have to check my day book. Half the people in Culverton had the influenza. I called on some of them, naturally."

"'Course, if what they're saying's right, she never was sick." Mrs. Fleck shook her strawberry-blond head. "Be a shame if she had ol' Doc Partridge to attend her. He ain't fit to deliver mail, let alone babies."

"Mrs. Fleck, you're a woman of sense," Ned began. "If you could do your part to convince other women that this is definitely not Miss Mayhew's baby—"

"I'm no party to gossip, Dr. Castle. I just thought you should know." She turned her back on him and picked up an insolently painted china dog and began to rub his acid-green head. "I gotta get on with my dusting, Doctor. If you'll excuse me?" she added with a return of her frigid company manner.

Ned went on his way to the office, trying to convince himself that Mrs. Fleck had gotten confused. Surely no one harbored the slightest suspicion that Petey could be Millicent's illegitimate baby. The very thought would make a cat laugh. He wondered if Millicent had laughed when she heard this story. So efficient was the Culverton gossip chain that he felt certain she'd heard all the dirt by now.

He had no clients that morning until he heard a slow step mounting the exterior staircase. Having nothing to do once he'd dusted his books and instruments, gladly taking Mrs. Fleck for a good example though not a wife, Ned gallantly opened his door for the patient. His sister, her face red, her hand pressed to her heart, stood on the landing. "Why . . ." she began and stopped to take a few deep breaths. "Why must your office be on the second floor?"

"Come on in," he said, taking her by the elbow. "Have a seat."

"Thank you, Ned. Carrying this baby around is getting to be more and more of a problem."

"If it's any consolation to you, you look more beautiful pregnant than most women do on their wedding day. I like your dress."

"Thank you, kind sir," she said, smoothing out the finely woven green wool. "If you talked to more women like that, you'd be married by now."

"Don't start," he said. "I've heard all I want to on that subject. Would you believe—"

"I take it that you've heard the latest gossip," Antonia said.

"Yes, stupid isn't it? Any contractions yet?"

"Just those practice ones you've been telling me about. And don't change the subject."

"Are they getting any stronger?"

"No. That's not why I've come to talk to you."

"All the same . . ." Ned looked at her with the penetrating glance of the physician, not the half-exasperated, half-entertained glance of a devoted brother.

"I wish the only decent doctor in this town weren't my brother! I can't even bully you!"

"You never could."

"No, but I could blackmail you. Remember Allisa Biggett's twelfth birthday party?" She read his expression and grinned. "So do I. Wouldn't that be something for the ladies to titter over at their sewing circle?"

"All right," Ned said, crossing his arms. "What do you want to talk about?"

Antonia folded her hands in what passed these days for her lap. Her cornflower blue eyes were unwontedly serious. "Now, Ned, I want you to be honest with me."

"I'm always honest with you. I promised I would be, remember?"

There'd been an ugly time when Antonia was a few months shy of her twenty-first birthday. Their grandfather, called a tycoon by those who wanted to flatter him, a robber baron by those who hated him, had tried to force her into marriage with the son of an oil company plutocrat. Lucas Redmond had turned out to be a rotter of the first magnitude, and possibly sexually deviant to boot. Even if he'd known of the groom's evil nature, Grandfather Castle would have still planned the match. Antonia had been willing to grant their grandfather the benefit of the doubt on that point; Ned had known better.

Except for Ned, their entire family had ranged themselves on Grandfather Castle's side. When the old man had tried to have Antonia institutionalized to break her spirit, it had been Ned who had warned her. He had also helped to heal the breach between Antonia and their parents, though it had taken a long time.

"Very well," Antonia said, keeping her gaze fixed firmly on her brother's eyes. "Answer yes or no. Are you trifling with Millicent Mayhew?"

"No."

"Is there any chance at all that baby is yours?"

"Antonia, I shouldn't have to be telling you this, since

you obviously know it already, but in case you forgot all those books you read . . . in order for Miss Mayhew to get pregnant, certain 'things' had to happen."

"Ned!"

He went on, disregarding her blushes. ". . . unless one is going to accept the existence of a miracle, which I categorically refuse to do unless I absolutely have to. Now, for all I know Miss Mayhew has been carrying on with everything in pants, but I'm willing to lay you long odds that she is untouched."

Rather less untouched than she'd been two days ago, but he would gladly take all the blame for that. However, on the bright side, nothing they'd done yesterday could possibly make a baby.

Antonia said, "That goes without saying. I don't know Millicent Mayhew at all well, but I doubt she's the sort of girl who throws her heart ahead of her head."

Two days ago Ned would have been willing to stake his professional reputation on the fact that Millicent Mayhew was a cold, passionless wench. Now, with the memory of her softly pressing against him in the darkness, he couldn't be so certain. He found his own actions even more perplexing than hers. Why had he kissed her? Curiosity? Desire? There had to be a reason. Every action had a reason.

"Ned," his sister said after a moment when she, too, seemed busy with her own thoughts. "You're not really happy here in Culverton, are you?"

"Of course, I am. . . ."

She held up her hand to stem his instinctive protest. With a sad smile she reminded him, "Answer yes or no."

"Yes, I am happy in Culverton. It's just . . . complicated. We in the East have this picture of life out here as simple, basic, down-to-earth. Who knew there was more conflict and acrimony in choosing church curtains than in the whole Civil War?"

"I don't care to live through another month like that, that's for certain."

"And take this marriage nonsense. I never thought for an

instant that I'd spend more time trying to keep myself out of the matrimonial noose than I would treating patients."

"I did warn you. . . ."

"I didn't believe you," Ned admitted. "Who would have? A whole town devoted to the principle that marriage is the happiest of all human conditions? It sounded like an exaggeration. It *should* have turned out to be one."

"You can't say they haven't had their successes. . . ."

"Yes, I know. You."

"No, not just me. There's Jake, too. He's happy, much happier than he was before he got married, though I say it who shouldn't."

"I wonder what criminals think when the marshal of this town is patently the happiest man in it."

"There's not much crime in Culverton."

"I know. Every male for a hundred miles has heard that he's safer out of this town than in it. Unless he wants to be married in a week, that is. What crime is worth a lifetime of servitude to one woman?"

Antonia gladly accepted Ned's arm to get out of her chair. "Some day you'll meet a nice girl and go over like a tower built on sand. Then you'll pray for a longer lifetime in which to serve."

"Not me," he said confidently as he escorted her to the door. Then he heard the sound of hurrying feet clattering up his office stairway. "Sounds like an emergency," he said and moved quickly to open the door.

Millicent Mayhew, her black hair tumbling down from its high knot, stood on the other side. Dust marred the black of her heavy skirt, and her cheeks were flushed with the exertion. Even through his concern, Ned thought she looked magnificent.

Antonia reacted first. "Miss Mayhew! There's nothing wrong with Petey?"

"No. He's fine. He's with Mrs. Cotton." Her voice came in gasps while she pressed her hand to her chest.

"Come in and sit down. Ned, get a glass of water."

Millicent allowed Antonia Faraday to take her arm to lead

her to a chair. "Not used to running," she gasped apologetically.

"That's all right. Here, sip this."

Over the edge of the glass Millicent sought for Ned. He stood back and let his sister tend her. After a gulp of water Millicent gently pushed Antonia's hand away. "Thank you; that's enough."

She sat up. "Dr. Castle, I came at once. You have to help me. . . . I don't mean that, exactly. But this is your problem, too. Do you know what they're saying about . . . about you and me?"

"I've just told him," Antonia said gently. "Of course, for anyone who knows you two really well it's obviously fantastic to imagine that there could *ever* be anything of the sort going on. Why, you don't even like each other! You've fought like cats and dogs ever since—"

Ned put his hand on his sister's shoulder. "You'll have to forgive her, Miss Mayhew. She was absent when they taught diplomacy at her school." He saw the slight confusion nestle between her dark brows and said softly, "I mean, she's not very tactful."

Millicent didn't know whether to be grateful for the explanation or angry that he thought she needed one. She focused on Antonia, though she could feel the doctor's gaze like a physical touch. "Yes, we've fought. All the more reason why folks shouldn't be talking the way they are." Suddenly she burst out, "And they were all so nice yesterday!"

She leaned forward, her elbows on her knees, her cheek cradled in her hand. "I don't understand folks," she said. "Yesterday they were giving with both hands; today, they're laughing at me."

"At us," Ned said. He left his sister's side and went down on one knee in front of Millicent. "You're not alone in this. I will help you fight it, though I don't know what we can do."

His handsome face looked older when it took on a serious expression, but no less handsome. Millicent knew the dangers of trusting any man, let alone one who looked like one of Satan's angels, especially when he had tempted her once already.

His hair had fallen in front of his ear when he cocked his head to the side to look at her. Millicent had to fight her hand. It wanted to reach out and brush the golden strands back into place. She could almost feel the soft tickle against her palm, and a fierce curiosity seized her, a longing to know whether it would feel as good as she imagined.

She heard a slight cough and glanced up. Antonia gazed at her brother, a strangely calculating look on her lovely features, as though she were doing sums in her head. Then the two women's gazes collided. Antonia Faraday smiled warmly.

"Well, I better be getting home. Jake doesn't like it if I stay out too much. Honestly, he thinks I'm such a fragile blossom that I'll break in a spring breeze. No, don't get up, Ned. I'm not so doddery that I can't manage to go down the same stairs I came up."

Still talking, she hurried out. On the doorstep she paused to give Millicent and Ned a last wave before continuing, with remarkable chipperness, on down the stairs.

"What was that about?" Ned wondered. "She was practically babbling. Antonia never babbles. She lectures, scolds, upbraids, and wears out a brother's resistance, but she never babbles."

"Pregnancy can change a woman's whole spirit."

"Yes. I know." He started to get up, realizing he looked ridiculous. Then Millicent laid her hand gently on his shoulder. A leaf coming to rest on his shoulder would have been heavier, yet he felt her as though she touched his naked skin.

"Thank you," she said. "For offering to help me out. But—"

"Now I'm serious," he answered, reaching up to take her hand so that he held it in a loose clasp. The fact that she didn't instantly pull away did something to Ned's insides, making him feel warm, connected, and, above all, needed.

"I'm serious," he repeated in a low, sincere voice. "You're not in this alone. I'm in it with you."

"Actually, I'm in it with three of you."

Ned wondered whether he should gently, very gently, press his lips to her wrist. Deciding reluctantly against it, he missed what she said and had to ask her to repeat herself.

"Town gossip has been nice enough to pick me three potential fathers for my baby. You're one of 'em."

"And the others?" He felt an unexpected anger flare up. He'd never been jealous, didn't believe in jealousy. Two people in love belonged together. They shouldn't require the admiration or pleasure of others. Yet the idea that nosy people were speculating about Millicent being lovers with any of a series of men was enough to make him see red, literally.

Millicent specified the other suspects for him. "There was a feller come around about the right time. Travels in horse doings. Traces, curry combs, and the like. I can't rightly remember ever laying eyes on him, but that means nothing. They'll have me in every barn with him before the week's out."

"And the other one?"

Millicent's cheeks, which had grown pale, brightened. A smile broke and trembled on her lips. "It's not really funny, I guess, but I sure laughed when I heard about this one. Some folks are hinting that the father might be Mayor Wilmot!"

8

MILLICENT, RECOVERED FROM her dash to the doctor's office, gently disengaged her hand from Ned's grasp. She stood up and, to hide her face and her feelings, went over to the window. When Ned looked into her eyes, she could feel a pressure at her heart, like a dam about to burst its bounds. She knew it came from being lonely, this desire to tell him everything. If she wished for one thing in this world, it would be for someone to share her burdens.

Yesterday, for a moment, she'd had a hope that there would be more friendship than charity in the kindness of her neighbors. Today's rumors had ruined her hopes.

"They're all talking as hard as they can go. You can hear 'em in the houses and the streets, all whispering."

"It's not that bad." She could tell from the sound of his voice that he'd risen and now stood behind her.

"You don't know. You've never faced this kind of thing before."

"And you have?"

"You don't know," she said again. "They'll make half-truths do for whole, and what they can't piece together, they'll throw out. Truth . . ." She shook her head, letting it fall loose, for she lacked the will to control it.

"Millicent," he began, sliding his hand down her arm. He took her hand and tried to turn her toward him. "Tell me . . ."

She let him hold her hand, but she leaned her forehead

against the cool glass. "I shouldn't have come here. It only makes everything they're saying look true."

Somehow, though, when she'd heard the full measure of what the others were saying, Ned's office had been the only place she thought of to go. She told herself now that she'd only been concerned for his reputation, but now she felt desperately afraid that she had another reason. Just looking at him made her feel more confident, more alive.

Millicent said, "I promised to look after Petey, or I'd just leave town."

"There's no reason someone else can't be found to care for the child, just until we find his mother."

She pulled her hand free and cradled it against her chest, protecting it with the other curled around it. His touch still seemed to encircle her hand, just as his kiss had stayed on her lips for hours after he'd gone. "I promised I'd take care of him. I mean to."

"Very well. We'll just have to think of some way to disprove these rumors."

"Might as well try to stop a fire from smoking," she said resignedly. "I've been told by three different people that they don't believe a word of it, they just 'thought I should know.'" She mimicked their sanctimonious, falsely sympathetic tones.

"It takes a friend and an enemy working together to really hurt you," Ned said, unable to repress a smile at her impersonation. "An enemy to malign you and a friend to tell you about it."

"Malign? What's that? Talkin' mean?"

Ned nodded, then looked thoughtful. "You know . . ."

He walked around behind his desk and slid open a drawer. He withdrew a fat hardbound book. "I'd like you to have this."

Millicent looked at it warily, her shoulders slanted. "What is it?"

"Take it," he said, pushing it toward her.

The red leather binding had changed color in places through long handling. "It's fat enough to be a Bible," she said, looking at the cracked gold print on the binding. "Dic . . . tion . . . ary?"

"If I use another word you don't know, you look it up in there. All the words are grouped by their first letter. If you know the first three letters of any word, you can look it up in a few moments. Go on; try 'malign.' M—A—L . . ."

She put the book down on the desk and very slowly and carefully raised the cover, feeling rather as though it contained a mess of dynamite with the fuse set. Some spiky black writing, very tight and small, marked the inside cover. Aloud, she read, " 'To Edwin, on the cel . . . celebration of his tenth birthday, Aunt Alicia.' "

She closed it. "I can't take it."

"Of course you can. I have another." He smiled, his blue eyes twinkling like stars on a summer night. "I wouldn't confess this to just anyone, but I'm probably the worst speller in the world!"

"You? But you know all sorts of fancy words."

He shrugged. "Just because I have a good-sized vocabulary doesn't mean I can spell all the words I know. At school I always got marked down for poor spelling. But I came up with a clever system. I developed poor handwriting. That way no one could tell if I was spelling words correctly or not."

Millicent could imagine him a small boy with hair so thick that it would never lie down, even more unruly and assertive than now. "Did it work?" she asked. "Did you get away with it?"

"Yes. And no. I didn't get marked down for spelling any more. But my penmanship grades . . ." He made a face as though he'd bit into a sour apple.

Laughter burst from Millicent's lips, taking her totally by surprise. Immediately she pressed her cool hands against her flaming cheeks. She'd forgotten the sound of her own laughter.

Her eyes went at once to Ned and then went wide. Her laughter had blown his out. What she saw in his face was pure purpose, the look a hungry hunter keeps for the prey that will sustain his life. The dark eagerness in his shining blue eyes took her by surprise. She had not believed him to have any darkness in his soul, not even the darkness of the hunger of a man for a woman.

With slow, padding footsteps, Ned came around the edge of his big desk. Millicent began to back up, each foot feeling the floor behind her as she slid them along. "I'd better get back," she said, her heart fluttering.

His eyes didn't change. They remained fixed on her mouth. Remembering how he'd kissed her, Millicent knew if he took another one, he would knock a big enough hole in her self-restraint that a wagon and four-horse team could drive through it. Determined not to let that happen, Millicent stopped backing up. Holding her arms out stiffly in front of her, she said, "Stop!"

He kept coming on until her hands rested flat against his chest. She could feel the tension in the hard planes of muscle beneath his suit and fancy shirt. "Stop what?" he asked.

"I . . . I don't mean to be foolish, Dr. Castle. Maybe I'm taking too much for granted, but I don't mean to be foolish."

"Foolish? What have you got to be foolish about, Miss Mayhew?"

Raised to be honest, Millicent said, "You."

The tension she could feel went up another notch. His chest felt as hard as hickory beneath her hands, moving with the deep breaths he took. For the first time in her life Millicent found herself intensely curious about the appearance of a man's body. She blushed for her thoughts. Not even Dan Redpath had gotten her thinking like that, and he'd been her husband-to-be.

"It's all wrong," she said.

"I know it."

"You don't even *like* me, and I . . ."

"And you?"

"I can't feel this way! I don't dare!" She whispered the words and closed her eyes against the burn of tears.

His hands came up to her waist. Slowly he drew her in. Millicent let her arms relax, allowed Ned to bring her head to his shoulder. She lay limply against him, letting him take her weight.

"Tell me," he said again, his lips moving against her temple.

She shuddered with relief. She hadn't wanted to be shattered again by a kiss. "I've said enough," she murmured.

"For you, maybe." His voice whispered so softly against the strands of her loosened hair.

Millicent recognized temptation when she saw it, even when it consisted only of the temptation to lay down a burden for a while. The thought of not having to fight this new battle alone made her yearn toward him. With Ned to fend off embarrassing questions, Millicent knew she might be able to keep the tenor of her lonely life intact.

She tried to free herself, but his arms were gently strong. "Let me go," she said against his collar. "If someone came up the stairs now, they'd believe everything!"

"Then you'd better tell me what's troubling you, Millicent, before they show up." The humor had come back into his voice, as though holding her in fond but restrictive arms had dashed cold water over the ardor she'd seen burning in his sky-blue eyes. He had himself under control. Millicent could very nearly be certain she felt comforted by this, though it felt more like disappointment.

"It's a long story. . . ."

"So far, it's been a slow day at the office."

This time, when she tried to put space between them, he allowed it. "You'd better get comfortable then," she said, nodding toward his padded leather chair.

She liked his big desk made of some reddish wood. It had a solid look, as though nothing could budge it. Through the opened door she could glimpse a leather examining couch in the other room. That could only belong to a doctor. However, his office might belong to anyone: a lawyer, a banker, a saloon owner. She could forget he was a doctor, used to looking inside people, and pretend that Ned could just be her good friend, a better friend than she'd ever known. They put aside their opposition over how to treat the sick, if only for this moment.

"I don't know how much Mrs. Cotton has told you about me."

"Not much. She said your grandmother was her best friend."

"That's right. Jenny Laurie was her name. She's the one who gave me the receipts that make you so angry."

The fingers of his right hand drummed the desktop once. "We can skip that."

Millicent suddenly found it easy to smile. "She died about four years ago come August. I was twenty-four, and she was my only relative in these parts still livin'. My parents didn't have luck; they got married young, and things just seemed to go from bad to worse. I was only four when they died, one right after the other."

"And your grandmother couldn't save them?"

She shook her head. "I thought you didn't want to talk about that."

"Go on and tell me what happened after your grandmother died."

"Wait a minute. She hadn't gotten the receipts all straight yet, and she hadn't written 'em down yet, either. That came later. That's how come she could leave 'em to me. I couldn't of remembered half of them if they hadn't been written down."

"Of course not. Why, for myself . . ." He waved his hand at the black-bound books on the shelf behind him.

"After she died," Millicent said, "I got awful itchy feet. I'd been taking care of Gran for a couple of years, and I guess I wanted to strike out and make my own way. So I wrote some letters to a miner out in Colorado who wanted to get married."

"You were a mail-order bride?"

She looked past him, remembering. "Dan wrote some awful pretty letters to me, once we started writing once a week. We seemed to think just alike on so many things. So I decided to go West. Dan told me it would be a while before we could marry, but we figured with the two of us working out there, we could get married in a year or two." She glanced at Ned and saw his forehead had furrowed lines.

"I don't want you thinkin' there was anything *wrong*. Dan worked his very own claim—silver mining. His idea was that I'd work in town, washing or cooking, or something that the miners would pay good for. More folks made their fortunes that way than with a pick and shovel."

Satisfied that Ned had no more reason to be shocked, Millicent said, "I sure enjoyed that trip out there. And everything was just like Dan had said. Wild, free, exciting!"

"What was Dan like?"

"Like?" Surprised, Millicent found she had to think hard to bring to mind the image of the man she had once intended, in all seriousness, to marry.

"Not much to look at," she said at last. "Kind of sandy hair and a sight too much nose for his face. But he was strong from the mining, and a pretty face isn't always . . ." She caught herself and slid a glance toward Ned. "But he was kind," she added. "At least, that's what I thought."

This time his fist showed his feelings. It tightened, and pounded once or twice on the leather blotter, as though he couldn't manage to keep it still. "What happened then?"

Millicent looked down into her lap. The hard part started here. She had to face the fact that he would, in all likelihood, never talk to her again after this, let alone touch her.

"I got a job in an eatery, washing dishes at first, then waiting tables, and finally cooking. I was there for two years. I forgot to tell you that this town was owned by the biggest mine around and by the family that ran it. There was the Colonel, though what he was colonel of I never did hear tell. The Colonel had one son. He thought the sun rose and set in him, and the moon didn't dare shine too bright on his face."

No words came from Ned this time to help her over the hard spots. Millicent took a deep breath. Still without looking at him, she went on.

"Also working at this same place as me was a girl named Emily Sharpless. She was awful sweet and pretty, kind of like your sister. We shared a room where we worked. Well, the colonel's boy started coming around . . . he wasn't really a boy. He must of been about my age then, but was so spoiled and coddled, he didn't seem half as old. The trouble started when Emily said 'no.' He didn't seem to think she meant it, but she was going to get married to a boy working on the tailings."

Millicent passed a hand over her brow as sweat prickled on her skin. She'd never spoken of that dreadful night to a soul. Talking about it now made her feel as if she relived every moment. She could smell the oil soap she'd been using to clean some trays. The smell competed with the reek of an oil lamp. It had been late fall and even the afternoons were dark.

She'd just gotten up and stretched, her hands in the small of her back, when she'd heard the cry from upstairs. Every time she remembered how she'd hesitated before going to investigate, she wondered if it had made any difference. If she'd been quicker, would she have been able to stop the evil about to happen? Her worst nightmares always began at that moment, when she'd faltered.

"I saw him leave our room, clear as day, because I'd brought the lamp with me. He all but fell over the threshold, and when he picked himself up, I saw his face. He had a long mark on it, bleeding free. I'd heard something clang as he tripped, and the knife skidded down that bare hall right to my feet. The blood on it looked black in the yellow light. Soon as I saw it, I knew what he'd done. I called out, 'Emily! Emily!' but I knew she wasn't ever going to hear me again in this world."

"My God. You could have been . . ."

She shook her head slowly. "He scrambled up anyhow and ran past me, knocking me aside. By then, some of the other folks had come out, but all they saw was his back, nothing to swear to. I don't know who was first to go into Emily's room. He'd . . . he'd cut her. . . ." She put up a trembling hand to the base of her throat.

"Millicent, stop."

But she couldn't. What she'd told him was bad telling and worse remembering, but the next part made the first part look easy. "Of course, I told what I'd seen. She'd been my friend. We had in all arranged that we were going to see each other married. She even had her wedding dress all ready. They . . . they buried her in it."

The flowers and veil had hidden the terrible wound in her throat, and the undertaker's wife had used a delicate hand with rouge to disguise the too-pale cheeks. There'd been a long procession to the barren and hideous graveyard, for Emily had been loved by all who knew her.

Millicent said, "I knew something was wrong when the sheriff wouldn't arrest the colonel's boy. Then I lost my job; not that I could have stood . . ."

When Ned tried to stop her again, she held up her hand. "Things just started going from bad to worse. Then worse yet. I told you the town was owned by the Colonel. Seems a lot of the people were too. Even my friends . . . the people I thought were my friends started talking about me . . . how I did more than cook and clean at the eatery. Soon I couldn't go anywhere by day, even by night. . . . They threw rocks . . . even the children threw rocks. . . ."

He jumped out of his chair and came around to her. Bending over her, he put his strong arm around her shoulders. Millicent tried so hard to stay stiff, but she could feel her resolve and her long distrust melting drip by drip, like an icicle in the sun.

She gathered her strength and went on. "Even Dan . . ." She felt the tremor that went through Ned at the mention of her intended.

"What did he do?"

"He came to town when the snows got too bad at the diggings. At first he tried to persuade me that I'd been mistaken, that I'd seen someone else in the hall that night."

"At first?" He muttered something else, but Millicent's ears were filled with the sound of his heart beating. She listened to it, and somehow the things she related got pushed a precious little bit further away.

"I think the death threats came next, either that or the threats to scar my face. That reminds me. The colonel's boy said the scratches on his face came from a prostitute named

Nelly Ray. She described in detail how he got them—her word against mine."

"But surely, someone like that—"

"By now most folks believed I was no better. Dan began to bully me, to shout at me, to shake me. I couldn't believe he could act that way. I'd known him for close on two years!" The hurtful wonder remained, duller now but still there. She didn't know if it would ever go away completely.

"It just got worse and worse," she said miserably. "Then a group of men broke into the tiny house I'd found that someone was willing to rent me. I wasn't home."

"Thank God."

She hardly heard him. "They destroyed everything I owned, even . . . even Dan's letters. And only Dan and Emily had known where I'd kept them. I was so alone . . . so scared and alone."

"But they tried this . . . this murderer, didn't they?"

Millicent shook her head wearily against his coat. Then with a reluctance she could feel in the stiff unbending of her fingers, she let go of him. She stood up, shaking off his comforting arm. Turning, she looked him right in the eyes.

"They didn't ever try him for Emily's murder, though I knew he was guilty as sin. They couldn't try him because the most important witness left town before the trial. I ran away. They'd beaten me, and I ran."

9

$\mathcal{I}$T TOOK ALL the strength Ned had to let Millicent walk out of his office by herself. He now knew why she lived so alone. Her trust in people had been destroyed by her very strength of character. He could understand not wanting to risk that betrayal another time. So she forced her strength to turn inward, not realizing, or perhaps no longer caring, that it would eat her alive.

After he couldn't see her any more from the window, he returned to his desk and sat down. He always thought better with his heels higher than his head. The habit had become so automatic that two grooves in the shape of his bootheels had begun to engrave themselves on the desktop.

Ned had just enough imagination to picture the weeks of torment Millicent must have suffered. Though she had not mentioned the length of time between the murder and her flight, he guessed it would have been more than a few days. A woman like that wouldn't be scared off easily. Weeks of unrelenting terror might do it. Compounded with the betrayal of the man she'd obviously loved, it had proved too much for her.

To think it had all begun with whispers, and now once again slanderous rumors had made her a target of every loose tongue in town. Ned wondered whether his brother-in-law had learned enough law through the textbooks he constantly studied to represent Millicent in a slander case. How could she win it? There were too many people talking too much.

He did the only sensible thing under the circumstances. He went to Mrs. Cotton.

"We been expecting you, Neddy. Come on in and set."

Millicent sat in the kitchen rocker, feeding Petey. The sun dazzled in the window behind her, lighting up her dark hair with soft red gleams. The child in her arms was wrapped in a pale green blanket, and the swath of color across her body seemed to brighten her skin and eyes.

Ned pictured her in a certain dress of emerald silk and black lace he'd seen in the dressmaker's window. Of course, so long as the earth went around the sun, Millicent would never accept the gift of a dress from a man; no respectable woman would take something like that except from a close relation or husband. So Ned had to be satisfied with his imagination. He found it a poor substitute.

Millicent said, "Mrs. Cotton has an idea on how to help us with these stories. You're not going to like it."

"Let me be the judge of that," he replied, remembering the sweet pressure of her body against his as he'd held her. Then he met Mrs. Cotton's wise eyes and wondered how much of his thoughts his face gave away.

"I was a fool," she said unexpectedly. "I should have known better than to think anybody's gonna put a *clean* reading on Millicent's finding that child. One thing about folks you can't change. If they can't find something bad to say, they'll make something up. It ain't Christian, but it sure is human."

Ned added grimly, "One thing you can say for the people in this town, they certainly are human."

He tried hard to not look at Millicent, keeping his neck stiff. Yet every time he let himself relax a little bit, his eyes sought her out. Whether from telling him the secret that had pressed on her, or just from holding Petey in her arms again, she seemed more tranquil than he had ever seen her. Her shoulders were not braced up and rigid. The frown between her curving black brows hadn't disappeared yet, but it had lessened.

Except when she looked directly at him. Then the carved lines were back, just as deeply cut. As though he could read her mind, he knew exactly what she worried about. Would he tell? Would he want to talk about what she'd told him? Or could he let it lie? Ned wished for some way to reassure her.

Mrs. Cotton said, "The way I figure things, the best thing you could do would be to get married out of hand."

"What?" Ned demanded.

"Told you that you wouldn't like it," Millicent said as she rocked the startled baby.

"You want a cup of coffee, Neddy? Might help your nerves."

"No! I mean, no, thank you, Mrs. Cotton. If you wouldn't mind explaining—"

She chuckled dryly, folding her arms across her stomach as though she were holding in her laughter. "I thought he'd be out of here like a scared he-rabbit," she said to Millicent.

"Wouldn't suit his pride," the younger woman answered. "'Sides, I reckon his pants would split if he should run."

"Maybe you're right. They do wear 'em tight these days. Does a poor ol' woman's heart good."

Self-consciously, Ned crossed his legs. His pants were not too tight; the peg-leg trouser was what all fashionable men wore. "Next time I call," he said with an assumption of calm, "I'll wear overalls. Now, if you wouldn't mind explaining this idea . . ."

"The way I see it," Mrs. Cotton said, "most folks will be so glad to see the two of you married, that'll be all they talk about. In case you couldn't guess it yourselves, you two are somethin' of a town disgrace. *One* youngster that ain't married is a dare of sorts. But there ain't no excuse for *two*. 'Specially with them being . . . you should pardon the word . . . of the opposite sex from each other. It'll seem only natural to some folks if you do get married."

Ned said, "Isn't it more likely that people will simply assume that I am, rather tardily, doing right by Miss Mayhew? It seems to me that to act as you suggest means *more* rumors and innuendo, not less."

Once again, as though he weren't there, Mrs. Cotton turned to Millicent. "I declare he's just as cute as can be when he starts talking so a body can't understand a word."

Millicent looked at him, and for a moment he saw the glimmer of a laugh in her eyes. "Maybe we could borrow that Diction-thing book."

Holding on to his slippery temper with both hands, Ned said, "Answer the question. Won't people's assumption that Petey is mine, or rather, ours, be confirmed by our marriage?"

"Don't worry about that. Folks just love a man doing the right thing by his gal, however late."

Millicent said, "I've told Mrs. Cotton that I won't hear of it. But she thought you ought to hear what she thinks. After all, you're a doctor. You gotta think about what folks say about you."

"Your reputation is every bit as important as mine, Miss Mayhew." So far, he'd done nothing to protect it. On the contrary, on at least two occasions, he'd acted in such a way to besmirch it.

"That's what I say," Mrs. Cotton said. "Now, mind you, some folks say that a milliner is on the path of destruction anyway, what with feeding women's vanity an' all. But I never could tell why a bonnet or a pretty little hat was such a sin. You shouldn't oughta think 'bout such things in church, but how's a girl gonna find a man if she don't gussy up some?"

"Some men have more discernment than others," Ned said. "Some of us don't require a fancy hat to catch our interest. A pair of intelligent eyes or cleverness in speech—"

"Don't mean nothing next to a nice ankle or a setup of glossy ringlets under a brim." Mrs. Cotton finished his sentence, snatching the words off his lips.

"Women are just the same," Millicent said softly. "We like a feller to look nice."

Ned saw the surprised gleam in Mrs. Cotton's eyes when she heard Millicent's comment. Very quickly that gleam turned to hope. Ned knew with a certainty that came from his bones that Mrs. Cotton's blue eyes would soon turn in hope and encouragement to him.

He cleared his throat and said, "I don't think the time has come yet for such drastic measures as marriage. Surely all this foolishness will die down shortly. The people of Culverton will find something else to talk about in no time. Anyone on the verge of getting married, Mrs. Cotton? That's always good for a few days of discussion."

"Not that I heard tell of. 'Course, there's Mrs. Fleck. . . ."

"Er . . . Mrs. Fleck?" No one could have overheard her all but propose to him this morning.

"I heard tell she might have her eye on somebody. One of her boarders in fact. Her old man's been gone . . . let's see . . . nigh on four years now. Time she found that boy another father. Someone who won't let him work so blamed hard."

Millicent put the sated baby to her shoulder and began to pat and rub his back. "I like the look of her boy. He's always smiling when he runs an errand in the store. What's his name? Something grand, isn't it?"

That, as much as anything, brought home to Ned how Millicent had isolated herself from her own community. The boy had perhaps been happy to be called Egbert as a youngster. But the battles when he'd grown older and begun to demand a change had rung up and down the streets of Culverton. It seemed so pathetic that Millicent hadn't heard a word of the struggle. What else had she missed? Picnics, socials, barn raisings, and corn shuckings? All the simple rural pleasures that he himself took a secret, boyish delight in.

She lived an almost entirely separate life, and Ned began to wonder why. Did they all know what had happened to her in Colorado? Or was Millicent's withdrawal so deep that they hadn't wanted to impinge on it? They didn't seem to have any problem with contacting her should they need one of her "cures," yet they didn't seem to talk to her outside of their need.

The baby burped as explosively as a shaken champagne bottle. Ned saw the expression of alarm on Millicent's face as she looked down at her unprotected shoulder. "Oh, dear."

"A little cold water will get that out," Mrs. Cotton said. "And I've got some of this patent spot remover upstairs. You come along with me. Give the baby to Neddy. He might as well get used to holding one. He'll have plenty of his own one day."

Millicent walked over to him and bent down over him, her clean scent and the fragrance of her hair falling around him. Her eyes were focused on the baby as she slipped him gently into Ned's arms. Then the lids lifted and he could see the flecks in the irises, like granules of gold reflecting the sunlight in the peaty depths of a brook.

Then she went off with Mrs. Cotton, leaving him unprotected and alone with the little stranger in his arms. The slate-colored eyes fixed on him with a mild curiosity. Ned cleared his throat.

"Erm . . . pleasant weather we're having, after the rain."

He'd held babies before, of course, wriggling, new-wet bits of humanity. But someone had always been there, an aunt or a father, to take the newborn from the doctor's arms almost before the baby exhaled its first breath. In the course of his practice, he'd held older children, but they'd usually been too sick to be away from their mothers for more than a moment's worth of diagnosis.

He had never held one in his arms for any length of time, not without someone there to take the baby away the moment it cried.

"Um, Miss Mayhew seems very fond of you. . . ."

Ned tensed as Petey writhed and yawned, the tiny mouth opening lengthwise, rather than in an O. The translucent lids batted closed. For a moment Petey struggled against the onset of sleep. He opened his eyes wide and stared up at Ned. Then again they closed. Instantly the tiny baby relaxed, his face falling in toward Ned's silk coat.

Chuckling softly so not to wake him, Ned added, "So I'm not a fascinating conversationalist. . . . I'll remind you of this when you're older."

Ned sat and watched the shadows darken as they crept over the Cottons' yard. The sweet scent of some early blossom floated in the back door. Mothers' voices called their young ones home, some sweetly, some shrilly. Culverton didn't have the wonder of nightfall on the boulevards of Paris, or the beauty of sunset over the fabled peaks of the Alps, but in exchange it had a great feeling of peace.

Peace, that is, until two men clumped up the backstairs and opened the door wider than a crack. It squeaked. A deep, strong voice said, "Ain't that cute?"

The other voice, older by its gravelly tone, said, "Looks mighty natural. Let's be quiet. Don't want to wake either of 'em up."

"I'm not asleep," Ned said, "no thanks to you. I've heard quieter clog dancing."

The judge moved about his kitchen, lighting two oil lamps. He sniffed the air and prodded the stove. "I bet you won't go home to a cold stove, Jake," he said mournfully. "That wife of yours knows how to fill her man's belly."

"You don't look like you're doing so badly." Jake glanced at the judge's straining waistcoat.

Ned mentioned the coffee in the plum-colored pot, but the judge just sighed. "Coffee's all right in its place, but it ain't vittles. But nothing's the same around here anymore. Time was a man's wife wouldn't 'low him to go hungry after a hard day's work."

"Well," said Mrs. Cotton from the doorway, "if you'd *do* a hard day's work, I reckon you'd find food here when you get home." She stalked across the floor and feinted a slap at the judge's hand as he lifted the lid off the cookie jar. "Behave yourself! You don't want to go and spoil your appetite."

"My appetite can't spoil," Judge Cotton said. "'Sides, don't seem to be nothing for it to spoil *for*."

"That's all you know. Why, if I know Antonia, she's slaving away at this very minute. She asked us for supper, old man, and you're not going to ruin it by stuffing your face now."

"Antonia's cooking?" the judge asked with a grin. "Some of them fancy dishes, I hope."

"I didn't ask her. Now trot on and put on a clean shirt and

collar." She paid no attention to the judge's groan. "And be quiet! I just got Millicent to take a lie-down on the spare room bed. Poor child," she said, turning to Ned. "She was up half the night feeding that baby."

He shook his head. "I guess someone ought to have mentioned two o'clock feedings."

"Oh, she's glad to do it. But there's no denying it takes it out of you." She turned her sharp blue eyes toward the marshal. Jake had been standing in the corner, grinning at the Cottons' talk. He'd once confided in Ned that he thought them better entertainment than a magic lantern show.

Now, though, he straightened up as though under a reviewing general's eye. Ned could have sworn he saw his brother-in-law's right hand twitch, as though about to throw a salute.

Mrs. Cotton asked, "Any luck?"

"No, ma'am. I spoke to Doc Partridge this morning. He was pretty well out of it, as usual, but he didn't remember delivering any babies in the last couple weeks, except a couple out at Handfast."

Those reflector-bright blue eyes swiveled to burn into Ned's. "Why aren't you delivering the babies at Handfast?"

"I would . . . I have . . . I mean, of course, if I'm called, I go. I have no reason not to go."

"Not because they're black?"

"I don't care . . . every mother and child deserves the best care available."

Jake stepped in. "Ned was out dealing with patients when the father came into town. He didn't want to go for Doc Partridge . . . who would? . . . but he said the babies were coming fast. Twins, as it turned out, so he didn't have time to look around for Ned."

"You saw the father?"

"I rode out there just to check. The way Doc Partridge is these days those kids could have been Swedes and he wouldn't have been able to tell the difference."

"It's a shame. I remember him. . . ." She shrugged. "Been a long time, but he was a good man once. Sober, he still could be. But the drink's got him for good, I'm afraid."

Ned said, "I'll go out there tomorrow to check on the mother and children. Doc Partridge's medical skills are somewhat behind even Millicent Mayhew's."

"Millicent would make a fine doctor," Mrs. Cotton said. "If she could get the schooling." She seemed to think about it for a moment and then dismissed it with a shake of her head. "Getting back to the matter at hand . . ."

Jake continued. "As long as I was in that part of town, I checked the saloon and Miss Annie's. She had a girl leave town a couple of months ago who'd gotten . . ." He choked over the first word that came to mind and substituted another. "She'd gotten into trouble, but she went off with a man long before her time. That's according to Miss Annie."

"I'd take her word for it over a matter like that. I reckon she must know about as much about it as anyone in town. Nobody else in her house?"

"No, ma'am. They're careful, she says."

"I reckon she knows a sight about that, too."

Ned's cheeks burned, and Jake didn't appear any too comfortable in the face of this plain speaking. But Mrs. Cotton only frowned and rubbed her right hand up and down her left arm. "I did hope . . . Well, if it isn't one of Miss Annie's girls and Doc Partridge doesn't know anything about it, I guess there's only one answer."

When neither man answered, she rolled her eyes. "Don't you see? That means she's got to be someone who hasn't been in trouble before. I'll bet she never had anything to do with a man except once and that's how she ended up in that spot. My heart goes out to her, whoever she is."

"Somebody like me?"

Millicent walked in, her dark clothes seeming to absorb some of the light. Ned jumped to his feet, and the baby started to cry. Jake started to speak but couldn't be heard. Mrs. Cotton crossed the room and took Petey from Ned's limp hands. Efficiently she began to quiet the baby by rocking.

Without looking up, she said, "Of course not, child. Lands, do you think I wouldn't be able to tell if it was you? I'm not that blind, crazy, stupid, or sweet-tempered . . . not yet. Here, you let me keep him while you run across and get redd up."

"Redd up? Why?"

"'Cause Mrs. Faraday said to be sure and bring you 'long to supper with the rest of us."

"Oh, no . . . I couldn't. . . ."

"And not to trouble showing my face if I come without you."

Millicent smiled, sweetly, shyly. A dimple, as furtive as a ghost, appeared and disappeared in her cheek. "I don't think Mrs. Faraday would ever say something like that."

"You callin' me a liar, child?"

Ned added, "You don't know how harsh my sister can be. A tartar! Isn't she, Jake?"

"Absolutely!" Jake said, imperiling his immortal soul. "She's turned out to be a regular household tyrant. Henpecked, that's what I am."

The dimple came back. Ned watched it, torn between delight in its appearance and jealousy that he alone had not been the one to call it forth. Then he wondered why he would feel jealous of Miss Mayhew.

"Now, trot on," Mrs. Cotton said to her. "Seems all I do these days is tell folks to get clean. And you two fellers could do with a washrag cross your faces. You're handsome boys, but you'd be all the better for a wash. Oh, my. Oh, yes."

10

MILLICENT AND MRS. Cotton cleared the table while Antonia Faraday rocked Petey. "That's a mighty good baby," Mrs. Cotton said. "Visited a mite, and then . . . *pfft!* Off to sleep."

"I hope he won't be up all night," Millicent said pessimistically.

"You should have taken that nap, like I told you."

"I never can sleep in the daytime." If she started taking naps, then she wouldn't be tired enough to sleep without dreams. "I don't mind getting up, not really. After all, it's kind of nice to be needed."

Now, why in the name of all that was kind and natural did she have to go looking at Ned Castle as she said it? And as if that weren't bad enough, what cause did she have to color up when he glanced her way? Just because she'd been musing over the kiss he'd given her in the dark didn't mean *he'd* given it a second thought. He probably hadn't, as a matter of fact. He'd kissed so many women that they most likely blurred in his mind so he'd be hard-pressed to choose one over another.

From her corner Antonia said, "I feel so lazy watching you work."

"You just bide," Mrs. Cotton said. "You'll have enough to do soon as that child comes along."

"She'll have help," the marshal said.

"Who from? You?" Mrs. Cotton put her hands on her hips and laughed. "There never was, nor never will be, a man who's any good with babies. Oh, you can quiet one if you hold it, but when it comes to changing those diapers, every last man I ever met was gone with the wind."

"You don't have much opinion of us men," Ned said, tipping his chair back on two legs.

"You're all right in your place," Mrs. Cotton allowed.

"Guess where our place is, gentlemen," Judge Cotton said, packing down the tobacco in his pipe with his blunt thumb. As he held the match over the bowl, he winked.

Antonia giggled. "Oh, yes. I'll grant Jake that without hesitation."

"Thank you for the testimonial, Mrs. Faraday," her husband said with a half-bow.

Millicent muttered, "I'll serve the pie," and hurried from the room. Though she hoped she didn't have a prudish streak, she'd never seen such goings-on. The marshal and his pretty bride seemed to share a warmth of affection unlike any married couple she'd ever known. A body couldn't take seriously even their complaints about each other. Not with the marshal taking every chance to squeeze his wife around her thickened waist, or to touch her hand or hair in passing.

As for the Cottons, she might snipe at him, and the judge seem resigned to it, but there again, they indulged in secret kisses and touches. One pair married only two short years; the other for forty-seven. Millicent didn't know which couple confused her more. How long was love supposed to last? What about all those couples who seemed scarcely able to tolerate each other? Was it an act, like the one the Cottons put on?

The door to the kitchen opened and Ned walked in. He, too, looked a bit flushed in the face. "It's getting wonderfully free in there. I may be a doctor, but some things should be private between a husband and wife."

"You can help me serve the pie."

"Thank you. I'll get the plates."

As he reached up for them, he said, "I don't want you to think I'm narrow-minded or anything. . . ."

"No, of course not. I . . . I get embarrassed, too. Mrs.

Cotton talks as if I know . . ." Her words stumbled and stopped.

"I'm sure she doesn't think you're anything but innocent, Miss Mayhew."

Though she realized that he had no reason to be hinting the opposite, she felt she had to justify herself. "Well, I am, as a matter of fact. I mean, my grandmother told me . . . things. But I don't 'know' them myself, if you understand what I'm saying."

"Yes, I understand completely. Now I, on the other hand, have both kinds of knowledge, but even I am embarrassed by the freedom of speech out here. Back home in Connecticut, I didn't even know where eggs came from until I was twelve."

"Now me, I've always known where eggs come from," she said, smiling at the very idea of such ignorance. "Growing up out here, stands to reason."

"I suppose everyone's life is sheltered in some ways."

She sliced into the pie, remembering at last why she held a knife. "Is it true you've been all over the world?"

"No. But I've been over more than a little of it. Parts of it are very beautiful."

Whether tone of his voice or a flicker of his eyes gave it away, Millicent couldn't tell. Suddenly she knew he didn't talk about buildings or cities but about her. He thought she was beautiful. Of course he couldn't be more wrong. Beautiful meant pink and gold, feminine and sweet, like Mrs. Faraday. Gawky, as dark as an Indian, prickly like a porcupine, she could never be beautiful. Then Millicent remembered he'd kissed her.

"Why . . . ?"

Hurriedly, to cover herself, she asked, "How big a piece do you want?"

"Oh, I'm greedy. If it were up to me, I'd take the whole thing."

He covered her hand as she prepared to sink the knife in again. "Why what?"

"I didn't say 'why.' I said 'pie.' How big a piece of pie do you want?"

Her voice trembled. She didn't know the tremble waited to come out, or she would have put a stop to it. Her hand trembled, too, a little, under his. Without quite realizing it, she'd begun to breathe faster, taking in the male fragrance of his warm skin with each pant.

His breath moved the tendrils of hair escaping from her twisted bun. She heard her name, so softly she couldn't be sure a moment later that she'd heard it at all. His other hand came around and rested, flat and smooth, against the middle of her dress. It seemed to sink right through her clothing, so she could feel the heat on her skin.

"Why?" she asked again, in a soft, unfamiliar voice. "Why do you make me feel like this? You don't even like me."

"No, I don't. But I admire you. I respect you. And, for some reason I cannot fathom, I want you."

He had to feel the tremor that went through her then, as those words whispered at her ear seemed to pass by all the machinery of her mind and go straight into her body. Her knees got weak and shaky. If he hadn't been holding her, she would have sunk to the floor.

She waited a moment, leaning back against his shoulder, waited for him to take action. Instead, he released her and stepped away, after making sure she could stand.

"It's outrageous, of course," he said, turning away. "This situation with the baby, our names being linked, puts this desire I have for you out of the question. It's ironic." He paused. "*Ironic* means . . . the opposite of what one might have expected."

"Thank you," she said in all seriousness.

"But it is ironic, isn't it? The one single woman in town I can't have is the one I . . ." He turned toward her with his sudden need to make himself clear showing in every line of his body. "I don't mean marriage, Millicent."

"I know that. I'm not the right kind of woman for you. Not to marry."

He laughed, a short bark without amusement. "And you're not the kind for anything else, either."

"No."

She turned back to cutting pie and scooping it out, an ordinary occupation that contrasted so strangely with their talk. Yet this preserved peach pie was just as real as the feelings between them.

Ned laughed again, more warmly. "Funny, I can't think of another woman in Culverton who wouldn't have slapped my face for saying that."

"What good would that do? I don't want to make you mad."

"Better not to let our emotions get out of control? Maybe you're right. All I know is it's difficult not to kiss you."

"Why did you?"

"I don't . . . no, that's not true. I wanted to see if you would be as cold in my arms as you seemed to be the rest of the time. I was wrong. And foolish. I should have suffered my curiosity, rather than suffer what I'm feeling now. Is there anything worse than to want what you can't have?"

She put the plates, each bearing a slice of golden fruit in golden crust, on a tray. "Oh, yes. Having someone you don't want, that's worse. Or being wanted by someone you don't want."

"Millicent! I don't believe that. It wouldn't be this difficult if you felt nothing for me."

Turning to back out of the door, she gazed at him with sad eyes. "The worst thing of all is wanting and knowing you're wanted, too. And not being able to have is worse still when you can't give."

As she handed around the dessert, she thought how strange to be able to talk straight at another person, and that other person a man. Once upon a time, a long time ago, she would have flirted with Ned. She'd been a talented flirt, leading boys on with alternating coolness and warmth until they didn't know if they were on their heads or their heels. All the girls had learned how to flirt at Culverton's small school, almost before they knew the name of the first president. There'd been a few boys who'd been wild for her, all long since married of course.

To be seen treating a boy as a friend and an equal in those

days had been thought more shocking than being arch and coy. But when she talked with Ned, their hearts seemed to speak directly to each other. They could be as honest as untaught children.

Millicent couldn't recall ever being so honest with Dan Redpath. They'd been too busy trying to impress each other with their charms. With a sad smile Millicent remembered how sweetly feminine she'd been in those early days in Colorado. How she would primp and practice fetching expressions in front of the mirror.

Yet here she seemed to have beguiled Ned without using a single art. *This must be irony,* she thought.

On the other side of the room Antonia leaned to the side and asked her brother, "So, what went on in there?"

"Where? And what makes you think anything went on?"

"How often does it take half an hour to cut six pieces of pie?"

"I'm sure you won't take it amiss if I suggest you mind your own business, dear sister. Dear *little* sister."

"It would help if you'd stop staring at her."

He forced his gaze to his plate. "She's an interesting person."

"Pretty, too. It's a pity she doesn't dress in colors. A nice cherry-red ribbon in her hair would make a world of difference to her."

"She's all right," he said. Then, quietly yet forcefully, he added, "Don't meddle, Antonia. She's all right as she is."

Instead of being suitably impressed with his intensity, his sister just clicked her tongue as though all her suspicions were confirmed. Then, in a serious tone, she said, "This is a dreadful mess the two of you are in. What are you going to do?"

"It's not just me. Some people seem to think Mayor Wilmot could be responsible for Petey."

"Him? Mrs. Wilmot never lets him out of her sight long enough for him to . . . to . . ."

"No, there's no delicate way of saying it," Ned said to save her time.

"Besides, I can't imagine Millicent falling for anyone

with a mustache like that! Imagine how it would prickle!"
She glanced at her husband and a dreamy look drifted across
her pretty features.

Ned sighed and looked toward the ceiling. "You were
saying?"

"They'll all forget about the mayor in a day or two. It's
going to be your problem, Ned, I feel it in my bones. What
are you going to do about it?"

"Mrs. Cotton thinks we should get married."

Antonia let out a shriek and clapped her hands together.
Her plate and fork slid to the ground. Everyone looked
around. She opened her mouth to explain, when she caught
the full force of Ned's glare. Instead of making the an-
nouncement, she smiled and said, "I forgot I haven't got a
lap. Ned, would you . . . ?"

He stood up, put his own plate on the chair, and knelt to
pick up the dish. In an undertone he said, "Of course we're
not going to do it. It's preposterous."

"You might as well give in now. If Mrs. Cotton says you
should get married, you might as well just do it."

"Grant me a little more backbone than that. Plus, there is
Millicent . . . Miss Mayhew . . . to consider. She doesn't
want to marry me any more than I want to marry her."

"Then why does she look at you the way you look at her
when you don't think she's watching?"

Ned rubbed his forehead with his free hand as he stood
up. "Could you write that down for me? I may not be able
to sleep tonight, and I find a word puzzle a great help with
insomnia."

Antonia just wrinkled her nose at him. "Mrs. Cotton will
get her way. You just wait and see. Are you going to walk
Millicent home tonight?"

"I hope I'll act like a gentleman," he said stiffly. He
carried his plate and hers into the kitchen. Only he and
Millicent knew how far from gentlemanly his behavior had
been. Perhaps on the walk home he'd find a chance to assure
her that he did not usually behave so boorishly. Not in all his
relationships with women had he ever been anything but
charming, passionate, and uninvolved emotionally. Grab-

bing girls and kissing them senseless held no appeal for him; he liked finesse.

Yet whenever Millicent looked at him with those eyes like clear tea, he found himself disregarding all his sophistication. He spoke to her as though he were a schoolboy in the throes of his first affair, blurting out whatever came to mind. No delicacy, no poise. Just raw feeling. It frightened him.

On their way to Antonia and Jake's house, the three men had walked together, discussing the problem before them. Mrs. Cotton and Millicent had strolled along behind, Petey in Millicent's arms. He'd been awake and alert but quiet, his slate-blue eyes seemingly fixed on the darkening sky above the whispering treetops.

Now he slept on Millicent's shoulder, a surprisingly heavy bundle but a very dear one. Mrs. Cotton and the judge walked ahead, lost in the dark, except for an occasional gleam of her white blouse or a giggle. Once they heard her say, "Lands!" and the judge's intimate laughter.

When Mrs. Cotton had turned down the marshal's offer of a ride, Millicent, young and strong, hadn't felt right about asking for it. Meeting Ned's eyes, she'd known he'd felt the same way.

Their conversation stopped as soon as the friendly lamplight of the Faradays' home had been cut off by the closing door. Millicent understood how dangerous it might be to talk to Ned. Things had a way of just exploding out of her. Better not to say anything rather than to say too much.

Ned, on the other hand, seemed to have no objection to having too much to say. Out of nowhere, he started a stiff little lecture on proper child nutrition. "Straight cow's milk isn't really enough. Wilmot's carries that lactated food, doesn't it? You should buy some. It has malt in it and will help him gain weight. Also, I noticed you brought out a bottle at supper. How many times have you fed him today?"

"I don't know." Lifting up the baby to settle him more comfortably, Millicent said, "But I don't think weight gain is going to be a problem."

"You need to keep careful track of how much and how

often he eats. A baby of his age should only require feeding every four hours."

"Every four hours?" She shook her head. "That don't sound right. I know I fed him today more often than that."

"Well, don't."

The moonlight glowed strongly enough to show a skeptical smile. So Millicent made sure that she hid hers behind Petey's downy head. "Just 'don't'? And how am I supposed to explain that to him? 'Sorry if you scream the place down 'cause you're hungry . . . Dr. Castle said you can't eat for two hours yet.'"

"If he's crying in between, he can't be hungry. You don't do him any favors by feeding him except every four hours." Maybe some derisive sound escaped her lips, for he said on a rising tone, "I happen to have studied this very subject with Dr. Seitz of Vienna. A world-renowned authority on children and their health. He says that a mother who feeds her child on demand might as well poison him."

"And what does Mrs. Seitz say?"

"That's unimportant."

"Of course it would be, to you." Before he could take her up on that, she said, "I bet this professor goes off to teach school and leaves her alone with their babies. I bet she feeds 'em when they're hungry and just tells her husband different when he comes home."

"This is nonsense," he said. She could tell by his walk, the steps coming down quicker and harder, that he'd begun to get hot under the collar. "Professor Seitz has studied this for years. He has made precise calculations on the rate an infant's stomach empties. His conclusions admit of no doubt. A baby should be fed no more often than every four hours."

"All the same, I bet Mrs. Seitz—"

"There is no Mrs. Seitz," he said sharply.

Millicent nodded as he proved her guess. "That's kind of what I figured. I bet there are no little Seitzes, either."

"As he's not married . . . as a matter of fact when I studied with him, he was in his early seventies." As another murmur of voices from ahead reached them, Ned added sourly, "Not that his age has anything to do with the matter."

"Sound like a pair of turtledoves settlin' down under the eaves on a rainy evening." Millicent sighed. "Must be nice."

"Don't change your mind about marriage, Miss Mayhew. I have no intention of changing mine. I am completely comfortable the way I am."

"That goes for me, too. Besides, *I'm* not the one who suggested we get married. Mrs. Cotton came up with that all on her own." Millicent started to feel the prickle of anger on her skin, as irritating as sweat.

"As long as we remain determined to be no more than friends, she can't pressure us into marrying. After all, we are free citizens with our own ideas and souls. Just because Culverton has this ridiculous reputation—"

"Are we friends?" Millicent asked.

"What?"

"Doesn't seem to me that we're friends."

He stopped and put out his hand to stop her. She couldn't shake him off without disturbing Petey so she let his hand stay on her arm. He couldn't have been aware that his thumb moved in a lazy circular pattern on her sleeve or that it caused her insides to liquefy. The night air flowed cool and soft over her skin, but she felt too warm.

"We are friends," he said, yet she could hear the doubt in his voice. "Or, at the least, we are allies. That's it. We are allies. A common defense against a common foe."

"And the foe is . . . Mrs. Cotton. I can't agree to that."

"No, not Mrs. Cotton. What she represents. Marriage. Especially marriage to each other."

Millicent nodded. "Sounds good. But I think there's one thing Mrs. Cotton said that you might find interestin'. If we marry each other, we don't ever have to be pestered again."

"That is an incentive," he said. Then she heard him laugh, and suddenly she plunged into a deep pit of worry. Why should his laughter at the thought of marrying her make her feel so dejected?

11

THE NEXT MORNING, as she glanced in the mirror to be sure her hat sat straight on her severely restrained hair, Millicent couldn't help but be disturbed by what she saw. Despite hopping up three times in the night to tend to Petey, she had color in her cheeks and a brightness in her eyes. Whenever she'd slept last night, she had lived in wonderful dreams. Dreams of flying, of Ned Castle's kiss repeated again and again, dreams of beautiful palaces where she raised crowds of children.

But it had not been the flying or the palaces that had put such color in her drab face.

She glanced down at the floor, where Petey lay kicking in his basket. "We don't have to let on to a soul, do we? It's nobody's business what I dream about."

All the same, she didn't know how she'd look Ned in the face when she met him today. Not with images of the two of them closely embracing still fresh in her mind. The funny thing was that he'd kissed her right here in reality, in this hall, but it hadn't been where they'd kissed last night. In her dreams the kisses had taken place under the open sky, in broad daylight.

Millicent blushed again, remembering. On the whole, she couldn't be sure she didn't almost prefer dreams about Beaver's Break, Colorado. They might frighten her, bringing her suddenly awake in the middle of the night, but at least she had the comfort of knowing she saw images of the unlucky past. A dream might very well predict the future. Or a wish, her heart whispered.

Picking up the basket and giving Petey an absent smile, she told herself not to be so foolish. Listening to her heart only got her into trouble.

She paused after she stepped outside onto the narrow porch and took a moment to cover the baby a little more fully with the blanket. Her smile warming, she brushed his feathery hair. He was the latest trouble her heart had led her into, and standing in the slowly strengthening spring sunshine, she didn't mind the least little bit.

As she turned to lock her door, she heard a rustling noise to her left as though something moved among the spring foliage. Millicent looked up and said in a sudden loud voice, "Scat! Go on, cat, git!"

A pity the snow had all gone; she could have thrown a snowball at the pesky thing. Of all the necessary tasks involved in keeping up a house, removing cat leavings from her flower bed ranked lowest among her least favorite. After changing the mustardy diapers that Petey created, she definitely did not feel much like cleaning up after anything else.

"I don't need more of *that* in my life, right now. You're teaching me all I care to know." She gazed down at him with mock severity. After only a moment she laughed for real.

Even in the two days she had had him she could see such a change in him. His eyes held hers a little longer. He smiled more readily. This morning, when she'd given him his bottle, he had made an uncontrolled, utterly endearing attempt to touch her cheek.

When Millicent put her hand on the gate, once again she paused. She felt a strange reluctance to go out onto the boardwalk. Today, her gate seemed to be more than the boundary between her yard and the world outside. It represented the borderline between a world of contentment, limited though it might be, and a larger world of censure, humiliation, and contempt.

She found it hard enough to go on every day with the

burden of her memories. At least she'd always had the comfort of knowing that she'd come home to a place where people had known her family. She had walked among them in outward peace, however tumultuous her soul.

Now these same people were talking about her as hard as they could. They speculated on her moral worth and passed judgment. She had to go out there and face them, to deal with them as she always had. Women would come and discuss hats they wanted to see on their heads. She would create them quickly. Surely no one cared about anything other than her ability to do her job well.

Despite this rallying talk, Millicent still could not bring herself to open that gate. "Perhaps Mrs. Wilmot will give me another day off to get settled," she said, apparently to the baby, but really to herself. "And tomorrow's Sunday, so I don't have to go in until Monday. I'll be able to do it Monday. I'll do it Monday."

"You do talk to yourself."

Ned leaned on the fence, his ankles in their shiny boots crossed just so, his elbow supporting him. He looked as though he'd been there a long time. His grin as he met her eyes seemed to tell her she looked a perfect fool.

The hot blood that ran under Millicent's skin turned it red. It did the same for her temper. "I do not talk to myself. I was talking to Petey. Unless one of your fine professors tells you a woman shouldn't talk to a baby?"

"No, they'd encourage it. Herr Doktor Reiner, for instance, would be thrilled that you don't talk 'baby talk.' He says that no child can grow up to be a rational adult if all he hears is the mush that passes for speech when people talk to children."

"Is that so? Now, don't tell me your mother never talked soft and sweet to you?"

"Of course . . ." He straightened up from his languid attitude with a snap to his spine. "That's beside the point."

Smiling as she realized she had a chance now to score off the clever doctor, Millicent tossed her head and said, "That proves it. I don't guess you'll be named as a 'rational' adult any time soon."

Before she could finish reaching for the gate, Ned had pulled it open toward him. Millicent walked straight through, the baby's basket snuggled in one curved arm.

"You've decided to go to Wilmot's Store after all?"

"It's where I work."

"With Petey?"

"When I talked to Mrs. Wilmot the first day I had him, she said I could bring him."

Ned fell into step beside her. "This would be *before* everyone started wondering what man was so obliging to you."

"Obliging?"

"Obliging enough to leave you with his baby."

"I wish you would stop talking like you've got a hot potato in your mouth and just tell me what you mean."

She'd noticed last night that their paces matched as they walked along, giving her a nice feeling of equality. Now, however, he sped along, marching as though he were angry. She had to trot a little to keep up. Petey didn't care for the increased shaking of his basket. He began to screw up his face as though in a moment he'd let loose with a yell.

"I mean that Mrs. Wilmot may have changed her mind about having the baby and you at the store. After all, people are now suggesting that it might be Mr. Wilmot's baby."

"Well, it isn't." Her tone admitted no doubt. She slowed down. Let him keep to her pace.

"You sound very sure of that. Whose baby is it?"

"How would I know that? Unless I were . . ." She caught her breath on a cry of mingled hurt and outrage. "Don't you start with me, Dr. Castle. Just don't you start."

"I didn't mean it that way. . . ."

"I think you did!"

"But you've got to realize that there's bound to be someone who'll ask you to your face."

Millicent said defiantly, "Just let 'em! I'll give them the same answer I'm giving you! I don't know who this baby belonged to in the past. To tell the truth and shame the devil, I don't much care. He's mine now."

Petey started to holler then, a rising and breaking cry that sounded all the louder for being outside. Before Millicent could put the basket down, Ned slipped his hands in and took the baby out. He put him to his shoulder, the basket sliding, and began to pat and rub the tiny back.

"Wassa matta?" he crooned. "Nassy ol' grown-ups makin' too much noise for you? There, now. There, now, Petey-petey."

Millicent folded her arms, opening her mouth to make a crushing comment regarding his use of baby talk. Then she caught the eye of several ladies whose baskets held not babies, but their morning's shopping. Forcing a smile that must have looked like a Halloween pumpkin's, she waved slightly and then clapped that hand to her cheek.

"You'd better put him back," she said, trying not to move her lips too much.

Ned said, "He's all right. I'll carry him for a while."

"I'm not talking about his crying. I'm talking about the gossip. You start making a fuss over him, and they'll all be certain-sure that you're the father."

"Nobody's out yet."

"Just half the town," she replied, nodding again toward the interested group of three. "Standing not a hundred feet away on the other side of the street. Three of the biggest talkers in this town, and one of 'em is married to the all-time champion tattletale, Mr. Grapplin. Everybody going in or coming out of the depot will know you picked that child up and draw some mighty interestin' conclusions."

Ned said, "Oh, my God," with a fervor that religion couldn't have bettered. He leaned down to put Petey back into his basket. But the moment the child came away from his shoulder, the gulping whine became once more full-fledged shrieks.

Snapping upright once more, Ned said, "I guess I'm going to carry him."

"I guess you are. Well, let's not dawdle, then."

Pausing only to pick up the trailing end of the blanket and wrap it around Petey, Millicent set off. She tried to pretend that she walked in a crowd, and couldn't be responsible for whoever walked beside her. A proper lady wouldn't even acknowledge such a stranger with a glance. But she couldn't help looking, though she told herself she had to check on Petey.

Judging by the doctor's expression, he pretended he walked alone in the middle of a desert. He kept his eyes fixed on the horizon. She could see the tight muscles bulge in his jaw above the stiff collar of his shirt.

Millicent realized she'd never yet seen Ned Castle dressed sloppily or slipshod. He always looked comfortable, but always dressed correctly, too. After a lifetime of farmers who wore nothing but overalls, or miners in mail-order jeans, she found him refreshing. Of course, the judge always dressed fancy, too, but not with the neatness or class of the doctor. Besides, everyone agreed that Ned Castle was a fine-looking young man, and nobody but Mrs. Cotton had ever thought that about the judge.

"I guess you've got a lot of calls to make today," she said.

"You're talking to me, then? Aren't you afraid of what people will say?"

"No point in marching along like a couple of soldiers on parade, is there?"

"No. And I don't have any calls to make today."

"I just wondered 'cause you're dressed so sharp," she explained. Then she glanced at him again, noting the bitter tone in his voice. "Why don't you?"

"Because no one has asked me, and those that asked me before have sent polite messages saying how much better they are feeling."

"Even Mrs. George?" she ventured to ask, knowing that nothing short of death would keep her from trying to catch an eligible mate for her daughter.

"Her message was among the first. Her leg is so much improved, she says, that she won't be home for my visit as she is going for a long walk."

"But she never walks anywhere if she can help it—oh!"

"Exactly. I don't mind her so much . . . her illnesses are all imaginary, or mostly so. It's the other people—the ones I can help. If they don't let me, there's nothing I can do."

"They'll come around in time."

"Will they? I can think of at least one who doesn't have the luxury of waiting until I'm seen to be morally upright."

"Mr. Landis? You're worried about his arm?"

Ned nodded stiffly. "Exactly. I'm afraid it's cancer. If I don't operate soon . . ."

"Can't you tell him that?"

"I did. He was supposed to come in today so I could tell him when. But sure enough, he sent his son over with a message that . . . I don't recall what lame excuse he chose to use. I was tempted to tell his boy that if he wanted to keep his father with him, he'd talk sense to him."

"Why didn't you?"

"It wouldn't have been professional."

Millicent said, "I guess you have to consider that kind of thing."

Ned stopped in front of Wilmot's Store. "Here," he said. "He's asleep."

But as he lifted Petey away from his body, Millicent saw the large wet stain on Ned's fine blue coat. "Oh, dear," she said, taking the baby. "I'm sorry."

When Ned glanced down, a wry smile twisted his lips. "Why shouldn't Petey do that? Everyone else in town is doing the same, if only figuratively." Meeting her eyes, he said, "I mean, they're not actually doing it, but they might as well be."

"I didn't reckon they were all standing around in a circle." She smiled to show she didn't mind his telling her what a word meant. Actually, she liked it. She knew there were many more words in the world than she had the chance to hear or use. A talk with Ned Castle was an education in itself.

"I hope they'll come to their senses soon," Ned said. "I'm responsible for the general health of this community. Besides, I'm lazy." In answer to her questioning look, he said, "If I don't keep up with it, I'll have to work ten times as hard later catching up. That's not my idea of a good time."

"What is?"

She saw how, when he ran his hand back through his hair, the strands fell thickly through his fingers. Inside her black mesh gloves, her fingers twitched as though they, too, felt the tickling fall of his hair.

"I like to read," he said. "When I was younger, I raced horses . . . not professionally but among my friends. Now I settle for Abendego. He's just right for pulling my gig and doesn't seem to mind being rousted out in the middle of the night. But if I ever have a home of my own, I'd like to own some blood stock again."

"I like horses, too. We never could afford one, but I used to dream about having one for myself."

Mentioning dreams reminded Millicent of the ones she'd lived through last night. In those dreams Ned hadn't spoken a word, just slipped his arm around her waist and pulled her up tight against his hard body. Then, after a single instant of looking more deeply into her eyes than any other person ever had, he'd kissed her.

"I . . . I better be gettin' in," Millicent said. "Thanks for . . . for carrying Petey. I . . ."

She trotted up the steps to the entrance to Wilmot's Store, leaving him looking up at her in surprise at the suddenness of her leave-taking. The last thing Millicent saw before she went into the near-dark of the store was the sunlight shining on his fair hair, turning it to gold.

Millicent walked straight to the back of the store to take off her coat, put on her smock, and—in a change from routine—apply cold water to the back of her neck. The chill seemed to help restore her shattered morale. She still held the soaked handkerchief there when the door to the change office opened and Mrs. Wilmot looked out.

"Oh, it's you, Millicent. Come in."

Stopping only to pick up the baby's basket, Millicent went in. Ever since she'd awakened this morning, she'd been hiding her dread over this interview. Not because she feared Mrs. Wilmot, or even worried that she wouldn't allow Petey to stay in the store during working hours.

The rumors about her and Mr. Wilmot must have reached

his wife by now. This meeting must be as embarrassing for her as it was for Millicent, possibly worse. It would require great tact to get through it without hurting anyone's feelings, and Millicent knew she had no tact. Honesty didn't have the same effect on people as smooth-talking.

"Sit down, Millicent." Mrs. Wilmot took her seat in front of the large rolltop desk pushed against the wall. The ledgers and invoices of the business were all around. Mrs. Wilmot traced her finger down the column of numbers in the book that lay open on the desk while Millicent got settled.

Then she spun around in the spring-seated chair and leveled a straight gaze at Millicent. "This child . . ."

"He isn't your husband's."

"My dear! I didn't imagine for a moment that he was."

"Good. Is there anything else? I've got a lot . . ."

Mrs. Wilmot's frigid face thawed a little. "I'm sure you've heard what people are saying."

"It's hard to miss," Millicent grumbled.

"I want you to know that I don't believe a word of it. You say that you found the child; very well, you found him. I have known you for a long time, most of your life in fact. I don't think you are the kind of girl who gets herself into trouble. Certainly, you wouldn't entangle a married man in anything unseemly."

"What kind of a girl gets herself into trouble, Mrs. Wilmot? I've always wanted to know."

Suddenly Mrs. Wilmot chuckled and Millicent relaxed. She'd always liked the older woman. Though her large family kept her busy, she always offered her help in the store when a lot of customers had come in, and she gave Millicent a generous percentage off on prices. Though Mr. Wilmot was the nominal owner of Wilmot's Store, his duties as mayor kept him out of it more often than not. Millicent didn't see how he would have had time to carry on with any woman other than his wife.

"What kind of a girl? Well, a girl like me . . . I mean, like I used to be. You probably don't remember. . . ."

"I remember how pretty you were. My grandmother always said you were the prettiest girl in Culverton when I was little."

"Yes, I think I can say without vanity that I was." She ran her fingers over the back of her mottled hand. "But children change that, don't they? If we knew that when we were girls, we never would have been in such a hurry to get them."

Mrs. Wilmot shook her head. "I shouldn't tell you this, but Mr. Wilmot and I didn't wait until we were married."

"Grandmother said that, too."

"Oh, I suppose some of the older women remember; that kind of thing is meat and drink to them. I'm not ashamed of it. But that's how I know you are innocent of what these rumors say."

"I don't understand," Millicent said.

Mrs. Wilmot gave a little laugh as she leaned back in her chair. "Well, I mean . . . I was a heedless, passionate girl then. If someone told me 'no,' I couldn't wait to disobey. I never stopped to consider the outcome of anything I chose to do. I ran wild; my mother couldn't do a thing with me. When Mr. Wilmot and I met, well, caution was one of the first things we threw to the wind. Of course, we meant all the while to get married, it just seemed so foolish to wait and . . . along came the first baby before we knew where we were at."

She shook her head at her memories and then leaned forward again to tap Millicent on the knee. "You're not like that, Millicent. You're . . . sensible. Down-to-earth in all the ways that matter. I can't imagine you losing your head and letting yourself be run away with."

"You mean, I'm not passionate?" Millicent didn't know if she liked the sound of that. Did it mean dried up, past all hope, an old maid born not made?

"You're not a fool. I was. I don't regret it. The first time . . ." Mrs. Wilmot's dark brown eyes stared through half-closed lids at something only she could see. Then she shook herself and said, "Not to mention that I've worked with you ever since you came home. Even if you were to throw yourself away on some man, it wouldn't be my husband, or anyone's husband for that matter. You wouldn't think it was right."

"It wouldn't be. I mean, when people make promises to each other, it's not right for somebody else to come in and try to bust it up." Then she added, more for truth's sake than to hearten Mrs. Wilmot, "Besides, Mr. Wilmot isn't exactly . . . That is . . . I mean . . ."

Mrs. Wilmot smiled. "Maybe not now, but once upon a time he was wonderful. Anyway . . . I just wanted you to know that I have no doubt that you found this baby exactly as you said. I shall tell anyone who asks me that I believe in you."

"Thank you." Millicent stood up, taking the handle of the basket in her hand. "I think I should warn you, though. Some folks may not want me to help them or to buy hats from me. An awful lot of people think I am all those things you say I'm not."

"I know. But we'll manage to get along without their business, if we have to. I've talked all this over with Mr. Wilmot. He thinks it'll look worse if we let you go than if we keep . . . I hope you're not upset by that. My husband has to think about those kinds of things."

"No. I'm too practical to mind it in other folks."

Mrs. Wilmot's words were in the back of Millicent's mind all day. They mingled there with Ned's explanation that he'd kissed her only because he wanted to judge if her coldness went all the way through.

Darryl, at seventeen the Wilmots' second oldest son, helped out in the store. Usually, he didn't have much to say for himself. His mother explained that he tended to be moody, a lot more than usual over the last several months. She said he was impatient to get away to college in the fall.

Today, though, he seemed to have lost his reserve. Maybe the baby softened him, for he played with Petey a few times when things were slow. Darryl chatted with Millicent about the weather, his friends, and his plans for the future, which seemed only vaguely to involve college. Taken aback by this sudden sociability, Millicent did her best to be interested and friendly in return.

At the end of the day, as Millicent stood outside while he locked the front door, Darryl said, "I always knew you'd turn out to be nice, Miss Mayhew." Then he turned red as a radish and bolted away.

Carrying Petey home, the empty bottles clinking in the bottom of his basket, Millicent asked herself just how forbidding she seemed. So far, other people's impressions had not been flattering. Mrs. Wilmot thought she was so level-headed as to be dreary. Darryl thought she needed the benefit of the doubt to be thought nice, until today. Ned thought she had a heart as cold as a witch's.

She told herself what Ned Castle thought didn't matter. Yet she wondered if her present problem could be traced to some fault of her own. If she'd been more open with the people of her hometown, would more of them have supported her now? If she hadn't been so afraid to let people into her heart, maybe more of them would believe her pure. But how could she have accepted their friendship? If she'd been open with them, they would know she preferred to run from trouble. Better to be misjudged than to be judged a coward.

Her spirits completely depressed, Millicent dragged herself and Petey home. The sky to the west was streaked with lemon-yellow and orange. The first sad songs of the cicadas, which would become a full orchestra by August, had begun to whine in the air. Millicent wished with all her heart that a hot dinner waited ready for her, and more than that, she wished for someone to talk to and a pair of arms to hold her tight, blocking out the cold.

She had pushed open her gate and had begun to walk up the path when she heard running footsteps banging away along the boardwalk. Turning, she peered into the gathering darkness.

Then, with a rushing noise she remembered all too well, a rock flew. Millicent gasped and cowered down, covering the basket with her body. The first rock disappeared into the darkness. The second shivered a window on the front of the house.

The footsteps pounded away. Millicent heard two sets, or thought she did, through the roaring rush of blood in her head. One set followed the other with only a few seconds in between. Someone ran down the boardwalk, while the other crashed through her backyard.

12

MILLICENT FELT AS though her head were floating a few inches away from her body. She reached out to bring it back but found instead that her fingers caressed smooth, cool cloth. Somehow she knew instinctively that she held the lapel of a man's coat.

His arm felt strong as a railroad tie beneath her. Every time she drew a deep breath, her front parts pressed against his body. He smelled like coffee and lemons. Ever so faintly came the smell of menthol through the other scents. It told her, plain as print, that Dr. Castle held her against his heart.

It would have been wise, perhaps, to push him away, to let him know without a doubt that she had become mistress of herself once more. Instead, she closed her eyes and let her body go a little more limp, sneaking a few more moments of comfort.

Then she heard the sharp tone in his voice as he answered the faraway buzz that meant other people's voices. She realized dimly that it had been his biting response to some question that had brought her back to wherever she'd gone after the rock had flown.

"I don't care if you have to roust every boy in this town! You find the little son of a . . . excuse me, Mrs. Cotton."

"Don't mind me," she said. "I may not say it like that, but I'm sure enough thinkin' it."

"You just find him, Jake. I won't trouble the court's docket with his punishment."

"I already cut me a stout switch," Mrs. Cotton added.

"We'll learn the little monster, and his parents, too, if he's got any that'll claim him."

Though she still didn't seem able to open her eyes, Millicent could tell by their voices that they stood above her. All except the doctor, whose voice thrummed in the surface beside her ear. Funny how it didn't matter to her what he said, so long as he would go on speaking. She wished she could stay like this forever, so comfortable and at ease.

"You better git Miss Mayhew inside, Neddy; it's starting to get a mite chilly. Wouldn't be surprised to see we're in for another thunder-walloper."

"She's all right. She's awake now."

How did he know?

His fingers were gentle on her face as he tilted her chin up. Millicent lifted her heavy eyelids and found him gazing down at her, an encouraging smile tugging at the corners of his mouth. The lock of hair over his forehead had fallen into his eyes, making him look not only younger but more compassionate. His eyes were affectionate as they dwelled on her, as if all his irony had blown away.

He said, "You're not hurt. The rock didn't hit you."

At first these words sounded like statements of fact. But Millicent thought a hint of appeal had come into his eyes.

"No," she said. "I'm all right. I think."

"Should I carry you?" he asked, his arms tightening.

Exquisitely comfortable, Millicent wanted to nod. It would be wonderful to be swept up in his arms and carried away. Then she recalled that others stood by, in all likelihood watching every twitch she made. Self-consciousness returning, she shook her head and pushed ever so slightly at Ned's solid chest. "I'm all right," she repeated. "I can walk."

She realized she lay across Ned's lap, sprawling really, in a pose that would have led anyone to suspect the worst about their association. The way he held her, the way she seemed to have melted into him could be called "cuddling" or even "canoodling." Once Millicent saw this, she scrambled around to stand up, not caring that she ground her skirt into the wet grass of her front yard.

"Where's Petey?" she asked, coming fully to her senses.

"Right here, child," Mrs. Cotton said. "Out like a light, poor lamb. But he's not hurt."

Eager to judge for herself, Millicent stepped quickly across the walk to Mrs. Cotton's side. Too quickly, perhaps, for she suddenly felt light-headed again. She stopped, putting her hands out as she swayed.

"Here now," Jake Faraday said. Being the closest, he stepped to her side in one stride of his long legs. He put a hand on her shoulder and peered down from his lanky height into her face. "Reckon you need to sit down, Miss Mayhew."

"Thank you, Marshal," she said, blinking at him. "What happened? I must of fainted, or something."

"Something like that," the marshal said with the smile that had won him many hearts before he gave his own to Antonia. Despite her wooziness, Millicent warmed under his smile the way a plant blossomed in the sun. He said, "Just tell me what you remember."

"I'd just come home from the store," Millicent said slowly. "I opened the gate. . . ." She glanced at it, remembering.

As her gaze went past Ned, she wondered why he looked like a thundercloud. His lips were tight, his brow all rumpled, and his eyes looked ready to shoot lightning at Marshal Faraday. What had the marshal done to offend his brother-in-law?

She stared at Ned with her head cocked to the side for a moment. It occurred to her that Ned might not like another man touching her. Though she sternly told herself he had no right to be jealous, she still stepped away, out of reach of the marshal's comforting hand on her shoulder.

Quickly she went on with her story. "Then there was a . . . a rock. It shattered a window, and somebody ran away."

"Which way?"

"Down the walk, I think. Or through the backyard. I don't know. I can't be sure. I dropped to the ground soon as I knew what was happenin'. And my poor window!"

She'd turned to look up at Jake again and caught sight of the damage past his head. Only two pieces of jagged glass remained in the rectangle, a black hole reflecting no moonlight, as blank and unsightly as a missing tooth.

"Looks worse than it is," he reassured her. "A piece of glass, that's all. Tell you what. I'll stop by tomorrow and fix it."

"The judge can do it," Mrs. Cotton said. "After all, it's our house."

"Oh, Mrs. Cotton," Millicent said, guilt settling on her. "Of course, I can pay for the . . ."

"Lands, why should you? Once we find the little heathen that done it, he'll pay for it. Important thing now is to get it fixed so you and this angel can sleep without a draft whistling past your beds. If Jake don't get to it in the morning, I'll have Vernon come by after we all get home from church."

Walking forward, Ned said, "Why wait? It can't be later than eight-thirty. I'll go ask Mayor Wilmot to open and cut me a piece of glass. I'm sure to find some putty at Mrs. Fleck's. Miss Mayhew and the baby won't have to sleep even one night in a draft."

He glanced up at his brother-in-law, and Millicent could swear she saw his expression grow hard and unfriendly. "Call it a prescription, if you like."

"On the grounds that it's unhealthy to sleep with a broken window in the house?" Jake suggested. Then he chuckled. "I'd listen to your medical man, Miss Mayhew. Well, I better get 'long if I'm going to catch the little bas . . . son of a gun."

"Yes," Ned said. "Hadn't you." He followed Jake, his firm jaw set with determination. The glance Ned threw at Millicent might have been calculated to put her back up, for it dismissed her as being of no worth.

Mrs. Cotton said somewhat hastily, "Well! I'll take the mite inside and then help you clean up the glass, Millicent. But don't you hurry if you don't feel right, hear?"

Millicent said, "I am feeling a bit woozy." Without saying anything else, she walked up to her front porch and sank down on the steps. Mud had spoilt her dress, in addition to a tear diagonally across the front; what did a little dampness matter?

As Mrs. Cotton came up past her, Millicent said, "Thanks for everything. I . . . I don't know how I'd get through all this without you."

She felt a brushing touch on her disheveled hair as the older woman stepped up on the porch. "Never you mind thankin' me. I got to honor my promise to your grandmother. I told Jeanie I'd look out for you, and I will."

"When did you promise that?" Millicent asked, curious despite her weakness.

"When you came home from Colorado."

"But . . . Grandma was dead then. Dead two years and more."

"Well, what in tarnation has that to say to anythin'? We was friends. That don't end 'cause one of you got your notice."

"I wouldn't know." Millicent leaned her aching head against the railing. "I haven't got any friends."

"You've got more than you know, child. Ain't you learned that yet?"

The vibration of her footsteps faded on the porch floor.

Millicent peered into the hastening dark, trying to see the men down by the gate. Their voices came to her like those of disembodied spirits, faint, far-off, and indistinguishable from the breeze. She wondered dully what they were talking about.

Then the breeze shifted around and she could hear.

"What the devil does that mean?" The marshal's voice, loud and tight with anger, rang out.

"Exactly what you think it does. If I hear one word about the two of you, that star won't save you from me."

Millicent looked around wildly. Should she call Mrs. Cotton? She could make anyone see reason.

"In case it slipped your mind, I'm a married man."

"That's right. Married to my sister. I think that gives me the right to be concerned."

Suddenly the marshal laughed and dropped his voice so

low that she couldn't hear it. She realized she leaned forward anxiously, trying to catch his words. Then Ned laughed, too.

Millicent let out the breath she'd been holding and inhaled the moist evening air, trying to get her emotions back under control. She had no reason to believe Ned and Jake had been talking about her. But her breaths became shakier instead of stronger as her eyes began to burn with the tears she never could allow to fall. She tried to stand up, impatient with her weakness, but had to grab the railing as she swayed unsteadily.

"Damn it," said Ned, his voice preceding him. "You're the most irritating female I've ever known!"

Then he appeared, materializing out of nothing, for his dark suit blended with the night. Ned strode up to her, taking the porch steps in what seemed a single stretch. She started back wildly, but he took no notice.

He drove his arm around her waist and pulled her hard and strong against him. "Now quit pretending you don't feel like hell, Millicent, and sit down again."

He sat down. She had no choice but to come down, too. Ned absorbed the shock as they hit the step, but she found herself once more on his lap. "Now," he said in a voice that came from between his teeth. "Put your head on my shoulder and pretend you're just a weak, defenseless, God-help-me *normal* woman, will you please?"

"You'd hate that," she said drowsily, her usual inhibitions failing to safeguard her thoughts.

"At least I know where I am with women like that. By God, Millicent, you've got me to where I don't know my *gluteus maximus* from my *humerus*. And no, I won't translate that."

She smiled up at him. "I can guess."

Putting up a languid hand, she delicately sought out and removed the pins from her loosened hair. She shook it free, letting it fall over his arm, heavy as a velvet stole. The shiver that went through him at that whispering touch should have put her on her guard. Instead, she gazed up at him as the smile faded from her lips.

"It's all wrong," he groaned even as he lifted her up.

Utterly different than the first kiss in the hall, or her dream kisses, Ned seized her in the embrace of a man goaded into testing his limits and hers.

Her arms were caught by her sides, wrapped in his hungry hold, so she couldn't reach up to him. She could only try to show him her willingness by taking what he gave her.

He stroked into her mouth, and at first that was too much, but then she thought it just fine. She felt a shiver start deep within her, rising to the surface of her skin like a river of fire bursting through a lake of ice.

Then he freed one of her arms, as he impatiently sought out her breast with his hand. Instead of recoiling, she threw her arm around his neck, dragging him downward, keeping him locked to her. She searched his mouth with her tongue, clumsily imitating what he did, and the heat flickering over her skin grew more intense when she heard his moan, knowing she caused it.

Millicent couldn't force a single thought into her mind, swamped by a whirlwind of sensations. His juicy mouth on hers, the sandpaper scratch of his shadowed face, the rustle where his hand brushed the soft wool of her dress, and the unbearable delight of his firm touch on her breast sent her mind reeling away from rationality.

She sobbed with pleasure, forgetting to be silent. Frightening to be so far out of control, but exhilarating. She couldn't breathe, but she could fly.

Ned looked down at her, his greedy eyes absorbing all of her. Her face glowed white against the blackness of her dress and the night, so that she seemed like a phantasm, or a witch. A witch, perhaps, with her eyes aglow over some spell. The spell she cast on him entwined around him. Even as he sank down to taste her mouth again, he felt the enchantment flourish.

Through the coarse stuff of her dress, her nipple hardened against his hand. He fumbled for the buttons on her dress, wanting to show her more of her own response, knowing as he did it that he had no excuses for the bad behavior he wanted to commit. She was a virgin; he'd swear to it.

Moreover, she struggled under enough burdens. Already everyone in town suspected her of doing exactly what he wanted to do with her.

If anyone saw them now, they'd both be ruined in this town. But the thought of stopping, of drawing away from the heat and the desire, struck him like a physical blow. One more kiss, he promised himself, just one more.

Ned dragged his hand away from her bodice and congratulated himself on his strength of character. Then Millicent arched up, a wail, half-protest, half-pleasure, coming from her softly opened mouth. Without thinking, he'd stroked down over her gently rounded stomach and into her lap.

He couldn't pretend this wasn't what he wanted. Nor could he really think that he took advantage of her. Not when every move she made, every soft cry, told him of her willing participation in her own seduction.

Once again, he kissed her. Like a child eating sweets, he promised himself just one more. And one more after that.

Only when he found himself lifting against her as mindlessly as an animal could Ned stop. Summoning up all his self-discipline, he pressed his cheek to hers. He could feel her heartbeat repeating in the hand that curved around the back of his neck.

"I was jealous," he said, the words as unexpected to him as to her. "Jake touched you; you looked at him . . . I don't know. I've *never* been jealous. I didn't believe I could be jealous. It's crazy."

Millicent replied only by moving her fingertips gently through the short hair at the back of his neck, the gentle motion keeping him focused on his need. He wanted her to stop and hoped she never would.

"It's only crazy like this with you, Millicent. Other women . . . I can't even remember that there ever were any. . . ."

Suddenly she laughed, a rich, womanly sound in the dark. "Always the gentleman . . ."

"Not tonight." He sat up, letting her hand fall away from his nape.

She moved, too, sliding away across his lap in a foam of skirts, to sit beside him. Ned closed his eyes against the torture, gritting his teeth to stop the howls from escaping.

"I want you," he said, surprising himself again. "I'm sorry. I shouldn't say that."

"Even if it's true?"

"The truer it is, the less I should express it. God, Millicent, don't you realize . . . ?"

"Of course I do. I'm no dummy. We're all wrong for each other."

"Completely wrong. I don't know why I should have any interest in you at all. Besides the fact that you're so beautiful that you knock men down like dominoes . . ."

"Huh? Maybe you're talking 'bout somebody else."

He reached out to her. He swore to himself he only wanted to take her hand. Yet, when his arm fit so naturally around her shoulders, it seemed wrong not to pull her in against him. The night might be damp, after all, and she'd just had a frightening experience. She needed warmth and comfort, though those things did not occur to him when she pressed her face into his neck.

"You're as beautiful as a witch," he whispered earnestly.

"Witches are ugly. With warts."

"You're thinking of ordinary witches. I'm thinking of sorceresses and enchantresses. That's what you are. Casting spells on unsuspecting men, enslaving them."

"You talk pretty," she said on a sigh, her lips moving against his sensitive throat. She mumbled something else. When he asked her to repeat it, she tossed back her hair and said, "What are we going to do?"

"Fix your window. Then we'll talk to Mrs. Cotton. Of course."

The window took no time at all, once Ned managed to measure the opening accurately. He had trouble with that because Millicent helped him. Every time he looked at her, his hands shook. Finally he'd been forced to ask her to leave. She smiled at him as she went out as if to say she knew exactly why he couldn't measure a simple square accurately.

After stopping to look in on Petey, sound asleep with his fist under his chin, Ned went down to Millicent's cheerless kitchen. After they both rejected Mrs. Cotton's suggestion for a quick marriage, she shrugged and said, "Neddy, so you don't want to marry her. It wouldn't hurt you just to woo her a bit."

Millicent echoed Mrs. Cotton. "Woo?" she asked, sounding like a confused owl.

"Why not? Nobody's going to believe that Neddy's out to buy the cow if he already got all the milk for nothing. So if he comes around with a few flowers, a bag of penny candy, and walks you and Petey home from church on Sundays . . . you can use our parlor to set in since it won't look right you lettin' him into your house after dark . . . again."

Ned wondered how much Mrs. Cotton saw with that guileless gaze, exceeded in apparent innocence only by her baby-faced husband. Yet a wilier judge had never taken the oath of office. How much of that reputation did he owe to his mild-tempered, devious wife?

Millicent put her elbows on the table, resting her forehead on the heels of her palms. "That still leaves two problems," she said. "Even if Dr. Castle would do it."

"Mayor Wilmot and that traveling man?"

Nodding, Millicent said, "You know how folks are. If Dr. Castle starts coming around, they'll say he's just tomcatting. Going where someone else has already been."

With his teeth grinding, Ned said, "Just let one person say anything of the kind to my face!"

Mrs. Cotton chuckled. "Why, you wouldn't hit a lady, would you? The men ain't talking. They don't care. It's the women that are making your lives hell. Stop them, and you'll stop these stories."

Ned threw up his hands. "All right. All right. Miss Mayhew, will you do me the favor of allowing me to escort you to church tomorrow?"

She raised her amber eyes, and he felt the pull of this attraction, like the power of a magnet on an iron filing. The iron didn't have any more choice in the matter than the magnet. Instantly he remembered the feel of her firm breast filling his hand. Maybe something of it showed in his face, for her eyes went wide as her cheeks flushed. Mrs. Cotton sat and grinned.

"Say 'yes' and the poor man can get home to bed."

"Yes."

13

"*WE LOOK LIKE* a magazine cover," Millicent muttered as she and Ned entered the church.

"'The Perfect American Family,'" he replied, without moving his lips. "That was the idea. Look at them looking at us."

"I feel like an elephant in the circus."

"Oh, I don't think they'll throw peanuts. . . ."

"Of course they won't! Hymnals throw easier," she said.

As they shuffled crabwise along the pew, Millicent attempted to ignore the whispering voices all around her. Even the Reverend Mr. Budgell, a man younger than his title would lead one to believe, opened the door to his robing room to glance out. His eyes grew round as he saw Millicent and Ned Castle sitting down together.

She could feel every stare like a hot match head pressed against her skin. "I don't know about this, Ned."

"Too late now. Here, take Petey."

He passed her the baby. As soon as the wriggling fellow settled in her arms, she felt calmer. Still, as always when she had somehow become the center of attention, Millicent wanted to crawl away and hide. Under the pews would be good. Maybe she could slip down there. Probably Ned would do the same. Then he might kiss her again, or daringly, she might kiss him. The smooth, hard muscles of his arms would close around her, bending her back. . . .

Millicent hadn't the slightest hope that the blush that stained her face would go unnoticed. She'd daydreamed in church before, even dozed off once when Mr. Budgell had started discussing the Amalekites, the Arbites, and the Arelites. But she had never imagined herself sharing wild kisses on the floor of the church with the town doctor. Shocked at her own wanton imagination, Millicent shifted slightly on the hard bench to put a little distance between her thigh and Ned's.

He refused to let that gap widen. Without moving, he suddenly seemed to take up more space. His legs were a little wider apart, his elbows crossing the line, his hand sliding over on the seat so that every wiggle of his little finger would brush her leg.

Resigned to Ned's playing his part well, she fumbled in her carpetbag for Petey's bottle. Millicent looked down at the baby, concentrating on the sweet little nose, the wide eyes, the utter, unexpected charm of a toothless grin. Petey had awakened this morning with a gurgle of laughter. When she'd gone over to his cradle to see why he laughed, a sunbeam made her smile, too. They'd shared the joy of a sunlight streaming in through a gap in the curtains. For that brief time she'd known what it meant to be truly happy.

She raised her eyes to Ned. He stared down at the two of them, his bright blue eyes hooded as he contemplated his thoughts. He looked troubled, his lips set as though against some pain, his forehead harrowed with concern. She wondered if he even saw her and Petey or if they were just in his line of sight while he busied himself with reflections.

Then he grinned, a silent laugh, and met her eyes. "Will you snap my nose off if I ask you how long since you last fed him? Or am I safe?"

"You're safe. He had some at daybreak, but not very much. He's a good eater, as a rule, but he had a lot last night so he's probably hungry again now."

"Four hours?"

"Pretty close. 'Course, my clock gains."

Then the preacher mounted the dais to stand behind the lectern. He announced the hymn and Ned reached for the book. His face became serious, mature, and above all, calm. She felt she knew him well, this man she'd sometimes kissed and often irritated. Completely wrong for her, of course, and looking at him now a single conclusion leaped out at her.

She was in love with him.

Shaken, she failed to hold the bottle steady, and it dropped from her suddenly nerveless fingers. Fortunately, it only bounced instead of shattering. Deprived of his late breakfast, Petey sent up a howl that cut right across the first verse of "Mercy we pray, Sweet Jesus."

Mrs. Prentiss, two rows ahead, bent down without missing a beat. She passed the milk bottle back, through the hands of Mrs. Landler's youngest girl. Millicent mouthed "thank you" to the both of them, and they nodded.

Fitting the bottle, now half-filled with bubbles, to Petey's wide-open mouth, Millicent cajoled him into taking it. A few good sucks and the baby settled down again. Despite the singing voices filling the air, the church seemed peaceful again now that he'd stopped. Millicent could think again.

She could not be in love with Ned Castle. Over time she'd pared her life down to the size and shape she could manage best. Her instincts of self-preservation showing themselves, she dismally realized that to add man-woman love to her life would break down all her barriers. She would be left without defenses, vulnerable again to heartaches.

Only a fool fell for a man who'd made it absolutely clear that he did not want anything to do with love. Millicent turned her head to study Ned, hoping to convince herself that she, in fact, was no fool.

He was above average handsome, especially compared to the other men of Culverton. Smart, too. Charming, but always with sincerity. He had depth, compassion, humor. . . . Millicent had to remind herself that she searched for reasons *not* to be crazy about him.

Ned touched his tie. Then he shot his cuffs. Passing his tongue unobtrusively over his teeth, he frowned at her. "What?"

She only shrugged. "Nothing. I'm just thinkin'."

Several ladies in the row ahead turned around to glare them into silence. Millicent smiled radiantly and scooted closer to Ned. His hand came down on her knee, and they all saw it.

Down at the other end of their pew, Mrs. Cotton leaned forward to put the hymnal back, her sharp eyes shooting a glance at them. What she saw must have pleased her, for she smiled like a puppet-maker when the dolls turn out just right.

As young Mr. Budgell addressed heaven from the pulpit, Millicent prayed for help. She might rescue a foundling child without suffering a single regret; taking on an opinionated thirty-year-old professional man couldn't be considered for a moment. She might be a fool, but she was not crazy!

She raised her eyes to him again. Let her find just one flaw, she prayed. Just a hair out of place, a spot of egg on his shirt, something! Let her see him as a slob, or a beast, or a lecher. Anything but the right man for her.

The sun shone down through the blue and red window above the pulpit. The beam came directly down to settle around her and Ned. She blinked in the wine-colored light and saw that he had become haloed by the clear blue glow. Millicent shut her eyes tight and swiftly reminded the Lord that when she'd asked for a sign, she'd had something a bit more negative in mind.

Ned's challenging blue eyes met hers when she opened them, studying her the same way she gazed at him. She looked away first, a flutter at her heart. Millicent told herself that she had to be careful. If she didn't act just as usual, he'd guess. After hearing all he had to say about marriage, she knew how he'd take the news that she'd fallen for him. In all likelihood, she'd never see him again, let alone be swept up in his arms.

With all her heart Millicent wished she could brave the eyes of her neighbors and walk out of the church. She needed fresh air to blow this fancy out of her head. She wasn't in love with Ned Castle. She refused to be in love with Ned Castle. To feel that way would be to court nothing but disaster. She had to be strong and hope she'd get over this giddy feeling as quickly as she would if she'd been taken with a bad cold.

After church Millicent and Ned went out in the crowd. He stopped to shake the minister's hand. "Fine sermon today. Really impressive."

"Why, thank you, Doctor." Mr. Budgell was still young enough to be gratified by a compliment from an unexpected source without wondering about its consequences. "I think I may say I'm not too unhappy with it."

"It was just right," Ned said, but the preacher had already turned from him to Millicent. "Is this the young man I've heard so much about?"

Millicent half-turned so Mr. Budgell could see the baby's face, pressed against her shoulder. He said, "A fine young feller," but his voice and his eyes showed his sorrow. "He'll grow up to be a boy anyone could be proud of."

"I hope so," she said. Instinctively she cuddled Petey more possessively. Mr. Budgell and his wife didn't have any babies yet, and despite Mrs. Cotton's pronouncement that Mary Lou was "handless," Millicent knew how much they wanted children. If she hadn't been so intent on keeping Petey for herself, undoubtedly the Budgells would have gotten him. Maybe that would have been best; she had no intention of finding out.

Then Ned said, "We don't want to hold anyone up. Good afternoon. My best to your wife."

"Want to bet half the congregation's going to follow us home?" she asked as soon as they were down the steps, out of earshot of anyone else.

"I never bet against a certainty." Without asking, he leaned down and hooked the carpetbag out of her hand. "Does he need changing?"

"Of course. But he can wait till we're home." He glanced casually over his shoulder. "Don't look now, but we seem to be leading a parade."

"They'll be hauling out their pocket watches next. I reckon half of 'em will time how long you stay."

"Am I going to stay?"

"You'd better. Don't want to disappoint anybody."

"Millicent," he said. "Slow down. Mrs. Drake's having trouble keeping up."

She realized she'd been storming along as if she'd left a cake in the oven. Forcing herself to moderate her steps, she managed a stroll. "How's that?"

"Better. I know . . . it isn't easy. I realize how much you probably hate this."

"Yep. But I hate the thought of starving to death even more. Nobody bought a hat yesterday."

"Didn't you say you had several orders . . . oh. You mean like me and my patients."

"That's right. Heard from a lot of women who 'changed their minds.' Mrs. Cotton says a milliner isn't supposed to have a good reputation but—"

"She said that? Of course you need a good reputation! And I'm not going to spoil yours."

"I thought that was the idea," Millicent said. "Not exactly that, but you know what I mean. Seems there's a first time for everythin'. I never heard of ruining a reputation to save it, but that's what we're doing, isn't it?"

"I'm not supposed to ruin yours in actuality," Ned said. "Just make people believe I'm on fire to do exactly that."

"If you can pull that off," she said, trying not to sound too bitter, "you'll have to give up doctorin' for the stage."

"Don't overestimate the difficulty." Ned held open her gate for her. From beneath the brim of her hat, she glanced up at him in startled astonishment. He smiled down at her in a way that made her heart speed up. She couldn't believe the warmth and longing in his eyes existed for the sake of their audience alone. Or maybe, she warned herself, she didn't choose to believe that.

He said, "I'm having a tough time keeping my hands to myself, Millicent. I think about last night. . . ."

"So do I," she admitted. "But Mrs. Cotton is right. We've got to be careful. Everybody's talkin' about us now for real. If we slip up, nobody's going to give us the benefit of the doubt."

"Would that be so bad?"

Once again she gaped at him. "You bet. It would

be . . . well, you know a lot of fancy words. Come up with one that means as bad as bad can be."

"Disastrous? Catastrophic?"

"Sounds good enough to be bad. We both depend on these folks coming to us with their money. It may not be much, but it keeps the wolf from the door. If they don't think we're decent and trustworthy, we'll be starving in the street come winter."

"So for them to think we're honest, we're going to have to lie, right?"

"Right." Millicent shrugged again and put her foot on the first step of her porch. Ned hooked two fingers around her elbow and stayed her. "What?" she asked.

"Do you have to go in so soon? I thought we might sit out for a while. Talk."

"Talk? What about?"

"Just things," he said. He slipped his hand into hers and tugged gently. "Come on."

Millicent turned back, summoned by the gentle persuasion of his voice. Then he added, "Besides, I don't think this crowd has had its money's worth yet."

Looking up and past him, she saw that quite a few members of the community seemed to find something to occupy them at this end of town. Several ladies, in their broad-brimmed hats and white gloves, were calling on Mrs. Cotton, despite the fact that she hadn't even left the church grounds yet. Though they rapped meekly enough on her door, those with the best view craned their necks for a glimpse of Millicent and Ned.

Raising her hand, Millicent twiddled her fingers at them, then turned abruptly to Ned to hiss, "I'm not going to be a raree show! They looked their fill at the church! I'm surprised you could tell the preacher he gave a good sermon. With all the gossiping going on, I couldn't hear a word he said."

"Neither could I. But it never hurts to praise a preacher's sermons."

"That's lying!"

"It's been a lying kind of a day," Ned admitted. "Why

don't we forget about it? Come sit with me in your backyard. They won't be able to see a thing except from the Cottons' yard."

"And what makes you think that window wouldn't be jam-packed in two shakes? Let's do it the way we talked about it, okay?"

"Very well."

His hand fell away from her elbow. Instead he laid it gently on Petey's back. "He behaved himself in church."

"As long as he's fed, he's happy. I wonder. . . ."

"What is it?"

"Nothing. Only, I was thinking about his mother today. Have you heard anything? Has the marshal . . . ?"

"I don't know. He's asking some questions around. The family at Handfast that had the babies have them all accounted for. The midwife there—do you know Miss Nancy Callahan?"

"Sure. She comes by for my raspberry tea."

He rolled his eyes at this mention of a folk remedy, but went on with his story. "She says that she hasn't been called to any pregnant women in the last two months. However, she did say that a girl visited her several months ago who was pregnant. She remembers because the girl was white."

"Did she get her name?"

Ned shook his head. "Miss Callahan says the girl told a story about just passing through and doesn't think the name she gave was her own."

"Why not?"

"Miss Callahan says she can always tell when women are lying. She says she doubted the girl was even married, though she wore a ring. It kept sliding off the girl's finger, and as she was only about seventeen, it didn't seem probable that she'd lost so much weight since marrying."

"Maybe I'll head out to Handfast and talk to Miss Nancy myself. She's probably about out of . . ." She let her voice trail off, fearful of letting someone else's secret out.

"Out of what?" he asked, his tone darkening. "What witch's brew are you giving her for her patients? Hemlock? Wolfsbane?"

"Nothing like that. It's not for her patients. The raspberry tea is, of course. Grandmother said it helped to ease labor."

"Balderdash!"

The baby jerked against Millicent's shoulder. "Look," she said, trying to remain reasonable. "Let's not talk about this now. We'll only get to fratching."

"Oh, that's right. We mustn't spoil the illusion of my infatuation with you. But I hope you realize, Millicent, that you are playing with people's lives. You can do a great deal of harm with your 'remedies.'"

He stepped away from her, letting his eyes play over her body. She saw anger and possibly contempt in his expression. It pricked her. Without pausing to wonder why he could rile her more easily than any other person she knew, she said, "You say that every time. You come storming in with your science and your fancy words and you don't do a bit more good than me and my grandma's receipts."

"That's a preposterous thing to say."

"Is it? We are all of us in God's hands, Dr. Castle. You, me, Petey, everybody. What I do and what you do are exactly the same . . . God's work. We're just the instruments."

"I had no notion you were so religious, Miss Mayhew."

"Just because I haven't had much luck in my life doesn't mean I don't believe. I've been witness to too many miracles *not* to believe. My grandma told me never to take the glory myself, to always be sure and give the praise to the one who ordains the cures." She saw his sneer and her hand fairly itched to wipe it off. If she hadn't been holding Petey, she would have done it.

Instead, she narrowed her eyes at him and asked, "If you don't believe, then you're just a two-faced lying devil."

"The word you are searching for is *hypocrite*."

"I wouldn't know. I'm just an ignorant female with a book of cures."

She didn't give him a chance to walk away from her. Turning about abruptly, she stepped up onto the porch while fumbling in her pocket for her key. She heard his footsteps on the gravel. For a moment she felt a sick dropping of her heart, but they came closer instead of fading away.

"Let me," he said, reaching around her to take the silver key. She tried to jerk it out of range, her anger making her petty. The key dropped.

Millicent gasped and started to bend for it. Petey startled, his arms jerking, so she halted and came upright.

"I'll get it," Ned said, leaning his stick against the porch rail. As Millicent moved out of his way, her skirt swung and brushed the key into the crack between two boards.

They stared at each other, drawn together by the willful behavior of an inanimate object.

"Clumsy," he admonished, but with a smile starting at the back of his eyes.

"If you hadn't . . . oh, never mind. Now what am I going to do?"

"Maybe there's a window open."

"Nope. Not since you fixed that one last night."

"The back door?" Her expression told him the answer. "Why do you lock up? Because of Colorado?"

"I just feel safer knowing nobody can get in."

"Nobody wants to get in, do they? It's not like you're keeping diamonds under the bed."

"Of course not. They're in the flour canister where they belong."

"And the crown jewels of Marie Antoinette are under the stove."

"Nope, they'd get too hot to wear. They're safe in my top dresser drawer. Who was Marie? She sure had a pretty name."

"It matched her face, or so I hear. She was a luckless queen of France." Ned ticked the ferrule of his stick against the gap. "It appears that the only thing to do is crawl under your porch and retrieve the key. Do you have a nickel? Or a penny would do."

"No. How could you get it back with a nickel?"

He grinned at her. "Simple . . . heads, you go. Tails, I do. In case you haven't noticed, this suit is nearly new."

"And my dress isn't. But I tell you what. Heads, you go. Tails, I don't. There are spiders under there, you know."

Millicent hoped that the spectators, still milling around trying to overhear what they'd been quarreling about, heard Ned's laughter. They certainly saw him hitch up his trouser legs as he knelt on the ground before going into the cobwebbed dark beneath her front porch.

As she looked over the railing at him, he said, "I hope you appreciate this, Miss Mayhew. I don't go crawling around under porches for every woman I know."

"Just the clumsy ones? Okay, I'll rap on the boards above where the key went through, so you know whereabouts to look."

"That's a good idea." He peered into the sun-striped darkness, coughing a little at the musty odor. "Not my idea of a suitable Sunday activity, but here goes."

After a moment or two, she called to him. "Is it awful?"

He coughed. "Dirty, that's all. And wet. And . . . ugh."

"What? Are you okay?"

"Nothing. Just put my face through a spiderweb."

Millicent screwed up her own face just thinking about it. "Was the spider home?"

"Thanks, Millicent. Now I can feel him walking around on my hair. Am I near where the key went through?" She tapped with her heel on the boards. Muffled, his voice rose. "I can't see a thing. I'll feel around."

"I sure admire you for doing this, Ned. Maybe I can do you a favor one of these days."

"I'll remember that. Are you sure this is the right place?"

"I think so."

Putting her hand under Petey's bottom to move him farther up her shoulder, she realized he'd soaked through his clothes. "Have you found it yet? Petey needs changing."

"So do I," he said. "My knees are waterlogged. And no, I . . . wait. Got it!"

"Good."

When he stood up, all his predictions came true. He had a dusty web clinging to his now dark brown hair, his coat and collar were smeared over most of their surface, and his trousers had definitely lost their sharp crease, ground away by mud and dirt. However, in his now unspeakably dirty hand glinted a small silver key.

"Maybe I'll reconsider locking my door," Millicent said handsomely.

"You do that. I'm going home to take a bath."

Ever the gentleman, he still came up the stairs to unlock the door for her. Feeling guilty about their argument, Millicent paused as she went in.

"I want you to know something," she started to say. But how could she tell him, baldly, face-to-face, that she'd try not to burden him with her love? She couldn't compare him to a cold she wanted to cure, though he'd understand that notion at once. When he scowled at her with ice chips instead of eyes, she found it easy to pretend her feelings were imaginary.

However, when he stood before her, filthy through doing her a service, she felt such a spring of love bubbling up in her heart that she wanted to wear a brick in her hat so her head wouldn't fly away.

"What?" he asked. He held his shoulders as if he were striving to avoid touching his clothes, even from the inside.

"Just . . ." Swiftly she thought of something else she could say. "Just that what I mean to take to Miss Callahan is some cold tea and sage water. Her hair's been turning gray, and she wanted something to fight it. That's all."

Ned put out his hand as though he'd touch her cheek. Then, looking at the leaf-mold that clung to his skin, he dropped his hand without making contact. "I appreciate your telling me that, Millicent. Don't worry. I won't let on to a soul that Miss Callahan's hair color isn't natural."

"I know you won't."

"Because you trust me?"

"I know you're a gentleman," she said.

"You still believe that? Even after last night?"

"All the more because of last night. If you weren't a gentleman, everybody in town would have known about it when you left the house late in the morning."

He laughed a little, wonderingly. "What did I ever do to

deserve . . . I'd better hurry home. I think this mud is starting to dry. Listen, Millicent, about our plan . . ."

Once again she looked past him at their audience, now growing somewhat desperate for excuses to still be lingering in the street. Several ladies were pretending to admire the plants just rising through the soil down by her front fence. Considering that most of them were no taller than a pinkie, the ladies were having a hard time working up enthusiasm. The men, luckier than the women, had started a spitting contest.

They were all of them, however, talking and watching.

Millicent said, "I think our plan is going fine. If you want more sparks, though, show up here tonight after suppertime."

"Millicent . . ."

"To make it good, I oughta throw my arms around your neck or something, but I can't with the baby."

"And I'm not exactly fragranced like the rose," Ned added. "All right. I'll see you after supper."

"Good. Mrs. Cotton will be here, too."

She thought he looked a little bit downcast by that news, but no doubt her fancy had played another pixie trick on her.

14

"*THAT DIDN'T GO* very good, did it?" Mrs. Cotton came in the back door as soon as she finished supper. "Just what was the problem?"

Millicent looked up from the cup of tea she nursed at the table. The fragrant steam did more to restore her spirits than the taste. "About what you'd expect. He's as stubborn as Mrs. Clancy's mule when it comes to doctoring."

"What started you off on that trail? Don't you know better . . . ? I mean, he's just a man, and they've got to be handled just so."

"He makes me mad," Millicent explained. "He's so danged ornery. It's got to be his way, just his way, all the time."

Mrs. Cotton's bright eyes fixed on Millicent. Under that gaze, she felt like a cow caught in the reflector lamp of an oncoming train. There didn't seem to be any place to run to.

The older woman said, "First thing to learn when you're dealing with menfolks is not to let 'em 'make' you feel anything. What you feel is your business. Now, some women manage their men by screaming and shouting and carrying on. Others go about it sneaky, talking about their 'nerves' and their 'spasms' till the poor fellers don't know where they're at. I reckon you're like me and you wouldn't stoop to such monkey tricks."

"I don't want to manage Dr. Castle. It's not like I'm fixing to marry him."

"No, but he's good practice for the feller you'll marry one of these long-come-shorts, ain't he?"

"Practice?"

"Sure. I figure if you can handle a hard-bitten proposition like Neddy, you can handle just about any other son of a gun out there."

Millicent shook her head. "I'll never marry."

Mrs. Cotton snorted. "And I'm the Queen of Russia. If you don't want to get married, child, you better stop sparking on the front porch with Neddy."

"You saw that last night?"

"Saw, and heard. Now, don't go blushin'. It's perfectly natural. You're healthy and he's awful nice-looking. Stands to reason the pair of you might spark a bit. I kinda figured all the arguing you two do might just be covering up what you really want to be doing with each other. It was only a matter of time before you started in on the kissin' and huggin'."

"Then you're smarter than we are. The first time I was more surprised than a hound dog bitten by a fish."

"The first time? That boy moves pretty quick once you get his attention, don't he? But I gotta warn you, Millicent, it's a lot easier to start canoodling than it is to quit."

Millicent dismissed that suggestion with "I don't think I'll have too much trouble. After all, I was engaged once. We spent some time kissing, and I didn't mind it a bit when I had to go without. Or Dan, for that matter."

As she said it, she realized she spoke the truth. Though the manner of their parting had been frightening, Millicent knew now that if Emily hadn't been murdered, she and Dan still would not have married. If they'd really wanted to do it, they'd have done it right off, bad times, little money, and distance notwithstanding. If it hadn't been for her fear, she probably would have forgotten all about Dan by now.

"Maybe, maybe. But Neddy's no dirty miner. He's a well set-up, sweet-smelling, sweet-talking man who knows what's what! After all, stands to reason a doctor would know where all the important bits are. Oh, my. Oh, yes." Mrs. Cotton fanned herself with her hand. "Who's to say but his lovemakin' might not be the kind you can't get enough of? Then what're you goin' to do when it's gone?"

Millicent had often been shocked by Mrs. Cotton's plain speaking, but this time she'd gone too far. "I'm not planning to go to bed with the man!"

"Maybe you oughta think about that. After all, he'd make a good first lover."

"Mrs. Cotton!"

"Oh, you young things are so serious! If I was a pretty young thing like you, dang me for a turtle if I wouldn't flirt with every man I saw, and maybe more than flirt. After all, once you're married, your fun's over."

"Not by what I saw comin' home from the Faradays' house the other night."

Now Mrs. Cotton's cheeks turned a pretty rose. "Oh, that. That's just on account of . . . Well, to tell the truth, Vernon can still get me a-goin' with just a look. Any more of that tea ready?"

"Help yourself." Millicent brooded a moment and then asked, "If you think marriage is the end of a girl's fun, why are you so bound and determined to see everybody hitched up?"

"Because it's good for people, 'specially for men. It steadies 'em, gives 'em an interest in life besides smoking, spitting, and watching the crops sprout. Just where do you think this country would be if folks stopped getting married?"

She sat down across from Millicent, the warm cup cradled in her hands. "It's a duty. It's all the better if you're in love, of course. Nothing like love to smooth out the rough spots. Naturally you should have some respect for the man, or you'll be unhappy. But everyone who can should get married. It's civilizing."

"For the men, you mean."

"Them, too. But for women as well. I mean, no offense, child, but look at you. You're as pretty as a picture. But you dress worse than any woman I ever saw. Even your hats are plain, and that's bad business if nothing else."

Millicent plucked at her collar. "I . . ."

"I know, I know. You had the heart and soul kicked out of you, and black just suited your mood. But, honey, I'm purely sick to death of it. Ain't you?"

Wearily Millicent nodded. "I would have changed long ago only . . ."

"You don't have any money?"

"That, too. Mostly, though, I was thinkin' how folks would talk if I made a sudden change in what I wear."

"But that's just it!" Mrs. Cotton cried. "We want 'em to talk about you, but in the way we want 'em to. So changing your clothes will just be part of it. They'll think you're changing your feathers 'cause it's spring and 'cause of Neddy. I wish I'd thought of this sooner. You could have worn fine feathers to church today and really got 'em going." She drained off her tea in a few swallows. "Let's go see what else you got up in the attic."

She stood up. Then, with a sudden gesture, she silenced Millicent's halfhearted protests. "Put out that lamp, child."

Something in her tone insisted that Millicent obey and at once. She reached for the lamp's key and turned down the wick, drowning the light. "What is it?" she asked, tension making her whisper.

"I don't know. I'm thinking your peeper's back."

"What? Where?" Millicent surged out of her chair, turning toward the windows.

"I swear I saw something moving out there. Too big to be a cat."

Together the women approached the window. Millicent's eyes hadn't yet adjusted to the darkness. The window could be seen as no more than a slightly paler gleam against the wall of the kitchen. The memory of all the times she'd lain awake, starting at the creak of a settling board, listening with all her might to the night until she thought her ears must be growing as big as a donkey's, came back to her. She caught Mrs. Cotton by the slack of her gingham sleeve.

"Come on," she whispered. "Let's get upstairs and lock ourselves in. Ned will be along soon. He'll scare the louse off."

"I don't know 'bout you," Mrs. Cotton answered. "But

I'm right curious." She pried Millicent's frozen fingers away from her arm. She pushed open the back door with enough force to send it rebounding off the wall, right back in her face.

"Damnation!" she shouted and gave the door another wallop.

Millicent heard again the sound of running feet. Mrs. Cotton seemed sure to follow them, so Millicent grabbed her again. "He's getting away!" the older woman cried.

"Let him! Let him. I'm not going to go chasing him in the dark, and neither are you."

"I just wanted to see who it was. A man's got no right to be peering in folks' windows. Gives a town a bad name, a thing like that."

Ned showed up at the front door at about the same time Judge Cotton arrived in the back. They met in the kitchen, to find the women still questioning each other's judgment by the glow of the renewed lamp. Judge Cotton called a halt, raising his arms in their tight sleeves to get their attention.

"I'm right obliged, Miss Mayhew. I don't think there's any call for you to go catching the feller yourself, Mother. After all, that's the marshal's job. I'm going to suggest he stick a deputy here after dark, Miss Mayhew, so you don't need to be scared."

"I'm not scared for myself," Millicent explained. "And I don't need a deputy stomping on my flower beds. But I'd be grateful for the loan of your granddaddy's squirrel gun."

"No!" Ned said hastily. They all looked at him. He spread his hands as he lifted his shoulders in a shrug. "If you put a bullet in him, I'm going to have to take it out. Probing for bullets is one job I don't care for."

"Then what do you think I ought to do?" Millicent asked. "I can't have some stranger peeping in my windows every night."

"Of course not. Buy blinds."

"Blinds? You mean window shades?"

"She'd stifle," Judge Cotton protested. "You gotta keep the windows open if you want to let your pores breathe proper."

Mrs. Cotton muttered, "Three more years," and Millicent threw her a smile.

Ned felt nervous about that smile. He already wondered if he had turned into just another puppet with Mrs. Cotton pulling the strings. When the two women shared that smile, a smile that hinted at mutual secrets, he also wondered about Millicent. Perhaps her distaste for marriage had been devised like the bait for a trap, lulling him into a false sense of security. Perhaps he'd been her target all along, with Mrs. Cotton's connivance. It would explain why Millicent didn't get upset when he kissed her.

Any other woman would have. His cheeks should be stinging with slaps. But Millicent gave kisses as sweet and wild as uncultivated honey. Thinking about those moments on the front porch steps yesterday, Ned could hardly sit still. He wanted her with an ache as much mental as physical.

Even sitting together like this, with two people watching every move they made, all he could think about was the golden gleams of lamplight on her hair and how big and dark her eyes looked. His hands curled on his knees as he remembered sliding his palm over the rising . . .

"I'm sorry?" He glanced around the table. Someone had spoken his name.

"I said, do you want to teach Millicent how to play poker so we can pass the time with a game?" Judge Cotton let the cards ruffle through his hands, his wrists as supple as a professional cardsharp.

"Pass the time?"

Mrs. Cotton looked at him with mingled exasperation and pity in her gaze. "I reckon an hour's long enough to stay the first evening. We want 'em talking about you two, and not about a shotgun wedding."

Millicent and Ned exchanged a glance. In her eyes he read a kind of reluctant laughter overlying the fear that the peeper had renewed. He wanted to reach out and take her hand, but he dared not allow his fingers even that much of her skin.

She pulled her chair closer to the table. "What are we going to use for chips?"

"Crackers?" the judge proposed, making the cards "walk" over the backs of his fingers.

"Why do I feel sure I'm about to lose big?" Ned asked Mrs. Cotton, though his gaze followed Millicent, standing on tiptoe to get the crackers from the cupboard.

"The secret to gambling is never risk anything you don't care to lose." She smiled as the judge performed an elegant cascade. "That's enough fancy tricks now. Let me cut 'em."

"I'll be lucky if I have a cracker to my name when this is over," Millicent grumbled.

"Shall I teach you how to play?" Ned asked.

Millicent seemed to hesitate and catch Mrs. Cotton's eye. The older woman nodded blatantly. Millicent said, "Thank you, Ned. I'd like to learn."

The chairs around the table were mismatched, obvious castoffs of more fortunate townspeople. Ned stood up and walked around the table to take the chair closest to Millicent. It was far too short for the table's height, and she laughed to see his stalwart chin only inches off the tabletop.

He said, "I see you've accepted someone's chair-ity."

Millicent answered, "Ladies started bringing their own and didn't take them home."

The game got off to a slow start. The judge fidgeted each time Ned stopped play to explain a finer point to Millicent. Mrs. Cotton didn't seem to mind, even urging Ned to explain more fully. "Tell her about 'dead men's hand.'"

"Don't worry about that," Ned said quickly, seeing a flicker of apprehension in her topaz eyes. "It's just a figure of speech about aces and eights."

"Oh, I see. But why—?"

"Are we going to play or talk?" Judge Cotton asked, laying down cards with a flair.

Ned considered himself no stupider than the average male. All the same, it took him two hands before he understood that Millicent Mayhew had beginner's luck second to none. By the fourth hand he knew that someone had educated her before him, at least in the finer points of poker playing.

He tossed down his cards on the table, faceup. "All right. End of the lesson. Millicent, you're a fraud."

Her eyes sparkled in the lamplight as she threw him a laughing glance. "I know it. I learned to play in Colorado. But there's lots I don't know. Like why is it called dead man's hand?"

"Just a silly superstition. Aces and eights were the cards Wild Bill Hickok held the last game he played before he was murdered."

"Murdered? How awful." She glanced over her shoulder at the black glass of the window.

The judge as well as Ned picked up on the significance of that look. "You got no call to worry," Judge Cotton said. "I been on the bench a long time. I never seen one Peeping Tom that hurt anybody. Pitiful creeturs, most of 'em. Every now and then you'll get one that's a professional type even—you know. A dentist or a doctor or somebody. Them the ones that are really round the bend."

Ned flushed and crossed his legs under the table. "Speaking for the medical profession . . ."

"Ah, shucks . . . never knew but one such myself. I reckon doctors see enough of the outside of folks without wanting to watch 'em through windows. Say, Mother, do you remember ol' Walt Zamuche?"

"And the opera singer? She had him going strong. They found him outside her apartment, didn't they?"

As the judge and his wife discussed old scandals, Ned patted Millicent's knee under the table. "Don't worry," he said. "I'm sure there's an explanation."

He didn't want to tell her that the first peeper had been himself. There didn't seem to be any way to bring it up casually, and his image in the eyes of Culverton had fallen low enough without adding a charge of voyeurism. He didn't know who or what they'd seen in the backyard tonight. Maybe no more than a shadow and their already overworked imaginations supplied the rest. Prepared to believe someone did watch Millicent from the dark corners of her yard, they obligingly invented a peeper.

Of course if he suggested it, they'd deny such a thing

were possible. Funny how so many people preferred a bizarre explanation of things to a simple one.

From upstairs came a wailing cry that made everyone around the table jump. Millicent pushed her chair back. "Right on time."

The judge gathered up the cards. "Time we were going, Mother. Got to get an early start tomorrow. Getting too hot for the fish to bite much after noon." He squinted up at Ned. "Say, you wouldn't care to come along, would you? I got a spare rod."

"No, thanks. Miss Mayhew and I have an appointment to drive out to Handfast tomorrow."

"Going to see Miss Callahan 'bout that white girl she saw?"

"That's right." He looked at Millicent, getting a bottle of milk out of the window box.

As she filled up Petey's flask, she echoed what he had said. "That's right. I want to ask her some questions myself."

Mrs. Cotton offered, "I'll watch the little one if you like. Don't want to wear yourself out. She looks a mite peaky, don't you think, Neddy?"

"I wouldn't say that," he said and was gratified to see Millicent drop her eyes under his approval.

"I thought I'd take Petey along. Miss Callahan never could hold out against a little one. And I'm hopin' she might trace a likeness."

"Never seem to me that children look much like their folks till they grow up."

"Now, Mother, you remember how Nancy Vail's baby was the spittin' image of Dick Bryan . . . had the 'zact same nose from the day he was born."

"That's scandal, Vernon, and I won't be a party to it. 'Sides, you know darn well Dick Bryan and Joe Vail were second cousins. Just 'cause Nancy and Dick ran 'way together don't mean that wasn't Joe's baby."

"What a woman!" Judge Cotton said, rolling his eyes at the ceiling. "Believes the good in everybody."

"Lucky for you I do." Mrs. Cotton threw her husband a

saucy glance, then turned her attention again to Millicent. "Even if you take Petey 'long, I'll stop by first thing tomorrow to help you. After all, it's easier to get dressed if somebody's around to mind the child."

Something in Mrs. Cotton's emphasis on dress made Millicent's confusion deepen. Ned wondered what new plot they were hatching. Petey's crying increased and Millicent flew.

After a few minutes of fidgeting, Mrs. Cotton went upstairs to help. The judge gathered together his cards and once again began to shuffle them in elaborate ways. He didn't look at his hands; they seemed to operate without his conscious control.

Glancing up at Ned, he said conversationally, "You're doomed, you know."

"Doomed, sir?" Ned asked, absently feeling his coat pockets for a cigar that he'd left at home. "That's a strange choice of words."

"Is it? I been living with that woman for my entire adult life. I know when she's aiming to fix somebody up."

"From what I hear, you're no sluggard when it comes to finding mates for your friends. Jake and Antonia have told me how you brought them together by, to put it kindly, manipulating the law of the land."

The judge chuckled soundlessly. "Yep. I did that, all right. Good thing I did, too. Have you ever seen two folks happier or more crazy in love?"

"Never." Ned found himself listening for sounds from the floor above. "But I don't approve of your methods. Culverton seems to have gotten so used to taking shortcuts when it comes to marriage that you can't leave well enough alone. Not everyone wants to marry within hours of meeting, you know."

"What's the use in draggin' it out? If a man and a woman are right for each other, they should marry up quick. Love's like apple brown Betty. A whole lot tastier when it's hot."

"And if it cools after marriage? What then?"

"Son, I been blowing on the embers for forty some years. It stays hot if you keep the fire a-going. But the way you go at it, you ain't even put the apples in the pan yet! Hell, they ain't even peeled. What in thunder are you waiting for?"

Ned shrugged. "Maybe I'm just stubborn. Ever since I was a boy, the one sure way to make me balk was to tell me I *had* to do something. I know this about myself, but I don't seem to change. Perhaps I don't really want to."

"Then ain't it time you grew up? Now, I'm an old man, but I can see that something's going on between you and that gal upstairs. She ain't got no daddy, but I still got a shotgun. Don't make me use it."

At Ned's frown the judge laughed out loud, his stomach shaking under his shiny waistcoat. With chuckles still rolling up and down his body, he shaped the cards into a neat pile. "Cut, son."

Ned reached out. He showed his card. "Queen of hearts," he said. "And I'll bet they kicked you off a lot of riverboats in your youth."

"A goodly few."

Quickly the judge dealt five cards faceup, two aces, and three eights. One ace gleamed black, the spade. He took the face card from Ned's hand and laid it down on top of the others. "There's your choice, son. You don't have to die to be dead, you know. Walking around without anybody to love or to love you—that's the worst death I ever heard tell of."

"That's what I like about you, sir. You're subtle."

"Ain't nothing subtle about it. It's a choice, plain and simple. Now, that little girl upstairs mayn't be everything you ever wanted. But she's enough to keep you from turning into ol' Doc Partridge."

"Doc Partridge? I would never—"

"Look, Ned. I've known him for twenty years. When he came here, he was just like you. Hard-hearted as Pharaoh, with a smart mouth and too much book learning. You might say he was the only failure Mrs. Cotton and I ever had."

He looked down at his mottled, thickly veined hands and shook his head. Ned had never seen him more serious. "We tried—Lord knows we did. But none of the girls were good enough for him. This one was too talky, that one breathed with her mouth open, 'nother one's mother was too scary for him. And he got lonelier and meaner and harder, till nothing could make him feel anything but the bottle. One day he just crawled inside and never came out no more."

Then the judge looked up and those straight eyes went through Ned like a diamond-tipped drill. "Robbie Partridge was a good man, but he went sour because he never gave his heart a chance to grow. He's a warning to you, Ned. Remember him. Keep him in mind, 'cause I can see the same thing happening to you."

"To me? No, not likely." Ned had never been so uncomfortable in his life. He wanted to protest, to proclaim that he'd never turn into a sodden drunk or a celibate grump encased in a hard shell of sarcasm. Instead, he said, "I just want to be sure before I commit myself. Is that wrong?"

"No. But you shouldn't question so much that you talk yourself out of love.".

"If it's really love, how can you convince yourself that it isn't?" Ned addressed not Judge Cotton, but his own heart.

But the judge answered. "Seems to me somebody like you can talk yourself out of anything. Don't do it. Try talking yourself into something for a change."

15

WHEN NED RETURNED to Mrs. Fleck's boarding-house, the moon had long since dropped toward the horizon. If the sky was not yet gifted with the dawn, it at any rate no longer carried the full weight of the night.

Ned stood outside the front door, and a shiver raced over his body. At three o'clock in the morning, even spring seemed cold and unhealthy. A thin mist spun itself along the street, its touch as damp and disinterested as that of a long-dead hand.

"Who's there?" called a quavering voice.

"It's me. Dr. Castle."

"Doctor . . . !" Mrs. Fleck opened the door, poking out a candlestick. Its flickering light made the shadows fall upward, deepening the hollows of her face. She wore a brown flannel wrapper, the reversed collar held up to her chin, her pointed elbows clamped on a gray knit shawl. Her hair hung in two thin plaits, a girlish style that only served to emphasize the strong lines of her face.

"Well, for mercy's sake! Come in. Are your boots dry? Wipe 'em on the mat; that's what it's there for."

Obediently Ned did as she told him, being scolded all the while. "It isn't very considerate, I must say, coming in at this hour, rousting me from my bed. I work hard, I'll have you know, and if I can't expect consideration from my boarders, then there'll be some changes made, and it won't be me who makes them!"

"I'm very sorry, Mrs. Fleck," seemed to be the only acceptable thing to say.

It appeased her. She sniffed and said, "I suppose if I'm going to have a doctor as a boarder, I have to expect this kind of thing. After all, doctors can't always keep office hours. Was it a bad case?"

Ned thought about inventing a desperate illness and a patient at death's door, knowing that to admit the mundane truth would probably result in another peal being rung over him. However, the landlady would know by morning that there'd been no such patient, thanks to the efficiency of the Culverton grapevine. Ned gathered his courage. "I was out walking. I had some thinking to do."

"Walking? Until this hour of the morning? Well, I never! You'd think a man of your position would have more sense, not to mention consideration, than to come waking me up just because you forgot the time. I thought you were more of a gentleman than that! Well, I won't say any more about it, but I'm disappointed in you, Dr. Castle."

She went on not saying any more at some length. Ned nodded wearily. His legs ached and he'd like to get his boots off. He hadn't taken such a long tramp since his student days in Austria. Then he'd gone walking in the hills to clear his mind before exams or operations. Now, troubled by his tumultuous feelings, he reverted to the habit, turning left instead of right when he left Millicent's door. He had crossed the railroad tracks and headed out down the main road out of town.

How far had he walked in the time between? Only his tired legs gave him a clue. When he'd passed Millicent's house again, he'd seen that her bedroom light burned behind the curtains and had known that she was awake, too, as, no doubt, was Petey. Looking up at their window gave him a strange feeling, half-tender, half-panicked.

Mrs. Fleck broke in on his thoughts by saying, "You look tired, Dr. Castle." She hitched up her falling shawl and peered at him in the dim light. "If you were wanting something to eat, I could fry you a couple of eggs."

"No, thank you, Mrs. Fleck. I'm not hungry, just ready to go to sleep."

"Hmph. Suit yourself."

He smiled at her. He'd always had good effect from his smiles, though he warned himself against the moral failing of manipulating people with the charm he'd done nothing to earn. "I'm sorry to have bothered you. I hope you won't have any trouble going back to sleep."

Her dry lips curved. "Oh, well. I'm used to it. Up and down all night. You wouldn't believe the nights I haven't closed my eyes for so much as a wink."

"Insomnia, eh? Your mind races endlessly?"

"Something fierce. The only thing that'll lull me to sleep is one of Miss Mayhew's hop pillows. But I daren't use it for too long, you know."

Though Ned tapped his foot impatiently at this mention of Millicent's herb lore, he didn't dare risk Mrs. Fleck's further displeasure by making a rude comment. "Why don't you dare?"

"The first night or so I'm not troubled. I sleep like the dead. But after a few nights, I start having the most terribly lifelike dreams. Horrible, some of them. But even the nice ones are so real, I might as well be awake."

Ned shook his head slightly. "Why do you people go to her with these problems? I could have—"

"Well, she knows things, doesn't she?" She stepped closer to him. "I'm not saying you don't. There's just some things I feel more at ease talking to a woman about than a man. And it's not like Miss Mayhew charges an arm and a leg, either. . . ."

Mrs. Fleck grimaced at her lack of tact. "Not that you're expensive; I don't mind that. But Millicent doesn't charge anything for her help. When you're a widow who has to watch every cent, that's important."

"She doesn't charge? But I thought—"

"No, she's never taken money for her remedies. Sometimes I'd give her something . . . a pie maybe, or once I gave her an old pair of my shoes, but not money. She won't take it. Says her grandmother didn't leave her those receipts to make money off of them. Personally, I think she's foolish. When you have something other folks need, why not make a living at it? You do. I do, too. That's how I get my money, isn't it?"

"Yes," he said, too distracted to give a more conciliatory answer.

Mrs. Fleck sniffed again and shuffled off in her bedroom slippers. At her door she turned back and said, "What time do you want to be woken up? Or do you mean to sleep the whole day through?"

"No. I'd appreciate it if you would call me at eight, please, Mrs. Fleck."

"All right. I'll go tell Egbert to do it."

"I don't want you to wake him. I'll get up without him calling me."

"Don't be worried about Egbert. He has to get up in another hour anyway to start breakfast."

"All the more reason not to wake him now." When she opened her mouth to insist again he wouldn't be bothering her son, Ned let his eyes turn cold. "No, thank you," he said again firmly. "Egbert is a growing boy and needs long, uninterrupted sleep, good food, and plenty of exercise."

"You saying I don't raise my boy right?" Mrs. Fleck challenged.

"Certainly not. Just that I will not wake him up merely to tell him what time *I* wish to be awakened."

Half an hour later he still sat on the edge of his bed, gazing down at his feet. He didn't see the thin spot in the sock at the end of his big toe. Rather, he looked with his mind's eye at a threadbare carpet, a dress darned inconspicuously but visible to a trained observer, and a pinched, prematurely wary face. He would be stunned to learn that Millicent had more than two cents to rub together, recent charity—including cast-off chairs—or not.

Yet she gave away her medicaments, some of which had expensive ingredients like ambergris or paraffin, things which had to be bought. He doubted very much whether Mr. Wilmot took hop pillows or old shoes in exchange for the goods he had to pay shipping and freight on. Yet she gave away her remedies to anyone who needed them. Chaos!

He lay back, still in his shirt and trousers. If only he had a hop pillow! Something to quiet his mind, which tormented itself with questions, and to calm his spirit. He'd never met a woman who confused him more.

When he drove up to her house the next day in his gig, he realized again, and more forcefully, that what he felt could also be called desire.

Two women stood on the porch. One was certainly Mrs. Cotton, a white apron on over her black and white gingham dress. Then the other woman turned at the sound of his gig and waved to him. The quality of her wave, gay, carefree, and uninhibited, made him frown in confusion. That couldn't be Antonia, not with that hand-span slim waist, but who else would greet him like that?

Then the woman started down the steps toward him. His first clue to her identity was the rich dark hair coaxed into ringlets under the brim of an absurdly inadequate hat. He couldn't imagine how that tiny chip of straw stayed on those glossy curls, especially with the load of fruit and feathers she'd forced it to carry.

"Millicent?" he asked in wonder.

Slowly he wound the reins around the whip stand and climbed down. She stood on the other side of the gate, waiting for him to open it. At his marveling glance, she laughed. "Yes, it's really me. It's fair floored me, too."

"But how . . . and why?"

The heavy, concealing black dress had disappeared. Instead, she wore a gown of ecru muslin, tight around the waist, flowing in the skirt. The elbow sleeves showed off straight, smooth arms while the modestly scooped neckline revealed a soft white neck.

These things, the soft skin, the small waist, the smooth elbows, reminded Ned that Millicent's years were considerably less than her experience. At his question she laughed, her eyes sparkling but without a trace of flirtation or even embarrassment. The sound of genuine laughter issuing from her dusky red lips made Ned's head swim.

"The how's easy. Mrs. Cotton's sewing machine and an old dress. The why's a little more tangled. She thinks that folks might believe what we want 'em to if I look like this."

"Oh, of course."

Ned glanced over his shoulder at Mrs. Cotton. She waved at him, too, an encouraging wave that turned quickly into a dismissal.

He said, "I take it that Petey isn't coming with us today."

"No, Mrs. Cotton wouldn't let me bring him. It's a pretty day today, though, don't you think? She's promised to take him out in the yard and let him soak up some of this sunshine."

"Sounds good. And the day is pretty." Ned was surprised to see her cheeks flush. Had she heard something besides polite agreement in his voice? He warned himself to be more careful. He'd agreed to play a game with her, nothing more.

He helped her into the gig, trying to ignore the silkiness of her inner arm against his fingertips. The look he threw Mrs. Cotton had no gratitude in it.

As soon as he settled himself and took up the reins, Millicent said, "Do you mind driving to the store first? I want to show Mrs. Wilmot this hat."

"Did you make it?"

"Last night," Millicent said, waving to Mr. and Mrs. Budgell. Ned noticed how quickly they turned and stared after them, while an amazing number of people suddenly had business on their front steps or met an immediate need for fresh air that could only be met by throwing open a window to lean out. He only hoped no one would fall.

While Millicent ran into the store, Ned walked the horse down to the corner and back. Abendego didn't need the exercise; his legs would hardly stiffen in five minutes, but Ned didn't care to wait standing still. Already a crowd of small boys had gathered, whispering among themselves while their female counterparts, somewhat less grubby, occupied themselves with giggling.

Tooling back, Ned spotted a red-haired boy moving with no particular hurry along the boardwalk. Ned tightened his hands on the reins. As the bay gelding slowed, Ned called, "Ed? Ed Fleck?"

"Hey, Doc!" The boy came over, his long legs eating up the walkway section by section. "Heard you got in some hot water last night with Ma."

"I hope we didn't wake you." It would be too ironic if their "discussion" about whether to wake Ed had in fact awakened him.

"No. I'm a pretty heavy sleeper. Some of the other boarders told me about it." He showed his wide, slightly yellow teeth in a grin just this side of a laugh. "My ma sure can pitch into a feller," he said admiringly. "Gets so you don't know as you got a whole piece of skin left by the time she's done."

Ned cleared his throat. "Quite." Then he said, "Are you going somewhere? Would you like a lift?"

"Gee, thanks, but no, thanks. I don't have to get to any place." He took a step closer to the gig, a hint of worry clouding his freckled brow. "Say, Doc, you saw Ma last night. You think she was feelin' okay? You know, just as usual?"

"Seemed to be. Why?"

Ed shook his head. "She was actin' awful funny this morning. Wouldn't let me cook the breakfast, told me not to bother carrying the hot water up, and then . . ." He glanced both ways over his shoulder to be certain no one could overhear them.

"Yes?"

The boy stuck his hand in the slanting hip pocket of his ankle-showing jeans. He gave Ned just a glimpse of a shiny silver coin, hidden in his palm. "She gave me a whole nickel out of her stocking's foot and told me to go get myself some candy. Then she said I should make myself scarce for the rest of the day. I been trying to think what I done different, but I'm blessed if I can think of a thing."

Ned hid a smile, not wanting to belittle the boy's concern. "I don't think you need to be afraid, Ed. It doesn't sound as though your mother has lost her mind. Maybe she just decided that even a son needs a day off sometimes. Hop in the gig; I'm going back to the store now anyway."

"Gee, thanks." He sat in the front seat, proud as a triumphant Caesar in a golden chariot. Unlike Ned and Millicent, he seemed to thrive on the glances and stares he collected. "Look at Suzie Riley staring at me! Heck, last week she wouldn't give me the time of day and now . . . How do, Suzie?" he hollered, squinting in her direction.

Ned noticed the way the boy's eyes screwed up whenever he looked to where the sun shone. "Is the light bothering you?" he asked, instantly concerned.

"I got kind of a headache, that's all." Ed swiped his hand over his brow as though he were wiping off sweat.

"Maybe you should go home and take a rest."

"Heck, no! Can't waste my time doing that! I got a nickel to spend. Hey, maybe Suzie Riley'd like some of them bull's-eyes. That's her favorite candy."

"Now, how do you know that?" Ned asked, figuring that a headache didn't mean much if the boy could think about girls while he suffered from one.

"It's what she got kicked out of school one day for sucking during the Battle of Yorktown."

"Funny, she doesn't look that old."

He got a big-toothed grin for this pleasantry. "Thanks for the ride, Doc," Ed said as Ned pulled up on front of Wilmot's Store. "I never rode in a gig before," he confessed. "That's a fast horse, huh?"

"Fast enough. But not too fast. It doesn't do to turn over in a ditch on the way to a case."

"I never thought of that," Ed said, getting down. "I guess a doctor's got a lot of trouble most folks never think of."

Millicent stood waiting at the top of the steps, young Darryl Wilmot standing beside her. She broke off her conversation with him to greet Ned. "I thought you'd gone off and left me."

"Not yet."

Her lightweight skirts swung and belled as she came down the steps, while the sunlight gave her black curls reddish touches. Though Ned couldn't see Ed's face, he saw the rigidity that came into his boyish shoulders as he gazed up at her. He had apparently forgotten all about Suzie Riley.

Ned sighed. A case of puppy love would complicate an already involved situation. Of course, Ed was exactly the age to fall into a crush where only wiser heads would avoid the trap. Then he caught a glimpse of Millicent's slim ankle as she raised her skirt slightly to step into the gig. He found himself wondering if age and wisdom offered any protection after all.

Millicent gave the boy a friendly but distant smile. Instantly he snapped to, offering his hand for Millicent's support, pushing her skirt away from the dirty wheel with the other. "Thank you . . . er . . ."

"Egbert, ma'am." Ned would have sworn that if the boy had a hat, he would have swept it off.

"Thank you, Egbert. You're Mrs. Fleck's son, aren't you? How is your mother?"

Once again the boy felt for the nickel in his pocket. But he didn't bring it out. "She's fine," he said, gazing up at Millicent with awe.

"I'll come by tonight for that verjuice, Miss Mayhew," Darryl Wilmot said as he stepped down to the boardwalk. Ned thought he saw in his eyes a determination not to be outdone by Ed Fleck. He sighed silently. What next? A duel over her affections in the middle of the street? Why was it always the young and inexperienced who fell for impossible women?

"We'd better be going," Ned said. "See you later, Ed."

He didn't have to glance over his shoulder to know that the landlady's son still stood in the street, gazing after his newly lost heart. Darryl Wilmot, on the other hand, looked glumly into the street as if he'd lost a half-dollar.

"You've made a conquest," he said. "Or is it two?"

Millicent gave him a look of bright inquiry. "I'm sorry. What did you say?"

"Nothing. How did Mrs. Wilmot like your new hat?"

"She liked it!" In her excitement Millicent reached out and pressed his forearm. "She thinks if I do more like it, they'll sell quick. Not all the same, of course; nobody wants to go to church and see half a dozen people all wearing the same hat as you, but some in the same style. Feathers and flowers."

"You'll have to keep making the other kind for mourning."

"There's always a call for those," Millicent said, and Ned wished he could stop the gig, get down, and kick himself for darkening her delight.

The drove in silence down the red-clay road, the very one Ned had trod until the early hours. He mentioned that he'd been out until three.

"I'd be scared," Millicent said, casting an eye toward the stands of tall trees above them on the banks. "Lots of critters in these woods."

"I would have thought you spent a certain amount of time in the woods at night."

"Lands, why?"

This conversational gambit also hid snares. "Er, gathering herbs by the light of the moon, and such."

Millicent laughed. Strange how he'd once thought she never did, and now every time he heard that peal, he longed for it to be repeated. She said, "You've got some funny ideas. Sure, I wouldn't plant anything but by the moon, but I pick stuff whenever I need it. 'Sides, I'm not much good at night. It's all I can do to get up when Petey needs me."

"I saw your light on when I walked back."

"He's a pretty good baby. Some I heard of want to be fed about sixteen times a night. He only wakes up a couple of times. I don't mind getting up, but there's no doubt but what it makes me heavy-eyed the next day." She turned her head and smiled at him. "You must be tireder than a dog chasing a hundred rabbits if you were up half the night."

Ned shook his head. "As long as I keep going, I'm all right. It's something I learned about myself as a medical student. When I was training, I'd sometimes be up for forty-eight hours at a stretch. As long as I never sat down with nothing to do, as long as I kept my brain busy, I could do without sleep."

"But the second you sat down and let your mind wander, your face would hit the floor?"

"Just about."

"Now me, I like at least eight hours of sleep without waking. I'll sure be glad when Petey sleeps through the night."

Ned let that go, for the moment. He said, "Have you had lunch yet?"

"Lunch? Oh, dinner? No. What with getting this dress fixed and whatnot, the time just got away from me."

Pulling back on the reins, Ned slowed the horse. "Under the seat is a picnic basket. I marked down a likely spot for a picnic the last time I drove this way."

"You often have picnics?"

"I like to sit on the grass and read while I eat lunch when I'm out driving around to my patients. Gives me a chance to relax and clear my head."

"I like to go to the picnic grounds down by the creek when it's warm out. The storeroom at the Wilmot's Store's always so bunged up with stuff there isn't room to move."

"Next time . . ." He had been about to propose that they sometimes take lunch together, but he remembered that after a while they would have no more cause to be seen together.

The bank between the road and the edge ran smoothly here, with a few ruts that showed other tourists had chosen this spot for picnicking and other bucolic delights. As he drove up, Millicent caught her breath.

The grass shone with the intense green of spring seen only before the heat dries the blades to straw. Here and there among the green, yellow dandelions and nodding white daisies showed their festive heads. The meadow sloped down to a fast-running stream, screened by a few slender birch trees. Early bees darted among the flowers, enough to lend a gentle murmur to the breeze but not enough to be threatening.

Ned found himself looking more at Millicent than at the scenery. Her eyes took on a golden glow as she gazed around, while her hands, clasped at her bosom, seemed to express a joy too big for words.

"Pretty, isn't it?" he asked.

"Pretty? Yes, I guess so. Let's hurry and eat."

"Sure," he said, amused and confused. "I'll just tie Abendego in the shade."

She didn't wait for his help to get down. When he looked up from getting out the basket and a blanket, Millicent had gone down on her knees. "What are you doing?"

"These are just right," she answered, showing him a few yellow flowers in the palm of her hand.

"Dandelions? What for?"

"Wine, of course. Spring's the best time for making it. The flowers are still sweet and tender."

"Dandelion wine?" he asked the sky. "What next?"

She stood up, her skirt stained already by grass. "Lunch, I hope," she said with a serene smile.

Ned didn't know quite how it happened. The warm sunshine, the excellence of the picnic lunch, the ease he felt in her company, all might have contributed. Whatever the cause, he fell asleep in his shirtsleeves, his head most pleasantly pillowed in Millicent's lap.

The first sign of returning consciousness was the gentle touch of her cool fingertips drawing across his forehead. He felt certain she'd been doing that for some time, but he only realized it in the moments before his eyes opened. He raised one eyelid, just enough to see her.

First of all, and disappointingly, she did not gaze down at him with tender, romantic dreams in her eyes. Instead, she stared off into the distance, her face calm but her mind obviously preoccupied. Her caressing touch had no more meaning behind it than it would if she were absently stroking a house cat.

"Millicent," he said, surprised to hear such steely determination in his tone. He softened his voice. "Millicent?"

"Yes, Ned?"

"Do you remember that I kissed you?"

Instantly he noted with satisfaction how her chest began to rise and fall more rapidly. He could be certain now that he had her attention fixed exactly where he wanted it, on him. There'd been kisses between them, laced with a volatile mixture of animosity and hunger, but his motivation had changed radically. He no longer wanted her despite his better judgment. He wanted her now just because she was Millicent.

Ned reached up and touched her cheek. An unmistakable shiver ran through her. "Do you remember?"

Her yes was hardly more than a shaken whisper.

"Don't you think it's about time to return the favor?"

16

$\mathcal{M}$ILLICENT FROZE, HER fingertips not even all the way across his forehead. She literally could not believe her ears. She blinked at him, but the picture before her eyes remained the same. Ned, his blue eyes twinkling, had just challenged her to kiss him.

It would serve him right if she jumped to her feet and left his head to bang into the ground. She'd do it, too, in a hot second, if it weren't for the fact that her left foot had fallen asleep. She'd be the one crashing down if she tried to stand, and then he'd gloat that his outrageous request had brought her to her knees.

Millicent coaxed a beguiling smile onto her lips. "Why, sure," she said, and had the satisfaction of seeing him taken aback. Then, to her horror, his bright eyes darkened and the touch on her cheek hardened.

"Well, come on," he said, his voice deep and enticing.

Millicent realized the time had come to pay the piper. The clutch in her abdomen could have been mistaken for fear if she had not known better. This was wanting, not pure and not simple, but all too real.

She leaned down as far as she could go; a very uncomfortable position. Then he lifted up and they met in the middle. This time they skipped the sweet kisses and went straight to the kind of tongue-tangling embrace that had haunted her dreams since Saturday.

She felt herself being drawn down. Suddenly she could bend that way, or any way, so long as he continued his tender invasion. Then his hands were hard against her shoulders as he held her off. "Wait, wait a moment," he said.

Muttering some protest, she tried to reach him. Slippery as an eel, he moved his shoulders off her lap. Suddenly, without remembering how she got there, Millicent lay on top of him, their bodies meeting at every point. Her hair came down and spilled around his face.

She watched him move into it, rubbing the silky strands against his face, his eyes closing with bliss. Pressing kisses into his skin, she tasted him and heard the low groan in his chest. She didn't know whether to laugh with pleasure or cry out.

Then Ned began to move his hands on her, those talented hands that knew so much more than she had ever been allowed to learn. Over her back the pressure varied, now light, now strong. Then he moved down farther, to her waist, and she rose and fell on his body to the stroke of his hands.

"Millicent, my God," he said, his voice dark. "You don't know. . . ."

"Yes, I think so."

He rolled with her. Suddenly she could see the sky past his shoulders and he rose up strong above her. She ran her hands up his arms, feeling the muscles tense beneath his shirt. Then he gathered her in his arms, scattering kisses over her face and throat.

Millicent closed her eyes and gave herself up. The heat bloomed in her as she clutched at his back. "Oh, my," she breathed, turning her head aside to let him nip at the tender flesh of her throat. She called his name as she moved restlessly underneath him. She should have been crushed by his weight, but she felt fine. His hands cradled her head as he tasted her mouth again.

Somehow his shirt came adrift and her fingertips found the smooth skin of his back. He stopped kissing her, lifting his head up, his eyes closing in pleasure. She watched his face intently as she stroked him. "That's heavenly," he said. Then he gazed down at her. "But not exactly what I want."

He rolled to the side and propped himself up with his head on one hand, his elbow on the blanket. Millicent turned to face him, her eyes questioning. "You're a grown man," she said. "I don't guess that kissin' is all you had in mind."

Slowly he shook his head. "It isn't."

Millicent knew that if she made so much as a move in his direction he'd be justified in thinking she wanted what he wanted. Facing her desire squarely, Millicent admitted that he wouldn't be wrong. She said hesitantly, trying the words on for size, "I want . . ."

"Yes?" He reached out with one finger and traced a line over her parted lips, then down over her chin and throat to flirt wickedly with the scoop neck of her dress. Millicent found her words fleeing as she focused on that teasing finger. It affected her the way a lighted match affects straw. It might start in one place but could spread in an instant to ravage the whole barn.

"I want your hands on me," she said wonderingly. For a moment the leaping hunger in his eyes let her see herself as he saw her, tumbled and heated with the longing she felt growing inside her. But there were things she needed to say first. "I just need more than that."

"Believe me, I'm willing to supply whatever you need." His mouth twisted in a smile, both tender and superior, while at the same time filled with the unsatisfied ache she felt herself.

She never wanted anything so much as to kiss him, but she'd been taught to strike only fair bargains. To kiss him again would be to promise more than she could pay. But because it hurt too much not to touch him, she laid her hand against his chest, right over his steady heartbeat. Somehow, touching him there seemed to lend her the strength she needed to say what needed to be said.

"I guess I'm afraid."

"Perfectly understandable. But if you'll trust me . . ."

"I do. I do trust you, Ned. It's just . . . we're gettin' awful close to milk territory here."

"Excuse me? What's milk territory? Cows?"

"Sort of. You know what they say about getting the milk for free?"

At first his smile widened. Then he nodded reluctantly.

"Mrs. Cotton's homely metaphor," he muttered. "And she's absolutely right. Damn it." He rolled over onto his back, flinging his arm across his eyes.

"Ned?"

"Just give me a moment," he said thickly. "I'll be sane again in a minute."

"I'm sorry."

"Don't be. It's not your fault."

"It's not yours, either. I'm willin' to share the load."

"No, this one's all mine. You're the woman; you don't have anything to reproach yourself for."

Millicent wished he'd show his face. She found it easier to explain herself to a pair of eyes. "I'm not reproaching myself. I just don't want to be dishonest."

"Dishonest?"

"Promising something to you that I can't give is dishonest, don't you figure?"

"It's not your fault," he said again. "I shouldn't have pressed you for it, knowing you couldn't give me what I wanted."

He took his arm away and turned to look at her. At once she wished he'd cover them again. She felt as if she could look into his soul and see her own reflected there. Her whole body tightened in response to the stark yearning in his eyes. Regrets might lie on the other side of making love with him, but they didn't seem important compared with the regret of not taking this chance.

"We'd better go," he said, starting to sit up.

"Ned . . ." Once again, more boldly, she ran her hand up his arm to the full stretch of her own reach. She slipped her finger under his tie and tugged on the end.

"Now, Millicent, you really don't want to do that."

The easiest way to bring him to her seemed to be to wrap his tie about her hand and pull. She underestimated her strength. He came down fast, only stopping himself by an outthrust hand.

"You said I should 'return the favor,' didn't you?"

"I was only . . . I didn't think you would."

"Think again."

She moved against him, telling him without words that her doubts were no longer important. Giving him her mouth, she didn't wait for him to take the initiative. Whether the hot sun had seeped into her body or her longing had reached its peak, she felt too warm and too alive.

Treasuring his groan like a prize, she linked her arms around his neck as he took over the kiss. He sought out her breasts with his hands, clasping gently. Millicent gasped and twisted in delighted shock.

The sunlight dazzled her, even through closed eyelids. She heard his breaths and the words he murmured, disjointed, passionate, mingling with the low throbbing of the bees. When he moved away, she protested wordlessly.

"I'm caught, honey," he said, tugging at her enveloping skirt. "Wait a minute."

He levered himself upward, putting one hand down on the blanket for balance. Then he snatched it away as though it had been burnt. "Damnation!"

He tottered, fell back, and crashed with a grunt on his side. Millicent came up on her elbow, too surprised to do anything but blink at him.

Rather slowly, pain etching lines beneath his eyes, Ned sat up. He turned over his hand and peered closely at the palm. He flicked something that had been crushed away with his left forefinger.

Millicent looked at his hand, too, as she pushed the tumbled fall of her hair off her face. "What happened?"

"Bee sting."

He held his hand out for her inspection. A tiny white trail straggled away from the red spot of the sting. She cradled his hand in hers, bringing it in against her bosom to hold it steady. "I'll take care of it. Hold still."

Pinching with her fingernails, she grasped hold of the sting and whipped it out. "There . . ."

"Ouch!" He tried to clench his fist and pull away. She opened her hand to let him go.

"Don't be a baby. It's gone. You ought to spit on it."

"Spit on it? What on earth for?"

"Takes away the pain. You must of been bee stung before. What do you usually do?"

"I don't spend much time lolling in meadows. I can't remember the last time I was stung, but I'm sure I never spit on it."

"Then I'll get some salt to draw out the poison."

She had already begun digging in the picnic basket when he said, "Don't fuss. There's no poison involved. It's just the point of impact that hurts; precisely and no more than if I'd run a needle into my hand."

Millicent began to gather her hair up, but she paused to glance at him sideways. "Of course there's poison," she said matter-of-factly. "Folks don't swell up and die from a sewing needle, and I've seen it happen with bee stings."

"I suppose that could happen, rarely."

Glancing around for her pins, Millicent added, "Good thing it's rarely. It's not a sight I'd care to see twice."

"I don't suppose you would. So, salt and spit are your suggestions?"

"That or . . . well, most folks will tell you that the only other thing that works is the juice from a honeysuckle vine."

"The honeysuckle vine?"

Millicent had had little hope that he'd go on making love to her after the bee interfered, but when she heard the disbelieving tone of his voice, that little hope died. Trying to keep things light, she said, "You know, you sneer better than any man I ever saw."

"I'm sorry. I didn't mean to sneer at you."

"Why not? It's what you've been doing ever since we met. We might as well face facts, Ned. There's never going to be any kind of a future for you and me."

"Were you thinking that there might be?"

His voice sounded so calm and indifferent that the question amounted to an insult. Her cheeks flew all their flags as she said, "When a girl can't go on a little drive without the feller being all over her like a duck on a june bug, she starts wondering if . . . well, you know what if."

She got up and went down to the water's edge in search of honeysuckle for a stubborn man's hand. The farther away she went from him, the harder it became to hold back the tears that stung in her eyes worse than bee stings. She wanted him and that was bad. Worse still, she loved him.

The very thought made her gasp for breath. Loving him when he behaved badly meant she had more trouble than even she had realized. She did not think she could talk herself out of it this time. If it happened only when he was being nice, that was a mild case and could be fought.

This time, though, he'd been rude and she still loved him. He could sneer at her all he liked, and she still loved him, though she didn't imagine for a solitary second that she'd take too much of it without giving something back.

Millicent glanced over her shoulder. Ned did not gaze at her with repentance in his eyes. Far from it. He'd flopped back down on the blanket and stared at the sky.

She watched him for a moment, a dim fear stirring. Bob McKrimmon had died from a wasp's sting when she was a child. She remembered seeing him fall down in the schoolyard, thrashing around and gasping for breath.

But Ned only lay there, quite still. After a minute he threw his arm once more over his eyes as though unable to bear the sight of so much blue above him. He looked so lonesome that she had to fight the feet that longed to carry her to him.

Millicent found the vine wrapping itself around a young tree, the flowers on it upraised like the trumpets of a conquering army that fought in silence. She snapped off the trefoil leaves, leaving the flowers, though she breathed in deeply of their scent. The bees were busy here, too, working their tiny bodies, striped like men's bathing suits, in and out of the flowers. They didn't bother her; she'd never been stung yet.

She came back up the hill, hating that her footsteps hurried. It was a terrible thing to be in love with a man when he didn't care for you. He wanted her, yes, but she had no hope that she could turn that into something else. Lust was lust and a sin. Could she find a way to turn a sin into a virtue?

"Here," she said, holding out the leaves. "Squeeze the

juice out of them, unless you want to have a sore hand for the next week."

"You were right about one thing," he said, gazing up at her. "Spit works."

"Don't be so surprised. I know so many remedies, it makes sense that one or two of 'em ought to work."

"Millicent . . ." he said, a half-laughing, half-pleading note coming into his voice.

"I'll see to the horse. You're not going to be able to drive." She let the green leaves drift down onto the blanket before she turned away.

Their trip into Handfast turned out to be pointless. The midwife had been called away to tend two women at the same farm some miles out of town. "Even if we knew where to look," Ned said, "she wouldn't have time to talk with us. Believe me, I know. I've been in that situation."

"Better you than me. I never want to tackle that! I'm no midwife."

At least he'd begun to talk again, Millicent thought. The silences had stretched long and hard between them, broken only by the clomping of Abendego's hooves.

Her satisfaction died a quick death. Once out of the small town, which looked the way Culverton had twenty years ago, Ned seemed to lock his lips with a key. When she thought how not an hour ago she had been free to explore his mouth as she liked, she could have hunkered down and cried a river.

Millicent hated to think what Mrs. Cotton would say about this disastrous day. She suffered no illusion that the quick-witted woman would not guess just how miserably everything had gone wrong. She wished she could just sneak into her home. Even the thought of Petey waiting for her failed to cheer her up.

Though she didn't want to trap Ned into marriage, Millicent had been warmed by the admiration in his eyes when he'd first seen her that morning. She'd put a little more swing than usual in the managing of her skirts. Now she knew it had been nothing more than an old-fashioned wish to catch his notice. She'd done so, but it had brought her nothing but a brief roll in the grass. She wondered if she'd ever really know what she wanted.

Ned walked her to her door. She knew he only did it because he'd been raised to be a gentleman. Otherwise, he would have probably driven off in a swirling cloud of dust.

Turning, she looked up into his face. "It's all right if you want to forget the whole thing."

"What whole thing?"

She could have stamped her foot in frustration over his thickheadedness. "Everything," she explained. "Petey and I will manage this mess somehow."

"Give up the cow plot? Never." As his smile faded, he reached out to take her hand. She began to meet him halfway, and then withdrew, feeling her safety depending on not touching him right now.

To make an explanation, she asked him, "How's your sting?"

"Better."

She refused to let her eyes meet his. "I'd better go in. Petey's probably missed me."

"Millicent . . ."

"I should go."

"What are you going to do when his mother comes back?"

She felt like a fool. Here she'd been worrying over what he'd say and then he said that! Suddenly she felt anger like an itch under her skin. "Why worry over something that's not going to happen?" she demanded, and she didn't care if he understood her double meaning.

"You don't think she's coming back? You'd be foolish—"

"You may be right, Dr. Castle. I've been a fool already more times than I can count. What makes you think she will come back?" She wouldn't let him speak. "The marshal, the judge, and pretty near every other breathing creature in this town's been looking for her, and they've not seen hide nor hair of her. She's cleared out; long gone by now. And Petey's mine."

"If the situation were reversed, Millicent, you'd be back for your child."

"I wouldn't have given him up in the first place!" she flared. Then she jerked open the door and went in, letting it slam in Ned's face.

Mrs. Cotton lay asleep on the coverlet in Millicent's room. The slow rattle of her exhalations filled the room with its homely melody. But beyond a quick glance, Millicent barely noticed the older woman.

She stepped, delicately as a deer, over the bare floorboards, avoiding by long practice the ones that squeaked or groaned. Reaching into the cradle, she drew back the blanket to gaze on Petey's tiny face. A small bubble had formed between his puckering lips.

As she watched, the baby sighed and wrinkled his forehead. Millicent smiled. When she thought of Ned, a bubbling mixture of indignation and love seemed to boil over within her. When she looked at Petey, serenity flooded her. If she could only feel that way about Ned, she'd know that she truly loved him.

She lay the blanket down across the baby again, smoothing the fabric over his chest. Suddenly cold as with a warning, she found herself watching her hands as they ran over the soft fleece. Something was wrong. This was not Petey's blanket.

17

SHE SNATCHED IT up and held it close to her eyes. The snowy color, the warp and weft, all different. She'd never seen this blanket before.

Closing her eyes, Millicent fought to control herself. Panic would not serve her. In all likelihood Mrs. Cotton had brought this blanket, after knitting it herself. All she had to do now was wake her to ask her.

Millicent crossed the room and touched Mrs. Cotton's shoulder. Somehow she managed to touch lightly, not grip to the bone the way her frightened brain urged.

"Mrs. Cotton," she said in a gentle voice.

The rattling snores caught for an instant, then went on. "Mrs. Cotton?" Millicent repeated a bit more forcefully. She shook the sharp shoulder. "Wake up."

Frowning, she crossed to where the lamp burned low. She remembered how tired and out of breath Mrs. Cotton had become even climbing the stairs in her own house. Had caring for Petey taxed her too much? Maybe her heart . . .

She brought the lamp close to the older woman's face. Sighing in relief, Millicent realized Mrs. Cotton's expression had nothing in common with the drawn face of someone at death's door, but rather the dimpling delight of someone in a dream too wonderful to leave lightly.

Then Mrs. Cotton laughed, right out loud, without waking. "Oh, Vernon!" she said in a voice as coy as a schoolgirl's.

Millicent blushed for her friend. Putting the lamp down

on the table, she wondered what to do. She hated to wake Mrs. Cotton from such a nice dream, but at the same time she needed to ask about the blanket.

She looked at it again. The soft white wool had been knitted in a pretty lockstitch that looked like flowers. It had heft and warmth without being too heavy for a baby. Surely if Mrs. Cotton had been working on this blanket for Petey, she would have mentioned it?

A hair sparkled in the light, glistening among the twisted strands of wool. Millicent caught it between her fingers and drew it out from the pattern. The lamplight burned golden. Millicent couldn't tell if the hair was gray-white like Mrs. Cotton's or blond. That revelation would have to wait until the clear light of day.

Nonetheless, this single reminder of whoever had made the blanket turned Millicent's heart cold. She knew that Mrs. Cotton had never created it. Somehow she knew the truth.

Forgetting her qualms, Millicent called Mrs. Cotton's name. She crossed the room and shook her shoulder gently yet determinedly. It took two more tries to wake Mrs. Cotton, yet even so she awoke with a self-satisfied smile. Then she blinked and focused on Millicent.

"You back already?" She yawned, patted it away, and apologized before asking, "What went wrong?"

"Nothing . . . I mean, let's talk about that later. Look, did you bring this for Petey?"

"Bring what?" She blinked shortsightedly at the blanket thrust under her nose. "Lands, child," she protested, pushing Millicent's hand off to a decent distance. "I can't see a thing close to without my spectacles. Now, then . . ."

She peered at the blanket Millicent showed to her. "Pretty work. Small needles. Who made it?"

"That's what I'm asking you. Did you make it?"

"No, I don't have time to knit in the spring. Too much else happening. Which reminds me . . . my back flower bed is a disgrace under a merciful sky. I'd be ashamed to have the rain see it when it falls there, and that's a fact."

"Mrs. Cotton," Millicent said, trying to keep from following her down the garden path. "Did anyone call while I was gone?"

"Why, yes, a few folks . . ." She sat up in bed, concentrating on the problem at hand. Counting on her fingers, she mumbled, "Mrs. Wilmot, Mrs. Budgell . . . I let them hold Petey, I knew you wouldn't mind. . . . Miss Winthrop, Mrs. George and Lucy . . . My, she's taking things hard or her mother's dishing it out; I ought to do something for that child. It's a shame Ned won't look at her."

"You had a lot of visitors then?" Which of them had tucked a new blanket around Petey without bothering to mention their generosity to Mrs. Cotton?

"Not too many. Just enough to keep Petey and me from being bored. We were glad when the last of them cleared out, though. He'd started getting cranky."

"Do you have any idea who brought this blanket then? Did any of them come up here?"

"Why, no, I don't believe so." As she blinked up at Millicent, Mrs. Cotton's eyes came into snapping focus. "You don't think . . . his mother?"

"Who else could it have been?"

Mrs. Cotton pushed back the coverlet and sat up. A grimace of pain crossed her features, tightening her mouth. She put her hands to the small of her back and pressed. "Child, you keep sleeping on this old mattress, you'll wind up twisted as a knot. You've got more lumps in here than in a bride's biscuits."

"Never mind that," Millicent said, repressing an urge to apologize. "Tell me if you saw anything, or heard anything."

"I wish I could, but I don't know that I can. Taking care of Petey kind of took it out of me. By the time he finally nodded off, you know I was ready to take a nap myself. Once my head hit the pillow, a herd of elephants could have wandered through here and I wouldn't have opened my eyes. What time is it, anyhow?"

"Sundown."

"My stars, Vernon must be thinkin' the bears et me!"

"I'm sorry I stayed so late. We stopped and had a picnic down in Parson's Meadow."

"Oh?" Now Mrs. Cotton leaned forward, enthralled. "What happened?"

"Nothing." Millicent felt glad she had the lamp at her back. Mrs. Cotton could spot a blush at twenty paces.

"That's too bad. I didn't reckon the boy was *that* slow."

"Well, it doesn't matter now. The important thing is to find out who left this blanket. Since the sun's just now going down, she must have left it here in broad daylight. Maybe somebody saw her. Is the judge at home?"

"I don't know. He might have sloped off to do some fishing. Poot Harvey told him yesterday that they were biting down at the crick."

"Then I'll go to Marshal Faraday. He can start asking around. Do you mind staying with Petey a mite longer?"

"Lands, no. So long as you don't mind me taking him over to my house. I better start supper. Vernon's a mild sort as a rule, but there's no denying he likes his meals to be on the table when he comes home."

Millicent wrapped the blanket up in brown paper, tying it with a string. She took a fleecy shawl for her shoulders, as the night closed down over the town and the muslin dress was not so warm as her black one.

The new jail, in the basement of the Quincannon Memorial City Hall, did not have the homelike air of the previous jail. However, the big brick building had become one of the sights of Culverton, and the townsfolk were burstingly proud of it. Once they'd fixed the problems with the doors, which now stayed locked instead of swinging wide at a touch, Culverton felt itself ready for any desperate criminals that didn't have the sense to stay out of town.

Millicent, along with most of the other women in town, had been of the opinion that the money would have been better spent on civic improvements, like sidewalks or a new schoolhouse. When the old school had burned to the ground two years ago, nearly taking Antonia Faraday and Jenny Dakers with it, the ladies of the town got their new schoolhouse. But the sidewalks still had to wait.

Though Millicent hadn't approved of the new city hall, now she felt glad to see the symmetrical facade, the windows all aglow with reflections of the setting sun. The very look of it gave her confidence. The marshal would soon find Petey's mother, no doubt about it.

With that thought, Millicent sat down heavily on the pale concrete steps. Ned—Ned of all people!—wanted her to imagine herself in that unknown mother's place. Maybe she was young, frightened of what people might say if they knew she had borne a baby. Maybe she was alone, dwelling in an otherwise empty house. Maybe she had no one to help her . . . and was probably too proud to ask for the human love and compassion she needed.

Millicent had no difficulty imagining herself that girl. She found it all too easy. No, she had never borne a child out of wedlock, as she must assume Petey's mother had. However, she knew full well how hard one woman might find it to stand against public opinion, to be pointed at, to be made an outcast.

For whatever reason, Petey's mother had decided that giving her child away would give him a better life than her keeping him. Millicent's imagination stopped short at trying to picture the agony of that choice. How many times had the girl turned back to take one last glimpse of her baby son in the basket before finally going away into that rainy night? Could more drops have possibly fallen from the sky than from her eyes?

The part of Millicent that wanted to hide the blanket, hide every evidence of Petey's mother's visit, curled up in shame. For the first time, she accepted that they needed to find Petey's mother for her sake, as much as for Petey's. A girl in that circumstance might do any desperate thing to escape her pain.

Filled with resolution, Millicent stood up and entered through the jail door. What she found there sent her back out into the street within a few moments.

She ran through the streets, her shawl flapping. Most people were safe indoors, out of the mists that rose up as the heat of the spring day faded. In any case, she saw no one she recognized, though a slurred voice called after her, "What's your hurry, sweetheart?"

The windows of Mrs. Fleck's boardinghouse were a welcome sight, with the light showing through the slots in the closed shutters. Millicent caught hold of the brass knocker and clanked it against the wooden door. While she waited for someone to answer, she bent double, hands on her knees, to slow her panting breath. Her heart hurt, it beat so strongly.

It seemed a long time before someone came to the door. Millicent did not know the young man who opened the door a crack to peer out with one eye the color of a faded pair of overalls.

She asked, "Is Dr. Castle here?"

The blue eye sparked with interest. "Is there an emergency?"

Even nodding seemed a waste of breath but Millicent managed one. She moved forward, expecting to be let in, but the owner of the pale blue eye only said, "Do you want to come in?"

"I want Dr. Castle."

"He's awful busy. The landlady's son's sick."

"Ed . . . I mean, Egbert?"

"That's right." The half of the pale lips she could see got licked. "They say he's going to die."

Millicent decided that standing here meekly would not get her what she wanted. She put her hand flat against the door and began to push inexorably forward. As impressive as a string bean and about the same proportion so far as height and weight, the man fell back, with a protesting, "Hey!"

Then she was in the dingy hall, the full smell of cabbage and corned beef coming at her like a drowning wave. Turning to the string bean, she demanded, "Where's Ed's room?"

The young man just pointed skyward.

"Is the doctor there?"

He nodded, rolling his eyes at her as if she were a madwoman. Millicent looked him up and down, and if anything that long slow regard made him even more nervous. "I guess I could show you. . . ." he stammered.

"Do."

Mrs. Fleck sat beside her son's bed, her worry hidden in a frown. Her eyes flicked constantly between Ned, stooping over Egbert, and Egbert's flushed face. When they lighted on Millicent, she stared for an instant before putting her finger to her pale lips.

Ned held one end of a strange, nearly heart-shaped device against Egbert's bared chest. From there, the thing flared into two halves, one of which went in each of Ned's ears. Millicent saw him move the dark wooden end of the device around the area of Egbert's heart, silently.

Sitting up on the edge of the bed, Ned said, "Well, that wasn't so bad. Good, strong heartbeat and sound lungs."

The boy smiled without opening his eyes. He had a cool compress over his forehead. With his vibrant red hair covered he seemed to have lost all his animation. His freckles stood out like burn holes against his pale skin.

Millicent said, "Excuse me, Dr. Castle?"

Ned turned around, but more surprisingly, Egbert opened his eyes. His smile widened. "Hello, Miss Mayhew," he croaked.

"Hello, Egbert. I'm sorry you're not feeling up to snuff."

"Oh, I'll be all right. . . ."

His mother said, "I'm glad you've come, Millicent. Who told you Egbert was sick?"

"No one . . . I mean, I didn't know that he was sick, too. I came to find Dr. Castle."

She didn't like what she saw in Ned's expression. His face seemed to have hardened the moment he saw her, losing the gentleness she'd seen in his posture while tending Egbert. But when she made it clear she hadn't come to meddle, his squared shoulders relaxed. "What is it?"

Millicent hesitated.

"Just a moment, then." He turned again to Mrs. Fleck. "He'll be all right in a day or two. Just a cold."

"But his fever?"

"It's mild. A few days of bedrest . . ." He stood up, put the tube in his open bag, and snapped the bag closed. He smiled down at the boy. "At least now we know why you had a headache earlier. Take some of the tonic I'll send over—about a wineglass full every few hours, please, Mrs. Fleck."

Egbert asked, his eyes closing against the pain of speaking from a sore throat, "Is it awful?"

"Not too bad," Ned answered reassuringly. "It's got a touch of whisky in it."

"Really?" Even sick, that thought cheered Egbert up. "I've never had any before."

Mrs. Fleck squeezed her son's hand and stood to walk out into the hall with the doctor. Millicent followed.

Ned said, "He'll be all right. And"—he lowered his voice—"don't worry; there really isn't anything in the tonic but tonic."

Mrs. Fleck nodded, and Millicent marveled at how a few confident words could change her attitude. Though still concerned for her son, she drew a deep breath as though some burden had fallen from her shoulders. Millicent didn't want to alarm anyone, so she kept the news she'd brought to herself for a moment longer.

When the landlady went back into her son's room, Millicent said softly, "I was just down at the jail, Ned. You'd better get over there, quick."

"What were you . . . ? Why? What's wrong?"

"I hate to say it, but I don't think Ed there's got just a summer cold a mite early."

"Oh." He folded his arms and leaned against the wall. "And what has led you to this conclusion?"

Millicent took a breath and held it, counting to ten. "Now don't go all stuffy on me. Egbert had a headache, right? Then what happened?"

"He complained of aching joints and a fever. Then he became nauseated . . . which means—"

"He threw up. . . . Don't look so surprised."

Ned nodded in acknowledgment of her small success.

"And you call that a cold?"

"What would you call it?"

"I don't know . . . but your brother-in-law's got it, too. And so do both his deputies. They're at the jail now. And nauseated don't cover it . . . not by a mile. We're going to need mops, lots of mops before we're done."

She followed him down the stairs and out into the street. He glanced at her over his shoulder and asked, "What do you think you are doing?"

"Following you."

"Why?"

"Because it's dark."

He paused and allowed her to come up to him. Then he reached out to take her hand. Passing it under his elbow, Ned said, "You're not afraid of the dark."

"No . . . not usually. But lately . . . rocks and stuff, you know."

"Oh, that." He walked on, moderating his pace to hers. "Ed mentioned that while he was out today, he found out who did it. You don't have to worry anymore. Ed will get the money for the window from the culprit."

"That's nice of him. I'm surprised. I know his ma, of course, but I never have had much to do with Ed."

Ned said dryly, "It seems that in Ed you have a champion."

"I wish I'd known that before. I would have thanked him for his trouble."

"You'll have plenty of time to thank him later."

It did not smell good at the jail. Even Millicent, who had tended sick people often, held a fold of her shawl to her mouth. Ned, on the other hand, paid no attention. He strode into the first cell, where a gray-haired older man lay moaning on the cot.

"Hiya, Doc."

"Feeling low, Pete?"

"Lower'n a snake's belly in a ditch." The deputy lay still while Ned laid his hand on the man's forehead. "You don't have to tell me, I got a fever."

"That's right. But just to be sure, I'll take your temperature."

The deputy's gray eyes narrowed as Ned opened his black

bag. "You ain't got one of them big there-mometers in there, do you? They used one of them ten-inchers on me when I got shot at Vicksburg, and I ain't goin' to——"

"No, no." Ned opened the wooden box he brought out. "See," he said, lifting out the glass tube with care. "It's not even six inches long."

"Oh. That's okay then. Them ten-inch things took nigh 'un forever as I recollect."

He lay back down on his cot and opened his mouth to take the thermometer. Millicent snuck a peak into Ned's squarish black bag. Before she could ask any questions, however, he said, "Maybe you should find Jake and Caleb. Tell them I'll be in to see them in a few minutes."

She found the younger deputy, Caleb, asleep, facedown on a cot in another cell. Squinting against the stink, she carried out the sick pail that stood beside his head. He had rolled over on his back by the time she'd gotten back. The ceiling seemed to fascinate him. He hardly moved his gaze away from it when she walked in and put the empty bucket back at his side.

"Are you all right?"

"My back hurts."

"Dr. Castle will be here in a minute." He didn't react except to close his eyes and groan. "Do you know where the marshal is? I can't find him."

After a moment Caleb said, "Dunno. Heard him a while back. Sick as a . . ."

He rolled over and was sick. Millicent scurried out to dampen a towel for him. When she returned, he lay on his side, holding his stomach and groaning. She wiped his mouth and forehead, hoping she wouldn't disgrace herself.

Caleb looked up at her with glistening eyes. "Thanks, Miss Mayhew. I wish my wife was here."

"Where is she?"

"Gone to visit her mother in Nesslerode. Won't be back for a week. I surely hate to die without her here."

"You won't die," Millicent responded automatically. Suspecting food poisoning, she asked another question. "What did you have to eat today, Caleb?"

His white face seemed to turn slightly green, like the belly of a fish, at this mention of food. "Not enough," he said, pressing his hands against his stomach. "I'm empty."

"Did you all three eat the same things?"

He shook his head, lolling against the scratchy ticking of the pillow. "Nope. I brought along some fricasseed chicken my wife left. Pete had what his old lady fixed him, and I don't figure the boss had time to eat. He went over to the Forks today, looking for that mother what's gone missin'." Caleb stopped talking. She saw his prominent Adam's apple rise and fall as he swallowed.

"I'm going to look for the marshal. You lie still."

He shook his head. "I think the boss went home, Miss Mayhew. I heard him . . . you know . . . sicking up, but I'm pretty sure he went home after that. Crawling, maybe."

Ned came in to hear the last part of this. His eyes met Millicent's. A dawning alarm lived at the back of them. Yet his manner to Caleb did not vary from what it had been to Pete, Mrs. Fleck, and Ed. Calmness, a readiness to listen, a sense of competence that brought tranquillity to a troubled mind. Even Millicent, who could grasp better than anyone the magnitude of the epidemic here, felt some of that comfort.

"I see Miss Mayhew brought you a cool cloth. Excellent. Put it on your forehead. It will help with the fever."

"I'll get one for Pete, too," she offered. She went out of the cell but hovered in the hall, just out of sight.

After a moment, as she expected, Ned made an excuse to his patient and joined her.

"What the hell is going on?" he demanded in a muted shout. "Three men sick, all with the same symptoms. Do you suppose Ed came here today? I'd guess food poisoning except that according to what I found out—"

"They didn't eat any of the same foods," Millicent said.

"You asked about that?"

"It seemed to be the right question."

She saw with what effort he forced down his temper. "You're right. It was. I just wish Jake hadn't headed for home. If this is contagious—"

"Contagious?"

"Passing through the air, from person to person."

"Oh, yes, Grandma told me about that."

"*She* did? Where did she learn about that? Never mind. Look, the whole town could come down with it."

"It's the grippe, isn't it?"

"That's right. Only doctors call it influenza these days."

"Grippe's not so bad. Even if a lot of folks get it, they'll be all right. . . ."

He shook his head, not as though she had said something stupid. More regretfully, as though he had bad news. "This looks worse than your ordinary influenza, Millicent. I've seen similar cases before. The painful joints, the headaches, the nausea . . . When I studied in Vienna, I saw this kind of disease sweep through the city. The doctors were helpless. All any of us could do was strive to make our patients as comfortable as possible while it ran its course. It killed a lot of people before it disappeared as suddenly as it had come."

"Killed people?" Millicent thought of her neighbors, who'd shown their caring time and again, even in the face of her unresponsiveness. She forgot the recent trouble they'd caused her and considered only what she could do now.

Ned said, "The fevers are the worst of it. If they can just make it through those . . ."

Instinctively Millicent moved closer to Ned. He raised his arm and wrapped it around her shoulders. They stood like that for all too brief a time, giving and receiving comfort. Then she drew away from his strong body.

She asked, "Do you want me to go find Jake? Maybe he didn't go home. If he's as sick as those two deputies, he could have passed out halfway there."

"Yes, go. But . . . don't talk to anyone. I don't want a panic here. Is Mrs. Cotton still looking after Petey?"

She nodded and then caught her breath. Not only had she not told Ned about the mysterious blanket, she had also forgotten a complaint Mrs. Cotton had made. "Ned, can a backache be a sign of this . . . sickness?"

"Certainly. Any unusual ache or pain can be a symptom. You don't—"

"No, not me. But Mrs. Cotton's back hurt when she woke up. And she's been with Petey all day."

18

$\mathcal{N}$ED HARDLY WAITED five minutes before he left the jail. Caleb and Pete were sleeping, or giving good imitations of it. The night grew blacker by the minute. He stood outside, trying to sight the light from the lantern Millicent had taken along. She must have gone.

"Good!" Ned said and started off at a jog-trot toward her house. At least he could count on Millicent doing her duty before running back to see what was happening at home.

No lights were on at her house, but as he stood in the street he could see a faint glow lighting the hedges toward the back of the Cottons' house. He dashed up to the front door and knocked loudly.

He heard muttering and a crash. "Judge? Judge, it's me, Doc . . . Ned Castle."

"Ned?" The judge peered out, in his shirtsleeves. "Ned, don't you know what time it is? Here's my wife stuck with this baby, so I had to get supper on the table myself. I can't cook nothing but fish hash, and if there's one thing I purely hate, it's fish hash. . . ."

"Yes, Judge," Ned said, pushing inside. "Where is your wife?"

"In the kitchen, naturally. Where else . . . ? Stand still a minute; let a body talk!"

Ned found Mrs. Cotton sitting contentedly with a lap full of darning beside a warm stove. "Good evening," he said, in answer to her mild-eyed look. "I . . . uh . . . is Petey around?"

"He's asleep, in the spare room. What do you want him for?"

"Just checking on him. You know, I'm concerned for his health."

"No need," Mrs. Cotton answered, a puzzled expression inching onto her face. "I been taking care of other folks' young'uns for some little time, now."

"I didn't mean—"

"I figured maybe you come about that blanket Millicent found today. I been feeling mighty low and ashamed of myself 'cause of that. Fancy, somebody walkin' right in under my nose and leaving it."

"Very nice," Ned said, not paying attention. "You're feeling all right yourself, I hope, Mrs. Cotton?"

"Never better."

"You don't have a headache from doing close work without a strong light?"

"Of course not. It's the strong light that hurts 'em." She watched him prowl around for another moment and then burst out with "What in the name of the Holy Hannah are you doing, Neddy? I seen just that look on a dog's face when he forgot where he buried his bone."

Ned had to resist the urge to scratch behind his ears. "Anybody call today?"

"That's just what Millicent asked me. She wanted to know about the blanket. Why do you want to know?"

Ned wanted to ask what blanket she referred to, but he was too busy thinking of an answer. At last he decided to settle for the truth. Before long, someone would come by to tell her that sickness had struck this town she'd helped to build from nothing but forest. He only briefly wondered at no one having told her yet.

"We may have an epidemic of influenza in town," he said bluntly. "The deputies are down with it, and so is Ed Fleck. I wanted to be sure that neither you nor Petey had caught it."

"Influenza? What's that when it's at home?" the judge asked.

"Millicent called it 'grippe.'"

The two older people looked at each other without

speaking. Ned wondered if after such a long time together two people could read each other's minds. In which case, why did he sometimes feel that he understood Millicent even when she was silent? Right now, for instance, she wasn't even in the room, yet he could feel her worry and her determination just as though she were next to him.

Mrs. Cotton moved the mending off her lap. "Just wait till I get a wrap," she said.

The judge stepped forward. "Now, Mother . . ." he began.

"I can't stay and let my hands be idle when there's folks ailing, Vernon."

Ned said quickly, "Really, Mrs. Cotton, there's no need for you to nurse anyone. I think Millicent will help out."

"Of course she will, I should of thought of it," she said. Her eyes brightened for a moment, and Ned felt a twinge of worry. She only looked like that when she scented matrimony.

Almost at once, however, she returned to the subject at hand. "Let's see . . . Caleb and Pete . . . the Fleck boy . . . Anybody else?"

"Not yet."

"There will be. This mist we been having every night what does it. Gets into the lungs; mucks 'em up."

Ned decided not to argue with her. There were many prominent members of his profession who believed illnesses came from so called "bad air," just as there were those who believed that only man-to-man contact spread sickness. The first group wanted to "sanitize" all dwellings, with an emphasis on clean water; the second desired to "quarantine" all sick people or those who had the potential for spreading disease, sometimes permanently. Ned himself fell somewhere between the two camps, always an unpopular and difficult position to be in.

Mrs. Cotton asked, "What 'bout Jake? Has he got it?"

"I don't know yet. We can't find him."

"Where can he have gone to? Probably went home, I'd guess. Well, if he gets it, it's my best corset to a plugged nickel that Antonia will get it, too." It sounded as though Mrs. Cotton might hold that middle ground as well.

"I'm afraid she might. What effect that will have on her child, I cannot guess."

"We'll hope for the best and prepare for the worst. How bad is everybody? Sicking up? Feverish?"

"Yes, ma'am. The two deputies seem to be less sick than Ed, though that may just be because they have not been sick as long. He was falling ill when I saw him this morning. I should have seen that. . . ."

"Maybe you had something else on your mind. Like a picnic?"

"I should have had my mind on my duty."

"Now, don't go kicking yourself, Neddy. Even a doctor's got to have some time to do his courtin' . . . that is, his *pretend* courtin'. . . ."

He grinned, reluctantly. Perhaps the judge could read his wife so well because sometimes she made a pane of glass seem opaque in comparison. "I better get back to work. I just wanted to be certain you and Petey were all right."

"I'm too old and he's too young to be bothered with the grippe. And the judge there is just too blamed mean to let any ol' fever catch on him."

"That's right," Judge Cotton confirmed. "Didn't I come through the cholera seventeen years ago without so much as a sniffle? I remember . . ." For a moment his air of self-congratulation dimmed. He cleared his throat and muttered, "That was a bad time; don't want nothing like that again. . . . Where are you putting the folks as got it?"

"Putting them?"

"Well, yes," Mrs. Cotton said, giving Ned the kind of encouraging look a teacher gives a backward student. "You can't take care of 'em if they're scattered all over the town, can you? You ought to get them all together in one place, both for your sake and so if other folks need help they know where to find you without wasting time."

The judge said, "Might as well use the City Hall. Nobody's using any of it but the jail and courthouse, and I ain't had a case in two weeks, so I don't see how we're goin' to be needing either of 'em for a spell."

"That's the ticket, Vernon. 'Sides, the deputies are already there, so that's a couple you ain't got to move. Now, we're gonna need beds, blankets, food, and water. . . . I reckon you'd better go see the mayor, Vernon. Wilmot's not good for much, but he can make a speech like blue blazes. Not to mention he's got that stack of Rebel blankets he's been hoarding since the war. Tell him now's the time to break 'em out."

She caught Ned's wondering glance. "He kind of ran to both sides there for a while."

Mrs. Cotton went to get her husband's coat. The judge came closer to Ned to speak softly, glancing after his wife to be certain she couldn't hear him. "What should I be on the lookout for, Ned? If she gets sick, I mean."

Ned knew that if he wanted to save his sanity, he had to cut himself off from other people's worry. If he didn't, their fear and sorrow would overwhelm him, making it impossible to do his work. Yet, looking into the judge's frightened eyes, he realized for the first time how deeply connected he'd become to the people of Culverton. A week ago he would have denied it, claiming that he didn't even know if he wanted to stay. He thought of Millicent again and knew this change of heart could be laid in part at her door.

He put his hand on the judge's shoulder. "Just keep an eye on her. If she seems feverish or sick to her stomach, call me. Same thing for Petey. Millicent may be back tonight; I'm hoping she'll stay and help out."

"She will," the judge said. "Mother said she would, and if there's one thing she knows, it's folks."

Mrs. Cotton came back, a heavy wool coat hanging from her hand. "Now, you wrap up, Vernon. Here's your scarf and your cap."

"If I'm calling on the mayor, I ought to wear my silk 'un," he complained.

"That don't keep your head near warm enough. Don't take Neddy here as a model. Your mother must have had a time keeping you healthy. I swan I've never seen you yet with a hat on."

Ned smoothed down his hair. "Can't wear 'em. But at least I'll never go bald."

"Is that my problem?" the judge asked, running his fingers through his sparse crop.

"Hair needs to breathe to be healthy," Ned said, throwing the judge a wink.

"That's it, Mother. No more hats for me."

"Well, you'll wear one tonight if I have to chase you down and nail it to your head. Now, get along, you two. There's work to be doin'."

The two men stood together for a moment on the walkway outside the Cottons' front gate. "She seems fine," Ned said when the judge had heaved a sigh dug up from the depths of his soul.

"I surely hope so. I been worried about her now for some time. She takes these spells where she comes over all dizzy-like and has to sit down."

"She hasn't mentioned feeling unwell to me."

Ned saw a glimmer of a smile on the other man's face. "Not to rile you, Ned, but she doesn't think you can do much for her. She sees you as a boy, you know."

"A not very bright boy . . ." Ned amended.

"Maybe it'd be different if you was . . ."

"Let me guess. . . ."

"Married."

The judge stuck out his hand, and Ned solemnly shook it. The two men turned away without speaking, preparing to go their separate ways. But then, low over the wind, a moan floated through the air, as bodiless as a ghost. Ned felt a prickle on the back of his neck.

Turning back, the judge said in a low voice to Ned, "What was that? A cat? Or maybe . . . do you think it's the peeper?"

But Ned didn't answer. Listening hard, his eyes on the ground, he waited to hear if the sound would be repeated. When, after a moment or two, he heard nothing, he called, "Millicent?"

"Hey, you don't think . . ."

Glancing up, Ned said, "Get a lantern, will you, Judge?"

"Sure . . . sure thing."

Ned reached over the top of the gate to tug the latch

string. Since he knew the "peeper" was no one but himself, it followed that Millicent must be here somewhere. She'd probably come to check on Petey and then had fallen ill. He pictured her lying on the damp, cold ground and began to walk up the path more quickly, calling her name again on a note that even to himself sounded panicky.

He heard another groan and then a choked coughing, coming from the porch. The dim light coming from a moon buried in clouds revealed a dark figure sitting, hunched over, on the steps. "Millicent!"

He reached her and knelt down by her side. He slid his hand over her shoulder. The instant he touched her, he knew that this was not Millicent. He snatched back his hand, more appalled by the flash of knowledge—knowledge that could not be supported by any visible fact—than by his potentially misunderstood caress of a totally strange woman.

"Who are you?"

She only shook her head and groaned again, her shoulders bowed under the weight of her pain. A faint beam of moonlight fell down through a parting cloud. Ned saw that the hair that tumbled over the girl's shoulders reflected back even this subdued light in a way that Millicent's rich dark hair never could. The girl was a blonde.

Ned reasoned that he must have seen her hair without realizing it. His mind had acted too quickly for him to follow knowingly, telling him that someone other than Millicent sat there. It had not been through any mystical understanding. He'd been foolish to imagine anything else.

Suddenly the girl bent forward, putting her forehead against his arm. "I . . . oh, merciful Jesus!"

By the time Judge Cotton came back with the lantern, Mrs. Cotton in tow, the girl was wiping her mouth on Ned's handkerchief. She shrank back from the light, her hand shielding her eyes.

Mrs. Cotton's first words flabbergasted Ned. They were words he never dreamed he'd hear from her. She leaned down close to the girl, her sharp eyes as curious as a young cat's. "I don't know you, do I, child?"

*   *   *

Millicent found Jake Faraday halfway to his little house at the edge of the woods. She'd been calling his name steadily for half an hour, but she found him by tripping over his legs. He sat upright against a tree trunk, and he didn't make a sound even when the toes of her boots hit his calf. At first she'd thought a tree root had tripped her until she stood up, brushing off her grimed hands.

Her first thought was *Oh, mercy, don't let him be dead!* She knelt and said, "Marshal Faraday? Jake?"

Dull eyes rolled toward her. "I know you."

"Yes, it's Millicent Mayhew. Can you walk?"

"Sure." She waited for him to get up. "You mean, now?"

"If you don't mind."

Another moment passed. "Sorry," he said. "Don't think so." He leaned his head back against the tree trunk, his eyes closing slowly but inexorably, as though he no longer had any power to control them.

Millicent didn't try to budge him. She knew her female strength would be useless against the substantially built marshal. She couldn't begin to lift him, let alone drag him back to town. Neither, however, could she leave him here long enough to go back and get help. Already his big frame began to shake with fever.

"You wait here," she said. She made him lean forward, draping her shawl around him. It covered his shoulders but didn't stretch to close across the front. He crossed his arms on his chest, grasping the sides of the shawl, as his teeth began to chatter. Despite his size and the jut of his jaw, he looked as helpless as Petey.

"I'll get help."

As she stood up, one heavy hand came up to grasp her skirt. "Don't tell Antonia," he said, his voice strained and rasping. "Don't want her to know. Baby . . ."

His hand opened and fell to thud into the earth. Millicent left the lantern and set out down the road. Both Ned and Jake wanted to protect Antonia. Millicent did, too, but she did not approve of keeping a woman in the dark, especially if she expected her husband to come home. Thinking of the alarm Antonia must be feeling, Millicent caught up her skirts and ran.

"You'll never be able to lift him by yourself." Antonia's first reaction to the news Millicent panted out surprised her by being a calm acceptance. "Sit down and catch your breath a minute while I figure out what to do for him."

Millicent nodded and sat on a chair. The big red plush sofa in the middle of the main room had fascinated her when she'd been there for supper, but she felt a little leery of sitting on it. It didn't look like the sort of furniture married people ought to own, though she'd seen sofas like it in Colorado, in the sort of places a respectable girl was supposed to walk right on by. A lot, however, could be seen through windows just in passing.

"I'll have to help you with him." The petite blonde put her fists on her narrow hips as she thought out ways and means.

"I don't mean to be rude, Mrs. Faraday, but in your condition, hadn't you better—"

"My condition? Have you been talking to my brother?"

Millicent nodded, and Antonia laughed at her shamefaced expression.

"Well, why shouldn't you talk to him? But he doesn't have much opinion of me, does he? He still thinks of me as his flighty little sister who has to be coddled. I bet he told you not to tell me about this."

"So did Jake just now. It was about the only thing he did say. I do believe he's worrying more about you than himself."

"Men!" She went into the bedroom and came out quickly with a dark blue wool coat on. It wouldn't close in front anymore than Millicent's shawl had closed around her husband's shoulders, but it had style. She also wore a dark hat that Millicent recognized as being from the hands of a master milliner.

"Can you saddle a horse?" Antonia asked. "I think that would be the best thing. . . ."

"Of course, but we can't get your husband on a horse by

ourselves. . . ." She accepted Antonia's aid without any further hesitation.

"You leave that to me."

The marshal's big black horse looked as intimidating as the clouds hanging low in the sky. Millicent caught her breath as the highly vulnerable Antonia went up to the stall where he looked over the half-door. "There you go, boy," she said, holding up a sugar lump on the flat of her palm.

The horse lipped it off as gently as an old dog licking a loved child's face. The next time Antonia gave him the bit and worked the reins over the twitching ears. The horse obligingly lowered his head so she could reach him.

"I can't lift the saddle myself."

Millicent found the black horse to be as easy and obedient for her as for Antonia. He had none of less well-tempered animals' naughty tricks. He didn't hold his breath so that she couldn't cinch the saddle tight, he didn't dance out of range just as she got the tongue through the loop, or slash his tail at the rude person who tried to saddle him.

He also walked as docile as a dog on a lead behind the two women. Antonia carried a second lantern, peering beyond its circle to try to catch sight of her husband. "It's not far," Millicent said for the second time.

"He's never been sick since we got married," Antonia said, her voice less confident out here in the woods. "He's so big I think he just scares the evil spirits away."

"Evil spirits?"

Despite her worry, Antonia smiled. "Not real ones. Jake spent some time as an Indian fighter, and he picked up some of their ideas."

"I didn't know that about your husband."

"Oh, Jake's one of those deep waters we've been warned about. You know. Still waters run deep? Ned's another."

"Do you think so? I don't find Ned very deep."

"No? I bet you think he's just one of those happy-go-lucky men who never have a care. Really, Millicent . . ."

"That's not the way I think of him at all," Millicent answered, warmed and softened by Antonia's use of her first name. It seemed to imply that the acquaintance started over dinner last week might grow into a friendship. Millicent didn't dare hope for any closer relationship, like that of a sister by marriage.

She said, "I know Ned feels things down deep inside. But he's not going to let me or anyone see."

Antonia clicked her tongue against her teeth and flapped her free hand. "Men are all like that. You wouldn't believe how much trouble I had making Jake stand still long enough for him to catch me." Her smile faded. "That's one of his favorite jokes."

Though not the kind of person who felt comfortable displaying affection, Millicent slipped her arm around Antonia's shoulders and gave a squeeze. "He'll be all right. Ned will give him a tonic, or a purge, and he'll be fine."

"Thank you," Antonia said, squeezing back. "I only hope you're right."

As soon as they came upon the fallen lawman, Antonia went over to him and knelt down in the moist grass and wet earth. She grasped his slack hand and called his name. When he made no sign of hearing her, she looked up at Millicent in confusion. Her eyes were filling with tears that she made every effort to keep from falling. "Is he . . . ?"

Millicent felt for the pulse the way her grandmother had shown her. "Rapid and shallow," she said. "Best thing to do is get him to where Ned can watch over him. The City Hall's the best place. Caleb and Pete are already there unless Ned sent them home."

"Shouldn't we just take him home?"

"No . . . my house, maybe. But there are going to be a lot of people sick in this town by morning, I feel it in my bones. Best if we make things easy on Ned."

"Yes. You're right."

"Goodness," Millicent added, gazing down at the six-foot-three frame of the man at her feet. "What did you want to marry such a big man for? If I ever marry, I'll pick someone I can toss over my shoulder if he sickens on a night like this."

Smiling despite the tears that had overflowed her control,

Antonia said, "I was thinking about other kinds of nights when I married him. And I can't start complaining now."

They tried to pick him up, but his upper body was too heavy for them and his lower body just dangled. Finally Antonia played her last card. She took a deep, deep breath and said quickly in a loud, rough tone, "All right, all right, rise and shine your boots, boys. Ten'shun! Dress parade . . . mount!"

Jake pushed himself up from the ground and headed for his horse at a blind stumbling run. Millicent stared to see the big man, a moment ago nearly comatose, racing for a horse as if for his life and mounting with an easy swing of his left leg over the saddle. Then he sat, still as a mountain, his back perfectly straight.

"Once in the army . . ." Antonia said, a touch snidely. But then she closed her eyes to offer prayers of thanksgiving.

Ned came out to meet them on the steps of the jail as they tried to persuade Jake to dismount. The marshal noisily protested this unmilitary action. Millicent had never been so glad to see anyone in her life.

"He thinks he's in the army," she whispered. "And he doesn't want to come down."

"Why don't you just tell him to?"

"Antonia can't remember what they say. You don't know, do you?"

"No, the army is one experience I am glad to have missed."

"Then how do we get him down?"

"Let nature take its course." He pointed and Millicent turned to see the big man swaying in the saddle in wider and wider arcs. Ned stepped over, judging with his eyes the proper distance, direction, and probably speed with which the marshal would fall.

He held out his arms and braced his legs. All the same, the force of his brother-in-law's fall knocked him to the ground.

With Ned's help, the two women managed to carry the marshal into the jail. After arranging Jake on an iron cot, Ned turned to his sister. "You go home now, Antonia.

There's nothing you can do, and it's best for the baby if you're not here."

"Let me worry about the baby. Right now my husband needs me, and so do you. How many patients do you have right now?"

"Five, but only four of them are here."

"Five? And you're going to care for them all by yourself."

Millicent didn't wait for him to say he didn't need anyone's help. She said, "I'll be here, Antonia. There won't be anything you can do for your husband that I won't do."

Knowing Ned glared at her, she added, "But if you don't want to go back to your house . . . it's kind of lonely there . . . you can stay in mine. I don't figure I'll be gettin' home again till this is over."

Someone called for Dr. Castle, then, and all three of them looked toward the door. Mr. Grapplin, the stationmaster, held his pretty young wife in his arms, she lying against his shoulder as limp as cooked lettuce.

19

THEY MOVED THE ailing women upstairs as soon as they had beds for them. The lower level, where the men were housed, had already come close to capacity, with every cell containing two or more men. People brought their relatives in and, instantly seeing the need, went home for any extra cots, quilts, and supplies they could spare.

Ned's hardest job was persuading people that they would do no good by staying by their loved one's bedside. He'd seen hospitals where the nurses and doctors couldn't even get to the patient for the crowd of concerned family.

"It makes things too difficult," he explained to Millicent when she protested.

"But folks need to see friendly faces when they're feeling ill," she said, her arm around Mrs. Fleck's shoulders.

"I won't get in your way, Dr. Castle. But if anything was to happen . . . and me not there . . ." The landlady's pleading eyes went huge with the horror that she imagined. Catching back a sob, she pressed the back of her hand against her teeth so hard that they must have cut the flesh.

Ned wanted to be kind, but he had so much to do. Already his back and arms ached as though he'd been beaten with sticks. It had been more than three hours since he'd first walked into the jail. He looked helplessly at Millicent, hoping she'd know what to say.

She bent close to Mrs. Fleck's lopsided bonnet and said gently, "Most people are going to my house after they come here. Why don't you join them? Mrs. Cotton's there."

"Oh, I don't know. . . ." Mrs. Fleck spoke wearily, as though even that were too much effort, though at the same time she leaned back to sneak a look into the cell where her son moved restlessly on his bed.

Millicent turned Mrs. Fleck around and started walking with her to the door. "There's no one there who doesn't know exactly what you're going through, Mrs. Fleck. They've all got folks in here, all feeling just as low about them as you feel about Egbert. You go along and talk to 'em. Maybe you can make them feel a might more hopeful, seeing as we figure Egbert's had it longest. He'll be getting better first, too . . . you'll see."

Her voice soothed like a mother's. The little stream of unassertive kindly chatter could be listened to without any effort, when any effort at all seemed too much. Even Ned, fuming at her promises when he knew how hard they'd be to keep, couldn't keep from relaxing the strained muscles in his neck.

Mrs. Wilmot came out of the cell where one of her sons lay sick, though less severely so than Egbert. At once Millicent looked up and smiled, saying, "Oh, Mrs. Wilmot. Would you mind very much seeing Mrs. Fleck to my house? She don't feel up to going back to her own place."

Ned admired her deft diplomacy. The two mothers saw in each other a fount of comfort. Ned, a cynic, thought he saw each woman deciding in the same moment that she bore up much better than the other. And yet, he realized he forced himself to be cynical rather than feeling genuine distrust. When Mrs. Fleck and Mrs. Wilmot cried on each other's shoulders, their weeping mingled with that of the patients, he felt a breaking wave of shame crash over him.

Millicent came toward him as soon as they left. Her pace changed from a near-funeral glide as she escorted Mrs. Fleck to a brisk, swinging stride as she faced the task at hand.

To his surprise, Ned realized that he might not be so exhausted as he'd thought. He looked at her as though he'd never seen her before, yet he recognized every line of her lithe body. The way her shoulders and hips moved, the full freedom of her steps, the confident cock of her head, combined to render him amazed and silent.

Her full skirt had been marked when she'd knelt in the rotting leaves, the same ones that had clung to the back of Jake's shirt. Her hair had sprung loose from its bun, leaving crinkled strands for her to blow impatiently off her face. Yet under the dirty dress, her figure would have made a monk whistle. Ned's celibacy went the way of all flesh when the lamp on the floor illuminated the silhouette of her legs clearly beneath the muslin. If she wore a petticoat, it must have been muslin, too.

She put out her hands as she came near. He took them and held them lightly, knowing that if he allowed anything beyond that innocent touch, he'd be lost.

Her fingers returned the light pressure as she looked up into his face, trust shining in her eyes. "What are we going to do?" she asked in a near-whisper. "There's so many sick. . . ."

Keep your mind on the task at hand, Ned warned himself. *Ignore her pink lips and her soft skin. Ignore, too, that womanly heart so full of the devotion you need.*

"It's the fevers we have to watch for," he said after clearing his throat. "I've asked for ice to be bought from Mr. Schultz. The judge and the mayor have gone out to his farm."

"I remember him from when I was a little girl. I used to love watching them cut the blocks from his pond in the winter. He'll give them the ice."

"I hope so. We can use it to cool water for the patients. Give them as much water as they want, and if they don't want it, give it to them anyway."

His hands tightened without his thinking about it, and he drew her closer. "I appreciate your willingness to help out here, Millicent. It's not a pleasant task, I know."

"What else could I do? Other women have as much experience, but I . . ."

His lips moved against her hair. What fragrance perfumed her hair, as haunting as a half-remembered tune? "Yes? What about you?"

"I'm the only one that can work with you."

"Am I so difficult?" He told himself that a kiss pressed to her temple wouldn't exactly commit him to anything.

"No, but they still haven't made up their minds about you . . . and me. . . ."

He cupped her head in his hands, bringing up her chin. "Have you made up your mind?"

He kissed her soft mouth, gently, tenderly, persuasively. A long night stretched before him, filled with the basic bodily nursing that was the most exhausting kind of medical care. He needed this moment with Millicent, her lips eager under his, to remind them both that the human body was capable of pleasure as well as illness.

Treasuring up each breathless whisper of his name, he stroked with tender fingertips the delicate outer edge of her ears. She shivered, then grinned up into his eyes for a moment before nipping playfully at his lower lip. Then she placed her hands flat against his chest and moved away.

"Someone will see us. Besides, I'm sure somebody needs me."

"Right here," he said, feeling happier than any doctor with a jail full of patients ought to feel.

"Somebody sick," she amended.

"I'm sure I could work up a few symptoms. . . ."

Millicent stepped nimbly out of range of his questing hands. "Let's be serious, here, if we can."

"It's a strain. . . . Okay." He raised his hands in a gesture of grudging surrender. "Just so long as you realize this is only a postponement until after this crisis."

"Okay." She dropped her lashes over her sparkling eyes and then raised them again to fix him with a straightforward look. "Have you anything you can give them besides ice water? Everyone's complaining of sore joints and head-aches. If we could just take care of that, then folks could sleep maybe. Sleep's the best thing for them, right now."

"Yes, I've been thinking about it, and all I dare safely prescribe is a paregoric with a little laudanum. Unfortunately, I don't have enough to dose everyone."

"Can't you make some?"

"It's not just a matter of picking a few berries, Millicent."
As soon as the words left his lips, together with a wry tone
easily mistakable for sarcasm, he regretted them. He could
feel her retreating inside, though she hadn't taken a single
step away from him. Ned rushed to make some amend.

"Look, why don't you give the sickest people the stuff
I've got with me? I'll go back to my office and mix up
another batch as quickly as I can."

"All right. Who should I give it to?"

"You decide. I trust you to do what's right."

The sparkle in her eyes when he'd kissed her was nothing
compared to the diamond stars that shone there now. Ned
could have kicked himself for being so blind to her needs.
Of course she wanted to hear that he trusted her to do the
right thing. She had lost all faith in herself to deal with other
people after that debacle in Bear's Creek or whatever the
rotten little people of that place had called their rotten little
town. He could help her, just as he could help the sick.

"I do trust you," he repeated. "Utterly."

"Where's the paregoric?" she asked, holding her head up
with a new sense of pride that, oddly enough, he felt almost
as much as she did.

He didn't see her again for a long time. When he returned
from mixing up a kettle-full of camphorated mixture, she
had gone away to work among the women. Ned kept busy,
bringing water, refreshing the ice, and working his thermometer until he thought the thing might break from the
strain.

Yet all the time, Millicent filled his thoughts. Like a
lantern in his mind, bright and shining, the thought of her
illuminated parts of himself he'd kept dark for too long. He
earned a reputation that night for a gentle bedside manner
that made him laugh ruefully when he heard about it later.

When midnight came, the men in the jail had finally
quieted down. He stood by the window in the outer office,
the shutters thrown open, and looked out into the night, only
vaguely wishing for a cigar. Then someone spoke to him out
of the darkness, a rasping voice painful to listen to. But the
harsh tone didn't come from vomiting, like so many of the

voices he'd heard this night. This voice had earned its grating texture by endless drinks, scoured to dryness by the harshness of rotgut whisky.

"Yes, it's me," Ned said. "Doc Partridge?"

The man shuffled forward into the lantern light shed by the open window. He screwed up his eyes and peered from under his raised hand. "I came up 'cause I heard about what's happening."

"I've got fifteen men and about as many women here, all sick as they can be."

Ol' Doc Partridge—Ned realized with a sense of shock that his predecessor couldn't be more than fifty—licked his dry lips, strangely like a little boy who desperately wanted to be asked to play, despite his gray hair and sprouting cheeks. He had tugged up the collar of his ragged coat to conceal the fact that he wore no shirt over his grimy union suit. His wrists protruded nakedly from the sleeves and his boot sole flopped when he took an eager step forward.

"I don't suppose you could use . . ."

"Another pair of hands would be a godsend, man. Come in."

Ned went and opened the jailhouse door for him. Doc Partridge gave a nervous laugh as he stepped over the threshold. "I've been here once or twice of late, but always as a guest."

Quickly Ned said, "There's not much we can do for our patients right now. Just wait for the fevers to break."

Partridge nodded his head. "That's half the job," he said. "Waiting for fevers to break and babies to come. Never cared for waiting. Gives a man too much time to think."

Without appearing to do so, Ned took a quick, measuring look at Partridge's hands. They were clean, strangely out of keeping with his unkempt appearance. As a matter of fact, they looked as though they'd been washed only moments before, the edges of his sleeves still dark where water had splashed.

Partridge must have noticed the direction of Ned's glance after all, for he rubbed his palms together. "Even cleaned my fingernails," he said. "I may not be a doctor anymore, but I know that much has changed."

"No offense," Ned said, with a man-to-man smile.

"None taken. Don't blame you at all. Now, what can I do?"

Millicent had no time to rest or gaze out of windows. Used to sick-nursing from when her grandmother had been ill, as well as caring for Petey, she would have thought she could handle just about anything. How wrong could one person be?

"Millicent, could you . . . ?"

"Miss Mayhew, if you wouldn't mind . . ."

"Oh, God! Millicent!"

After a little while she began to wish that she had wings on her heels, for her arches and her back ached in shifts. But getting cranky would only put her in the wrong. She couldn't expect people as sick as this to be reasonable, so it stood to reason she had to be. She followed the doctor's orders to the letter, encouraging, cajoling, and insisting that they drink plenty of water. Some of her patients she suspected feigned sleep when she came by.

About midnight she sat on the cot of Amabelle Cartwright, twelve-year-old daughter of the town undertaker. The girl, not yet budding, had awakened with a nightmare. Millicent had gone in to comfort her and quiet her, so she wouldn't wake the others in the judge's chamber. There were three other girls in the spacious room, one in a spare cot, two on mattresses laid on the floor.

Amabelle had crawled onto Millicent's lap like a toddler, whimpering. She smoothed the sweat-stringy hair back from the girl's forehead, rocking her gently. Someday, no doubt, Petey would come looking for comfort in just this way, heavy with sleep, muddled with fragments of dreams that seemed to have escaped into the real world. She would offer him all she had in the way of security, her own body protection enough, at least from dreams.

"Petey . . ."

Deep in her own thoughts, for a moment the spoken word

did not register. Millicent stilled, Amabelle heavy against her shoulder. She decided she'd said it herself or had only believed she'd heard his name because he had been in her mind already.

She remembered the way he looked asleep in his cradle, his arms and legs flat against the mattress, his cheek pushed forward so his tiny lips pouted as though he were blowing her a kiss. Sometimes his bottom stuck up in the air, and she would grin at the sight of him, storing the image in her heart.

One of the girls on the floor shifted restlessly, throwing her arm over her blond head. A choked sound came from her throat as if she strangled on a cough.

Concerned that the girl was about to be sick again, Millicent maneuvered Amabelle off her lap to lay her down on her pillow. Amabelle made the same sort of half-spoken protest that the girl on the floor made, as if they were talking not so much in their sleep as from their deepest dreams. It was like hearing someone speak while under water.

Standing, Millicent held still and waited. She didn't want to interfere with anyone's sleep, for they needed it so. Amabelle quieted down and the girl on the other cot hadn't moved since Millicent had come in. Her breathing came deep and slow, without a hitch. The second girl on the floor also slept soundly, though every so often she'd kick out like a bullfrog swimming.

Millicent sighed. If no one here needed her anymore, she felt certain somebody in another room waited for her with fretful impatience.

She tiptoed toward the door, avoiding the fat roll of Turkish carpet lying between the desk and the door. The judge hadn't wanted anyone getting sick on the birthday present the Faradays had sent all the way to Chicago for. Millicent had just eased open the office door when she heard, "Petey!"

Which girl had said it?

The blonde on the floor said, "No!" and thrust out a hand as though warding something off. Her hands tightened into fists. "No, Mama, no!"

Millicent turned about and knelt down by the girl's side. The kindest thing to do would be to awaken her, gently. Grandma's receipt book had strict rules about waking sleepwalkers, but it said nothing about sleep-talkers. It might not be kind to let the girl stay in her nightmare, but Millicent wanted to hear more.

"Mustn't know . . . don't tell . . ." Millicent felt she heard the cry of a lonely spirit, a voice too private for another's ears.

Sweat gleamed on the girl's cheekbones and throat. Mottled red now by fever, her skin must have been naturally pale. Millicent could see the beating pulse of the blue vein at the girl's temple. Her blond hair lay spread loosely on the pillow, and the comforter she'd thrown aside revealed that she wore a chemise and petticoat buttoned together at the waist instead of the nightgowns the other female patients wore. Of course, their relations had brought those. Maybe no one knew that this girl was even here. Maybe no one would look for her.

When the girl spoke again, Millicent's knees were tight from kneeling so long on the hard pine floor. This time the sleeping girl said, "No, Papa! I don't . . ." It all trailed off into a frustrating murmur.

Millicent laid the back of her hand against the girl's hot forehead. Her hands were always a little colder than other folks'. "There, now," she said in as comforting a tone as she could manage. "There."

The girl sighed, as deep and as sorrowful as if all the evils in the world had found her. "It's not right," she said very softly but clearly.

"No, it isn't," Millicent agreed.

"Where am I to go?"

"I don't know. . . ."

"Oh . . ." The girl rolled over on her side, and Millicent had to move back. She did it in a crabwise manner, not wanting to rise until the girl had said something more.

Millicent waited, getting pins and needles in her feet. When the prickly feeling of numbness started spreading up her calves, Millicent decided on more direct action.

She leaned forward with great care, being careful not to overbalance. She had to put down her hand quickly once to stop from toppling over as she whispered, "What's wrong? Why are you sighing?"

No answer dropped from the girl's mouth. Millicent, highly critical, looked her over trying to decide if she were good enough to be Petey's mother. She couldn't be more than twenty, with the strong hands and forearms of a farm girl, sturdy despite her illness, though a little on the thin side. Feeling ill for a day or two would account for that as well as the bruiselike circles under her eyes. Millicent wondered if those eyes when opened would be a pretty slate blue.

Just as she stood up to allow some feeling back into her legs, the girl's voice came again, more mournful still. "Please . . . don't take him away. . . ."

Tears slipped from beneath the closed lids, dripping like sad spring rain from the girl's long eyelashes. Millicent did not have to rack her brains to remember who else had eyelashes like that, almost long enough to scrape the roof of his cradle.

Millicent left the room before she did something she might regret. She had to find Ned, to learn who had brought that girl in, and to settle for once and for all the question of Petey's future. Though she had to stop several times before she could go down the stairs to the jail, she answered each question or solved each difficulty with diplomacy or a glass of creek water.

She looked in every cell. Most held two or three men, lying fast asleep. How she wished their wives and daughters were as sensible. Though she conscientiously checked every room, underneath it all Millicent guessed where Ned would most likely be. Hovering over the bedside of Egbert Fleck, popularly known as Ed.

She peeked around the dividing wall between the cell on the end and the one next door. At once she hurried in. Instead of the calm scene she expected, she saw chaos.

Ned stood at the head of the bed, holding a spoon in his right hand. The color and most of all the smell gave the presence of paregoric away. She'd almost gotten used to the throat-closing odor of camphor by now, but not quite.

Egbert thrashed around on the bed. "Don't want it," he protested, slapping the spoon out of Ned's hand. The medicine left a black blot on the whitewashed wall.

"It will make you feel better," Ned promised.

"Want to die. . . ."

Millicent stood over him with her hands on her hips. "Die? Certainly not!"

Ned brushed the fallen hair out of his eyes with his other hand. He'd taken off his jacket, his tie dangled, his eyes were bloodshot and heavy. Millicent thought he looked like a god after a hard day's creation. "He won't die," he said, "but he'll feel much better after he's had a dose of this!"

"No. Won't take it."

"That's enough, young man," Millicent said. "You've got to take your medicine."

She walked over, took the spoon and bottle gently from Ned's hands. Steadily she poured out a new dose. "Catch his hands," she said to Ned and put the spoon to the boy's highly colored lips as soon as he did so. "Are you going to open your mouth?"

Ed said, "No . . ." Just as his lips closed around the long vowel sound, Millicent slipped in the spoon. Ed coughed and sputtered, protesting that he hadn't been ready, that it wasn't fair that the circus had started already; he wanted his money back. Sobbing weakly, he subsided into sleep.

Ned drew Millicent out of earshot of the bed. "It's bad," he said shortly. "His fever's pushing one hundred and four. Much more and he'll start having convulsions."

"Con . . . you mean . . . ?"

"Fits, I guess is as good a word as any."

"Fits? Fevers and fits?" she said to herself.

Ned went on without regarding her absentmindedness. "I'm going to have to send for his mother; she ought to know. Millicent, do you think you could possibly—"

"Listen, Ned," she said, taking him by the arm so tightly that he wondered if he would find little black bruises on his biceps the next day. "I know what you think of me and my works, but I think I saw something in Grandma's books about herbs."

"I've got sick people here, Millicent. Now is not the time to start planning a salad."

"Don't be so . . . what's the word? Irksome."

"Irksome? Is that the best you can do?"

"I'm in a hurry, Ned. Shush up and let me explain."

He laughed shortly. "Consider me shushed."

"I'm going to look in Grandma's book," she said. "If what I think I read is true, we might not have to worry so much about the fever. What I think you should worry about is how you're going to tell me about Petey's mother."

She had gone outside, swirling her shawl around her, before he could ask her what she meant. *He* didn't know anything about Petey's mother. He turned back toward Egbert, replacing the blankets around the boy. Now the hardest waiting began, either for the first convulsion to take over the boy's body or the first drops of sweat that would signal the breaking of the fever.

20

MILLICENT CAME BACK within fifteen minutes, a canning jar in her hand, half-full of the nastiest, sloppiest-looking mess that Ned had ever seen. Mrs. Fleck followed her close on her heels, her pale face haggard in the lamplight.

The landlady flung herself on her knees by her son's bedside. "Ed? Ed, it's Mama, sweetheart." She stroked her hand over his forehead. "He's burning up! Why does he have all these blankets?" she demanded, starting to pull them off.

"Don't do that, Mrs. Fleck," Ned said, putting his hand on her shoulder. "They'll help the fever to break."

Turning again to Millicent, he glanced down at the jar she held. "What the devil's that?"

"Willow-bark tea. The last batch my grandmother brewed."

"Willow-bark tea? For God's sake, Millicent, do we have to sink into the Middle Ages?"

She stood up to him like a tigress. "Do you have anything better to offer, Dr. Castle? Because if you do, I guess this is the time for it."

Ned shook his head, not because he didn't have anything to say, but because he was afraid of saying too much. Though he'd once smashed a bottle full of a mixture she'd brought to a bedside, he didn't want to do that again. He knew it would mean smashing the fragile understanding between them as well. He would have to trust her again, this time with an unknown elixir.

"All right then," she went on, just as if he'd offered another argument. "Lots of folks swear by this tea. It helped me when I was sick as a dog at the end of March. And even if it's no good, at least it means we tried. Whatever happens, at least we tried *something!*"

Ned stepped back to let her pass to Ed's side. "It's on your head then," he said in a whisper for her ears only. "Not mine."

"Don't worry about it," she said in a hard voice that rang like a steeple bell. "No one will blame you, no matter what."

She tasted the stuff herself, on a fingertip. "It's strong from sitting so long," she said, addressing herself to Mrs. Fleck, or the ceiling, anyone or anything besides Ned. "We'll give him half a spoonful, instead of a whole one. If it's not enough, we'll give him some more in an hour."

"I hope it works," Mrs. Fleck said fervently.

"Better pray," Millicent answered and flicked a glance toward Ned. "For Ed and me both," she added.

The thing, when it happened, did not come as a miracle in the sense that the change came instantaneously. Millicent gave the boy the tea—closer to syrup by now—from the jar with the same spoon as before. His mother got him to open his mouth this time. Then Millicent left the room to tend her patients, leaving the jar behind.

An hour passed, slowly. Every moment Ned expected to hear a cry from Mrs. Fleck, who remained with her son. Ned came back often from pacing in the hall or helping someone, only to find no change.

Then Mrs. Fleck said, "I think he's cooler. Feel."

Ned laid his hand on the boy's forehead. "No, I don't . . . Let me get my thermometer."

He didn't like taking people's temperatures when they were so ill. There'd been ugly stories when he'd been a student about fever patients biting the ends off thermometers. Ed submitted quietly, however.

Ned raised the glass tube to his eyes. The numbers were tiny, almost too small even for his excellent sight. "That can't be right," he said aloud. He shook the mercury down a second time.

"What is it?"

"One hundred and two, or nearly that anyway."

He shot a puzzled glance toward the muck in the jar.
"No . . . it's impossible. It must have been that last dose
of paregoric. It must have been. . . ."

In that case, however, his scientific mind argued back,
*how is it that none of your other patients, into whom you've
been ladling paregoric as though it were soup, have shown
a similar improvement?*

"He *is* better, isn't he, Dr. Castle?" Mrs. Fleck asked,
looking between his face and the glass tube in his hands.

"What? Oh, yes. He seems to be. Needs watching still, of
course."

He'd do it, by Godfrey!

Half the male patients in the jail were awakened half an
hour later by Dr. Castle. He took their temperature, making
a notation on a scrap of paper. Then he gave them a spoonful
of something that smelled and tasted like swampwater.
Later still, he woke them again to take their temperature
once more. At the same time he took two sets of temperatures from the other patients, the ones he had not dosed with
willow-bark tea.

Millicent heard the complaints as she reached the lower
level on her errand for more ice. A voice floated out into the
hall from the cell nearest the staircase, "Just dozed off, too,
when he comes around *again* with that there thing, tellin'
me to open my mouth for it."

Millicent peered in the cell. There were two beds set up
in it, piled with gray blankets that she recognized from
Wilmot's storeroom.

"Happened to me, too," the other patient complained
shakily. "Took forever to get it to work, too. . . ."

"Quit grousing." The grizzled man in the ragged jacket
straightened up from the head of the bed, where he'd been
shaking out one man's pillow. "You always were one for
sour-mouthing other people, Bill Cobbett. Hey, don't you
still owe me for that last child you and your wife had?"

"I . . . I paid you, didn't I, Doc? Sure, sure I did."

"Dr. Partridge?" Millicent asked uncertainly.

He turned around and she recognized him. He'd once been tall and straight, an ebony column in his dark suit and high silk hat, a frightening figure to a child. Now he looked more like an object of pity.

"I'm Millicent Mayhew. Roberta Mayhew's granddaughter?"

He nodded. "Yes, I see a likeness. Your grandmother was one of the finest women I ever knew. I was sorry to hear of her death."

"Thank you." He must have been drunk the day she died, and just as drunk every day thereafter. Yet some remnants of gentlemanly behavior lingered. Millicent wondered if he could teach Ned Castle a few things.

"If you're looking for Dr. Castle—" he began.

"I'm not. I'm looking for ice. . . ."

"He's in the marshal's office, correlating some figures."

"Figures?"

"Temperatures. It seems willow-bark tea may lower fevers."

He coughed then, his shoulders shaking. When the spasms passed, he drew his hand over his mouth, the pressure of his fingers pulling his lips to one side. "Working hard gives a man a thirst, doesn't it, Miss Mayhew?"

She didn't answer. A fever ailed him for which her grandmother had known no cure. Perhaps Doc Partridge saw pity in her eyes, for he ducked his head, avoiding her gaze. "The marshal's office is at the end of the hall."

Ned only raised his head from the desk when Millicent stood beside him, casting her shadow over him. "You should lie down," she said gently. "It's pretty quiet now. You could sleep for an hour or two."

"I could sleep for fifteen years," he said, straightening up. He rubbed the back of his neck as he twisted the kinks out of his shoulders.

"Let me," she said, coming around behind him.

His shoulders were wide from front to back as well as across his body. Her fingers were hardly up to covering so much territory, but she tried her best, while he sighed under her hands. Millicent concentrated on bringing him this pleasure, expressing how much she loved him through the motions of her hands. Even when he was being so stubborn he could give lessons to a mule, she still loved him.

"It's not fair," he said, closing his eyes in painful bliss. "You've been working just as hard as I have. The second you're finished with me, it's your turn."

"You tempt me. I might stop now." Millicent lifted her hands an inch away from his shirted back.

"No, don't." Without turning, he reached above and around his shoulder, capturing her hand, and dragging back to the twanging tendons in his neck. "Right there. God, that's good."

She loved how she could make his voice crack with a touch. What would he do if she leaned down and kissed the top of his ear? A prickle of excitement ran over her skin like the touch of his hands.

"You really ought to lie down," she said again, the sultriness of her tone a complete surprise to her.

"After I'm done recording these temperatures."

"What temperatures? The ones Doc Partridge mentioned? About the fevers?"

The muscles in his neck that had relaxed jumped back into tension. She could feel the change under her hands. "He told you about that?"

"Shouldn't he have?"

"No, it's not a secret. I just wanted to know for sure."

"Know what?"

"Whether or not your tea works, I mean *really* works."

"I told you it did. And Ed's better, isn't he?"

"Yes, he's better. His temperature is still high but not dangerous."

"Well, that's a blessing, anyhow. Then I'll go ahead and give the tea to everybody now?"

"No, you can't."

"What? If it works, then everyone has a right to it. I can't keep it to myself; it wouldn't be charitable."

"Millicent, I just want to make sure the stuff works. The best way to do that is to keep one set of patients free of whatever it is we're testing. You see . . ." He paused while he tried to think of how to explain the scientific method in language she would understand.

But she leaped on what he'd said already. "You're planning to keep some folks sick? Why in heaven's name would you want to do that? You're a doctor."

"No, you don't understand. How can you? Science is completely alien to your way of thinking."

"Because I'm a woman? I'll have you know——"

He waved both hands at her while screwing up his eyes as though he found her suggestion painful. "No, it's got nothing to do with your sex. It's just . . ." He pushed his hair back while he thought. Then he said, more calmly, "Look, science . . . science has to know *why*. That's the basic question."

"Why?" she asked disbelievingly.

"Look, do you know why I became a doctor?" He went on without waiting. "When I was a boy, I used to drive my governesses wild with my ceaseless asking why. 'Why is the sky blue?' 'Why aren't there flowers in the winter?' 'Why do people die?' At some point they'd usually say, 'Because God made them like that.' It never satisfied me. It still doesn't."

"And you became a doctor to find out?"

"Among other reasons, yes. But mostly because it seemed the best way to find out most, if not all, of my 'whys?' How was I to know that every answer leads to another question? For you, it is enough to say, this plant cures or alleviates this problem, therefore we'll use it. But for me, for science, that isn't enough. I still want to know why."

"Maybe you need to have more faith."

"Religion is only more unanswered questions."

"I didn't say religion. I said faith. Have faith that your questions will be answered one day and maybe they won't torment you so much."

He laughed dryly. "That's not good enough. Take this stuff." He tapped the jar so that it gave out a faint ring. "How do I know it works?"

"Well, you saw Ed Fleck's fever go down, didn't you?"

"But how do I know that this concoction was responsible?"

"You just do."

"See what I mean? It could be a coincidence or a fluke. The only way to know for sure is to experiment. The best experiment is one in which not even the doctor knows which group of patients got which substance. It's called a blind test. I can't do that here; I'd need more help."

"What's next best?"

"I give half of a selected group the tea and the other half nothing but what I've been giving them. Then I compare their temperatures to each other. If there's a difference, and all other variables are the same, then the only variable that is different must be responsible for the change. Do you understand that?"

"And then you give the second group the tea?"

"No, they'll never get it. That would invalidate the test."

She stared at him, trying to see his point of view and failing utterly. She whispered her thought, "What if someone dies . . . ?"

Ned clasped and unclasped his hands in a gesture of resignation and silently shook his head.

"I want to understand," she said. "Truly and for certain I do. But I can't. Those aren't just folks out there. They're your neighbors. They'd be your friends if you'd let them."

"You're a fine one to talk to me about that, Millicent. Are they your friends?"

"It's not for want of their tryin' to be. I just . . . At least I'm standing up for them now."

"You don't have to stand up for them against me, Millicent."

He stood up and came around the corner of the marshal's desk. She shrank back from him as if he'd become horrible to her. "Oh, come on," he said, catching her hands. "I know it sounds cruel and I know how much you hate any kind of cruelty, but think for a minute. If willow-bark tea works to stop fevers, think what a boon that could be for the whole world. People die from this kind of thing all the time, even small children. This experiment could be the first step in stopping that."

"Not at the price of one of my neighbors' lives," she said, her determination softly stated but completely sincere.

"And all those other people out in the world, Millicent? You might not know them, but aren't they your neighbors, too? Or does your compassion stop at the city limits?"

She tried to pull her hands free, but it didn't serve her for he had an arm around her waist. "You twist everything around," she protested, struggling feebly. "I don't know the rights and wrongs of it; you're too smart."

"I'm not so smart," he said, his voice taking on a dangerously tender note that had the effect of stilling her struggles while her mental panic increased.

Only she knew how close she was to giving in to him physically; if he kissed her now he'd know it, too. There would be no way to keep him from knowing it, for, despite her resentment over his professional callousness, Millicent knew that if he kissed her again, she'd give him her heart along with her lips.

"Please don't," she said, her voice tight with tears she did not want to shed.

Perhaps he realized that she meant it, for he released her at once. "You're right. This isn't the time for . . . what is it Mrs. Cotton calls it? Canoodling?"

"No. It isn't."

"Now, wait a minute," he said in response to her tone. He put his crooked finger under her chin and tilted it up so he could look into her eyes. "Don't get any funny ideas, Millicent. We're still—"

"Still what, Ned?" She tossed her head, freeing herself and turning away. "Friends? Or is it allies?"

"All of that. What else do you want from me?"

"Nothing. I don't want anything from you. Not that you have anything I want."

"Millicent . . ."

"Oh, just stop! We've let things go too far. I never should have let you kiss me in the first place."

"Why did you?"

"I don't know now. It seemed like a good idea, that's all."

"Yes, it did. And to me, it still seems like a good idea. You've fascinated me from the first, you know. There you were, this beautiful woman with no friends, no lover, not even family. I wondered about you, a woman of mystery in the heart of Culverton, a town that seemed to talk every other mystery to death."

"You do talk sweet, Dr. Castle." Millicent kept her back to him, afraid of his discernment. He came up close behind her, talking softly.

"I was fascinated," he said again. "Until you started getting in my way."

"Oh? I can make it so you're not troubled anymore."

He laid his hands gently on her shoulders, began moving his thumbs in a circle on the stressed muscles. Millicent felt her insides melt as she leaned against the pressure.

Ned went on speaking, each word in keeping with this on-again, off-again seduction they had between them. "I disliked you then, but I couldn't stop thinking about you. You were driving me crazy and even I didn't know why. The first time I kissed you wasn't the first time I'd wanted you, Millicent."

She had no answer to that but a sigh.

His voice held a smile. "What are we going to do about it? The way I see it, we've got just two choices. . . ."

"Always so clear-minded," she said driftingly.

"We can part, or we can make love."

"Impossible."

"Which one?"

"Either one."

"You're right," he said, bringing her against his body, his arms sweeping around her waist. "But if we go on like this, one of us is going to wind up insane, and I'm afraid it's going to be me."

"I've beaten you to it." She turned in the circle of his arms, her skirts hiking in a twisted bunch. "Oh, Ned. I don't want to be in love with you."

"Are you?"

"I . . ." At the last instant she showed yellow. "I don't know. Sometimes I think I might be, and then . . ."

"Then I make you crazy again? Now you know how I feel."

She looked up into his eyes, the blue of the windswept sky, and saw that he, too, stood hesitating on the very brink of love. If she were clever, she'd know how to make him fall for her. Among all her grandmother's receipts, there had not been a formula for attracting the right man.

"Ned," she began, forestalling the kiss she saw he intended. "Will it ruin your experiment if we give the willow-bark tea to all the women and girls upstairs? At least we could help them."

After a moment's thought, while Millicent held her breath, he agreed. "But only if I can take their temperatures before and after."

Loving him then, she laughed up into his face. "You're impossible yourself, you know that?"

"So I've been told. Now kiss me."

21

WHILE FOLLOWING MILLICENT upstairs, carrying the tea jar, his thermometer case, and a notebook, Ned asked, "What did you mean about Petey's mother before?"

Millicent stopped short, carefully holding on to the banister as she looked down at him. "I think she's here."

She told him what the blond girl had said while in a fever. "She definitely said his name and something about not telling her father. What does that sound like to you?"

"It could mean anything," he said, just to reassure her. "Think about it. Her beau's name might be Petey, and she could have quite a different reason for not wanting Papa to know." When she looked blank, he said teasingly, "I'm willing to show you what I mean any time you say the word."

With the half-exasperated, half-charmed smile she kept only for him, Millicent said, "Be serious. I want you to see her and tell me who brought her here. If she's awake, I think we ought to find out her name and where she lives. Then we can ask Mrs. Cotton about her. She knows everything about everyone."

"Not quite everyone. There was this girl last night . . . I found her on your doorstep of all places."

"You don't suppose . . . She might have come to my house before. I kept feeling like there was somebody watching me."

Ned cleared his throat but felt no overwhelming impulse

to confess his part in her "peeper" scare. "Let's go ask some questions," he suggested.

The white light of dawn brightened the windows of the judge's chamber. Amabelle Cartwright blinked and sat up when Millicent opened the door. "Is it time to get up?" she asked.

"No, honey, go back to sleep," Millicent whispered automatically. To Ned, behind her, she said softly, "She's the one on the left."

But the blanket on the mattress lay flat and smooth without anyone under it. Her mind slowed by lack of sleep, Millicent stared for a long time at the bed unable to believe what she saw. Once she even gave it a furtive pat, just to be sure her eyes were not fooling her.

"Amabelle," Millicent said, still keeping her tone moderate though only by a great effort. "Where's the other girl that was here?"

The twelve-year-old yawned. "I don't know. Out back, maybe?"

Ned asked, "How are you feeling this morning, Amabelle?"

The girl winced as she moved her arms. "Everything still hurts," she said in surprise.

"Yes, it will for a while, but I have something now that night help."

"Yeww, what's that?"

The other two girls still in the room sat up then, bleary-eyed and full of complaints. "What's going on? Can't you see we're tryin' to sleep?"

Ned called Millicent over from the desk, where she seemed to be looking for something. "What are you looking for?"

"There was a dress here last night, hanging off the judge's chair as if to dry. I can't see it now."

"I saw it. That girl put it on," the other girl who was bedded down on the floor said. "She slid out of here a while ago, moaning and sighing fit to wake the dead."

"Didn't wake me," the second girl boasted.

"See?"

Millicent asked, "Did the girl say anything? Did she see you had woken up?"

"No, she didn't say a word that made any sense. Tell you true, I don't reckon she felt any stronger than I do, and if someone told me I had to get dressed and walk, I'd purely break down and cry."

Millicent waited until Ned had finished taking their temperatures, recording each figure carefully in his book. Then, despite their protests over the taste, he dosed them with the willow-bark tea. He consoled them by saying that their breakfast would be along soon. After that, he bowed Millicent out through the door ahead of himself.

"What are we going to do about that girl, Ned?"

"There's nothing we can do, not right now."

"But she's out there somewhere, sick."

"And there's close to twenty more, right here, just as sick. We'll take care of them first, then when we have someone here to take over, we can do something about her. All right?"

"I guess so. But . . . there's one more thing, though it's not for me to say. . . ."

"What?" He took her hand in a gentle clasp, swinging it lightly. "Go on."

"Don't you think you ought to give that thermometer a rub with something after you stick it in somebody's mouth?"

He looked startled. "To shine it up?"

"To clean it off," she stated, with maybe a hair more emphasis than he thought really necessary.

"It's clean. Would you like to see?"

"No, I believe you. It's just that I wouldn't want something under my tongue that's been in somebody else's mouth, especially if they've been sicking up all night."

"Squeamish? You?"

"A person's stomach is only as strong as his head, or is it the other way around?"

"You are tired," Ned said, stealing his arm around her waist. "You should go rest; I can do the rest of these patients myself."

"What if the girl does turn out to be Petey's mother . . . his *real* mother . . . ?"

He tried to make his voice soothing and persuasive. "Everything will keep until later. You're exhausted, Millicent. Come to think of it, so am I. As much as it pains me to admit it, you could lie down next to me right now and be as safe from ravishment as if you were on an iceberg adrift in the North Sea."

"Okay, then, let's go to the boardinghouse."

"What? Why would you want to go there?"

"You have a bed, don't you? And going to bed is the only thing I'm interested in right now."

Amazing how even her commonplace attitude had an arousing effect on him. Ned mentally reviewed, with astonishing speed, just how disarranged his room had been when he'd left it that morning. He didn't believe it was too disreputable, but his bed was only big enough for one. That image, of them both squeezed together on his narrow bed, made his earlier interest in her look on a level with a schoolboy's first innocent realization that there are two sexes for a very good reason. Reasons he had no business picturing.

"I will gladly lend you my latchkey, Millicent, if you feel you won't get what you need—I mean, if you think you won't get enough rest at your house."

"You haven't seen my house. This jail is less crowded. Every woman who has a husband, child, or distant cousin sick in here has made my house their home. I don't even have any bacon fat left—when I ran over there last night, they were frying doughnuts!"

"Did you bring any with you? I think my stomach has forgotten its proper function in life, it's been so long since I ate."

"Mine, too. Were you lying when you said breakfast would be here soon? Or did you make some arrangements to feed everybody?"

"I'm relying on Mrs. Cotton. She won't have forgotten about us."

He was right. As they were giving the last dose of tea in

the jar to Maisie Grapplin, they heard a loud halloo from the front hall. When they came down the stairs, folks were coming in, their arms laden with baskets and dinner pails. Some men were carrying sawhorses and planks to make tables. Mayor Wilmot led the way, pushing a wheelbarrow across the parquet floor. The wheelbarrow overflowed with bed trays.

Millicent had eyes only for Mrs. Cotton, who carried Petey on her shoulder. She left Ned to greet the helpers and to yearn after a hot meal, while she made her way through the crowd.

"Land sakes, child, you look like a stewed string bean. Didn't you get a wink of sleep last night?"

"I kept busy," Millicent answered, reaching for the baby. Cradling him in her arms, she said in wonder, "He *couldn't* have gotten bigger just since yesterday!"

Petey kicked lightly through his long dress, reaching for her with spread fingers. "There you are, oh, there you are!" Millicent said delightedly. "Look, he's smiling at me."

"Of course he is. I never believe it's just gas." She smiled kindly at Millicent. "I brung his bottle along. I reckoned you'd like to feed him."

"Oh, yes, thank you. But not with all this racket."

They'd begun hammering something under the tall windows that ran along one side of the entrance hall. Ned stood over there, talking animatedly with the judge. Millicent tried to attract his attention, but he didn't look her way.

Mrs. Cotton took her by the arm and said, "Why not go outside and sit on the steps? It's quieter and the fresh air'll do you a world of good."

Watching Petey eat revived her more than the fresh spring morning. Millicent rocked him gently and watched with hungry eyes his growing contentment.

"I think he missed you," Mrs. Cotton said, sitting next to them on the stone steps.

"Do you?" Millicent said eagerly. "Do you really think so?"

"It's natural to miss folks who love you and who you love. Little Petey never takes his milk like that from me."

"I think he does like me." In a softer, more reflective tone, Millicent said, "He's done so much for me."

"For you? What could a baby do for you?"

Millicent met the older woman's eyes and smiled wisely. "You know exactly what I mean, Mrs. Cotton. I was turning into a sour old maiden lady with about as much niceness in me as you'll find in a stone in your shoe. Now . . . things have changed."

She expected Mrs. Cotton to mention Ned, but the older woman surprised her. "I figured that child might be the making of you."

"Then you don't think I did the wrong thing in keeping him?"

"Why, no. I never thought that. But . . ." As though a cloud had come over, Mrs. Cotton's friendly face grew concerned. "But you'd be doing a wrong thing in a-keepin' him permanent."

"Why?" Millicent asked, cuddling the baby closer.

"You missed him last night, and you've only had the caring of him. What must his mother be feelin', who had the carrying of him? How she must miss him now. You've gotten his first smiles."

"Everyone talks about his mother as though she's a suffering saint. We don't even know . . ." The memory of that girl's troubled face, her frightened words, came back to Millicent. She knew that if she didn't do everything possible to help that girl those images would haunt her forever. Petey's mother did want him, wanted him desperately.

"What is it, child?"

"That girl you and Ned found last night, on my doorstep. Is she the one, do you reckon?"

"I reckon. She wouldn't give her name. Sick as she was, she held it back. As soon as everyone's been given breakfast, I'm going to have a talk with her."

"She might be gone."

"Gone?" Mrs. Cotton repeated. "Where to?"

"Wherever she came from. Look, was she wearing a gray homespun dress? And she was blond, or fair anyway?"

"That's her."

"Well, she's gone. Still sick, too."

"Have you looked for her?"

"No. Ned and I have been busy."

Mrs. Cotton shook her head. "It's a bad business. You'll have to keep a sharp eye out for her, and if she comes to your house again, you're going to have to coax her in."

"My house?"

"Of course. She's been there a time or two already. She's bound to come back to see him." She put out a hand to twitch Petey's blanket closer to his trunk. "Such a little lamb. We'll get your mama back soon, don't you fret. And a papa, too, if we have to comb the woods for him."

"That's right," Millicent said in some surprise. "There must be a father around, too, mustn't there?"

"For sure—unless somebody's planning to write another Testament," Mrs. Cotton said with a roguish grin.

"Millicent?" Ned called from the doorway behind them. Both women looked around to see him balancing two plates of breakfast on his forearms. Mrs. Cotton jumped up, amazingly spry, and helped him. However, Ned still brought the second plate and put it at Millicent's side. "Do you want coffee?" he asked.

"Sounds good. I take it with milk if they've brought any."

"I'll see. Would you care for some coffee as well, Mrs. Cotton?" he asked as he left.

"No, thank you. Sends me out back too much."

Mrs. Cotton had that inquisitive look in her eye when she sat down again. "Well!"

"Now, don't start thinkin'. . . ."

"Me? I'm not thinking a thing!" But Mrs. Cotton's smile held the bright expectation of a child seeing a long-wanted gift on Christmas morning.

"It wasn't easy, last night," Millicent explained. "I guess we just decided to be friendly."

"Friendly? Or friendlier still?"

"Ned's been good to me. It can't be easy for him, after all, our names being linked by everyone in town with a tongue."

"That's certain. 'Specially as he comes from such a fine family."

"Yes. He does?"

Mrs. Cotton nodded. "Yes, indeed. I met them when Antonia and Jake got hitched. Fine folks. More cash in hand than a banker, I'll be bound. And such clothes! My, his mother's dress must have been hand-spun by a silkworm."

"I kind of forgot about his family, I guess," Millicent said sadly and softly.

Mrs. Cotton went on. "Yes, it's right kind of Neddy to take the trouble to see your reputation don't come to harm. Of course, I don't say all the hugging and kissing you've been doing was strictly necessary, but I guess folks expect it."

"There hasn't been that much," Millicent said, though she knew her pink cheeks gave her away. She put Petey to her shoulder and started patting his back. Little bubbles began escaping from his lips, and he grinned toothlessly as they tickled their way up.

"Not that much! Well, if you say so. But from what I hear, he can't hardly keep his hands to himself. Maybe it's about time you two had your quarrel."

"What quarrel?"

"You remember. You don't want to have to marry the boy, and if you keep going on like you've been, you'll have to."

"Now, wait a minute! This was your idea. . . ."

"'Course it was. But I never figured on you and Neddy *enjoying* it so much. Why, you don't mean to tell me that you haven't liked it, that you just been kissin' him to make things look right? Oh, now, I never meant——"

"What's going on?" Ned asked, carrying two thick mugs of coffee down the stairs. Millicent couldn't sustain his glance, but the sight of the cold fried fish and boiled eggs on her plate didn't give her anything more appealing to look at. He turned toward Mrs. Cotton.

"Is everything all right?" he asked.

"Oh, yes. I was just telling Millicent here how everyone's all but forgotten about her being Petey's mama. It sounds a mite heartless, maybe, but this sickness everybody's got is a blessing in disguise for you two."

"I'm afraid I'm too tired to appreciate it," Ned said, sipping the coffee. "How is it a blessing?"

"Nobody's talking about you, 'cept to say how grateful they are for your being here. So now . . ."

"Mrs. Cotton suggests that we have a big fight so we can stop pretending to be courtin'." She slanted her eyes sideways at him, wanting to see how he'd take the suggestion.

To her disappointment, he didn't seem to fume at all. Instead, he just looked thoughtful. "Yes, I remember we said that. You think the time is right, then?"

"That's right. Maybe you can fight about what happened last night. You didn't get fresh, did you, Neddy?"

"Did I, Millicent?"

"No, you were kind of a slow-coach, come to think of it."

Mrs. Cotton said, "That's too bad. Maybe you'll do better tonight."

"I'll do my best," he promised. "Aren't you hungry, Millicent?"

"I'm too tired to be hungry," she said. "Mrs. Cotton, I hate to ask but—"

"I'll be glad to keep Petey as long as you like. Makes me feel young again, though the judge doesn't agree. He's the laziest . . . Never mind. You two get some sleep."

Millicent asked, "What are we going to do about Petey's mother? We should look for her."

"A search should be made," Ned said. "I don't know how bad she was, but she could make herself much worse if she went far."

Mrs. Cotton nodded soberly. "I'll get the judge to tell folks to be on the watch. A girl, off her head, wandering off in the night . . . Everyone will turn out for her."

"It was this morning, we think. . . ." Millicent said.

"We'll find her," Mrs. Cotton said with confidence. She stood up, shaking out her full skirts. "I best get along and see what's what with the breakfast. You want to keep that child, or are you going to fall asleep on him?"

Millicent blinked stupidly. "What?"

"I'll take him," Ned said, reaching for the baby. "Until you're ready to go home, Mrs. Cotton."

He took the gold pen from his vest pocket and showed it to Petey. The baby promptly tried to bring the enticing object to his mouth. "I'm not sure," Ned said. "Does spit harm gold?"

"Won't do it any good," Millicent guessed. She could have watched the man she loved play with the baby she adored all day. Ned seemed to have a natural knack for taking care of little ones, as well as grown-ups. If they got married, how would Ned feel about fathering a whole brood?

She shook herself out of that pleasant dream. They'd talked about many things, including feelings, and teased each other more than a little about the attraction between them, an attraction rapidly becoming yearning. Neither one of them, however, had said one solitary word that could refer to marriage.

She'd never hidden her low opinion of that state. Ned's view wasn't much higher. Imagine the laughter if they actually did find themselves married, and to each other, after giving every appearance of affection. Culverton as a whole would laugh itself into fits if they thought the doctor and Miss Mayhew had given way to a love-match.

Deep in these uncongenial thoughts, Millicent only just noted the haze on the horizon. Then she focused on it. At first she thought smoke mounted up into the sky and laid a hand on Ned's sleeve to draw his attention.

"That's all we need," he said. "A fire. What next? We've had pestilence."

"Shouldn't we tell the others?"

"Wait a minute," he said, paying no attention. "That doesn't look like smoke. It looks like . . . dust. Someone must be driving hell for leather to raise a dust on the road today."

"They must need a doctor fearful bad. Maybe more people coming here. Here, let me have Petey. You better get your bag."

The wagon drew up before the City Hall with wheels

slewing in the gravel drive. The two mules that drew it were winded, the fierce breathing shaking their rib cages. The wagon's boards were warped and hard-worn.

Millicent looked at the driver. Shoe leather that had been in salt for forty years looked more flexible than the man who stepped down from the buckboard. He wore simple overalls with nothing underneath but tanned hide. His jaw and brow were like extruded rock, his eyebrows growing like a plant clinging to the edge of a sea cliff. Beneath the brim of his sweat-stained straw hat, he had eyes the color of the lead used to make pistol balls.

"This where they've set up a hospital?" he asked through narrow lips that hardly moved.

"Yes," Millicent said. She'd stood up the moment the wagon came into view. Now she cradled Petey on one hip while she gazed down at the stranger with cool eyes.

"Where's the doctor?" he asked, his tone as unforgiving and hard as his profile.

"Inside, getting something to eat. I . . . I'm part of the hospital, too. Maybe I can help you."

The man didn't bother to contradict her, just gave his head a very slight shake as if his neck were stiff. Millicent understood with perfect clarity where she stood in his world. She didn't even have a wedding ring, which would have given her a place, even if a low one. Until then, in the eyes of most people she had no more status than a child.

Taking courage to face another rebuff, she said, "Is someone sick? Do you have them with you?"

"If you know where the doctor is, then fetch him out, woman. Don't stand there catching flies in your mouth."

Millicent's chin went up. "And you take your hat off when you're talking to a lady. Don't snap orders, and don't call me woman. I'm Miss Mayhew. Dr. Castle will be back in a moment or two. If you'd like to come in . . ."

"Harlot."

Millicent felt certain she'd simply misheard. After all, it wasn't a word she'd heard very often. As a matter of fact, she felt fairly certain that she'd never heard the word before, outside of the Bible. "*What* did you say?"

The judge came bouncing down the stairs, his long coat flapping in the breeze, Ned following more sedately behind him. The judge knew no restraints when it came to flying off the handle. "What do you mean disturbing folks this way, Vogel? I'm still judge of this court, and if you don't want to spend tonight in this very jail . . ."

Ned tapped the judge on the shoulder. "No room," he said. His whisper carried to Millicent, who felt no desire to laugh. Something about this man's eyes frightened her, they stared so fixedly at everything. She'd seen that look before, the stare of the frightened fanatic.

The judge went on without missing a beat. "What do you want around here? If you've come just to make trouble . . ."

The stranger drew himself up, squaring his shoulders. He addressed himself solely to Ned. "The name's Vogel and I'm lookin' for my daughter. She's got no business leaving the farm, and I aim to tell her so myself."

He cracked the knuckles of both hands by interlacing his fingers and suddenly twisting his arms so the palms turned outward. A barrage of snapping and clicking filled the soft morning air. "Fetch her out," he repeated. "I won't have her in that den of vice for another minute. I won't have her turning into a harlot like that one there."

He pointed straight at Millicent. "Her with her child of shame! There's no decency left in Culverton. You should have rid her out of town on a rail. That's what decent folks would do. That's what my daddy would've done. Rid her out of town on a rail and her brat, too."

While the townspeople who had come out of the entrance hall to see what the excitement was whispered and chattered among themselves, Millicent tried to marshal her thoughts into coherent patterns. "Mr. Vogel . . ." she began.

He raised one board-thick hand and said, "I won't stay to be corrupted. Where's my Sally?"

Though Millicent noticed that Ned's ears were bright red, the doctor introduced himself and asked, "What does your daughter look like, Mr. Vogel? Blonde, brunette, roan?"

"She has yaller hair," Mr. Vogel admitted. "Skinny thing, too pretty for her own good, 'bout seventeen."

"Hands, or years?"

"Years! She's not a horse."

"Oh, I thought she might take after her father . . . never mind. We did have a girl here who matched that description, pretty much. She left under her own power some time ago."

"I don't believe you!" Mr. Vogel made a charge up the step, but Ned seemed to be there first, taking Mr. Vogel's weight on his chest and throwing the big man into the pale spring grass.

Millicent wanted to applaud; the judge and those townspeople who had nothing better to do than to watch a brangle weren't so restrained. The clapping seemed to drive Vogel mad.

He jumped back into his wagon and shook out the reins. "It won't do you any good to hide her. I'm her father; she belongs to me until I find her a husband to obey. That's in the Good Book. If any of you ever read . . ."

Foolishly the Reverend Budgell, still loaded with trays at the entrance, said with dignity, "I have read the Bible from cover to cover. . . ."

Mr. Vogel made a rude noise and his mules started walking away. He shook a fist and said, "God help you if you find her first!"

22

$\mathcal{N}$OW THAT ALL the excitement was over, Petey began to cry. Millicent's attempts to comfort the baby were not helped by Judge Cotton, who danced around Ned saying, "You should have knocked him down, boy. You should have knocked him down!"

Ned said, "That's right. He's only fifteen years older than I am and half-crazy with worry. I should have knocked him down all right; that would have been fair."

"You don't know Vogel the way I do. He's a bully who hides behind the Word of God. His wife can't call her soul her own, and I thought he'd run off all his children with his hectoring ways. This Sally must be about the last of 'em. Hey, Mother?"

Mrs. Cotton, as usual on the spot when anything unusual happened, came down to him. She handed Millicent another bottle of milk, saying, "Give this to him. Maybe one wasn't enough."

"He's not . . ." The baby took the nipple and began sucking the milk down like a suction pump. "Oh, maybe he was. But that man scared him."

"Mother," Judge Cotton said, fairly jigging with the desire to attract her attention. "Mother, that girl was Vogel's youngest."

"No! I didn't know they had any after Joshua. If that don't beat all! That last boy nearly killed her; I never thought she'd have another."

"I've never heard of the Vogels," Millicent said.

"They live in the woods . . . a whole passel of 'em. Poor as a hard-pack dirt floor, from the oldest to the youngest. That was Einz . . . he's the orneriest son of one of the bullheadedest men I ever met in all my born days. I think Jake's had a couple of run-ins with some of Einz's brothers or cousins in the last year or two, come to think of it, but Einz himself keeps his nose clean, 'cept when he drinks."

"He didn't sound like a drinkin' man," Millicent said.

"No, this one found religion, of a sort. He don't sin no more, and I hear tell he's mighty hard on those that do."

Millicent glanced at Ned and found that he had the same enlightened expression on his face that she could feel on her own. Some of the things Sally Vogel had said made perfect sense now. Einz Vogel didn't have the appearance of a man who would be sympathetic to a daughter in trouble.

"We've got to find that girl," Millicent said.

"Some of the men are starting a search in a few minutes," Mrs. Cotton reassured her.

"I'll help," Ned said.

"No, you don't, Neddy Castle. Nor you, either, Millicent. Don't you two worry about that. Get along home and catch yourself some sleep. Your eyes look like burnt holes in a blanket, and your skin's waxier than the candle they come from."

"That put us in our place," Ned said.

"That's right. Now you give me that baby and git. You got to come back here tonight and do the same thing all over again."

"Everything?" Ned asked with a wicked wink.

"That's up to you," Mrs. Cotton replied, her merry eyes at odds with her prim mouth.

Too tired to work up a blush, Millicent kissed Petey's forehead and handed him back to Mrs. Cotton. "Are you sure you don't mind?" she asked, hesitating.

Ned took her arm. His tie askew, his vest unbuttoned and, with his hair tumbled and falling on his forehead, he thrilled her senses. "Come on," he said. "You can play mother later. Right now, sleep."

She went with him, though not without a backward glance. "He's so tiny and precious."

"And you don't want Vogel to have anything to do with him?"

"You read my mind, Ned, you know that?"

"It's not hard to do. But, listen, don't judge that man too harshly."

"Why, you heard the judge. Are you, of all people, defending—"

"No. For all I know, Vogel's a hound and not fit to live, but I wouldn't judge him on what we saw a few minutes ago. I mean, think about it. He's probably been looking for his daughter half the night, worrying every second he'll find her dead in a ditch. Then he comes here and finds a bunch of people who seem to be hiding her from him."

"We were telling him the truth. . . ."

"He doesn't know that. Right now, he probably doesn't care very much. Put yourself in his place. Pretend it's Petey you're looking for. How would you feel?"

The words dropped slowly. "Angry. Tired. Ready to hurt anyone who stands between me and my baby."

"Exactly. So maybe Vogel's a menace. But maybe he has a reason to be." He held her arm a little more closely against the warmth of his body and said, "Of course, that's just for now. If he's the same way after he finds Sally, I probably will knock him down, especially if he so much as twitches a toe in your direction."

"Thank you. I can tell you I don't much relish being called a harlot." She yawned, then apologized only to catch him doing exactly the same thing.

They walked on in a comfortable silence until they reached Millicent's house. She opened the front door and called, "Anyone there?"

The quality of the silence that came back had changed somehow. It sounded less the echoing emptiness of an underground cavern than the stillness of a house in which liveliness has been laid aside for the moment.

"I just hope no one's asleep in my bed," Millicent said. "If all three bears were snoring in it, I'd still climb into it."

"Maybe I should come in, just to check. . . ."

Millicent managed to get the door half-closed between them. Much safer to talk to Ned through a crack when he got that teasing, beckoning light in his eye. "I'll be fine," she said kindly but firmly.

"Millicent," he said coaxingly. "Now come on. How can we have a big argument if you won't even let me come in?"

"I don't want to argue with you right now. . . ."

"But Mrs. Cotton said we should." He didn't push against the door, trying to overcome her with his strength. Millicent thought she would probably have had more resistance against that, than the undermining effect of his smile.

"We don't have to do everything Mrs. Cotton said. She wants us to get married after all."

"Will marrying you get me inside your . . . house?"

"Go home and go to sleep, Dr. Castle."

"I see that smile."

"Wasn't a smile."

He pushed on the door, now that she no longer blocked the opening of it with her foot. Ned stepped inside the dim hallway, dark even at this hour of the morning. "Do you remember the first time I kissed you?"

"Yes . . ." Millicent said, backing up.

"You didn't kiss me back then, did you?"

She shook her head, unable to speak for the excitement that built within her. Maybe the time for games had come to an end. Maybe the time had come to fulfill the promises they'd both made, with their eyes wide open.

When the wall met her back, she had to stop retreating. She would have stopped in any case, unable to take another step in any direction because her·knees were trembling so. He put his hands on either side of her head against the wall and leaned forward, trapping her. She had plenty of time to escape.

Throwing her arms around his neck, she kissed him the way he wanted her to, with her whole heart and soul. Strange how waking the fire in him brought a flame to life in her.

"You're not tired?" she asked when he freed her lips to kiss the side of her throat.

His laugh had an intimate, masculine note that sent a sparkling thrill through her veins. "I'm exhausted," he said, his voice heavy and muffled. "But I don't seem to care."

He slid his hands around her neck, massaging lightly, his thumbs caressing her cheeks. Lightly, he kissed her open mouth. "Do you want me to go? All you have to do is tell me to go and I will."

"Then if I ask you to stay . . . ?"

He groaned and rested his forehead against hers for a moment. Then he kissed her again and again until she gasped, laughing with love.

Smiling under his kisses, she ran her shaking hands inside his open vest and started pulling his shirt out. "I want to touch you."

"You're not tired?" he asked, grinning.

"Tired doesn't even begin to describe it, but at the same time . . ." She twinkled up at him through her lashes.

Then she ran her hands over his skin, and the game they were playing came to its predestined end. She recognized the dazed intensity of his eyes, feeling the same fire burning in herself. His muscles were hard and tight. Her fingers curled in shock when she realized that her palms were being gently abraded by the hair that swirled over his chest.

"Don't stop," he said, his voice dark. "I've been waiting for you to do that. . . ."

He bent his head to take her lips. Millicent felt a jolt in her midsection like a zap of lightning. She strained to get closer to him, her hands slipping around his waist to cling to his back. Her dirty muslin dress seemed too heavy all of a sudden, as heavy as the blackest wool she owned. She began to long to be free of it.

Ned kissed her neck, her eyes, her mouth, letting his kisses fall randomly like spring rain. "How come you taste so good?" he whispered. "Why are you so beautiful?"

He didn't let her protest that she wasn't, stopping her mouth with kisses, long and sweet, hardening into passion. The only equal of his desire was her own. It made her restless, so she couldn't keep still. Her rapid breathing flowered into sound as his name formed in her thoughts over and over.

Millicent didn't know how they reached her bedroom; for all she could tell they'd floated mystically up the stairs. But when she opened her eyes, there they were, standing at the foot of her narrow bed. Her dress felt loose around her shoulders as Ned unbuttoned the long back.

She raised her arms to pull the remaining pins from her hair. The dark mass fell, cool and fluid against her skin. Ned's eyes lit up as he smoothed it with his hands, his fingers catching and tangling in the blackness. "I saw you like this once," he murmured.

"When?"

"One night . . ." His voice caught and he added, "In my dreams, I guess."

At least one button popped off his shirt as she fumbled with the unfamiliar right-hand arrangement of buttonhole and button. He stopped her then, pushing down her hands. "I have to be able to wear it home."

"I'll sew them back on after . . . afterward," and she knew her skin had darkened with a blush.

Through her opened curtains, the sunlight marked her bed in broad squares. Her dress slipping from her shoulders, Millicent walked out of range of Ned's reaching hands to seat herself on the edge of the bed, one leg bent beneath her. Self-consciously seductive, yet with eyes that could not quite meet his, she waited for him to come to her.

Ned drew one fingertip along the line of her jaw, noticing how even so innocent a touch made her quiver. "We can wait until we're married if you want."

"Married?" she said, as if asking him the meaning.

"Yes. I thought we would."

She laid one of her graceful hands on the base of her throat. "You thought we would get married . . . ?"

"I'm not a cad, Millicent. I don't intend to ravish you and then twirl my mustache as I disappear into the night. I don't want you to wind up like Sally Vogel."

"I see. It's kind of you."

"No, it's common sense. I . . . I want you very badly. Badly enough to imagine that once with you might not be enough."

"I don't know what you mean."

He sat down on the bed, a careful distance away. Knowing that what experience she'd had with men had not been stellar, Ned wanted to take his time. He needed to make sure she knew what she was getting into before he touched her satin skin again or lost himself in the torrid fascinations of her kisses. His body leaped ahead of his mind, and Ned fought a battle between his desire and his self-control that left nail marks in the palms of his hands. His voice, however, remained cool.

"Millicent," he began. "Now, don't be embarrassed. Do you know what happens between a man and a woman?"

Then she smiled and he began to feel like a little bit of a fool. It was a worldly-wise smile, like the Mona Lisa's, and it held a wisdom that left him in awe of the power of a woman.

"I'm not a child," she said. "Not even a young girl. I've been living and doctoring people for some time. What I don't know from my own life, I have heard tell. Also, my grandmother had a book about that kind of thing."

She took a deep breath that did things to the dress that clung to her upper body in defiance of gravity. With a look of devastating directness, Millicent said, "Do you want to take a peek at it?"

"At what?" Ned answered, trying to remember what a rational thinker he'd been before she'd cast the spell of love on him.

"My grandmother's marriage manual."

"I don't think . . ."

Her laughter warmed him even while it exasperated him. He reached out for her as though to wring her neck. She sank back onto the bed. He followed her and found himself where he most wanted to be in the world, in a bed looking into Millicent's eyes as they clouded with desire for him.

Ned knew he didn't want to marry her because he wanted her, or to forestall talk. He wanted her with him always because he had a nervous certainty that he would not live long without her. With her at his side he'd never sink back into bleak cynicism and cold rationality, but go on living in the world of human beings and their emotions. Now to get her to see that world as she'd shown it to him.

With deliberation Ned set out to open Millicent's eyes.

"What . . . ?" she breathed as he lifted over her, peeling off his coat, vest, and shirt in one.

"Getting undressed is part of the fun." He threw his clothes on the floor and sank down into the circle of her arms.

"I think you just broke your thermometer."

"It doesn't go high enough to register the temperature I've got."

She ran her hands over his shoulders and back. "Hmmm, fever all right." Sucking in a shocked breath as he freed her from the top edge of her chemise, she whispered, "It's catching."

Then his mouth moved on her breast, and she'd never in her life known anything to match the feel of it. Rough and strong, yet unbelievably tender, Ned might as well have lit a fuse. She should have been frightened, she thought wonderingly. Instead she looked forward to the eventual explosion. Everything might go sky-high, but what a ride it would be.

"Oh, my heavens," she said, twisting under him. Not to get away, but to get closer to the source of this feeling.

"It'll be all right," he said, lifting his head a moment.

"Yes, indeed." She arched under him as he tasted her again. Her fingernails scraped his back, and it was a revelation to her when he moaned. "Ned, that feels . . . oh, my goodness!"

With almost frightening suddenness, he rolled off of her and on to his side. "Give me a minute," he panted.

"What's wrong?" Millicent asked, propping herself on an elbow and reaching toward him with her other hand. He caught it before she could trace his chest.

"I need a minute to collect myself." He threw his arm

over his eyes and lay there, his lips moving to some silent phrase.

"What are you doing?" she demanded, feeling as though she'd been thrown into a cold-water bath.

He moved his arm to drape it around her neck. "I don't want to disappoint either one of us, so I have to control myself."

"Control yourself?" She thought it over. "No, I don't think so." Moving closer to the warmth of his body, so close that there was no room between them, she pushed her fingers through the thicket of hair on his chest, trailing them down over the sensitive flesh of his stomach. "You're a fine figure of a man, Dr. Castle."

She let her gaze wander over him with wanton curiosity from top to bottom. Then she stopped, goggled for a moment, and then looked away. His hands went to the buttons that marched down the front of his trousers. He seemed to hesitate. "Are you sure you wouldn't like to get married first?"

Her embarrassment almost overwhelmed her desire. She fought it and won. Though she blushed, she said, "You're not going to start that again, are you? I don't want to marry you; I want . . . I want . . ."

"Take your dress off," he suggested, "because I can't find you under all that."

She tried to get it off, but the skirt was too voluminous and the bodice too tight to pull off over her head. Finally, while he lay there grinning at her, she stood up on the bed and shook the dress down to her feet. When she stepped free of the swirling skirts, the laughter in his eyes had been replaced by fascination.

She unbuttoned her chemise and petticoat from each other and let the white skirt fall. Then she kicked dress and petticoat out of the bed and kneeled down, somewhat unsteadily, on the mattress. "Ned . . ."

"You really are the most beautiful woman alive. . . ."

She tugged at the hem of her chemise, suddenly shy. Her long stockings covered her to mid-thigh and her chemise was a modest garment. Other than those items, however, she was as nature made her.

"How does the rest come off?" Ned asked, his teasing grin reappearing, though his blue eyes were dark with serious purpose.

"The same way as your trousers."

Ned's gaze held a promise of things to come as he lazily overlooked what of Millicent had been revealed. He reached out to cover the dusky tip of one peeking breast, then slipped his hand around to her back. "Beautiful . . ."

A few moments later, dressed only in sunshine, they lay on top of the crumpled counterpane. Dazzled, Millicent closed her eyes, seeing sparks and flashes of light behind her eyelids. Ned touched her, delightful strokes of his sensitive hands running freely over her arms, her throat, her stomach, even the length of her legs, all the while kissing her with such passionate intensity that she could hardly breathe. Yet he circumvented her breasts, though he'd seemed to enjoy touching them and kissing them before.

Frustrated, for the hot pull she recognized now as excitement still intensified within her, she finally captured one of his hands and dragged it upward. She sighed with contentment as the pressure of his hand relieved some of her ache, yet a moment later, she felt unsettled and unsatisfied again. She snapped open her eyes and found him smiling at her as if in approval.

"Don't look at me like that."

"What should I do?"

"I don't know! You're the one who's done this before. There's got to be . . . more."

"Well, yes," he said softly.

He slid his hand, firmly, down the hard front of her thigh as he'd done before. But this time he angled in and drew back with just one finger touching her sensitized skin. Millicent understood where he would touch next, and she tensed in anticipation.

Just as he touched her intimately, he again took the tip of her breast into his mouth. The combination sent her mad. The whole world shrank and dwindled down to nothing but *feeling*, a feeling that took over her body and mind like a wave of fire. Ned alone remained, the master of a shattered universe.

Coming down from the crest, Millicent reached for him, but learned, when she looked into his eyes, that he didn't control the power. It controlled him.

His body was hard and heavy as he moved over her. Millicent thought she could hear the pounding of his heart. Instinctively she raised her knees to make him a refuge. Disappointingly, he didn't act at once to take what she offered.

He held himself up on rigid arms where muscles showed in high relief. Through grinding teeth, he said, "Do you . . . hear something? Like, someone at the door?"

A distant "Halloo?" proved him right.

Millicent realized in a horrifying flash that she had never locked the front door. She thought they might have as much as thirty seconds before whoever was downstairs came to look for her.

23

$\mathcal{N}$*ED HAD HIS* pants on, his socks in his pockets and his upper body clothed in the coat he'd dropped with his shirt and vest nested in it, in the same amount of time it took Millicent to slip on a nightgown. He'd just stomped his boots on and was finishing buttoning his shirt while she slid beneath the covers of her bed when Mrs. Wilmot opened the bedroom door. "Oh. I hope you're not ailing, Miss Mayhew?"

Ned thanked heaven for the instinct that had told him a thermometer could pass as an alibi. Remembering Millicent's reservations about the cleanliness of that instrument, he simple held it up and said, "No, her temperature seems to be normal."

"Are you sure, Doctor? Why, I've never seen her so flushed. I'm sure she must have a fever."

Millicent smiled with great friendliness, though Ned noticed she didn't dare look at him. "I'm just tired, Mrs. Wilmot. I hope you're not here because of Dave. He didn't seem near as sick as some of the others."

"Oh, that boy of mine's a trial. Sick as a dog, and he wants to play boats with his brothers. I'm stealing a minute from him just to let you know that Sally Vogel's been found."

Now Ned could exchange a glance with Millicent and not be afraid of bursting into laughter.

Mrs. Wilmot went on. "Yes, my son Darryl found her not half a mile away. It's a wonder her father didn't find her first . . . must be a miracle of providence, for she wasn't ten feet off the road. 'Course, Mrs. Cotton should have come to tell you herself—it's not like *she* has family at death's door, but you know her! She's got to be where the gossip's the best or she can't sleep nights."

"Is she alive?" Millicent asked.

"Sally? I think so. Terrible sick, of course." Mrs. Wilmot glanced at Ned. "My husband went to find you, Doctor. I think they'll need you."

Millicent sat up. "I'll get dressed."

"There's no need," Ned said. "You should stay right where you are. At least, until I can come back to check on you." His words were for Mrs. Wilmot's ears, but Millicent knew exactly what he meant.

Ned's eyes flicked over her. Despite knowing he'd seen all of her not five minutes before, something in his eyes made her want to raise the blanket to her chin. She felt marked by that look, branded.

He left with Mrs. Wilmot, and Millicent lay in bed, stunned. She'd known that what she felt for Ned was stronger than friendship and more impatient than appreciation. She'd called it love, but the power of their passion had taken her totally by surprise. When he took her in his arms, she seemed to lose every thought and be given over to a storm of emotion.

Millicent knew without a single doubt that the only reason she could still call herself a virgin was thanks to Mrs. Wilmot's impulse to stop by. She certainly hadn't made any struggle to hold on to her innocence. She even regretted that she still kept it.

She'd been kept from making love with Ned this time by an accident. The next time there might not be any interruption. The idea set off a ringing in her head that sounded less like an alarm than a celebration. She pressed her hands over her eyes, trying to calm down.

A sponge bath with cold water helped her regain her sense of balance. Then she called on Mrs. Cotton.

"I thought you'd be long asleep! Come on in. I bet I know what the trouble is. You're too tired to sleep! I git that way sometimes. Best thing is a glass o' hot milk. You set down and I'll fix you up some."

Millicent picked Petey up from his cradle. The baby didn't wake. She laid him against her chest and sat in the big rocking chair, watching his eyelids twitch in dreams. What did babies find to dream about? Endless bottles of milk, perhaps, with a multitude of kisses thrown in.

Mrs. Cotton said, "I reckon you heard they found Sally Vogel."

"Yes, Mrs. Wilmot stopped over to tell me."

"That gal . . . gossip's meat and drink to her! Always jabbering away like a magpie!" She stirred the milk in the saucepan. "If Sally does turn out to be Petey's mama, what are you going to do?"

"That depends on her, don't you think? After all, she might not admit it, or if she does, she might not want him back."

"That's true. One thing's certain; she won't want her pa to find out about it, not that there's any way to keep this thing a secret." She hurried to reassure Millicent as soon as she saw the distress in her eyes. "Now, don't you worry about Sally! Even if Jake's not on his feet yet, there's not a soul in this town who'd let Einz Vogel get near that girl. We'll take care of her as if she were our own."

"I never realized how important it is, to be part of a town."

Mrs. Cotton's voice held nothing but surprise. "Mercy, child, you've always been a part of this town! You always will be. You can't get away from us any more'n we can get away from you!"

"And Ned . . . ?"

"Oh, Neddy!" Mrs. Cotton chuckled. "Of course, he wasn't *born* here; he's an outsider. But plenty of folks who weren't born here belong here."

"Like the ones who've come from Europe?"

"That's right. We got some cuttings from some strange gardens around these parts, and they grow just as good as the natives. Ned's like that. He'll put down roots soon enough once he's married."

"I suppose he will," Millicent said thoughtfully.

"Of course, it's got to be the right girl. I can see now that Lucy George wouldn't do. She's too flighty. 'Sides, I understand she and Roscoe Benders might be making a match of it. So I was thinkin' of Netta Harbottle's oldest girl. . . ."

"Rena? But she's—"

"I know, I know." Mrs. Cotton poured the steaming milk into a glass. "She's only sixteen right *now*, but she's a mighty taking little thing. They grow up so fast these days. Oh, my. Oh, yes! The way I figure it, it might take Neddy another year or two to decide he wants a home and family. If that's so, he'll be the longest holdout we've ever had, but he'll come around. 'Specially if that pretty gal—"

"Mrs. Cotton, you ought to know that Ned's asked me to marry him a couple of times now."

The older woman spilled the milk as she put it down on the table. "Lands!" she said, jumping back from the splash. She snatched up a dishtowel and started mopping at the spreading lake of white.

Millicent sat and rocked her baby. He had the sweetest face in the world, his eyes shut so tight crinkles appeared at the corner of the lids. She passed her hand over the fuzz sprouting from the top of his head, smiling at the tickle.

"He asked you to marry him? When?"

"Right away, I think." Remembering how he'd asked her, she knew he hadn't wanted to wait any longer than necessary.

"I mean . . . when did he ask you?"

"When we came back from City Hall. We went into my house. . . ."

"I know . . ."

"And he asked me."

"Well!" Mrs. Cotton rubbed her hands together with glee. "Let's see. Today's Tuesday. . . ." She started counting on her fingers. "With a little luck, you could be married this Sunday. Good thing you can make your own veil. That's something I don't care to see borrowed, though I've known it done."

"Wait. I haven't said I'll marry him yet."

"What in tarnation are you waitin' for? A brass band and a chorus of angels?"

Millicent had to blink hard to dismiss the tears that threatened. "I just want him to tell me that he loves me."

Mrs. Cotton sat down heavily. "Don't we all, honey?" She leaned her head on her hand. "If that don't beat the Dutch! You figure Neddy would have more smarts than that, all the flirting he's done."

"He's not that bad. He wouldn't say anything he didn't mean with all his heart."

"You've got it pretty bad for him, ain't you?" Millicent nodded in dumb misery. "But you won't be the first to tell him, will you? I'm not sayin' you're wrong. You've got your pride, same as other folks."

"Besides, what if he doesn't love me? He'd look at me as if I'd lost my mind. . . . You know that look he gets when you've said something stupid?"

"Yes. Many's the time I've wanted to smack him for it, but never more than now. Of course, you know what it is. He's scared, scared as you are."

"I am scared." Petey wriggled and seemed to be trying to burrow closer to her. Millicent supported his back, moving her arm to a more comfortable position, already all pins and needles.

"I'm scared for a lot of reasons. He's a fine man, a doctor, and I'm just . . . me. He doesn't think much of Grandma's receipts or of me for using 'em. Not to mention, I don't think he's going to want to spend his whole life right here in Culverton, and I won't leave even when they carry me out feet first. I'm going to be in that churchyard till the last trump sounds and the smoke clears away."

"You'll see me there," Mrs. Cotton said with an approving wink. Then she drummed her fingers on the table. "Never mind all the reasons you can't marry Ned. Tell me the reasons you should."

Under those wise eyes Millicent found she could not lie. "I love him. He makes me crazy, but I love him like a house afire. When he touches me, I . . . I . . ."

"'Nough said. Give me a little bit of time to figure out what to do."

"The exposure didn't do her any good," Ned said, stepping out into the hall with the Reverend Mr. Budgell and the judge. "Her pulse is quick and thready; her lungs are noisy. It'll take more than luck to keep this from turning into pneumonia."

"I shall organize a prayer vigil," Mr. Budgell said firmly. "This girl will not leave this earth with a burden of sin on her shoulders. I trust in you, Dr. Castle. I know you'll act as the Lord commands."

"Thank you, Mr. Budgell. I'm sure your prayers will be very helpful."

Somehow he felt no need to roll his eyes or speak his cynicism aloud. Budgell might be overzealous and even sanctimonious at times, but his heart knew only kindness and love. However, he wouldn't permit long pastoral visits once his patient recovered. They might prove to be too much.

Turning to the judge, Ned said, "You're going to have to deal with her parents, Judge. I can't let this girl go home without knowing she'll good care. She needs to be kept warm, dry, and well-fed. She doesn't look as if she's been eating well lately."

"She shouldn't stay here, though. Besides, I don't think Einz would make as much a fuss if she were in a private home. He doesn't seem to have much faith in the government. Took a potshot at my clerk of the court once upon a time."

"I didn't know you had a clerk."

"I don't . . . now. Poor bastard."

"Why didn't Einz go to jail? If he murdered—"

"Who said anything about murder? My clerk got married to one of them widowed Baggage sisters. Man, I'm in favor of marriage but not to a black widow spider."

"I had no idea you were so particular. . . ."

Judge Cotton chuckled and patted Ned on the back as high as he could reach. "I'm going down to see Jake. When he's feeling more himself, I'll send him off to find Sally's man. If he's anywhere between Canada and Mexico, Jake will find him."

"I told Jake he'll be feeling better tomorrow, but I don't think he believed me. He'll be able to get up by Monday. By then the girl will be able to tell us where her man's gone, provided she knows."

"Provided she lives," Judge Cotton said, his pale lips tightening.

"She'll live," Ned affirmed with a confidence he hoped no one else could tell was half-assumed.

By noon he no longer needed a stethoscope to listen to Sally's lungs. Every time she inhaled, her chest resounded with a shaky wheezing that he knew as rhonchus. One of the ladies who helped him that day thought it sounded like a death rattle, and repeated her thought to everyone else. Thereafter, the other "nurses" tiptoed around her room like mutes at a funeral.

Though he hated to disturb Millicent's rest, Ned couldn't stand having the others around. Millicent might not be an optimist, not yet, still he wanted her solid sense, her unromantic views. Most of all he wanted to refresh himself with the sight of her.

She walked right up to him, where he sat dozing in a chair, and put her arms around him, pulling his head down to rest on the softness of her breast. "You're worn out," she said.

"I'm all right," he declared, though he made no attempt to move. He couldn't remember being so comfortable before.

"How's Sally? I heard . . ." Three people had told her the girl lay on death's door, and she'd only been in the building for five minutes.

"Her chest is congested and her fever's high. She's awakened once or twice, briefly. The last time she was delirious but said nothing that made any sense. On the bright side, she's taken water and some broth. Also on the bright side, there's only two men who are as sick as she is, and none of the other women. Some of them are feeling well enough to be troublesome."

"Well, I'm here to help. You should get some rest."

"This is nice." He rubbed his head tiredly against her. Millicent felt a surge of tenderness for him, mixed with the wish that he'd get the sleep he obviously craved.

"You can't do anyone any good if you're asleep on your feet. I'd send you back to sleep in my bed—"

"Not without you in it."

She smiled at him and combed her fingers through his thick soft hair. "There's a couple of empty beds here now."

"Did somebody die?" he said, sitting upright so suddenly she felt pushed back.

"No, no," she said soothingly. "Jake and Caleb felt too helpless lying down all the time."

"If they don't take things slow, they'll be right back in there."

"Jake won't mind if you nap in his bed. Go on. I'll look out for Sally Vogel."

When Ned came back in two hours, yawning but refreshed, Sally's condition had improved slightly. Millicent had propped the girl up in bed, so her breathing no longer shook her frail body. Yet Millicent reported that Sally still hadn't awakened.

She took Ned by the arm after he finished taking the girl's pulse and lead him out of earshot. "Ned, I'm right worried about that girl. She looks . . . broken-hearted. Like she's fading because she doesn't care to go on. Don't you see it?"

"That's just the illness. . . . She's probably in pain."

"Now, I've been at enough bedsides to know the difference," she said with a flash of impatience. Looking into her eyes, Ned saw Millicent's fear. He reached out and wrapped his arm loosely about her shoulder, giving her reassurance.

"Of course you would know. What do you want to do?"

"Would there be any danger to him if I brought Petey here?"

"You'd do that?"

Millicent turned her face toward the girl on the bed. Ned laid his warm hand on her cool cheek and raised her face. A glittering tear trembled on her dark lashes. She blinked and a drop like acid fell on the back of his hand. "I don't want to," she said. "But I think it's the right thing to do."

"I love you, Millicent Mayhew."

The words came from a full heart. She gave no sign that she'd heard.

"If she's Petey's mother, and I'm guessing that she is, her heart must be awful sore. That's why she came to see him and to leave that blanket for him. She doesn't want to lose him. She's just young and scared and sick."

"Get Petey," Ned said, kissing her hair. "We'll take care that he doesn't get sick, too."

A sad smile glimmered just for him, then Millicent opened the door. She had her head down and nearly ran over the dark young man who stood there, turning the brim of his hat over and over in his hands. "Darryl? You can't come in. . . ."

"I better," he said, his voice cracking. "I'm her feller."

He glanced up and down the hall. "My folks don't know about it. Nobody does."

Ned and Millicent exchanged an incredulous glance. "Then Petey's your son?" Millicent exclaimed. Sally moved and moaned behind her.

Instantly Millicent clapped her fingers to her lips. With a glance at Sally, she repeated her question more softly. "Petey's *your* son?"

Flushing, he nodded. "Yes'm. I didn't want her to give him to the Cottons, but Sally was too scared to tell her pa about me."

"Did he realize she was pregnant?" Ned asked, his face severe.

"He was working on the new Santa Fe line this winter. Down in New Mexico. Sally and her mother kept the baby till he came back, then her ma said they'd have to do something with him. Mr. Vogel's awful handy with his fists, and Sally's ma's scared of him. They both begged me not to tell him." He threw out his chest, though his anxious gaze returned to the wasted girl sleeping upright among the pillows. "I don't want you to think *I'm* scared of the ol' bustard, 'cause I'm not."

"Then why haven't you gotten married?" Millicent asked.

The boy's mouth tightened as he tried to keep from showing more emotion than a man should. "She won't do it. I've begged her and begged her, but she just won't do it. I told her she could come to my folks and be married from there, as proper as you please, but all she talks about is ruining me and dragging me down. You know, my ma wants me to go to college like Fred did."

"What do you want to do?" Ned asked, folding his arms.

"I want to stay here, run the store, and marry Sally. That's all I've ever wanted since I first saw her when we were just kids. Maybe she's not what my ma wants for me; she wants me to marry some fancy piece of goods, but I want Sally and our baby."

"Then you better do something about it."

The look Darryl Wilmot flashed at Ned spoke of inarticulate frustration and a belief that no one over twenty had any feelings at all. He said, "I almost had her agreeing to it when her father came back home. She's scared of him; I think for her mother's sake more than her own."

He walked over to the bedside, his steps as heavy and dragging as an old man's. Kneeling down, he took his lover's hand and his eyes closed in pain at the limp feel of it. "Come on, Sally," he pleaded. "Come on."

The girl lay motionless, only the wheezing in her chest letting them know she still lived.

Ned said to Millicent, "I don't suppose your grandmother . . . ?"

"Just the usual remedies. Warm wax on brown paper applied to the chest and back, elderflower wine, and sweating. I don't think they'll work this time."

"That's better than nothing. Which is exactly what I've got. I don't have anything to treat this. I've already tried paregoric and the willow-bark tea."

"Maybe they haven't had time to work yet."

"In two hours? I wonder if you're right. Maybe medicine isn't what she needs, so much as . . ." He glanced toward the bed. Darryl lay with his face pressed against Sally's hip, his shoulders shaking with the tears he could no longer keep back.

Millicent and Ned, without speaking, left the room to give Darryl the privacy he needed. She said, "I think Mayor Wilmot or his wife will be in Dave's room. They're going to have to know."

"I was thinking we might let Mrs. Cotton or the judge break it to them. A thing like that shouldn't come from people who are younger than they are."

"You're more'n likely right, Ned, but I'm thinking it's more important they find out quick, before Mr. Vogel shows up here."

"You think he'll come back?"

"Right soon. If you don't know somebody's already been out to his place to tell him his daughter's found, then you don't know Culverton as well as you should."

"I didn't think of that." He slid his hand down her arm and interlaced his fingers with hers. "I've got to get back in there. Millicent, when all this chaos is over, will you give me your answer?"

Now was not the time to turn all maidenly, but Millicent couldn't help being shy. When his voice took on that caressing note, the remembrance of his intimate touch came back as real as though it were happening all over again. "I don't know," she said. "There's so much to think about."

"There's only one thing that's important. I just found it out for myself. If you don't know what it is yet, take another look at poor Darryl Wilmot."

24

MILLICENT WALKED AS slowly as possible, trying to make the short walk from her house to the makeshift hospital last and last. She showed Petey, bundled in her arms against the sharp spring breeze, the waving leaves on the bending branches. She showed him the birds that sang and the slow-stepping turtle crossing the road. Above them all, the silver-white clouds rushed away before the wind, too far off and too big to be understood by someone so small.

Stopping outside the City Hall, unable to believe she'd gotten there so fast when all her heart said "slowly, slowly," Millicent kissed Petey's soft spot for the last time, feeling his heartbeat marking its own time. "You won't remember me," she whispered. "But I'll never forget you. You'll always be my first, my very best baby."

Petey looked at her with those wide, wise eyes and tried to grab her nose. Millicent sniffed and found it easy to smile for him after all. Holding him tenderly against her breast, she carried him up the steps and inside. The flight of stairs to the second floor was the longest she'd ever climbed.

She heard the ruckus before she'd gotten halfway down the hall. Petey heard it, too, his brows—hardly more than pencil lines—drawing together in fright. He opened his mouth and let out a yell that silenced the adults standing outside Sally's room.

The shock passed off, and instantly, Millicent found herself with two zealous grandmothers swooping down on her as though she were the last piece of pie at a picnic. One, imposing in black silk a-tremble with jet beads, came from the right. The other, heavyset in rough gray homespun as neat as a new pin, wheeled on her from the left. Millicent shrank back, but they weren't interested in her.

"There he is! My grandson!" Mrs. Wilmot exclaimed, reaching out.

"My sweetums! My little sweetums!" Shining tears marked the lined cheeks of the other lady, who could only be Mrs. Vogel. She also put her hands out.

Millicent seriously considered retreat, but did not believe she'd make it more than two steps before one of the grandmothers would tackle her. Besides, she'd come with a mission, and she intended to fulfill it, no matter what.

"Wait just a minute," she said, lifting Petey out of reach.

"Miss Mayhew! You can't mean to continue to deny me my grandson," Mrs. Wilmot said.

The kind and understanding woman who'd maintained her husband's innocence had vanished. Millicent knew that Mrs. Wilmot valued nothing in the world more than her family. A nameless baby could be overlooked; a member of the Wilmot family, no matter how derived, would be sacred to her.

Then Millicent looked into Mrs. Vogel's eyes. They were slate-blue, the exact shade as Petey's. Though she tried to put on an expression as haughty as Mrs. Wilmot's—what *had* they been saying to each other?—Millicent saw how love for the baby shone out of her. She said, "I think it's fair that Mrs. Vogel get to hold him. After all, you held him just a day or two ago, Mrs. Wilmot."

She would have sooner given away her heart. Yet from somewhere, Millicent found the strength not to snatch him back as the older woman gently lifted him out of her arms. Tears swelled up, cool and healing against her hot eyes.

Mrs. Vogel whispered "Thank you" as she gazed down at the baby.

Then Millicent felt a touch, so light and fleeting, against her back. She knew that touch so well that even a brush of his fingers told her who it was. Turning slowly, she looked up into Ned's face. His eyes were wet as he gazed down at her.

Then he raised his head to take in the group milling around Mrs. Vogel and the baby. "All right now," he said, his voice firm and decisive. "I have to tell you that it doesn't look good for Sally right now. She needs a lot of rest, lots of care. If you can't bury the hatchet long enough to see to her health, I can't be very encouraging."

Millicent saw varying expressions on the faces before her. Mrs. Wilmot seemed disapproving while the mayor had a hard look in his eyes that boded ill for anyone who meant to cause trouble. Mrs. Vogel dried her tears with the edge of Petey's new blanket and hushed him by rocking him against her shoulder. Millicent wanted to show her what he liked, but by biting hard on her lower lip she kept her silence.

Young Darryl Wilmot's red eyes and swollen nose told how he'd stayed by his girl's bedside until called out to tell his parents about his intentions toward the mother of their grandson. Now he straightened drooping shoulders and said in a ringing voice, "I don't care what any one of you says or does. Sally's getting well and we're getting married. You can try to stop us. Hell, *she* can tell me a hundred times she's not good enough for me, but I'm still going to marry her."

"Don't swear in front of your mother," Mayor Wilmot said through his mustache.

Mrs. Wilmot laughed, on a hysterical note. "He's going to marry that . . . that . . ."

Ned said, "Be careful, Mrs. Wilmot. Don't gamble more than you are willing to risk."

She said with false heartiness, "Really, Darryl, you're going too far. You don't have to get married. . . . We'll take good care of little Petey . . . um, why Petey?"

"He's named for my brother," Mrs. Vogel said. "Drowned at sea."

Darryl said, "Ma, I'm marrying her and that's final. I'd do it now, if she'd wake. Nothing nobody says is going to make a hair of difference. Yes, that goes for you, too!"

Millicent couldn't imagine why he threw those words at her and Ned. Then she heard the heavy steps behind her.

Ned's arm tightened around her waist as he stepped back, taking her along. Einz Vogel, his large hands twitching by his thighs, walked toward them. Close, too, she could see how his muscles strained against the worn flannel of his shirt. Even bigger close to than he'd seemed at a distance, his face settled into lines of discontentment.

"Where's Sally?" he growled. "I want to see my daughter."

Millicent wished Marshal Faraday were here or even the judge. Someone with authority to quell the seething anger of Mr. Vogel. Mr. Wilmot didn't seem very eager to scrap with his soon-to-be in-law, and though Darryl might be eager, Mr. Vogel outweighed him by fifty pounds. After working on a railroad, very little of Mr. Vogel represented fat. That left Ned to handle him.

But Millicent forgot about the only other male present, a male who could bring any human being to his knees.

Petey let out a gurgle of happiness. What had pleased him? Millicent wondered, feeling another pang at her heart as she realized afresh that his likes and dislikes were no longer her concern. When he cooed, she had to close her eyes against the cool drop of tears.

Mr. Vogel on the other hand stumbled forward. "What's that baby?" he demanded in a voice that shook as if with fear. "Whose . . . whose is it?"

"It's mine," Darryl said boldly. "Mine and Sally's."

Mr. Vogel rounded on the boy, his grizzled jaw thrust forward. "What? You and my Sally? Sinners, fornicators . . ." His denunciation faded away. "Where is she? Someone said she was sick."

His wife handed Petey to Mrs. Wilmot. Going up to her husband, who towered over her the way Jake Faraday topped Ned's sister, she laid her farm wife's red hand on his arm. "Yes, she is sick, Einz. The doctor says she might die."

"Die?"

Strange that such a burly man could suddenly look as helpless as a baby himself. He blinked around at the other people like an owl in the daylight. "Where's the doctor?"

Ned stepped out of his protective attitude toward Millicent. He put up his hands toward Mr. Vogel's face, and the other man jerked back, his fists rising in a boxer's stance.

"You'd better sit down," Ned said, gently pushing down the melon-sized fists. He put his hands up to Mr. Vogel's weather-worn face and pulled down the lower eyelids with his thumbs, one to either side. "You're all but exhausted, man. You'd better be careful. This influenza will knock you over if you let yourself get run down."

To Mrs. Vogel, Ned said, "It's too many shocks at once. Has your husband ever complained of chest pains?"

"Of course. He eats hearty."

"You'd better get off your feet," Ned said to Mr. Vogel. He threw a glance at Mr. Wilmot and Darryl. Like it or not, it looked as though they were about to become related to the disagreeable Mr. Vogel. They had better start caring for him.

The expression in Mr. Vogel's eyes had a lot in common with a miner who has been struck over the head with another miner's sluicing pan. He walked obediently between the two Wilmots, but he looked as if he had no idea that they were people he didn't like. They heard Darryl say, "I'll take good care of Sally and the baby. We'll get married on Sunday, if Sally is feeling well enough."

Mrs. Vogel said to Mrs. Wilmot, "He's a good boy. I don't know why Sally wouldn't take him, 'specially when she found out she was going to have this young'un."

Mrs. Wilmot primmed up her mouth, and Millicent held her breath. "I don't know why, either," she said at last. "But I finally understand why Darryl's been acting so moon-struck lately. I thought he had worms; it must have been love."

Ned said, "Mrs. Vogel, as Sally's doctor, I feel I have the right to ask . . . That is, Darryl told us that Sally said she was afraid of her father's anger."

"Did she? I'm not saying she didn't have a right to fear it. A man's liable to act mighty hard when he hears his daughter's expecting a bastard."

Millicent couldn't think of a tactful way to ask the question she had in mind. So she blurted, "Does your husband hit you, Mrs. Vogel?"

"Millicent!" Mrs. Wilmot protested. "What kind of a question is that to ask a lady and a stranger?"

Mrs. Vogel said, "I don't mind it. Yes, once or twice, when he was drunk he'd hit me. Though otherwise he was the best provider," she hastened to add. Then she said proudly, "Since he found the Lord, he's not touched a drop and swears he never will again. Sometimes he's a hard man, a powerful hard man, but he does not hit me, and he *never* struck the children."

Privately, Millicent thought she'd live in a ditch with spiders and frogs before staying with a man who hit her, drunk or not. She knew, however, that some women stayed on with their husbands no matter what, whether out of a sense of duty or a sense of helplessness. For Mrs. Vogel's sake, she felt glad that part of her married life had ended. Now for Sally . . .

"Bring the baby, Mrs. Wilmot. If you please."

While they'd been brangling in the hall, Mrs. Cotton had stayed in a chair by Sally Vogel's bedside. She glanced up from her lap, an open book that lay there. "Oh, good," she said. "You brought that baby along. I just was praying that somebody'd have the sense to do it." She closed the worn leather binding of the Bible she'd had since childhood and stood up.

They lay Petey across his mother's lap with a pillow to support his head. Sally's rough breathing did not change tempo. Her eyes did not open. She had sunk too deep into illness even for delirium. Mrs. Vogel pushed the sweat-soaked hair off her daughter's forehead and whispered, "It's your baby, Sally. He's right here."

The baby kicked lightly and made happy sounds. He turned his face toward her, burrowing slightly against her underthings. Sally didn't move, her face pale except for the dark marks like bruises under her eyes. Mrs. Vogel bit her lips and stumbled away, her trembling hand hiding her eyes.

Mrs. Wilmot guided Mrs. Vogel to a chair. "She'll be all right," she said, stumbling over the words. "I had an uncle who was ever so much worse once and he got better. And

Dr. Castle's very clever, you know. My next boy, Davey, is here, and Dr. Castle's taking excellent care of him."

Millicent saw Ned shake his head as though denying he deserved any praise. She slipped her hand into the curve of his arm, just to give him a little comfort. Her grandmother had always said that there were some folks you couldn't save, no matter how much medicine you ladled into them nor how much praying you did.

Maybe she'd been able to accept death. Using her wisdom, Millicent could, too. Yet she'd come to understand that Ned would fight with every weapon at hand and throw himself in the breach as well sooner than yield one inch to death. She held on to him a little tighter, for she knew how much he hated the powerlessness he felt.

Behind them, the door opened and Darryl peeked in. He walked to the side of the bed, looking down at his girl and child with an expression of utter hopelessness in his eyes. His hands came up to cover his eyes.

The miracle, when it happened, hardly registered with anyone present. Ned and Millicent were looking into each other's eyes, trying to share their strength, while Mrs. Vogel wept softly into a handkerchief Mrs. Wilmot had lent her. Mrs. Cotton prayed, her lined lips moving silently.

Petey lay on his mother's lap, starting to make fussing noises because nobody seemed interested in feeding him. Her heart heavy, Millicent turned to pick him up. She froze, her back still bent. Ned stepped over to see what she stared at.

Sally's hand turned over. Her fingers slowly opened, as if to cradle her son's head. Millicent, holding her breath for fear of diverting Sally's purpose, very gently pressed the girl's hand in to where Petey lay.

The weak fingers rested lightly on the fluff of Petey's hair. Raising her eyes to Sally's face, marked now by the faintest contraction of her brows, Millicent said, "It's your baby. Open your eyes and see him."

"Wake up, Sally," Darryl pleaded. "We can be together forever if you just wake up."

As though it took her a moment to translate what she

heard into some form she could understand, Sally did not wake up at once. Yet, so slowly that the coming of dawn would have seemed faster, intelligence and life returned to the girl's face. Her cheeks stayed pale with the gloss of sweat still on her skin, yet she stirred and opened her eyes.

She looked aimlessly around the room, plainly confused by the dark paneled walls and high molded ceiling of the clerk's office. Seeing Darryl standing beside her, she squinted as if to bring him into focus. "Darryl? I had such a funny dream. What time is it?"

Her mother laughed on a hysterical note. "She always asks that, first thing!"

But Sally didn't wait for the answer. She peered down toward her lap to where Petey, certain now that it was all a plot to keep him from his late morning snack, had begun to bawl. "Oh," she said again, "I had such a funny dream. Not true, though."

Millicent helped the girl raise her child in weakened arms. "Mrs. Wilmot, there's a bottle. . . ."

"No," Sally said. "I can . . ." She fumbled with the front of her chemise.

Glancing over her shoulder, Millicent looked to Ned to see if Sally should risk feeding Petey, as her illness had left her so haggard. But Ned did not stand behind her anymore.

"He went out," Mrs. Cotton said. "Don't you reckon you should follow him, maybe? We'll take care of Sally."

Millicent understood what Mrs. Cotton tried to express without coming right out and saying it. Petey was no longer her concern. He had a family . . . maybe more family than necessary, but one never knew. He didn't need Millicent anymore. The fact that Millicent still needed him didn't weigh in the balance of what was important.

With a last brush over Petey's soft arm, Millicent backed away. On the threshold she hesitated, unable for an instant to take that last step. But what was the use in looking back? She forced herself to go forward.

25

IN THE LONG shadows of evening, Ned pulled the latch string to open Millicent's gate. He noticed mounds of dark dirt, freshly turned over, spaced at even intervals all along the walkway. In imagination he saw Millicent working out her heartache by creating the potential for future life in her garden. He wondered how many of those lily bulbs were watered with her tears.

Millicent's house showed dark and still, as it had been before Petey had come into her life. Ned wished he'd been the one to bring light to it. However, he couldn't be jealous of a baby, not when little Petey had done so much for him as well as for Millicent.

Shifting his bouquet of Mrs. Wilmot's half-budded roses from one hand to the other, Ned straightened his tie and smoothed his hair with the flat of his palm. He tried to remember that they'd come as close to being lovers as made no difference, yet he still felt a prickle of nervous sweat. He had to do this just right, or Millicent might still refuse to be his forever.

When a voice addressed him out of the darkness, he almost jumped out of his skin.

"That you, Neddy?" From the porch next door, he heard the *creak-crick* of a rocking chair over the two-note violin song of the cicadas.

"Good evening, Mrs. Cotton."

"'Bout time you got here." He could glimpse her now, a plump motherly figure rocking away the minutes.

"I have patients, you know," he said defensively. "Besides, I thought she might like some time alone."

"Well," she said on a slow considering note. "I'm not sayin' you're wrong. She's got her pride, and she ain't one to let folks see her cry."

"No, she isn't." Once again, he wondered how much crying she'd done.

"Now, I'm no doctor, but I figure I know the best thing for that girl. It's—"

Ned interrupted Mrs. Cotton. "I am a doctor, and I know the best thing for her without a single doubt is . . . something I don't intend to discuss."

"Good boy," she said, chuckling. "Always said you was the smartest feller ever to hit this town." She stood up, wrapping up her knitting in a neat bundle. "It's a mighty nice evening. Be a moon later, I reckon."

"I wouldn't be at all surprised. Oh, Mrs. Cotton . . . ?"

"Yes, Neddy?" She paused, the front doorknob already in her hand.

"Is Sunday too soon, do you think? Or can Culverton manage to pull a wedding together in so short a time?"

"Oh, we can manage a wedding on less notice than that; you'll see if you keep on living here! But we don't need a whole lot of time for you two. Why, I understand some ladies have been baking since clear back to last Wednesday's prayer meeting." Her laughter, as fresh as a young girl's, floated out on the evening air for some time, even after Ned had gone into the cold, dark house next door.

He found a candlestick in the kitchen and lit the taper at the stove. Judging by the condition of the kitchen, Millicent hadn't bothered to eat anything. Her gardening gloves, marked with garden mold, were thrust anyhow in the crown of a plain straw hat. He found her canvas boots leaning against each other like drunken soldiers a few feet inside the back door.

Her stockings lay on the floor of the hall, like the discarded skins of depressed serpents. She'd obviously been too miserable to think of picking them up. He stepped on a fallen button and sent it spinning to the foot of the steps.

Shielding the candle's flame with a hand cupped around it, Ned climbed to the second floor. Seeing her dropped dress, his heart contracted, for it took him back to the moment when she'd fainted after her window had been shattered. She had lain just that limply in his arms.

Then he found her petticoat, her chemise, and her corset, all in a row a few feet apart. By now, Ned had an armload of her clothes, the cloth breathing out her faint scent. He couldn't help but realize that, sunk in misery or not, she must be naked by now.

Millicent lay on her side, one bare arm curving into her shoulder as elegantly as a trailing vine. Her dark hair spread across the pillow behind her. Ned drew a deep breath as happiness flooded his heart and soul at the sight of her.

He put her clothes on a chair and the candle in the middle of the barren floor. Then, taking his time, he removed his own clothing. Lifting the blanket, he slipped into the coolness of the sheets, pillowing his head on his arm.

Ned could feel the slight heat her body generated, and he sighed as it warmed his skin. There were long years ahead of nights like this, when he'd sneak in quietly after a late call or delivery, careful not to wake Millicent. Sometimes she would go on sleeping, no doubt. Other times, say in the depth of winter when he had to knock ten pounds of clinging snow off his hat, she would cuddle up against him, undeterred by the chill of his body.

Ned thought about the future and felt content. Though he could wish this would be one of those nights when Millicent draped herself over him, he could respect her weariness and her heartache. He could afford to wait, hard though it might be. He had years of lovemaking to look forward to. Of course, she hadn't accepted him yet, not formally. He closed his eyes and his dream of their married life passed into dreams of sleep.

Millicent awoke because the moon shone on her face through a chink in her cheap curtains. She raised herself on her arms, wondering why Petey had not cried yet. Then she remembered and pain crashed in on her again.

She swung her feet out of bed to go close the curtain but

found her bare knees more interesting. Where was her nightgown? That's right, she thought, reminding herself that she'd been so worn out that she'd just dropped her clothes willy-nilly on the way to bed. Though she knew leaving them lying around meant hard work with a sad iron in the morning, she felt too lethargic to do anything about it.

She stumbled to the curtain and smoothed the gap closed. Unfortunately, that opened another one. Hearing a muttered complaint, Millicent turned with great slowness toward the bed.

Ned sat up, the moonlight making him look as though he wore silver armor molded to the exact shape of his body. She'd seen pictures of such things in her books when she'd been at school. Roman heroes, like Horatius at the Bridge, had worn such armor.

Something warm began to grow inside her, near the region of her heart, at the sight of him. Though she had lost much today, she realized how much she'd gained as well. *After all,* she reasoned, *there are many different kinds of love.*

"I guess I should scream," she said with a slowly widening smile. "After all, there's a man in my bed."

"I'm sorry, Miss Mayhew, ma'am. All the other beds in town were plumb full up." He put up his hand and then said, dropping the country accent, "I can't raise a hat when I don't have one."

"Do you remember where you saw it last?"

"I do believe it was right here in this bed."

"Should I help you look for it?" she asked, coming closer. Deliberately, she put a little sashay in her walk, a little extra roll of her hips.

"Maybe you can find it more quickly than I can."

He slid his warm hand around the in-curve of her waist, and Millicent felt like a bottle of her homemade wine about ready to pop a cork. He pulled her closer still, guiding her to kneel on the bed. She closed her eyes against the shudderingly good feeling of Ned's hands running over her.

"Who's . . . who's minding the store?" she asked as he nuzzled the slope of her stomach.

"Doc Partridge is keeping an eye on things for me."

"Doc Partridge?"

Ned's voice dropped lower as he said, "He's promised not to touch a drop till I get back. I told him . . ." Millicent yipped at what he did with his teeth. Then she laughed on a softly intimate note. The combination of sensuality and laughter sent Ned's pulse to a level that, if he'd found it in a patient, would have meant a prescription of six months' bed rest. Ned didn't think he'd be getting much rest tonight.

Ned said, "I told him to expect me back by midnight."

"What time is it now?"

"Not midnight."

Taking advantage of her lack of balance, he pulled her down among the tangled sheets. Capturing her mouth with his, he silenced her laughter with a firmness that awoke her response. They rolled over together in a silence broken only by tiny sounds of pleasure.

Millicent ran her hands up his smoothly muscled arms, feeling the tickle of his hair on her palms. Every time she touched him, the love that swept through her left her awed. When he kissed the side of her neck, she gasped and then began to speak her thoughts aloud.

"I love it when I can touch you like this," she whispered, letting her fingers curve over his shoulders, then sweeping her palms down his warm back. "It makes me feel . . ."

"Me, too," he murmured. "Let me touch you, too."

"You do. You are."

Her body gave itself over to him, while her thoughts were consumed by perceptions she'd never realized before. She couldn't have said when he drew the dark pink of her breast into his mouth, or when he massaged the stiffened backs of her legs. Completely absorbed in sensation, she only knew that it all felt so wonderful, whether he tickled her ear with his breath or ran his fingertips over her stomach, making the goose pimples arise.

She did her best to give him something back. But Ned caught her hands when they would have sought to know more of his heavily aroused body. "Not tonight," he said.

"I'd go crazy, and tonight . . . tonight is for you, Millicent. There'll be plenty of time for everything else later."

"But I want . . ." Even naked with him, she could still screen her eyes with her lashes so he wouldn't think she'd become an absolute hussy. "I want you to feel . . . like this."

"Like what? How do you feel?" He ran his hand, smoothly yet firmly, up the quivering skin of her thigh. Touching her so softly, he sought out the secret wellspring of her greatest pleasures. Remembering what it had been like before, Millicent gave up any pretense of thinking and surrendered to the promise of his hands.

He moved his fingers the tiniest bit, and Millicent stiffened as if she'd glimpsed angels flying down rainbows out her kitchen window. "Oh, please. I want . . ." She couldn't catch her breath, which troubled her at first, but then breathing seemed utterly beside the point.

"You like that?" he said, his voice very soft yet with a note of surprised delight.

"What are you doing?"

"I'm not sure it has a name. I could look it up, if you'd like." He did it again and she clutched his shoulders. She couldn't hold still. Moving against his hand with timidity, still Millicent felt a wonderful heat blossoming with every touch. She bit her lips and tossed her head on the pillows, impatience growing along with passion.

No longer caring that his eyes never left her face, Millicent reached a zenith of delight and tumbled down the other side. For a moment, falling and flying became one. She soared away. Realizing dimly that Ned had not accompanied her, she returned for him.

Opening her eyes, she said, "Oh, I don't know what to say! I never . . . merciful heavens, I don't wonder anymore why people get married!"

Ned laughed. His chuckles spread, shaking the bed. Millicent, confused, blinked up at him, wanting to share his good humor but not understanding why he was laughing. Ned smoothed the hair off Millicent's forehead, smiling into her puzzled eyes. He said, still with a gasp, "You're a woman in a million. At least I know you're going to marry me for something besides my brain."

"I haven't said—"

He captured her face between his hands. "You are going to marry me. Please notice that I'm not making it a request. I'm never going to let you stay single."

Looking up into his eyes, Millicent held his gaze. "Why?" she asked.

"Because, like it or not, home remedies or not, prickly as a nettle or not, I love you."

She gave him no smile. "Try it again. Without the fancy trimmings. Need help? Listen. I love you."

Ned sank down and kissed her deeply, with an eager hunger that he'd not yet assuaged. Her lips did not answer, though a shuddering sigh ran through her. He knew she wanted him, knew she loved him, and also knew that this might turn out to be the first thoroughly equal marriage in the world. Always excepting the Cottons', of course.

He rested his forehead on hers and said, in a deep true voice that shook only a little, "I love you. I love you. As much as I hate repetition, I love you."

Watching her eyes fill with joy reminded him of seeing an apartment building at twilight as slowly, one by one, the gas light comes on until every window shines out, warming passers-by. He wanted to linger in that moment, watching her joy, but she had other ideas.

She ran her hands down his shoulders, over his back, and down to the fine male rear that was wasted even in peg-leg trousers. There she squeezed lightly, daringly, and Ned breathed in some extra oxygen to deal with the demands ahead. "What now?" she asked, her eyes bold.

He had no doubts about her readiness. It fairly announced itself, between the flush on her cheeks and chest and her sweetly spicy fragrance that he preferred to Parisian perfumes. In all honesty, however, he felt it necessary to be completely frank in their dealings.

"Millicent, you do know . . . I mean . . . it might not feel good . . . your virginity . . ." Somehow all his medical training had deserted him. He just couldn't say the words.

"Oh, that? I've heard about that. You may not know this, but women do talk among themselves."

"About that?"

Now it became her turn to laugh. "Sometimes we don't talk about anything else." She nibbled on his ear, a very sensitive spot for Ned, and he forgot what he meant to say.

He made it as easy as possible for her, bringing her to a second peak of pleasure before essaying the first advance. Then she repeated a motion of her hips that had gone over well when she'd walked to him. Ned lost control of himself. He surged forward, only to be stopped by a frail barrier.

He looked down into her face, to meet her glowing amber eyes. She bit her lip and then managed a shy smile. "Go on," she urged in a whisper. "It's what I want."

Ned hated the very thought of hurting her. He set his teeth and made a worse face than she did, which made her giggle. Millicent reached up to link her hands around the back of his neck. Together, they found the way.

Ned concentrated on her pleasure, trying to keep from tumbling over the cliff-edge himself. He could feel the sweat pooling on his back, cool as the air brushed over him. The sight of Millicent's lovely face as she met this new experience was almost too much for his self-control. He shut his eyes tightly but couldn't block out her image, her sounds, the wonder of it all.

For Millicent, she simply drowned in delight. She couldn't see, she couldn't think, and breathing became an afterthought. She couldn't keep quiet. She all but sang to him, giving him all the words of love she'd kept crammed in her heart.

Miraculously, he had words of his own. Lovely, poetic words that she knew she'd treasure until she died. Even if she became old and withered, she'd take those words out to bloom again. But the best was also the simplest. "Millicent, I love you."

He whispered it again and again as she felt more pleasure than the human body could hold. She twisted under him, seeking for some relief from this bounty he pressed on her.

Then she heard him say, "It's all right, Millicent. Let go. Just let go."

He touched her somehow, and the balance tipped, spilling over. Ned's shout of joy mingled with Millicent's small sounds, that soon turned to laughter.

Their engagement existed in hurried, snatched moments between late Tuesday night and early Sunday morning. Ned still had patients at the City Hall. Millicent helped him, but the sickest took up much time, leaving little for billing or even cooing.

If they did have a few free hours, sneaking off to Millicent's house for lovemaking always turned into going to someone's house for dinner or to a church event.

"We just want a part of you," Antonia said, clinging to her soon-to-be sister-in-law's arm. "You have all the years of your lives to talk to each other."

Ned began to suspect a plot; a sneaky underhanded conspiracy to keep him and Millicent apart until after the wedding. He chafed at the delay. Although he had realized for a long time that all he had to do to have Millicent in his bed was close his eyes—she always appeared in his dreams—the reality of her deliciousness once tasted made dreams seem more a torment than a comfort.

On the few occasions when he and Millicent had been alone, such as when walking back after the party Antonia threw them, Millicent seemed preoccupied. Even her kisses started as if they were absentminded, though after a few minutes she always seemed to perk up. Knowing what troubled her, Ned laid his plans and hoped they'd come off without a disaster of Biblical proportions.

Ed Fleck was on the mend. Though he'd merely mumbled his congratulations on the doctor's upcoming wedding, a visit from Suzie Riley had him realizing life might still be worthwhile, just now and again.

Sally had been moved to the Wilmot home, where Ned saw her twice a day. Darryl doted on her endlessly, and together they managed to care for Petey without involving Mrs. Wilmot. "Before too long, we mean to have a place of our own," Darryl had promised Ned. "Even if I can't work at the store 'cause of all the gossip . . ."

"It'll die," Ned promised. "In this town, there's always something else to talk about. I hear Roscoe Benders is courting Lucy George; that ought to be good for some diversion."

"Roscoe? I heard it was his brother Ezra."

"Very good," Ned said, nodding his head approvingly. "If anyone tries to say anything about you, Sally, or the baby, just switch them off onto Lucy."

Mr. Vogel had a bad case of influenza, Ned's prediction having come true. His wife nursed him devotedly, for which service Ned was grateful. Every time the burly backwoodsman saw the doctor, he tried to get his hands around Ned's throat. He seemed to blame Ned for his misfortunes, but Mrs. Vogel assured Ned that it was only because her husband was sick that he was violent. "When he's well, he'll pray for your soul, Doctor."

"I just hope he won't dispatch it first," Ned confided later to Millicent.

"I'll protect you," she vowed.

"Just promise to love, honor, and . . . will you obey?"

She turned a coquettish smile on him. "Since I doubt Mr. Budgell's willing to rewrite the vows just for us, I guess I will. But—"

"You don't have to tell me." Looking up and down the hall of the second floor, Ned put his hands on her waist and pulled her against his body. "I won't ask for obedience. How about willing cooperation?"

"Are the pair of you at it again?" Mrs. Cotton demanded.

"No!" Millicent said in frustration while Ned groaned. "But we'd like to be if we ever get the chance."

"Later. Right now you got to go try on your wedding dress. You're a sight taller than Mrs. Wilmot allowed for. I told her so, but she always knows best."

"Mrs. Wilmot?"

"Sent for it all the way to Chicago. Came in on the morning train."

"But . . . there's no way. It takes . . ." She started counting on her fingers.

Ned cleared his throat. "It seems, my love, that we were the only ones who didn't know we were getting married."

"That's the truth," Mrs. Cotton cackled.

Tears coming to her eyes, Millicent said, "I don't know why everyone should be so good to me."

Mrs. Cotton patted her hand. "Well, now, you work for the Wilmots. It's only right they should do something for you. 'Sides, since it looks like Sally won't be on her feet to get married herself this Sunday, maybe she can have the use of the dress after you're done with it."

"Of course."

"Come to think on it," Mrs. Cotton said, "we've been having so many of these here weddings where the bride ain't got a dress, maybe we ought to keep a supply on hand. . . . I'll have Vernon raise the subject at the next town council meeting."

She frowned for a moment and then shook her head, as though putting off the beautiful thought until a more appropriate time. "Come on, Millicent. They're all a-waiting for you. I'll stay and watch after the girls till you're . . ."

Suddenly Mrs. Cotton's cheeks were pale. She pressed her hand to her breastbone and seemed to totter.

Millicent put her arms around the older woman's waist to support her. "Mrs. Cotton! Ned!"

"I'm all right . . . don't . . . don't fuss."

Ned bent and picked her up. "Where's an empty cot?"

"Clerk's office," Millicent answered, trotting ahead to open the door.

By the time he'd laid Mrs. Cotton on the smooth coverlet, the spell was passing. "Don't fuss, Neddy," she said, tugging her wrist out from his hand. "I'm fine. My, it's been a few years since any man swept me up in his arms."

Her laughter died away on a sudden gasp of pain.

"Mrs. Cotton! Are you all right?"

She coughed a little. "Don't go worrying about me, Neddy. I'm fine."

"I want you to come see me professionally," he said

sternly. "You've got to stop scaring us. The judge has told me, as has Millicent, about your tiredness, your pain . . . if it's your heart, there are many new treatments . . ."

"Lands sakes!" Mrs. Cotton said abruptly. "I had no notion so many folks were taking an interest. There's nothing in the world wrong with me 'cept for turnips."

"Turnips?"

She nodded impatiently. "I love 'em when they're just up in the garden, no bigger than my thumb. Fry 'em up with a little salsify greens and butter, and nothing in the world or heaven tastes any better. But they give me the heartburn like I swallered a live coal. Not that I care much 'cause they taste so good going down. So all you folks just save your worry for when I'm on my deathbed. I'll be certain sure to let you know when that might be."

Ned met Millicent's eyes across the bed. Her lips twitched, and she covered them with her hand. But she couldn't keep her laughter from exploding.

Sunday's sun shone as any bride could wish. Millicent, stiff and suddenly frightened inside her gown of lace and cambric, sat across the aisle from Ned. She sat with the Cottons, while he sat with his sister and the recovering marshal.

She kept sneaking peeks at him under the brim of a white straw hat that she'd fixed up last night when sleep would not come. He sat in a relaxed attitude, his legs crossed. Only the continual tapping on his fingers on his knee gave away the state of *his* nerves. He didn't glance at her even a single time.

Mr. Budgell's sermon ran under an hour, for once. Then the moment had come. Millicent stood up, Judge Cotton holding her arm. Ned stepped to the front of the church to stand alone.

Mary Anne Budgell pumped the harmonium and the congregation began to sing. Millicent couldn't have named the tune, for her head seemed to buzz and her fingers in the judge's hand were cold and trembling. "Come on along," he said.

She stepped out blindly, spots and halos before her eyes.

A space cleared in the center of her vision, and she could see Ned. He wore a smile of such enduring tenderness and bliss as she came toward him that all her nervousness evaporated. With a confident tread, she came up to him and gave him her hand.

"Wait a minute," he said as Mr. Budgell lifted his book. "We need the best man."

Out of the side aisle stepped Darryl Wilmot, his hair slicked down hard. "Darryl?" Millicent asked.

"No," Ned said. "Look."

Darryl bent to take from his mother's arms a baby dressed in a blue serge skeleton suit. Petey kicked and grinned as his father lifted him, but he let out a gurgle of joy when he saw Millicent.

She tossed her flowers to Mrs. Cotton and held Petey during the ceremony. He stared around with his big blue eyes, good as gold, only giggling when Ned fished the ring out of a tiny pocket sewed to the front of Petey's jumper. As her new husband slid the gold circle onto her finger, Millicent realized that she'd lost nothing but her sorrows when she'd given her heart to the baby, to Ned, and to her home.

Culverton as a whole had a talent for throwing wedding suppers that would put a White House dinner to shame. As Ned strolled through the gathering dusk at the picnic grounds, his bride on his arm, he felt surrounded by goodwill. He said, "I only wish my parents could be here to see this."

"They promised to come as soon as they get back from Europe, didn't they?"

"Yes, but maybe if they were here they'd finally understand why two out of three of their children have decided to spend the rest of their lives here. Right now they think it's an interesting aberration that will wear off in time."

Millicent squeezed the muscles of his arm. "You know, we don't have to live here forever. I mean, I'd like to. But if you think we ought to move . . . go back East or wherever, I will."

"Love, honor and obey?"

"Well . . ." She smiled and the dimple in her cheek was new.

"Have you put on weight, Mrs. Castle?"

She laughed to hear her new name and admitted, "Yes. Since Tuesday night . . . you remember Tuesday night? . . . I've been eating like a horse."

"Good. There's slender and there's skinny, and I don't like skinny."

Her heel left a dusty impression on his carefully shined shoes. "Same to you, Doctor. I better not see a potbelly on you anytime soon."

"Or what?"

"Nothing. I'd love you no matter what. Lose your hair, lose your teeth . . . but not right away."

"Agreed. Now that that's settled, would you care for another piece of Mrs. Cotton's angel food cake before we retire for the evening?"

"Can we take it with us and eat it later? I'd like to retire now, to tell you the truth." Her pink cheeks and the entrancing circles her fingers made on the back of his hand told him that delay was unthinkable.

They sought Mrs. Cotton to thank her for all her kindnesses when Jake came thundering through the crowd to seize Ned by the arm. "Come on," he said, his authoritative voice going up half an octave.

"What is it? Stop pulling on me like a maddened ox and tell me what's up."

"Antonia," Jake said briefly. "Labor. Now."

"Go on," Millicent said. "I might as well learn now what it is to be a doctor's wife. I'll meet you at home. Unless you need me?"

"I always need you," he said as his brother-in-law all but carried him off bodily. "Wait at home."

Millicent waited up, passing on the fine wedding suit of lacy nightgown and matching robe, choosing a sturdy flannel gown and Mother Hubbard instead. She had plenty of cold leftovers from the wedding picnic, though she had a feeling Ned would need something nourishing and hot when he came home. Cooking in lace was impractical.

She wandered, while she waited for him. Every room in her cold house seemed different, and she wanted to enjoy the change. Though the paint and furniture were the same, the feeling had been transformed. No longer just a house, it had become a home, a place of contented refuge.

Seven hours later Ned found her asleep in the kitchen rocker. He went to her and sank down on the floor, putting his head on her knee. He felt the start that ran through her when she awakened, then, accepting, she stroked his hair. He'd expected a flurry of questions; she said nothing.

After a few minutes of comfort, he found words. "I saved them both," he said on a sigh. "A hard fight; the baby was big. Antonia stayed strong; Jake fainted. But they've got themselves a son now."

"That's wonderful. Are you hungry?"

He shook his head, hiding his tired eyes against her. "They wanted to name him after me. I said they could provided they convinced Mrs. Cotton to call *him* Neddy instead of me."

At her soft laughter Ned raised his head. "I like this coming home business."

"I like it, too."

"Give me a few minutes to wash up, all right?"

"Take your time." She stood up, a graceful figure in the lamplight. Her fingers trailed along his jaw, quickening the banked fires in his soul.

He rose, too, wrapping his arms around her. For a moment they just held each other, a warmth in the night, a kindness in the dark. There'd be times ahead when he would not win his "hard fights," but so long as he had these arms to come home to, the agony of his defeats would be shared and thus lessened.

"Come to bed," Millicent said, husky invitation in her voice. "If you're not too tired. . . ."

"Tired? I don't believe I know that word. Where's a dictionary?"

Epilogue

THE ONLY THING in Ned's life more difficult than helping Antonia deliver four babies was helping to deliver his own. After Antonia's first, she never had another moment's trouble, even with the twins, and he supposed he'd gotten spoiled. He'd thought he'd learned emotional detachment; he couldn't have been more wrong.

Finally Mrs. Cotton, older, grayer, but just as purposeful, had ordered him out of the room, saying she'd call him if she needed him. Even Millicent, her hair clinging damply to her cheeks, said, "Yes, please, Ned. Go on downstairs and talk to Jake."

Jake pushed Ned into a chair and a drink into his hand. "This is the worst part," he said cheerfully. "It never gets any better, either."

"How do you stand it?"

"Whisky. Drink up."

The alcohol burned his throat but did nothing to lessen his fear. "Why'd we do it?" he asked the glass. "We've gone along happy as a couple of hound dogs for nearly four years."

"But Millicent wanted kids, didn't she? All that stuff with Petey Wilmot . . . By the way, what an imp he's turning out to be! Only five years old and can talk more law than I can. Talked me out of tanning his hide last week when I caught him stealing doughnuts off Mrs. Pierce's window-sill. . . ."

Ned hadn't been listening, absently patting the dog beside

him. He said, "Sure, we both wanted children, but we never had any luck. Somehow things just didn't happen for us. . . ." He'd missed too many nights of lovemaking, keeping on his rounds, taking on other towns within a day's ride, by horse or train, where there was no doctor to be had.

Millicent had never complained, though he'd held her often enough when her monthly flow had begun, a crashing eternal disappointment. She'd stopped talking about children, and even managed to hide her pain when others had them. A devoted aunt and Sunday school teacher, she never again invested the kind of emotion in another woman's child that she had in Petey.

"Then that trip . . . we were so happy when finally she got pregnant."

When Millicent's nightmares had returned, Ned had advertised for a partner. The bright young woman he'd taken on had been a quick learner. Though Culverton hadn't yet made up its collective mind about a qualified lady physician, Ned didn't delay any longer. He'd booked passage for two on the first train going West. Millicent had protested vehemently at the very thought of a return to Beaver's Bend, yet her nightmares had lessened in frequency almost at once.

What Ned hadn't expected was the force of his own anger. The sight of the prosperous mining community, on a solid financial footing, had started a red rage in his soul. He'd wanted to fight every human who looked twice at Millicent. Which of them had been so cruel to her? The chubby one with a bowler hat sitting like a peanut on top of his jowled face? The sly woman with the stained apron? Or was this honest-eyed, gray-haired sheriff the one who'd refused to help her? They'd all looked at him askance, a young man with an obvious chip on his shoulder and a protective arm around his lovely wife.

The sheriff had explained matters to them over a cup of coffee in his office. Things had changed since Millicent lived there. He said that the mine owner, the Colonel, had sold his share of the concern when his son was found shot through the head.

"Shot himself?" Millicent exclaimed, meeting Ned's eyes.

"Yes, ma'am," the sheriff said. "Sorry if it was a shock. Did you know him?"

"No . . . I used to see him around, sometimes." She pressed a starched handkerchief to her lips. Ned laid a gentle hand on her back for moral support. "He was a wild boy."

"So most folks say. Not his pa, though. He claimed murder, but plenty of folks had heard the boy promise to kill himself on several evenings when he'd had too much to drink. One night he took aboard enough Dutch courage to do the job."

Glancing at Millicent, the sheriff went on, "Some folks say it was a murder he'd done that preyed on his mind. I even heard tell how this girl's ghost was a-haunting him, never giving him a moment's peace, but I don't believe in that stuff."

"Neither do I," Millicent said, but her eyes were hot with tears. She turned toward Ned and leaned her head on his shoulder, hiding her eyes.

The sheriff reached for the coffeepot on the small iron stove and gave it a questioning shake. Satisfied by the swish, he poured out another cup for Ned and himself. Millicent hadn't touched hers. "Course, it was all old news by the time I got this job."

Ned started to say, "Then you weren't living here when all that—"

"No, sir. The feller I replaced dropped down dead of a stroke couple of months after the boy shot himself. Funny, now that I think of it, 'most everyone in town nowadays is a newcomer, like me."

Millicent sat up straight, letting out a long sigh. With a trembling smile that Ned longed to kiss away, she said, "I've always thought this would be a nice town someday."

"Thank you, ma'am. There's a petition going around to change the name to Eagle's Mere. Folks think it's a sight classier. I wonder if you'd mind signing it."

"Not at all. I like that name very much."

After Millicent had signed and gone outside to breathe in the fresh air her husband prescribed, Ned asked in a low voice, "Anybody by the name of Dan Redpath living in these parts?"

The sheriff stroked his chin and flicked his eyes over Ned. "Yes, sir. Till last winter he lived in a shack up the mountain a piece."

"Where is he now? I'd very much like to have a little conversation with Mr. Redpath."

"Reckon you'll have to wait a sight for that, Dr. Castle. Soon as the ground thawed they done buried him. He froze to death during a snowstorm. Funny how so many folks from the early days up and died. Almost like something that was after 'em got 'em."

"Someday we will understand the awful power of a guilty conscience, Sheriff. Thank you for your time."

Emerging into the sun, Ned found his wife perched on the railing outside the sheriff's office. Her traveling bonnet hung by its ribbons down her back, and she swung a booted foot, showing a froth of petticoats. She looked about eighteen, not at all the staid, proper wife of a rising physician.

She gave him a sideways glance and then a provocative smile. Without saying a word, he took her hand and led her back to their hotel suite, a brand-new building at the other end of town from where Millicent used to work.

It never palled, their desire for each other. Sometime on that trip, maybe in "Eagle's Mere," maybe on another stop during their holiday, they'd created a baby. And now this . . .

"How do you stand it?" Ned asked his brother-in-law again.

The big man's face grew serious. "Every single time we have another baby I swear it'll be the last. I promise I'll be a monk, and mortify the flesh. I don't want to blame Antonia . . . that's a cad's trick, but let's just say my resolutions don't last real long when she sashays around the bedroom in next to nothing."

Jake smoothed back his graying hair. No longer the town marshal, he'd become the attorney he'd always planned to become. There was more than a little talk of running him for mayor when Mr. Wilmot finally retired. "So we keep on having kids," he said. "And I keep getting grayer."

"Well, I'll keep my resolution," Ned said firmly. "I'm not going through *this* again."

"Come on out on the porch and have a cigar," Jake said. "It'll calm your nerves."

"A cigar? I haven't had a cigar since . . . I can't remember when."

He'd forgotten the trick of lighting the flattish brown sausage. Soon, however, he had it drawing well. He took a deep drag and waited for the satisfaction to appear. Instead, he coughed, all but retching.

Jake said, "I think somebody's calling you."

Ned ran into the house, the door slamming behind him. Jake stepped on the smoldering cigar as he puffed on his own. "Waste of a good smoke," he said ruefully.

Dr. and Mrs. Castle's daughter came into the world at eight forty-five on a moonlit night in early May. Her father held her first as he did what needed to be done. "She's fine," he told Millicent. "All fingers and toes present and correct."

They laughed on a note close to tears as the baby cried, her lower lip trembling. As Millicent bared her breast and brought her daughter to it, Ned's tears did come. He went about his doctoring with them streaming down his face.

"I ain't never seen such a man," Mrs. Cotton said, rolling down her sleeves. "When I think what he used to be like, so stuffed he had to keep his head down at Thanksgiving . . ."

"Don't look at me," Millicent said, her voice a thread. "It's not my doing."

Mrs. Cotton huffed. "If it's not your fault, child, I don't know whose shoulders get the blame. I'll be back tomorrow morning to fix breakfast. You'll want a day or two in bed, but no longer, mind!"

"Ask her, Ned," Millicent said, adjusting things for the baby.

"Oh, yes. Mrs. Cotton," he asked formally. "We'd be so honored if you'd allow us to name her after you. After all you've done for us, it seems right."

"Oh, my. Oh, lands," Mrs. Cotton said. "I'd . . . I'd be most proud. Nobody ever done that before. . . ."

"Um, there's just one question. Everyone calls you Mrs. Cotton except for your husband, and he calls you Mother. What is your first name?"

"You know, it's been so long I all but forget it myself. But it's Charlotte. I never liked it much. My folks and family used to called me Lotta. But when I married Vernon, Lotta Cotton just . . . Now don't you go laughing at me!"

After he'd walked Mrs. Cotton home, Ned got into bed with his family, their dogs on the floor. He held little Charlotte on his chest and let Millicent doze. There might be happier men in the world at that moment, but he'd defy anyone to show him one. He spent a good hour marveling at the wonder of his child, counting eyelashes and admiring the tiny perfection of fingernails and toes.

Millicent awoke and saw him with his heart in his eyes. She stroked the tiny knee closest to her and whispered, "Hard to believe. . . ."

"Isn't it? But one is enough, Millicent. I don't want to have to go through that again."

"*You* don't? What were *you* doing that was so difficult?"

"Worrying and praying and swearing my life away if you'd just be all right."

She leaned her head against his shoulder. "All right. We'll see."

"Millicent . . ."

"We don't have to make up our minds right now, do we? Those books you had me read said we had three months of waiting before we could make love again."

"At least three months. Maybe longer if—"

"Say, who seduced who two weeks ago after church?"

"All right, I know I married a wanton woman."

"Darn right."

"But I've never been so frightened in my life. . . ." he said.

"Sssh." She placed her fingers over his mouth. "It's done with. We have a daughter to love and cherish. That's what's important now."

"You're right. Did you see her smile at me a little while ago? Yes, she did. A big smile like she knew who I was."

Millicent laughed, a fond, loving laugh, and snuggled into the curve of his arm. "We'll give her the best of everything."

"Absolutely," Ned said. "All our love . . ."

"All our love," Millicent repeated. In her depths of her mind she added, *And lots of brothers and sisters . . .*

Our Town ...where love is always right around the corner!

If you enjoyed this book, take advantage of this special offer. Subscribe now and get a

FREE
Historical Romance

No Obligation (a $4.50 value)

Each month the editors of True Value select the four *very best* novels from America's leading publishers of romantic fiction. Preview them in your home *Free* for 10 days. With the first four books you receive, we'll send you a FREE book as our introductory gift. No Obligation!

If for any reason you decide not to keep them, just return them and owe nothing. If you like them as much as we think you will, you'll pay just $4.00 each and save at *least* $.50 each off the cover price. (Your savings are *guaranteed* to be at least $2.00 each month.) There is NO postage and handling – or other hidden charges. There are no minimum number of books to buy and you may cancel at any time.

Send in the Coupon Below

To get your FREE historical romance fill out the coupon below and mail it today. As soon as we receive it we'll send you your FREE Book along with your first month's selections.